T0354343

AMERICA OCCUPIED

AMERICA OCCUPIED
THE DANARVIAN CHRONICLES, PART I

BY
S R LARSON

iUniverse, Inc.
New York Bloomington

iUniverse books may be ordered through booksellers or by contacting:

iUniverse
1663 Liberty Drive
Bloomington, IN 47403
www.iuniverse.com
1-800-Authors (1-800-288-4677)

Because of the dynamic nature of the Internet, any Web addresses or links contained in this book may have changed since publication and may no longer be valid. The views expressed in this work are solely those of the author and do not necessarily reflect the views of the publisher, and the publisher hereby disclaims any responsibility for them.

ISBN: 978-1-4401-3428-9 (sc)
ISBN: 978-1-4401-3429-6 (ebook)

Printed in the United States of America

iUniverse rev. date: 04/29/2009

May reality never surpass fiction

P R O L O G U E

Hello. Whoever you are who found this tape, please listen to it all the way through. Please hear me out... I am not insane or making any of this up. I swear to God that every word is true.

And when you get to the end, please follow my instructions on what to do with this tape. I... Thank you.

My name is Thora Jane Larson. Today is May thirty one, nineteen ninety three. It is Memorial Day. It is overcast here in Lindsborg. I think we're going to get some more rain.

I will be hiding this tape in the wall here, up in my attic, because I do not think I have much time left in freedom. I am not a criminal, please do not think that I have done anything wrong. I am an honest, hard working woman. I am a professor of archaeology at Hudson College. I'm an honest person...

This is the house I grew up in. My parents died last year and my sister has been caring for this house since then. I was considering buying it, maybe move back here. I just turned fifty, and I have no children. But my sister has five, and... well.

[Faint scratching sound in the background]

After what has happened these past few days, this... this past week, I doubt that I will ever move back here.

I am recording this tape so that someone... that's you... will hear it and let the world know what happened here. And why.

It all started ten days ago. On the first night after I flew out here

1

my niece, she's is a local police officer, she asked me what I knew about forensic science. Not much, I told her. She explained that just a week earlier, a local farmer, Albert Gorman up on the hill west of town, had found some... skeletons... when he was digging a new irrigation tunnel to some land he had bought.

The police started a homicide investigation, but the county coroner shut down the whole thing right away. He declared, on the spot, right there on site, that the cause of death of the bodies was accidental.

The skeletons... oh, God, I get goose bumps just thinking about them... they remained in the ground. My niece, Shelly, brought me out there to have a look.

I am telling you... It was... it was the most... frightening experience in my life.

[Faint scratching sound. A muted bump.]

There was one skeleton that was easy to spot. That's the one they thought was a murder victim. But as they started digging they found... well, other bones.

I-I-I... I have... never believed in UFOs. I'm an archaeologist, I deal with the documented past, not science-fiction. But those bones... they scared me. I can barely talk about them without shivering.

I don't know how to describe the creatures, the skeletons... but they were not humans.

Except for... oh, God... These creatures had... a... a spine that rose from their body. And a head... a – a human... a human head. With fangs. And the eye sockets were... big.

[Very faint bumps. Slow. Almost rhythmic. They stop.]

You think I'm crazy. Please don't. Please do not turn off this tape! Every bit of this is true! There are pictures of these skeletons, pictures that I took. I mailed them to a friend who is a professor of anthropological history at Empire University up in New York.

I took the pictures and we brought some bones in for DNA testing. I just got the DNA results today. When I picked them up, the analyst who had tested them stared at me without uttering a word. He looked like he had seen… a ghost.

I can't blame him.

[Low frequency humming in the background.]

These creatures are alien. They are… they have some DNA that resembles ours… perhaps that's why they have human heads… but…

All week we have been followed by strange men, probably from some government agency. They stopped us and harassed us a few days ago. Shelly was pretty tough with them. She is a police officer, and that shows. So they backed off a bit, but they've been here on my property and they have destroyed the grave and everything that was in it. As far as I know, at least. Fortunately they did not get hold of the DNA results. I've mailed them, with the pictures, to Betsy up in New York.

Two days ago two men who said they were from the Environmental Protection Agency came here and told me I had violated environmental law when I was investigating that grave. I told them to charge me, but they just wanted to let me know that they were watching me. And that if I had taken anything from that grave, there would be consequences.

[Background humming sound grows stronger.]

Yesterday a strange helicopter hovered over my house for twenty minutes. Then it went away and came back and flew over here for a half hour. It had no lights, no markings… It was…

Wait, I think they're coming. Up the driveway now… A van and a car… Yes, I recognize the van.

I've seen it before. They… they're parking outside, on my driveway. I guess… it's time. I'm going to stop here. Please bring this tape and tape recorder to Betsy Hammersmith. Today, May thirty one, nineteen ninety three, she is a professor at Empire Univer …

Oh, God! Oh, dear God! I-I… can't believe… I better… there is a way out… I'm going downsta…

Ah!! AAAH!!! AAAAAAAAAHHHHHH!!!!!!

2 0 0 9

Two young men ran down the hill, in the middle of the night, through the thick forest, right in the middle of the storm, with no paths to lead them, no signs to help. They ran, jumped, stumbled, fell and got up and kept on running. Their hearts pounded, their legs begged for a rest.

But there was no time to rest. Absolutely no time. They had to keep running. They had to run – or die. Die the most gruesome death anyone could imagine.

Unforgiving gusts rocked the trees hard, and forced the leaves and branches into a ghostly dance. The roaring wind ripped leaves off the trees and left naked branches that reached for the two men like the arms of the Grim Reaper. The moonlight bounced between the leaves and the branches and played a fool's game with them, painting shadows of nothing between black trees and staring rocks – sending their eyes looking here, looking there, looking everywhere for enemies, for danger... only to find nothing more than the taunting spirits of a deep, dark forest.

On this side of the hill the trees were so tall they embraced the stars, and their branches played catch-me-if-you-can with the frightened young men as they rushed, leaped, tumbled and staggered down the hill. And there was always that wind, that ghastly wind that blew life in to the shrubbery as they tore through in their desperate fight to reach the valley.

Arms scratched, shirts torn, hearts pounding and their feet in excruciating pain.

A creek came winding down the hill and cut off their path and forced them into blind jumps. As they landed on the other side, a shrieking sound ripped through the roaring wind, pierced their heads and sent chills of terror down their spines. And they begged, pleaded with the Gods for a merciful escape.

They got separated as they landed on the other side of the creek.

"Ayush!!" cried one of them, as he desperately searched for his friend. "Ayush!!!"

"Here!" Ayush replied, breathing heavily and grabbing his left leg as if it was hurt.

There was a long cut in his thigh, and dark green, almost black blood poured out from it.

"Get up!" Shahrem shouted at him.

Ayush grabbed a tree branch and tried to pull himself up, but the pain in his leg overwhelmed him. He stumbled and fell back to the ground, ripping the branch off the tree so it fell over his injured leg. He cried out in pain.

"I can't!" he said as his friend came over to him.

Shahrem removed the tree branch and tried to help his friend up. Ayush pushed him away and rolled over on his back.

"Go, go, Shahrem, go! You heard the beast... it's got our scent. That shrieking... it's calling on the males from its herd to come..."

"There is only one of them. It's just its instinct."

"Yes, but the soldiers are coming. They are letting it loose, and it will find us. Aargh!" He grabbed his leg again as the pain cut through his flesh. "And... and it will kill us. You know... what that means... you have seen it..."

"I know."

"Shahrem, go to the shuttle. I can delay them. The beast will find me and the soldiers won't realize that you've escaped until..."

"Shut up, Ayush! We're almost there!"

The shrieking laughter again... closer now.

Ayush looked up the hill. The beast was too clumsy to run through the woods, but once it had the scent of its prey it would pursue it relentlessly. And it was coming. It would only be a short while before it was here.

The beast was a horrific… creature. Many died of fear when it came for them.

Ayush turned to Shahrem and made a split second decision. He pulled out his hunting knife, grabbed his friend by the shirt and pointed the knife at his throat.

"Leave, Shahrem, or I'll kill you right now."

His voice was desperate, his eyes fixed on Shahrem with an almost supernatural determination. For a couple of seconds, Shahrem looked at Ayush in disbelief. He forgot all about the storm, the wild, raging wind, the beast that was coming for them.

Then he realized that Ayush was serious, that he meant every word he said. Ayush's death, as he himself was planning it, would be an honorable one. He just depended on Shahrem to make it happen.

"You can fly the shuttle" Ayush whispered, his words almost inaudible in the fierce wind.

A loud crack from a tree somewhere up the hill turned their attention to the beast that was coming their way. Shahrem shivered to his bones. He had seen… what it did to its prey… and his heart almost stopped when he realized what a gruesome death his friend was facing.

"Not even The Tyrant deserves to die that way" he shouted to his friend.

"I will be dying already when it gets here. Now go, or it will kill you first!"

Shahrem pulled away from his friend's grip, stood up and looked up the hill. Then he looked at Ayush. Ayush had turned the hunting knife at his own throat. He looked at Shahrem with a desperate request in his eyes, a plea to Shahrem to leave and save himself and the people waiting in the hidden shuttle.

Another loud crack, frighteningly close, got Shahrem moving.

"I will call upon the Gods for you!" he said to Ayush and left.

He ran off down the hill. He turned so the wind would not carry his scent directly toward the beast, and he tried to tell himself that the blood-chilling scream he heard was nothing but the angry wind ripping mercilessly through the forest.

Soon the hill flattened out and he was on softer ground. There were no more rocks, roots or tree branches to look out for. He could run faster.

There was a small pond ahead. His grandfather had taken him there when he was a kid. He could still remember swimming in it. Back then he still had skin between his digits on his hands and feet, but like all reptilians he lost it as he grew up.

The pond was almost gone, lost to plants that grew best in humidity and water. But the ground was still soft and if Shahrem did not look out he would trip and sink in to waist deep water.

Then he would be trapped. And the beast would come and... take him.

The shuttle was on the other side of the pond. He was almost there.

He turned around one last time, as if to say goodbye to Ayush.

Then he saw the eyes. He saw the eyes of the beast, up there among the trees. Two clusters of eyes, glowing green and vicious in the dark.

And the beast screamed again. It raised its head and screamed in triumph.

Ayush was gone. An unspeakable death by the most gruesome beast in the universe. 'You evil Tyrant, one day, it will be your turn' Shahrem thought and formed two claws with his hands. His people had used that gesture since before the dawn of civilization to show their enemies that they would fight to the last breath.

Then he turned again, ran into the deepest part of the valley and got in the shuttle. The others had already fired up its booster engines. They were ready for a lightning-fast take-off.

They took off in the blink of an eye and climbed fast. By the time the military scanners spotted them, they were already leaving the atmosphere.

Ayush's plan had worked. He had given his life for it. Now it was up to Shahrem to honor his sacrifice and bring freedom home to their people.

"Where do we go now?"

It was one of his fellow escapees. A young man, barely old enough to marry.

"As far as we can go" said Shahrem and tried to sound confident.

"But where?" the young man insisted. "We can't just fly around in space."

"Ayush told me about a couple of places…"

"You don't sound very confident."

"He was the one who knew… he had seen the maps."

Shahrem glanced at the young man and his young wife.

Then he noticed something.

She was pregnant.

And it would not be long before she would give birth.

"Look" the young man said and turned to Shahrem again. "I know you're doing your best, but… did Ayush give you any directions?"

"Yes" Shahrem half-lied. "There is a small supply station where we can land and get some supplies. It's a military outpost, but it has no permanent guards. Then we can go from there…"

"A military outpost? But that would trigger the alarm and they would come after us."

Shahrem thought for a moment. The young man's objection was valid. It would greatly increase the risk of them being caught.

"There is another option" he said. "But it's at least as risky, if not more."

"What is it?"

Shahrem glanced at him.

"There is… an inhabited world. About as far as we can fly."

"An inhabited world? I've never heard of it."

"They're not like us. They are bare-skins."

"Bare-skins? They really exist? I thought that was just a myth!"

"Yes, they do. Ayush knew all about it."

"But bare-skins… they don't like us reptilians, do they? I mean, the stories I've heard… and I certainly did not believe them… they said that bare-skins eat reptilians."

"I don't think that's true" Shahrem replied. "But it's either the bare-skin world or that military outpost."

The young man looked at his wife. She was weak, sitting on a bench looking like she could fall asleep any minute. She raised her right hand in an approving gesture.

"OK" the young man said to Shahrem. "Let's go for the bare-skin world."

2 0 1 0

This sector of space was desolate. Vast emptiness, very far between the stars. Almost no planetary systems... and only two worlds with intelligent life within three thousand light years.

A space craft made its way through the endless emptiness. It was a cargo ship, just big enough for two crew members and a little bit of cargo. It was not really built for long distance hauling. Its engines worked hard to keep it on course. Big stars had gravity fields that made the ship veer off course, and Cstoron, the most experienced pilot of the two onboard, had to make constant course adjustments. He had to shift power between the engines and make sure the gravimetric stabilizers were not overloaded.

If they were, it would be bad.

As if reading Cstoron's thoughts, Hwo remarked:

"Imagine getting stranded out here."

He was responsible for the navigation. He read their scanners and tried to plot the best course back home. It was not a whole lot of work, so he took the opportunity to slouch in his seat and stare out in the wild, wide, open space ahead of them.

"That's funny" Cstoron replied without a hint of a smile.

Unlike Hwo, Cstoron was constantly busy with something. He had an electronic notepad in his right hand and a pointer in his left hand. He moved it back and forth and pushed a button on the pointer every now and then. Each time he did, the notepad acknowledged with a muted beep.

"The funny thing" Hwo continued, "is that no one would ever come to our rescue."

He had put his feet up on an empty space on the instrument panel.

He giggled.

"The funniest part" he continued, "is that not a single soul back home would know where to come and look for us. No one has a clue where the Hell we are right now."

"Mr. Kelm does" Cstoron replied, with indifference in his voice.

Hwo glanced at him. Cstoron refused to look up from the notepad.

"And you seriously think he'd come looking for us?" Hwo asked rhetorically.

"With this cargo, he would" Cstoron replied matter-of-factly. "He's paid dearly for it."

The cargo. Hwo had tried to forget about their cargo...

"Yeah, I guess you're right" he mumbled and looked out the window again.

"Can you give me a navigation update?" Cstoron asked.

"What for? We're good for another two hours."

"The gravitational pull is pretty strong here. It's draining our engines. We might not have power enough to go through that big star cluster again."

Hwo slowly put his feet down and tapped a couple of buttons on one of the screens in front of him. The ship's scanners went to work and built an image of space ahead of them. He tapped a couple of more buttons and got two layers of data on top of the space map.

"Well" he said, "if we're going to coast around the big gravitational fields, we'd have to..."

He was interrupted by a loud bump behind them.

Hwo and Cstoron looked at each other.

"It can't be..." Hwo said.

"It can't..." Cstoron agreed. "But what else could it be?"

He turned on an overhead screen. Hwo leaned back as far as he could to see it. The screen was black.

"Turn on the lights back there" Hwo suggested.

"No. If it's awake it will go completely berserk."

Cstoron turned on the infra-scan. An image emerged on the screen.

They both shivered when they saw it.

"I'll never get used to seeing that... thing" Hwo whispered.

There was no doubt. The creature in their cargo bay was awake.

"How could it wake up?" Cstoron asked rhetorically. "They said it was sedated for five days."

"Maybe they didn't care too much" Hwo said.

"Why not?"

"Because they got their payment upfront. Why would they care if Mr. Kelm gets his new pet or not?"

Cstoron looked at him calmly.

"I guess that makes sense" he noted. "The question is, what do we do now?"

"Why?" Hwo asked. "That wall is strong enough to..."

Cstoron shook his head.

"It may hold for a few hours, but that thing is strong. Didn't you see the demonstrations they gave us? When they had it do all those tricks?"

"I... kind of couldn't stomach it" Hwo admitted. "I mean, I get goose bumps when I look at it."

"Goose bumps?"

"That's what we humanoids get when we get scared. My hair stands right up on my arms. What do you reptilians...?"

Hwo was interrupted again by another loud bump.

"It is definitely trying to break through that wall" Cstoron noted. "It's probably hungry."

"Oh, that's just wonderful. And we have three more days of flying to do. Excellent."

"To make things worse" Cstoron said calmly, "we have no extra sedative. So the only option is to kill it."

"What... are you out of your mind??"

"It's the only rational solution."

"Alright. I suggest you walk in to Mr. Kelm and tell him that 'Good afternoon, Master Kelm, we just wanted to let you know that we killed the most expensive pet you ever bought. Have a nice day.' Yeah, that's really good. And you think he's gonna let us walk out of his office alive?"

Cstoron looked at Hwo for a moment. It was obvious he had not thought of that part of the equation.

"We could just change course and head back to Danarvia instead" he suggested. "We can hide from him."

"And just how do you propose we enter Danarvian space? We pull up to the border patrol and show them that ..." and he pointed with his thumb over his shoulder, "that thingamagee... and say 'hey, guys, we just killed a pet that belongs to the biggest drug lord in the galaxy, and we're trying to escape his wrath. Wanna let us in?'. I don't think so, pal."

The beast charged hard against the thick wall that separated the cargo bay from the crew area. This time the ship actually shivered momentarily.

"And we can't open the cargo doors in open space" Cstoron noted. "Alright, what do you suggest we do?"

"I'm not sure" Hwo said. "But since we need to bring the beast to Mr. Kelm, period, and we can't do it right now..." and he glanced at his map screen, "there is really only one solution."

A blood-chilling scream came from the cargo bay.

"And what solution is that?" Cstoron asked, a bit excited for a change.

"We park the damned thing somewhere and come back for it later."

"Park it? What do you mean by that??"

"Here" Hwo said and loaded up his map screen on a screen in front of Cstoron. "See this planet here? It has the right type of atomsphere."

"And it's inhabited" Cstoron noted, rather sternly. "This thing will start eating the locals, and they..."

A loud bump was followed by a cracking sound and another blood-chilling scream.

"It's already breaking through that wall" Hwo said. "We'll dump it on some remote island somewhere, go home and get some sedatives and then come back and pick it up."

"It's a mad plan."

The cabin filled with the smell of the terrifying beast.

"Got a better idea?" Hwo asked.

Cstoron looked at him for a second.

"Alright" he said. "Let's do it."

"You get us there and I'll hold off the beast."

Hwo climbed out of his seat, pulled out a gun and went back into the service hallway. It ended where the crew stored their food, right up against the wall that separated them from the cargo bay.

He saw the crack in the wall. And one of the beast's claw-like feet was trying to make its way through the small opening.

Hwo froze for a second. He had lied to Cstoron. He had seen every single piece of the demonstrations that the Zoh'moorians had given. He had seen all of what the beast could do.

Even how it… consumed people.

It was the most horrifying event he had ever witnessed.

"Take this, you beast from Hell" he said and fired a shot at the claw.

The beast pulled back and was still for a moment. Hwo tried to listen to what it was doing in there. He did not hear anything.

"How long until we get to that planet?" he asked Cstoron.

"An hour."

"It's already broken through the wall. We don't have that much time."

As if to reinforce Hwo's fears, the beast stuck its claw out of the hole again, but this time it did not try to reach for anything.

This time, it tried to cut the hole bigger.

Hwo did not believe his eyes.

"You gotta be kidding me" he whispered.

He fired again. This time the beast did not move its claw at all. Hwo refused to believe that his high-charge energy weapon did not even hurt that beast. He fired again. Same result.

And the beast was actually able to cut the hole a little bit bigger.

It pulled the claw back in and moved around in there.

"How is it going?" Cstoron asked.

Hwo could hear the stress in his voice.

"Well, it's cutting its way through that damned wall" Hwo said.

He fired again, this time right in to the dark hole. Apparently he hit something sensitive, because the beast screamed and moved backward.

"Take that, you monster" Hwo said.

"What did you say?"

"Nothing. I think I hurt it. That should keep it quiet for a moment."

The beast was quiet. Hwo relaxed and lowered his gun.

"Yep" he said. "That sure took care of it."

"You sure you didn't kill it?" Cstoron asked.

"Well, you can always check the infra-scan."

"Maybe" Cstoron said.

He was busy avoiding collision course with a comet. Hwo turned and looked over his shoulder out in the open space.

"You're a good pilot" he noted.

"Thanks."

"Hey, you know what we could do when we get back home?"

"What?"

"We could participate in that race from…"

A deafening scream from the cargo bay was followed by a very loud bang from the cargo bay wall. Hwo turned on a dime, just in time to see a huge crack spread up and down from the hole in the wall.

And a thousand eyes on the beast's horrifying head stared at Hwo, right through the gap in the wall.

*   *   *

THE AMERICAN
UFO REPORT
SEPTEMBER 2010

THE INCIDENT AT JAMTLAND ZOO

As the only English language publication, The UFO Report can now bring the true story of the

**horrifying incident at Jamtland Zoo in Sweden
this past summer. We have interviewed dozens
of witnesses and examined forensic evidence
and two hours of video film. Our conclusion is
that the incident was caused by the landing of
an extra-terrestrial vessel.**

**And the escape, or release, of an extra-
terrestrial animal.**

Around 11:30 PM on a clear night in mid-July this
past summer hundreds of residents in the small,
rural city of Ostersund, Sweden, saw a strange object
descend from the sky. It landed on the top of a
mountain on an island in the lake next to Ostersund.
After a few minutes the object rose to the skies again
and vanished.

That was the beginning of a series of horrifying
events that would leave this peaceful rural community
shattered and devastated.

Within a half hour of the UFO landing on the mountain
top two women came walking up the ski slope of the
mountain. They were on their way home from a party
to their cousin's house on the other side. One of the
women never make it there.

She was killed by an animal so strange and vicious
it scared the other woman mad.

She is now in a mental institution. She screams of
horror through the nights and spends the days locked
up in her room. The only words she can say are: "She's
melting! She's melting!" and "Eyes! Go away!"

When she got to the cousin's house the cousin called
the police to report the other woman missing. A K-9
unit was dispatched but the dog refused to even enter
the wooded area on top of the mountain. The two
police officers left the dog in the patrol car and went
into the woods on their own. What they found has
been classified and the local police chief has issued a
blanket gag order for all officers who ever investigated
this and related incidents.

But with the help of a Swedish journalist the UFO

Report has been in contact with one police officer with good insight into the woman's vanishing. Here is an excerpt of our interview with him:

"It was very strange that the K-9 unit's dog did not want to enter the wooded area. That dog is experienced and has never behaved like that, before or after. The two officers found the place where Ann-Marie and Ylva had their encounter. They found no traces of Ylva, but they did find a large amount of a strange substance on the ground. There was also a strange odor all over the place."

"Did they retrieve any of the substance?"

"Yes."

"Was it analyzed?"

"The forensic expert who looked at it the day after said he had never seen anything like it."

"Can you describe it?"

"No. I never saw it. I spoke to N., one of the K-9 officers, and he described it as yellow blood."

"Yellow blood?"

"That's what he said."

"Were there any tests done on it?"

"I don't know. The entire case has been put under the highest level of classification. All documents were taken away by people from the national police headquarters in Stockholm."

"What happened to the investigation into Ylva's disappearance? What was the conclusion?"

"It was ended as inconclusive."

"When did that happen?"

"A week after she disappeared."

"Is that normal for a missing person case?"

"No. It happened after some military people, well, had paid a visit to the chief."

"The chief of police?"

"Yes. Soon after that the entire case file was retrieved, as I said, by some people who flew in from Stockholm."

This police officer also has good insight into the events that took place at the zoo that borders the wooded mountain area on the island.

"Two nights after Ylva disappeared something happened at the local zoo. Can you tell us about that?"

"Well, one morning a zoo worker found a very strange hole in the ground at the fence that surrounds the zoo. It kind of looked like a wolf had dug itself in underneath the fence."

"Was it like a tunnel under the fence?"

"Yes, the zoo officials investigated and found that someone, or something, had dug a tunnel under the fence. They poured sand into the hole."

"Had anything happened at the zoo that night?"

"They noticed that the animals nearby were very nervous. There were strange tracks in the dirt outside the exotic bird house."

"But they found no animal that could be responsible for the intrusion?"

"No. They opened the zoo as usual"

"It was an uneventful day?"

"Yes. But they put a 'round-the-clock night watch on duty just in case. And that... well, that's how they got the footage."

"The video?"

"Right."

The video that the officer referred to was taken by two night watchmen. One of them had a good camera phone, and it came to good use that night. The UFO Report has seen the footage. Four minutes of it is on YouTube, but we have also seen another eighty seconds that was captured by a surveillance camera.

The four minutes that is available on YouTube show the section of the zoo where the chimpanzees live. The chimps are very nervous over something. Then the camera pans to the right, toward the wall on the far side of the chimpanzee section. Some animal is trying to scale the wall. Strange paws or legs are visible. The two night watchmen run over in that direction, but they cannot get straight to where the animal is because of some storage sheds.

Once the camera man get to the last of the sheds he turns a corner, running. And he finds himself less than 20 feet from the animal.

He manages to focus the camera on the animal for four seconds before he drops it.

He captures images of a black animal, standing on rear legs, with what looks like extremities stretched out from the body.

The night watchmen stop on a dime. Somehow the animal realizes that they are behind it. That is when it turns around and the camera captures a snapshot of its head.

And its green eye clusters.

"We have been trying to find the two night watchmen to interview them, but we they are nowhere to be found."

"They were arrested the next day."

"Why?"

"I cannot elaborate on that."

"But you know what the charges are?"

"All I can tell you is that they won't be available for interviews for a long time."

The most frightening pictures are from the eighty seconds of surveillance camera from the moose section of the zoo. They were taken several hours later and show a walkway, a fence and parts of an open area where two moose stand next to a big bath tub with water.

Suddenly one of the moose, a female, runs away to the left. The other moose, a male, turns to the right and lowers his head. He has big horns and seems to show them off to warn an attacker.

Then something appears to the right. A dark entity crosses the walkway, stops at the fence and somehow makes a hole in it. The moose takes a couple of steps back, but keeps his head lowered.

The dark entity, which looks like it is walking on several legs, charges straight at the moose. The moose tries to hit the attacker with his horns, but the attacker forces him back with something that looks like big crab claws.

The attacker stops with the rear end of its body still visible to the camera. Slowly it walks forward and eventually disappears.

We asked the police officer about this footage.

"What happens here?"

"Uh... well, something attacks the moose and... well, all that was ever found was... well, the same kind of... uh, yellow blood that was found up on the mountain."

"What about the male moose?"

"It... all that was found was its rear legs."

"This entire incident, with the moose, is nowhere to be found in newspapers or TV news broadcasts. The zoo says they had to euthanize the male moose because it got sick."

"Well, now you've seen the footage, so I guess you understand why the truth has been kept from the public."

"And after this, the strange animal is never seen again?"

"No, but it took three more animals at the zoo."

"Why was there never a big hunt for the animal at the zoo?"

"Well, the city mayor and the owner of the zoo agreed that they didn't want to stir up a panic, so they did everything they could to cover it up."

"Was this beastly animal ever captured?"

"No. A secret military commando unit searched the zoo and the wooded mountain top for it. They were able to trace it to the opening of a big cave that runs very deep into the mountain."

"Did anyone ever go in to search for it?"

"Search for something that can kill a fully grown male moose? That can make a woman disappear without a trace? No thanks. Besides, that cave is enormous. It would take a major operation to go down there. So they sealed the entrance to it with concrete."

About ten days later the UFO returned. It was seen circling above the mountain, the island and over the entire city for two nights. There are numerous videos on YouTube of it.

The second night the air force scrambled jets that chased off the UFO. It was never seen again.

Just like the strange animal.

National Swedish government authorities refuse to even discuss the incident. Local authorities turn downright hostile when the incident is brought up. The UFO Report's reporter was threatened with arrest when he asked a representative at the mayor's office for comments.

This is one of the strangest UFO incidents we have ever reported on. It is also one of the most well-documented. There is no doubt that a UFO landed on the mountain outside Ostersund, Sweden. There is also no doubt that the UFO dropped off a strange, beastly creature that killed a woman and four animals at the zoo. Then the UFO came back and searched for the animal, without success.

The only question is: why? Why did they leave the beast there?

The UFO Report has asked two renowned UFO researchers.

Stanley Freeman, a former weapons technology expert with Boeing and prominent UFO scholar:

"Who knows what went on here? On the one hand, it seems like an experiment, but on the other hand, you don't plant an animal in a new environment and then just lose it. It doesn't stand up to scientific standards, and we have to assume that aliens are skilled in scientific methods. I really don't want to speculate here. What is clear, though, is that these events took place and that the Swedish government is carefully hiding the truth from the public."

Tom Welsh, senior editor of the UFO Report:

"What I fear we are dealing with here is a brazen biological weapons test. This could be a genetically modified predator that was planted into our environment to test its capabilities. If it turned out well, these animals might be used by the aliens as part of an invasion strategy. Imagine the panic it would cause among our civilian population if beastly creatures were let loose in our cities. It would disrupt our entire society."

2 0 1 1

It was raining that night. It was a hard rain that kept people off the highways. Especially the highways around Pointers Bridge, Colorado. The small town in the north west corner of the state never saw much traffic anyway, and on a cold, rainy September night it would be easier to find people jogging in Central Park than driving down isolated county roads in the Rockies.

The rain started when the sun set that day. As the people of Pointers Bridge sat down to have dinner they had no idea that their little town was going to be the scene of… well, some unusual events.

It all started when a black Crown Victoria rolled in from Maybell. It pulled up to the local Chevron station and the man in the passenger seat went inside to buy a couple of sodas.

"Jeff, want anything to drink?"

"Get me a Pepsi."

Jeff pretended to fill up the car – he used a credit card but only put three gallons in – while really scanning the area with a small, handheld motion detector.

When the other man came back Jeff replaced the nozzle and put the gas cap back on.

"Any activity?"

"No. Everything's cool."

"So we're good to go, then?"

"Yes."

"I'll call Ray."

The gas station was located on the edge of town. It was surrounded by open fields that sloped up toward high mountain tops. An isolated farm had cultivated most of the land between the slopes.

"This place is perfect" said Jeff.

The other man got in the car and made a phone call. He was on the phone for several minutes while Jeff stood leaning against the car and just looked around.

"What's the matter with you?" asked the phone caller when he got out of the car. "It's freezing here."

"I grew up in Maine. I don't mind the cold weather."

"I grew up in Jacksonville. I do mind the cold weather."

"So what did Ray say?"

"They will be here in half an hour."

"What does the weather report say?"

"It's gonna rain all night."

"Good. That will wipe out the tracks."

During the half hour they waited only one car passed them. The gas station attendant came out and told them he was closing for the night. The two men took the opportunity to buy some snacks for the drive back to Denver. Then they left the gas station and drove a mile back out of town where they stopped and let the engine run.

A couple of minutes passed.

"Where are they?"

"Want me to call Ray again?"

"Yeah."

"They're only five minutes late."

"What if… them… get here first?"

"We'll just tell them to wait."

"Oh yeah? And how do you tell them to do that? You don't even know their language."

"OK, I'll call Ray."

Suddenly the sound of a helicopter broke through the rain. The two men looked out the windshield. They did not see anything. Jeff got out and looked around. He could hear the helicopter just south of where he was – two helicopters, actually.

The other man got out.

"There" said Jeff and pointed.

Eventually they could make out the contours of two black helicopters with no lights or markings. The choppers stopped right above their car and hovered for a minute. One of the men pointed toward the field on the north side of the highway. He was not sure the pilot in the first chopper saw him, but after a few seconds the first one moved out above the field and landed. The second helicopter circled the field first and then set down a little bit farther way from the highway.

"All set."

"Well, Bruce, now we'll just have to wait, I guess."

"Have you ever seen one of… them?"

"Yep."

"What do they look like?"

"You really wanna know?"

"I'm curious."

"They look like…"

Their conversation was interrupted by a loud humming that came from almost right above them. They looked up despite the rain, but could not see anything. Their eyes went back and forth as the humming grew louder.

"There!" said Jeff and pointed up in the sky.

A dark grey object slowly descended through the rain. To the men's surprise it did not look like any flying saucer they had heard stories about. Instead, it looked almost like a small oil tanker from the underside. It descended slowly and folded out something that looked like landing gear. As it set down the humming died down and a couple of lights were lit up on its side.

Bruce and Jeff put on headsets. They listened in on an intense radio conversation as they watched the county road for traffic.

Something that looked like a large hatch opened right below the lights on the alien ship.

"Alright, folks, get the merchandise ready" a voice ordered over the radio. "Tango One to Watchdog, are we clear?"

"All clear" said Jeff.

"Tango Two, you are good to go" said the radio voice.

It was hard to see what went on over at the helicopters. They both knew what was supposed to happen, and as much as they would have liked to be there, all they could do was look on from over a hundred yards away.

"Tango Two, merchandise delivered."

The men by the car both felt a sting of disappointment. They were witnessing a historic event and were not allowed to come closer. As far as they knew, nothing like this had ever happened before. It was unique in human history. An alien ship landing on Earth and they had to stay far away.

It was worse than being allowed to feel your Christmas presents one day in adv…

"Alert! Alert! Merchandise escaped!"

"Tango One, did you just say…"

"One of them escaped! He's running toward the highway! Watchdog, Watchdog! Subject coming your way!"

"Copy that, Tango One! Bruce, get the motion detector!"

Bruce opened the passenger door and got out the motion detector. He fumbled with it for a moment.

"Is it on?!"

"Just a sec… Damn it…"

"Watchdog, do you see him?"

"That's a negative, Tango One, a negative so far. Bruce! Is it on?"

"Got it!"

Bruce raised the motion detector and pointed it toward the helicopters.

"I got… something… coming… uh, this way…"

"What are you talking about??"

"Well, it's not a human…"

"Of course it's not a human! It's an alien! Let me see!"

Jeff dashed around the car to Bruce and took the motion detector from him. He pointed it in the same direction that Bruce had pointed it.

"There" he said. "There's the alien. No, wait…"

"See what I mean?" Bruce said, revealing a sense of harm over Jeff's attitude.

"Alright, I'm sorry…" Jeff started.

He did not finish the sentence. They both stared at the motion detector and the sky. The alien was coming closer. He was only 50-60 feet away. And the alien vessel lifted off and started moving in their direction.

"They're gonna zap him" Bruce guessed.

"Zap? Zap him?? What kind of…"

The alien turned and ran parallel to the road. He was probably trying to reach a wooded area some hundred feet away. The alien ship quickly caught up with him. It sent a quick lightning-like strike down at the alien, who fell to the ground. Then the alien ship shot straight up and vanished into the clouds.

"They… zapped him" Jeff noted.

The radio chatter picked up again.

"Tango Two to Watchdog! Confirm the merchandise has been destroyed!"

"Copy that, Tango Two" said Jeff.

"I get a bad feeling every time they call people merchandise" said Bruce.

"Come on, let's go have a look" Jeff suggested with a voice that revealed that he agreed with Bruce.

With the motion detector pointed straight at the alien Bruce and Jeff left the highway and marched straight out in the grassy field. The ground was muddy thanks to the intense rain and Bruce complained about his shoes leaking water. Jeff told him to shut up and keep walking. Bruce ignored Jeff and reported that the alien was still lying on the ground.

"What kind of life form is he?" he asked.

"A reptilian."

"What's that?"

"Think of it as a human-size T-Rex."

"You're kidding, right?"

Of course Jeff was kidding. Once they got to the alien Bruce sighed of relief when he saw something that looked more like Kermit the Frog than a carnivorous dinosaur.

"He's dead, alright" Jeff noted.

"Watchdog to Tango One" Bruce yelled through the radio. "The... object is dead."

Before Tango One had copied the message, the alien opened his eyes and leaped to his feet. For a split second he stared Jeff and Bruce straight in the eyes, and Bruce felt a cold shiver down his spine. Jeff did not feel anything, except an urgent need to pull out his gun. He reached inside his trench coat, but the alien reptilian apparently realized what Jeff was up to. He made a one-eighty and his tail came flying straight at Jeff's head. It knocked Jeff over and made him fall onto Bruce, who dropped the motion detector and his radio at the same time.

Bruce was able to retain his balance and even managed to get his gun out. He aimed it straight at the alien's face.

Then the alien did something so unexpected that Bruce just stared at him with gaping mouth.

He reached down, picked up a small package of blankets and clothes from the ground and removed its top.

A small head, looking much like the alien's, appeared.

And the alien hugged the package... uh – the baby – and looked at Bruce.

"Mother of God" Bruce whispered and lowered his gun. "You have a baby."

The alien looked at Bruce. Bruce put his gun away.

"Hey... I have no idea why you're here and why that ship tried to zap you" he said. "But I'm not going to shoot someone who's got a baby to care for."

He pointed with his thumb toward the woods behind him, where the alien seemed to have been heading when the alien ship fired at him.

Or was it a her?

"Hey, take off if you want to" Bruce said. "I'm not gonna stop you."

As if he (or she) understood what Bruce was saying, the alien took a few steps past him, still watching Bruce. When he was safely past Bruce the alien took off running.

"Watchdog, Watchdog! This is Tango Two! Respond!"

Bruce suddenly heard the radio. He ear piece was still hanging off his shoulder. He put it back in and turned toward Jeff.

"You OK, buddy?"

"Yeah" Jeff mumbled and got up with Bruce's help.

"This is Watchdog" Bruce said. "Uh… the alien surprised us. He wasn't dead at all. He took off… uh, up toward our car. And past the road."

Jeff looked at Bruce with disbelief in his face.

"Hey, you're bleeding from your cheek, buddy" Bruce said.

"I was knocked over by that alien" Jeff said incredulously.

"Something to write home about" Bruce giggled.

"What happened to the alien?"

"He got away."

"Why didn't you stop him?"

"I'm not sure" Bruce lied. "I think he exercised some kind of mind trick on me."

                    *   *   *

"Madam Secretary, there is a phone call for you."

"Thanks, Molly."

The Secretary of Defense, Holly Stanton, picked up the phone on the desk in her office. It was far too late for her to be up working, but some things just could not wait.

"This is Holly Stanton."

"Ma'm Secretary…"

"Ray, how is the operation going?"

"The merchandise has been delivered."

"Good. That's excellent."

"There is just one problem."

"Ray, I don't have patience for any problems. You know that. What kind of problem are we looking at here?"

"Ma'm, one of the prisoners escaped, but…"

"You let one of them get away??"

"No, it was after they had been turned over to the Zoh'moorians. Somehow he was able to knock down one of their guards and run away. They fired on him from their ship."

"Good. So he died, then?"

"No. But the Zoh'moorians took off believing he died."

"So what happened to him??"

"He was able to get up and run away. I am preparing a manhunt..."

"No, don't do that."

"Ma'm?"

"If the Zoh'moorians think he's dead, we don't have to look like fools... you don't have to look like fools out there... for losing one of the prisoners."

"But ma'm, I think there is a good chance we could catch him."

"We are not going to launch a big manhunt up there. It would catch the attention of the public, and then sooner or later the president will know what we are doing. No. Let him get away. We'll pick him up nice and clean later."

"He's already survived for two years out in the open, ma'm."

"I know that Ray. Damn it, who do you think you're talking to?"

"Yes, of course. I'm sorry, ma'm. So we'll just call off this operation."

"That's right. And make sure everyone knows that the alien is dead. I don't want any rumors going around."

"Yes, ma'm."

Secretary Stanton hung up and leaned back in her seat. She had a wrinkle between her eyes. It meant she was not satisfied with what Ray had reported.

"Bad news?"

Holly Stanton looked up. Her wrinkle disappeared and was replaced by a warm smile.

"Oh, hi, Rhea, I didn't hear you come in."

"You look like you need some company."

"I need your company, Rhea."

"Well, let's go home. You can tell me all about the bad news on the way."

2 0 1 2

The briefing room was small and lacked windows. It was poorly furnished – it even had an old wooden table – and the air was dry and had a dusty smell to it. The climate control system had checked out a week earlier.

When Tahm Qaar entered the room he had already realized that this was an important meeting. His division secretary had told him that two of his commanding officers would be there, together with the agency's foremost expert on emerging civilizations.

It was a bit of a disappointment, though, that his bosses had located their meeting to this old shack. The campus of Advanced Retrieval, the intelligence agency of The Federation of Danarvia, was short on office space. Sometimes even extremely important meetings were held in this old shack that was ready to be torn down any day.

Tahm Qaar stopped briefly as he entered the room. There were four chairs around the table and not much room to get around behind them. The empty chair was on the far side of the table.

"Thanks for coming on such short notice" said Tahm Qaar's boss. "Have a seat."

"Thanks" said Tahm Qaar and tried to squeeze in behind the civilizations expert.

"Oh, I'm sorry" said the expert. "I'll just move over."

He was a reptilian, very overweight with a massive tail. He took heavy breaths as he got up and moved to the next chair. His moves were slow and it was easy to see that his weight was bothering him. He had difficulties controlling his tail as he sat down; the seats had openings in the back seat for reptilians to put their tail through, but they were normalized for, well, normal tails, not very fat ones.

"It's just my tail" the expert said wearily. "It won't fit the chairs anymore."

"You have a big tail, Rohm" said one of the bosses, also a reptilian. "Females think that's attractive."

"Tell that to my wife" Rohm sighed. "All she talks about is how I need to lose some weight."

"Thanks for the seat" Tahm Qaar said and sat down.

Rohm nodded to him.

"Let's get started" said the highest ranking boss, an albino human. "Rohm here is an expert on emerging civilizations."

"I've read some of your work, doctor" Tahm Qaar said, turning to Rohm with a gesture of respect. "Very impressive."

"Thank you."

"TQ, I know you've only been home a couple of months since your last assignment" said the albino. "So I hope you understand I am not at all happy to ask you to take on a new assignment."

Tham Qaar revealed his feelings for a moment, without saying anything.

"I know" the albino continued. "I know it's taking a toll on you being away from home. And I know you're scheduled for a home assignment now..."

"I was hoping to get a teaching job at the academy for the next year."

"You are entitled to that according to your contract" the reptilian boss added. "That's why we are not ordering you to take this job. We're asking you. If you say no, it won't be held against you."

"Your career with the agency is formidable" the albino continued. "You're one of our top five assignment commanders of all time."

"Thank you, sir."

"If you say no to this one we will make sure you get a good teaching job instead."

The room fell quiet. Tahm Qaar looked at his two bosses. His big, strong hands rested on the table in front of him. They had scars from decades of intelligence operations, assignments to dangerous worlds, even war zones. His memory spanned vastly different jobs. He had survived a mass execution on one assignment. On another he had purposely almost starved himself to death. He had killed people, he had been betrayed by pretended allies, he had fought insects the size of a grown man and searched for state secrets buried deep into the core of a seismically collapsing planet.

He could quit the Alien World Operations division, join the agency academy full time and say he had been there, done that, seen it all.

So why would he take on a new assignment?

His bosses knew why.

"Well…" Tahm Qaar said. "I'm curious. What's the assignment? I mean, it's gotta be something pretty good if you're calling me in for it."

The albino smiled briefly.

"You won't regret taking this assignment" he said.

"I didn't say I'll take it" Tahm Qaar replied, but they both knew he would not say no at this point.

"It's a world in sector KB" said the reptilian.

"KB? That's three sectors outside Danarvian space."

"It's a fairly low-advanced civilization" the albino continued. "Rohm, this is your area."

"Yes" said Rohm and consulted his notes. "This is a humanoid world with a Brix evolution index at no more than three. Split into multiple nations, no world government, and from what we have been able to tell they are not very good at respecting individual freedom. Big governments run the economy. Based on data we have been able to siphon off their global data network, we estimate that taxes are somewhere in the range of forty to fifty percent of the economy."

"What?!" Tahm Qaar almost cried out in an unusual outburst of emotions. "That's tyranny!"

"I think we can all agree on that" Rohm continued and nodded emphatically. "Their governments run everything from education to health care to retirement funds. But at least they have free elections in many countries. So what you have here is a classic case of government intruding on people's freedom and excusing it with free elections. A low Brix evolution level. I say three, not higher. But this is all based on electronic surveillance. No on-ground investigation yet."

"Media monitoring?"

"Media, computer-based communications, chatter. Our language division estimates there are well over a hundred languages on that world."

"How long have you studied them?"

"Two years."

"We want to put a ground team on that world" said the albino.

"Already?" Tahm Qaar said, surprised. "But the normal remote monitoring time is four years."

"Well..." the reptilian said and glanced at the albino. "There was a bit of an incident that made us accelerate."

"Eight months ago space troopers in the Felix sector picked up two young criminals" the albino said. "They had veered off a super-light speed corridor and were flying erratically around the Felix 242 system. It turned out they were errand boys for the Dream Web."

"A fraction of them has re-established itself in the Temptation Sea" the reptilian added.

"Ah, outside Danarvian space" Tahm Qaar noted.

"Right" the albino nodded. "They are pushing mind-enslaving drugs on at least two worlds out there, and local law enforcement is struggling to keep up with them. Since it's outside of our jurisdiction they can do pretty much what they want to. These two young men were on the run from the Dream Web. Apparently the leader of that Web fraction, a Mr. Kelm, is a collector of exotic animals. They had been sent to pick up some exotic species on a planet they said was located somewhere on the outskirts of the Temptation Sea, but their navigation computer quit working and they ended up on this world in the KB sector."

"They told the space troopers they ran out of food for the animal" said the reptilian. "So they landed on a remote island but the animal died of food poisoning."

"Since Mr. Kelm would kill them if they did not return with the animal they chose to run away" the albino concluded.

"Let me see if I get this right" Tahm Qaar said. "A drug lord sends two of his errand boys to some world to pick up an exotic animal. Their navigation system breaks down, they land on a civilized world way outside the Temptation Sea and manage to stay there with an exotic animal without being detected. Then the animal dies and they take off and fly all the way from KB to Felix, pretty much in the opposite direction than Temptation Sea, and they do it with a broken navigation system."

"No one believes their story" the albino said. "Except for the part about landing on the world in KB. That much we know they did. The problem is that if a couple of young criminals can use that world as a rest area it is only a matter of time before all sorts of people will go there with more or less sinister intentions."

"Like pushing mind-enslaving drugs" the reptilian added. "If we can accelerate the process and make formal contact we may be able to avoid what has happened in the Temptation Sea."

"I see" said Tahm Qaar.

"You have the usual time to prepare" the albino continued.

He paused and looked at Tahm Qaar.

"That is… if you accept the assignment, of course."

Tahm Qaar leaned back on his chair and smiled.

"Sure, damn it. I'll do it."

"Good" the albino smiled back. "Then we'll leave you with doctor Rohm. He can tell you all about Earth."

"Earth, sir?"

"That's what the indigenous people call their world" said Rohm.

"Weird name."

"So is Danarvia" the albino chuckled as he left the room.

*   *   *

The security measures at Wright Patterson Air Force Base were exceptional. Not only was the secretary of defense landing there, and not only did she have a former president – her brother – with her, but there was also a rumor going around that an alien ship would land at the base.

"Maybe it's the first contact" a master sergeant said to an airman first class.

The airman gave the master sergeant a funny look, forgetting his lower rank for a moment.

Darkness had fallen and all activity at the base had been suspended. All personnel that was not absolutely necessary had been sent home, but the security posts had double manning. Patrols around the air base had also been doubled. Phone calls in and out of the airbase were cut off, except for what was permitted at the A2 military alert level.

"Why is the base on A2 alert, sir?" asked another airman as he approached the master sergeant.

"A2 means 'attack on the United States is imminent'" said the sergeant, with a strangely relaxed tone in his voice. "Don't worry, son, we're not going to be attacked."

"So… why this high alert? It's just the defense secretary visiting."

His question was answered by a humming sound coming from above. They all looked up and tried to locate it. It seemed to come from everywhere.

"There!" said one of the airmen. "Look at that thing!"

The three men stared in awe at the vessel that slowly lowered itself from straight above the tarmac outside one of the major buildings on the base.

"That's no UFO" said the other airman, clearly disappointed.

"No UFO?" the sergeant asked, looking at him like he was talking to a whimsical kid.

"I mean… it's no flying saucer."

"Maybe it's a flying oil tanker" giggled the other airman.

"You guys are wearing me out" the sergeant sighed and walked over toward the building where he had his office.

The airmen stayed outside and watched how the alien vessel folded out some landing gear and set down.

"First contact" said one of them.

"Then where's the president?" asked the other.

"Out giving a speech somewhere."

He was right. President Barry Oslow was in Venezuela to give a speech and had no idea what was going on at Wright Patterson Air Force Base. His vice president was just as uninformed.

"The White House would go berserk if they knew about this" secretary of defense Holly Stanton whispered to her brother, former president Walter Stanton.

"Look, sis" said Walter Stanton, "we've kept this a secret for some time now. Nothing's gonna change there."

"Just remember… when you meet the Supreme General, greet him with 'ah'owee'a'. It means distinguished leader. And when you meet the Grand Leader himself you address him as 'kho'ram'schar'. Means something like the beloved master. It's important."

"What's even more important is the negotiations" Walter Stanton pointed out. "If I succeed…"

"The world will be at our feet" Holly Stanton smiled.

"Just make sure everyone thinks I'm in Europe. OK?"

"OK."

Former President Stanton gave his sister a kiss on the cheek and left the building. He walked out on the tarmac, chatted jovially with a couple of Secret Service agents and continued toward the alien craft that had now settled down and opened a hatch on the side. It had folded out a walkway and two beings, appearing to be soldiers, came out and took position on each side of the walkway.

Walter Stanton stopped briefly before he entered the walkway. He turned around and waived toward the windows where his sister stood. She waived back and felt a sting of worry.

So much depended on his trip. What if they had overlooked something? What if he displeased the Grand Leader?

What if he did not come back?

It is late May 2013.

The invasion of the United States of America is imminent.

CONSPIRACY

Vice president Holly Stanton was not a tall woman. She was quite possibly the shortest vice president that the United States had ever had. But it would be a bad mistake to think that her short height was somehow representative of how she fulfilled her duty as vice president. Anyone who made the mistake that they could talk above the her head just because she was short was in for an unpleasant surprise.

She was on top of any conversation, any issue, any social gathering. Whenever she walked in to a room, she owned it.

Nobody knew that better than Irwin Schwepp. He had worked with Holly Stanton ever since she was attorney general of New York way back in the early '90s. He had been with her through her years as a U.S. Senator and her campaign for president in 2008. She had lost the primaries to Barry Oslow.

Through a stroke of luck Oslow had appointed her secretary of defense. Some would say it was more than a stroke of luck – that she had something on him, something incriminating. But those were probably just rumors.

Then, in good time before the 2012 election, vice president Jeffrey Becker had declined to seek a second term with Oslow. No one really knew why, but some people noted that Holly Stanton looked extraordinarily happy the day Becker announced.

Who better suited to take his place than defense secretary Holly Stanton? Well, there were many names on that list, but somehow president Oslow felt compelled to choose Holly Stanton.

From the day Stanton took over the Department of Defense she had shown Oslow who was wearing the pants in his administration. After a few confrontations he had given in to her and basically let her run her own show from Pentagon. Now that she was vice president it was a poorly kept secret that Holly Stanton ran the White House.

President Oslow spent most of his time giving speeches around the world. He also wrote a column in the New York Times.

Holly Stanton was a cunning politician. Thanks in good part to Irwin and his ability to make things happen, she had effectively become the 45th president of the United States without being elected. She could operate from behind the scenes without having to take any official responsibilities.

It was a perfect position for her.

And Holly Stanton saw a future. A bright future. She had ambitions, far bigger than anyone could imagine.

She put a lot of faith in Irwin Schwepp to help her fulfill her ambitions. She needed him. She had shared many, many secrets with him and trusted him with doing things for her that nobody else knew about.

Except her brother, former president Walter Stanton.

Irwin knew that whenever he was called in to an early morning meeting with the president, it was serious business. And when her brother was there, too – then it was really serious.

He had been told to report to the Oval Office, which was a bit unusual. The vice president really did not use the Oval Office unless the president was abroad. And as far as Irwin knew, president Oslow was somewhere in New England.

But Irwin did not question the location of the meeting. He was a loyal servant. And Holly Stanton was his master.

When Irwin came in, Walter Stanton was standing by the bay window, right next to Holly. The former president's presence gave Irwin a clue that this meeting was even more important than he had thought. Something really big was going on. Probably an international crisis. Maybe a huge scandal with some big name in Congress.

Or maybe even with president Oslow.

Holly Stanton was looking out the window at the lawn. She looked short next to her 6'4" brother who, frankly, still looked very presidential. But Irwin was also struck by how much Walter Stanton had aged recently. He had been in Europe for six months not too long ago, and that trip seemed to have been a bit tough for him.

The Stanton siblings were talking about something when Irwin entered. Walt Stanton noticed Irwin, nodded to his sister and came over toward Irwin.

"Hi, Irwin" he said and offered his hand. "Been a while."

"Yes. I haven't seen you since before you went to Europe."

"Always busy, Irwin" Walt Stanton chuckled in a way only he could. "Always busy. Have a seat."

They sat down at a side table with a small couch and two armchairs. Walt Stanton took one of the armchairs and Irwin sat down on the couch. Holly Stanton came up to them and stopped behind her brother.

Irwin put his folder on the table. He had a notepad in it and some very exclusive pens.

"There's no need to take notes" Holly Stanton said and nodded toward the folder.

Unlike her brother, the vice president seemed uneasy. Her face was tense and she barely looked at Irwin as she sat down in the other armchair. Irwin had rarely seen her so tense and for a moment he wondered if he was going to be fired. He could not for the life of him see why, but you never knew with Holly Stanton.

Since she did not want him to take notes Irwin put away the folder on the couch next to him. He noticed that his hand was getting sweaty. The palm left an imprint on the cover of the folder.

Holly Stanton did not seem to notice how nervous he was, but Walt did. He took the lead in the conversation.

"We got something very important to talk about, Irwin. You've done a lot of good work for Holly over the years and that's why you're here now. She trusts you and so do I."

Irwin relaxed a bit. His job was not the topic of the meeting. But he was still a bit cautious. Holly Stanton was so nervous that there was no doubt in Irwin's mind that he was about to hear something Earth shattering.

He had done a lot of things for her, things that were so bad sometimes that if the general public ever got to hear about it, they would demand her impeached, even if it was before she became vice president.

Each time he had done such things he had been called in for an early morning meeting like this.

But never before had Holly Stanton looked so nervous.

"I'm always there for you" Irwin said quickly, looking at her.

For the first time since he walked in the room she actually looked at him. Her face was tense, her lips tight and her eyes cold as steel.

Irwin had a bad feeling about this one. His armpits got sweaty and he moved a pen he had in his right hand to his left hand and back just to ease some of the excitement.

"Irwin" said Holly Stanton quietly. "Do you remember our little meeting in Denver the day before Independence Day in 2009?"

Irwin's forehead wrinkled as he tried to remember the occasion.

"Yes…" he said. "Uh… yes, ma'm, I remember…"

"Do you remember the group of people we met with?"

"Yes, I do. It was the inner circle of the Bilderberg group. It was the first meeting of the One World campaign. You discussed how best we can promote a world government."

"We've been working on that ever since" said Walter Stanton. "I've been chairman of the working group. We've been advancing the plans for a world government for years now. And we're almost there."

He paused, as if to make sure that Irwin paid very close attention to his next words.

"Irwin…" he said slowly. "Do you remember how many people came to the meeting in Denver?"

"Yes" Irwin said, confused by the questions. "There were twelve people there, including me."

"Well, there was one more participant" Walter continued. "Someone you did not meet. Only four of the others met him."

Irwin waited. He felt a sting of excitement. There was no doubt Walter Stanton was revealing a very, very big secret.

"And... who was that?" Irwin asked.

Walter Stanton and his sister exchanged a quick look.

"Ambassador Hreutz, envoy for the Grand Leader of Zoh'moor."

"Who, sir?"

"Irwin..." Holly Stanton said, with an eerie calm in her voice. "We are ready to take over."

Irwin took a deep breath and raised his eyebrows.

"Well... ma'm... with all due respect, haven't we done that already? I mean, we're in the White House and the president isn't exactly working..."

Walt Stanton chuckled.

"We're not talking about that, Irwin" he said.

"I'm not following you, sir" Irwin admitted.

Holly Stanton explained:

"We're talking about creating a world government."

"But... how?" Irwin asked, sensing that there was something earth shattering coming down the pike.

With chilling calm in her voice Holly Stanton spelled it out for him.

"Our friends are coming" she said. "The Zoh'moorians. They're going to help us."

"The... who, ma'm?"

*   *   *

Advanced Information Retrieval Agency
Division of Alien World Operations
KB11-4-3 Earth Assignment Progress Report
Federation Universal Time Date Nomo 7372-09
Local Time Date KB11-4-3 May 24 2013
Chief Assignment Officer Tahm Qaar

KB 11-4-3 "Earth" assignment detail is now fully operational. All agents have been deployed and information retrieval is progressing as expected. Assignment headquarters is protected by Level Four security measures. Two cloaked satellites are in orbit and we have parked three cloaked surface-to-surface transport vessels in the upper atmosphere.

Our mission to investigate Earth for official contact is in full progress. The information environment is more favorable than initially expected. There is an abundance of local resources, even a fully developed information network called "the grid". The computer technology here has leaped in recent years but crystal-based computers are still not available. We expect to be independent of AWO support from now on.

Agents have blended in well. The physical similarity between our agents and Earthlings is strong. Physical differences are limited to different shapes of ears – Earthlings have somewhat larger elliptical ears – and there is a smaller variety of skin color among Earthlings. But the blending-in has been hassle free with the exception of my rookie agent, Goryell, who is a bit too interested in Earthling women. I have had a talk with him and he understands my concerns. On the upside, he has given us all a good overview of the culinary resources here. This should not be underestimated: it has helped us get comfortable in our daily lives and allowed us to stay away from our (still tasteless) AWO field meal rations.

We are based in the nation called United States of America, abbreviated USA or America. The USA is a federation of states. We are located in the state of New Mexico.

Our political evaluation group reports a complex pattern of nations and alliances across Earth, characteristic of a civilization at Brix Evolution Index step three. The leadership of America appears to be among the most advanced and our preliminary evaluation is that a first contact should be with the American government.

Addendum - Important!

Just this morning our signal monitoring satellite picked up an atypical transmission from Earth. It was directed toward coordinates in the outer rim of sector KB, toward the edge of the galaxy. The transmission was powered by particle boosters, a technology that is one or two steps above Earth's technological evolution according to the Brix index.

Earth has no off-world outposts. I therefore suggest that they may have made contact with a world located further out in this sector, who has shared their communications technology with Earth. Publicly accessible media resources here contain no information about any such contacts. Therefore, my conclusion is that such contacts are hidden under massive layers of secrecy.

Our databases have no information on the part of sector KB that borders the edge of the galaxy. I therefore recommend that a space mapping unit be deployed to this sector immediately.

A recording of the signal is attached to this message.
End report.

*　　*　　*

On Pendleton Street in Columbia, just off the University of South Carolina campus, was an old, worn-and-torn brick building that looked like it had survived a hundred battles. In a way it had. It was *The Flunked Final*, a student hangout with two bars, a dancing floor, game rooms, pool tables and a lot of atmosphere. It was owned by Gus, who had dropped out in junior year after flunking all his finals in the spring semester. He was too embarrassed to go home to Augusta, Georgia, so he decided to start a business in Columbia. He bought a blighted old fraternity house and opened it to all USC students.

Of course, he really was not allowed to serve alcohol to anyone under 21, but he had found a flaw in the South Carolina law that regulated alcohol sales that said that anyone who could "credibly show" that he was 21 could be served alcohol. So he applied his own definition of credibility and there was nothing the state could do about it. Not that they had not tried – they had sued him for serving alcohol to minors. He won, of course.

Gus was legendary among college students in the Columbia area and a hero to many libertarians. The American League of Young Libertarians always held their annual national conference at *The Flunked Final* – a four-day stretch of endless political debates, vintage computer games, wild parties and massive sleep deficits. Mostly, they got together to have fun, but many of them also went there because they wanted to build political networks. Some worked as Congressional staffers, others were elected to city councils or school districts. A couple of lucky ones worked for Paul Carlyle, the iconic libertarian member of the United States Senate.

But most of the Young Libertarians were students, undergraduate or in grad school. Like Jack, Todd, Ched, Walid and Alexis. They were all grad students from Schuyler University in Saratoga Springs, New York. They were members of the same local chapter of the Young Libertarians and worked hard on their Ph.D.'s. Even though they did not talk about it, there was some sort of competition between them about who could get the doctorate first.

Saturday night was the last night of the Young Libertarian convention. The air inside *The Flunked Final* was thick with smoke, random talk and loudspeakers filled with *Heartattack and Vine* by Tom Waits. At the bar on the ground floor Walt Widebelly was discussing *habeas corpus* with a cute blonde from Harvard Law School. Walt had wanted to go to law school, but he did not get in. So he had become a political science major and concentrated in constitutional theory. He considered himself a constitutional expert, especially in the First Amendment.

The cute blonde from Harvard told him she could not see what *habeas corpus* had to do with the First Amendment. Then she smiled, kissed him on the cheek and left.

Jack passed Walt Widebelly just as the blonde left.

"Hi, Walt" he said and put his hand on Walt's right shoulder. "Who's the babe?"

"Uh, just some blonde from Harvard."

"Too bad she left."

"It's the third blonde I try to pick up in two days who just walks away" Walt Widebelly complained. "Wonder what's wrong with me."

"Nothing's wrong with you" Jack said. "Some girls might find you a bit... ponderous, but..."

"You saying I'm fat?" Walt noted.

"I'm saying those weight-freaky blondes are out of your league, Walt. They're out of my league, too."

"Out of my league? Who's ever *in* my league? Do you know how long it's been since I had a decent date?"

"Trust me, Walt. You don't want that girl. Haven't you been paying attention? You've seen her over at the hotel at breakfast. She has dark rye bread for breakfast, lunch and dinner, and all she puts on her bread is a slice of tomato. She adds some lettuce for dinner to make the meal more interesting. I don't think she knows what cheese is. Can you actually picture yourself dating her without sharing her food habits?"

Walt's face turned pale. He shivered as he looked over to where the blonde had disappeared. But he did not see her. All he saw was a double cheese pizza flying away on the black wings of sorrow.

"There's nothing wrong with fat" Jack continued. "It's just that some gals are obsessed with it. They watch their Body Mass Index like you watch the stock market."

Walt laughed.

"Yeah, I guess you're right. I should find myself a... what was it you called me?"

"Ponderous."

"Yeah, a – ponderous – woman."

"Hey, Walt, I have a legal question for you."

Walt loved legal questions. He loved them so much he could almost taste them. In one of his secret daydreams he had grilled civic law for dinner.

"Sure" said Walt. "I love legal questions."

"What's the minimum sentence for breaking the law of gravity?"

"Well..." Walt started out, bravely searching his memory banks, until he realized that Jack was pulling his leg. "A-ha! Hey, that's a funny one. I gotta use it some time."

"Might yield a date or two" Jack smiled and headed upstairs.

The second floor was divided into a dance section and a section with tables and a bar. In the back corner of the table section, around a big, round table, sat a whole bunch of Jack's best libertarian friends. Todd, Ched, Walid and Alexis were already there. And Big Red Bob, Wolkenkratzer, Charon and Salto Waltz.

Oh, and Jack's biggest crush of all times: Jenny Blue Eyes.

Alexis was deeply involved in a discussion about the federal funds rate with Todd and Salto. The rest of them were more or less seriously engaged in an arm wrestling contest. Jack looked at Jenny, who was in graduate school in Pennsylvania, not too far from Schuyler University. She was writing a dissertation in finance and came from a very wealthy family. She was also an avid lacrosse player, remarkably good at arm wrestling and drop dead gorgeous.

"Jack!" cried Big Red Bob, whose smile always grew with his blood alcohol level. "C'mon over here!"

He pointed Jack to a seat next to him and grabbed an empty glass from the table. He poured Jack a beer from the nearest pitcher and toasted with him. Jack looked around and saluted them all. He took an extra long look at Jenny Blue Eyes who smiled back at him and made him nervous all the way from his stomach to his ears.

"Good you came" Big Red Bob said. "Ched and I were just debating what the answer is to the ultimate question."

Jack glanced at Ched Chatson. Ched was chain smoking as usual when he was drunk. He looked at Jack with high expectations. Unlike Big Red Bob, both Ched and Jack had read *The Hitchhiker's Guide to the Galaxy* and knew the answer.

"And why should I tell you that?" Jack asked. "What's in it for me?"

"Another big, fat beer" Big Red Bob said. "My treat."

"Deal! The answer to the ultimate question is forty two."

Ched looked at Big Red Bob with a smile on his face. Jack tried to ignore him. He had answered the question not because he wanted to make Ched happy, but because he shared Big Red Bob's taste for beer.

"Oh, so I lost that one" said Big Red Bob. "Well, that's life. How'ya been, Jack? Haven't seen much of you at the convention."

"Well, you know how politics can be."

"Yeah. Actually, I've spent most of my time here playing computer games."

He laughed a thundering laugh.

"Still in law school?" Jack asked.

"Still in" laughed Big Red Bob and raised his beer glass. "The problem with law school is not staying in. The problem, folks..." and he addressed the entire table, "The problem is getting out the other door. The graduate door, you know."

The entire table toasted, except Walid who did not drink. Todd Salmon was finishing his third Scotch while Alexis fired off another round of verbal ammo at Salto Waltz. Jack felt sorry for Salto. He was not even half as quick witted and verbally savvy as Alexis, and he had no clue what she was talking about.

Wolkenkratzer and Charon Outcaster engaged in arm wrestling. They were both about the same size. Wolkenkratzer had never been to a gym, but was still pretty good at arm wrestling. Charon had been to his campus gym many times but did not believe that his biceps were as strong as they actually were. Wolkenkratzer, on the other hand, was endlessly confident that he could beat the puny little Charon – who was actually two inches taller than Wolkenkratzer – just by imagining himself as a winner. He stared at Charon with a mean look on his face. Charon got nervous and suspected that anything might happen if he won. He failed to use the full strength of his muscles, but Wolkenkratzer still had to cheat to win.

Jenny Blue Eyes had fun watching Wolkenkratzer cheat himself to victory. Jack glanced at her and got nervous when she glanced back with a smile.

*   *   *

Senator Carlyle was driving a white Buick. As he pulled out from the parking lot, he waived and smiled at a group of people standing on the lawn on the driver's side of the car. They waived back and thanked him and called him both brave and "our next president". The old man honked and waved one last time before he made a left turn and accelerated down the street.

The weather was not very good, but there was still no rain. He did not like driving in the dark any more, but sometimes, he thought, 'you just have to step up to the plate'. His wife had a hip injury and could not drive him. And he did not want to bother anyone else with driving him.

As he passed through the next intersection the crowd dissolved and most people went back to their cars. No one noticed the dark grey Taurus that pulled out from a parking space along the street. It slowly passed the dissolving crowd until it was about fifty feet down the street. Then it sped up.

"Don't lose him, Craig."

"I'm not losing him, Irwin. Take it easy."

The white Buick's tail lights made a right turn two blocks down the street. The Taurus passed a light just as it turned red to keep up.

"Don't take any risks, Craig!"

"Easy. There's no cop around here."

"I don't care. We can't afford to get pulled over right now."

The white Buick made a left.

"What if he takes the interstate?"

"Craig, he's not taking the interstate. He never does. He thinks this route is a shortcut."

"Yeah. A damned slow one."

"Now, shut up and let me calibrate this thing."

They left the city and crossed a couple of cornfields. The road made a right turn and they came upon a wooded area. The Buick slowed down to under the speed limit.

"Alright, Craig. Slow down. Put a quarter mile between us. There's a long stretch here, almost a mile. See?"

"Yeah, I see it."

"The next turn is a left turn. As soon as his tail lights vanish, I'll push the button."

"And then we make a left onto that county road."

"Right."

They slowed down a bit more. A small flatbed truck came around the bend at the end of the stretch.

"Alright, let him pass before you make the turn."

"Irwin, he'll see the blast in his rearview mirror."

"So what? It's an accident."

The Buick reached the left turn. The flatbed had not yet passed the Taurus.

"Push the button, Irwin!"

"Not until the truck's passed us."

"But he's leaving the wooded area!"

"If we turn after the explosion, we'll look suspicious."

The truck slowed down as it approached the intersection.

"I'm gonna have to stop here!"

"No, just turn."

"Now?"

"Yes!"

The Taurus made a left turn on to the county road.

Irwin pushed the button.

"There" he said, relaxed.

The flatbed turned the opposite way. Apparently, the driver did not notice the explosion that followed when a small Semtex device tore the Buick's gas tank open and ignited the gasoline.

"May God have mercy on his soul" Craig chuckled.

Irwin glanced at him.

"You're so full of shit. Let's get outta here."

* * *

Todd knew all about Jack's crush on Jenny. He decided to offer his friend an ice-breaker.

"Jenny" he said and unintentionally pointed at her with the filter end of his cigarette. "Why don't you challenge Jack? He's a damned good arm wrestler."

"Good idea" she said and swapped chair with Todd to get next to Jack.

"Oh, well, maybe not a good idea, I mean bad idea, I mean..." Jack stumbled like an idiot, trying to ignore the smirk on Todd's face.

Jenny put her arm in position and looked Jack deep in his eyes. Jack got all sweaty and nervous. 'Dear God' he thought, 'why are you doing this to me?' 'Because you deserve it, you promiscuous, irresponsible little party animal' God replied.

"Huh?" said Jack.

"What?" said Jenny.

"Oh, never mind."

Jack blushed and Jenny smiled. Her blue eyes were so pretty that Jack was sure she'd get away with murder. Her hair was so blonde it simply could not be fake, her...

"Ten bucks on Jenny!" cried Big Red Bob behind Jack.

"Twenty!" said Wolkenkratzer.

"You don't have twenty bucks" Jack said and grabbed Jenny's hand.

"I'm betting Charon's twenty."

"What?" said Charon. "Hey, that's my money."

Not only was Jenny as pretty as any girl could be. She was also surprisingly strong for a girl her size. They looked one another deep in the eyes and began flexing their muscles.

"Ready, set, go!" Todd said.

On 'Go' Jenny smiled, formed the words 'I love you' with her lips and flirted intensely with Jack. Jack got all shaky, lost his concentration and focus and she smashed his hand on to the table.

Everyone cheered.

"Hey!" Jack said. "No fair! You cheated! You said you love me!"

That triggered a tsunami of laughter around the table. Except Salto Waltz.

"I won!" she said with a slightly naughty voice. "What's my prize?"

"No, no" Jack protested and shook his head. "Best out of three. Either that or I'll challenge you down in the pool room."

"I'll take the pool room."

"One hour."

She gave him a long look as she left. Big Red Bob put his big, nicotine-stained hand on Jack's shoulder.

"No more lonely nights for you, mister" he said.

"Man, that girl's got *cojones*" said Jack.

"Actually, she did cheat" said Big Red Bob. "Alexis told her to use that trick on you."

Jack looked at Alexis who blew a kiss at him from across the table.

"Well, thanks… I guess…" said Jack.

"My pleasure."

"No, no. My pleasure."

He refilled his beer glass.

"And Jenny's" he added.

Everyone laughed except Salto. Todd noticed Salto's lack of sense of humor. He decided that Salto could use a crash course in comedy.

"Salto" he said and leaned over toward him. "Can you tell me… what is the difference between an elephant?"

Salto stared at Todd with pale eyes.

"I beg your pardon?" he asked.

"What is the difference between an elephant?"

"Is this some kind of joke?" Salto asked suspiciously.

"That's right" Todd said and killed his cigarette. "What is it? The difference."

"What difference?"

"Between an elephant."

"An elephant and what?"

"Between an elephant" Todd repeated patiently.

"It can neither ride a bike" Ched Chatson filled in.

Everyone laughed except Salto.

"C'mon, Salto" said Todd. "It's a joke."

"It's funny" said Salto without the slightest hint of amusement.

Ched Chatson blew a couple of rings of smoke in Salto's direction. Salto got irritated and waived his hand in front of his face to evade it.

"Let him off the hook" said Big Red Bob. "Salto gave a great seminar on Robert Nozick's writings today."

"Yeah" Jack said. "Salto is a good guy. Hey, Salto, what do you want to do after grad school?"

"Get a job as a professor" Salto replied with a taint of relief and gratefulness for being rescued.

"Me too" said Alexis. "But I want to work for Senator Carlyle first."

"He's my idol!" Wolkenkratzer declared.

"He's damned good" Jack agreed. "He has introduced more tax cut bills in the senate than all the other Republicans together."

"He has the only plan to privatize Social Security" Alexis noted.

"All of it?" asked Big Red Bob.

"The whole thing."

"That's my guy."

"He's a freedom fighter" Jack added. "The best there is in Washington since Ron Paul."

"Is he running for president in 2016?" asked Todd.

"I bet" Jack said. "I hope."

"I met one of his staffers at a seminar today" said Alexis. "She said Carlyle is definitely going to run for president."

"Awesome!" Jack said.

As the night went on they enjoyed company, music and fair amounts of alcohol (some had more than fair amounts). Jack shot pool with Jenny Blue Eyes and won twice. When he tried to buy her a drink she said she had to go home and prepare for tomorrow's classes. When he said that tomorrow was a Sunday and that she was four states away from her school, she looked him deep in the eyes and said that he was a very smart young man and that she had a certain thing for very smart young men. Then she put a hand written note in his hand, left him and vanished out in the street.

He unfolded the note. '422' was all it said.

Damned! That woman! Two floors up from his hotel room.

This was going to be a long night.

He tried to re-unite with his friends, but it was not easy. Todd had already moved on to the next phase of the night and was nowhere to be found. Walid and Salto had withdrawn to a room in the attic to discuss John Rawls. Big Red Bob was throwing dart with a bunch of local students and was too drunk to even hit the dart board. And with a pending *rendez-vous* with Jenny Blue Eyes, Jack had no interest whatsoever in talking to Alexis, who was his old girlfriend from high school.

He was just about to leave when Ched Chatson grabbed his right arm. Jack turned and looked at him. Ched had smoked a good amount of pot and had one too many scotches.

"So tell me" Ched said, "what do you really think about legalization of marijuana?"

Jack turned to him and searched for a quick, witty comeback to get him out of the challenge. Ched knew that he and Jack were on different sides of that issue. They had discussed it a gazillion times. Jack was not in the mood for another verbal shoot-out over it, but he could not quite come up with a good excuse.

"You know what I think" he tried.

"I know what you think, but not why" Ched smiled, sensing Jack's reluctance to debate.

Jack was just about to come up with a lame excuse when Walid grabbed his other arm. Jack looked at him and was surprised to see that Walid did not look happy at all. On the contrary, he looked upset and – well, almost afraid.

"Jack" he said.

"What? What's the matter with you?"

"Jack, have you heard the news?"

"No. What news?"

"Senator Carlyle" Walid almost whispered through the loud music.

"What about him?"

"He's dead."

*   *   *

A summer night in Houma, Louisiana is steaming hot. It leaves you soaking wet, exhausted and in total loss of time and space. And it's dark. Pitch black.

You can leave the lights on if you want to.

Thor liked the summer nights in Houma. He liked them even more when he was with Miss Beth. She was just like the night – long, black, hot, intense and full of secrets. And she made him sweat without even getting out of bed.

She was called Miss Beth simply because her name was Elizabeth and she was from Mississippi. She worked afternoons at a bar in town serving beer, Cajun, alligator sausage and cheeseburgers to tourists. Thor had been dating her for almost a month and he wanted to continue dating her for as long as there were more dark nights in Houma.

He knew he would have to pack up in a couple of days and drive back home.

But right now, home was an eternity away. Right now, all that mattered was Miss Beth.

Thor was a pretty big guy, but at six-foot-four Miss Beth towered him by two inches. And she loved to tower him in bed, too.

She was in complete control. She set the pace. She decided where they were going, how fast, and when. She teased him, then let him come a little closer, a little deeper inside her secret world.

Then she stopped him, pushed him back a little, and teased him again.

She drove him nuts, and he loved every minute of it. He wanted her for all eternity.

The humid midnight heat was pouring in through the screen window. Down on the sidewalk, outside the bar where Miss Beth worked, some old blues junkie was singing *One Bourbon, One Scotch, One Beer.*

Up here in the bedroom, Thor was singing his love song for Miss Beth. She smiled, and gave him a little bit more. He sang another verse and she gave him more. Her sweat was dripping down on his face. She was hot. He was even hotter. She was strong and gentle. He worshipped her with his hands, let them wander off all over her as she took him for a another ride right in to the rainy, stormy, hot, humid Louisiana midnight.

She collapsed on top of him. He could barely breathe, but he didn't care. He held her so tight he thought they would become one.

She held him, too. She hugged him with both arms and legs, and gently rested her lips against his shoulder. He felt her breathe through her nose against his skin.

He closed his eyes and made the moment last. It would soon be over. Not just tonight, but all these nights would soon end.

Her breath calmed down. She kissed him on the neck and raised her head so she could look him in the eyes. He smiled. She smiled. He opened his mouth to say something.

"Hush" she whispered and put her index finger over his lips. "Let's make this last forever."

She was thinking the same as he was. She kissed him gently and then looked at him again.

"*Konmen to ye?*"

He looked confused. She smiled.

"*Mo laime toi*" she whispered. "It's Creole."

"I didn't know you speak Creole."

"Goes way back in my family. My great grandfather was an alligator hunter. He lived with the creoles."

"Cool job."

He caressed her gently. Her skin was wet and smooth. He let his fingertips follow the shapes in her skin. His thumbs reached her knees.

She laughed lightly.

"You're tickling me."

"Here?"

"Yeah."

He tickled her gently again. She laughed again.

"Stop it."

He did it again. She grabbed his arms by the wrists. She was surprisingly strong and pressed them down against the pillow behind him. She leaned forward and looked him straight in the eyes with a conspicuous smile on her lips.

"You naughty boy. I said stop it."

He played along and tried to break loose. She held him steady. He tried again, a little more power this time. But she still held him down.

He could break loose any time he wanted to. But he did not want to. He wanted her to hold him tight and pin him down in her bed so he would never have to leave.

Her face turned serious. She looked at him for a second, then she slid off him and sat next to him, resting her back against the wall right by the window.

"What?" he asked.

She looked down.

"When are you leaving?"

"Monday."

"It's Sunday tomorrow."

"Come with me."

She looked at him.

"You really mean that?"

"Of course."

She smiled and looked down again.

"I can't."

"You can find a job there."

"You know it's not that."

They looked at one another. Thor felt a surge of emotions. God, she was gorgeous!

He really loved her. He had never really loved anyone before he met her. Not this way. This was – real.

He took her hand and pulled her down. She laid down on her side, close enough so he could feel her heartbeat.

"I just wish things were different" he whispered in her ear.

"At least we have two more nights" she whispered back.

He nodded. That was always something.

Until his cell phone rang.

"Damned" he said and struggled to get it out of his pants.

They were all tied up in a mess on the floor.

The phone kept ringing.

"Is that your brother?" Miss Beth asked. "He called last night about this time."

"He did?"

"You had already fallen asleep" she smiled.

Thor found the phone and looked up at her.

"What did you tell him?"

"That you were my prisoner of passion."

Thor looked at the display.

"Oh, no" he said and answered it.

"Report for duty at noon Sunday" an all too familiar voice told him.

He ended the call and dropped the phone on the floor. Then he laid back and closed his eyes.

"Bad news" Miss Beth noted.

"I have to be in Atlanta in…" and he looked at the clock on the night stand, "…in eleven hours."

"That's a ten hour drive."

"I can do it in eight."

"You'd have to drive eighty all the way" she noted with a sad tone in her voice.

"I have a brand new BMW."

He looked at her. She looked at him.

"Come with me" he asked her again.

She shook her head.

"I can't" she whispered, with tears in her eyes.

"Oh, Beth" Thor said and caressed her face with his fingertips.

"Hold me" she whispered.

She was always so strong and independent. Never asked for help, never asked for support.

But not now. Now she was coming to him, asked him to hold her and assure her that he loved her.

She fell asleep in his arms. He lay awake for a while, holding her close. Then he gently let her lay down next to him. He turned off the light and tried to go to sleep on his side of the bed. It was not easy. He kept reaching out with his foot to feel Miss Beth's long, strong legs. She was sleeping like a baby, so she didn't notice his gentle touch.

He wanted to sleep at least for a couple of hours before he drove back to Atlanta. But it was hard. When he could not fall asleep on his side of the bed he turned around and moved close to her. He gently placed his nose up at her neck, so he could smell her hair and her skin. He shaped his body after hers, his legs bending with hers, his belly forming a cushion for her behind.

Then he could finally relax and fall asleep. At least for a couple of hours. Then he would have to rise, shine and drive.

All because of an imminent threat to the safety and security of the United States of America.

*   *   *

"White House, good morning."

"This is Irwin Schwepp, put me through to the vice president, please. Code Zebra Charlie Four Four Eight."

"One moment... Alright, Mr. Schwepp, I am connecting you now."

"Thanks."

"Good morning, Irwin."

"Good morning, Madam Vice President. I am sorry to call you at six in the morning. I just wanted to say that I will be back in Washington tonight."

"OK. What is the weather like in Saint Louis?"

"The weather is good here, ma'm."

"That's nice, Irwin. Very nice. And how is your cousin doing?"

"My cousin is sleeping, ma'm."

"Well, then, I will see you this afternoon."

"Yes, ma'm."

After the phone call Holly Stanton spent almost an hour in the bathroom and then another ten minutes deciding what to wear. First on her agenda was a meeting with the secretary of education. Then she had to go through a stack of legislative bills with her staffers. She also had to make some phone calls and plan a trip to China.

Just another boring day in the White House.

The phone rang. Her assistant answered.

"Ma'm, it's your brother."

"Thanks, Pedro, I will take it in my bedroom."

She went in, closed the door and took out a small black box from a drawer in her desk. The box was four by three inches and had two small wires attached to it. She plugged both wires in to small holes on her landline telephone. Then she switched on the box and picked up the receiver.

"Hi, Walt" she said quietly.

"Are you on the safe line?"

"Yes, I just hooked it up."

"Good. Has Irwin called yet?"

"Yes. Everything went well. Carlyle is dead."

"No witnesses?"

"He said the weather was nice."

"That's good. Well, that's a good start."

"We still have a lot to do, Walt. A lot of preparations for our friends' arrival."

"Don't worry, sis. We'll get there. Just make sure to call them and give them a positive update."

Holly Stanton hung up. She disconnected the black box and put it back in her drawer.

Her personal assistant knocked on the door.

"Yes?"

"Ma'm, the secretary of education has arrived, he is waiting in the Oval Office."

"Yes, thanks. Tell Sheila to entertain him for a moment. I have another phone call to make."

"Yes, ma'm."

The personal assistant left and closed the door. Sheila, her chief of staff, would keep the conversation going for a good ten minutes. That was all Holly Stanton needed to make that one last phone call.

Or maybe "phone call" was a bit of a stretch. She took out a small key from her purse and unlocked a drawer. She pulled out the drawer and lifted up an elliptical dark green console. It was the size of a small notebook computer but had markings on the top that no notebook computer had. She gently tapped the markings in a specific order. The top slowly converted from a solid cover into a flat screen. She placed the device before her on the desk and folded up the screen to a 45 degree angle. Then she touched four symbols in a certain order, waited a moment and touched them again in the opposite order.

The screen lit up and after a few seconds a face appeared.

She still had not gotten used to the face. It looked as if it was cut out of a bad horror movie. All dark green, with rugged lizard-like skin and scales all over the forehead. Two yellow eyes and a broad mouth that concealed sharp teeth that looked like they could tear through living flesh and break bones.

"Sir" Holly Stanton said. "Mr. Supreme General."

"Yes, Holly."

"I have good news."

"I hope so. We have had some setbacks recently that you are responsible for. Our Grand Leader is not happy about your setbacks."

"I apologize for those."

"You should express gratitude for his patience when you eventually have the honor to meet him."

"I certainly will, and please send my regards. I can report to you now that Operation Red Carpet has started. We have cut down the first tree already."

"That is satisfactory. Now make sure the operation proceeds as we have requested."

"I will, sir. Thanks again for your patience."

She terminated the communication and locked the device back in its drawer. Then she went out to the Oval Office to meet with the Secretary of Education.

"Hi, Larry, how are you?"

"I'm good, thanks, ma'm. How are you?"

"Good, Larry, good" said the vice president and sat down at the small table where they were going to have their little talk about education policy.

She listened politely. But she really did not care much what Larry was talking about. All she could think about was that he was the 14th tree on the list that they had made for Operation Red Carpet.

CONTACT

For being a special assignment agent with Advanced Retrieval, Tahm Qaar was almost too perfect. He had served on a hundred assignments on more worlds than he could keep track of. He had a Masters degree in anthropological psychology and had been six years in the special forces of Frontline Services, the Danarvian military. He had another Masters degree in interstellar diplomacy and was a seven-star grand master in the toughest martial arts form in the universe.

He was a good leader, had a flair for technology and an IQ somewhere above 200.

He was simply the perfect agent to be Chief Assignment Officer on this mission to Earth.

Except – he was getting old. And with age came a growing lack of creativity.

And he hated cheeseburgers. So when his young rookie agent Goryell brought him another Happy Meal from McDonald's for lunch, Tahm Qaar decided to have a talk with Goryell.

"Siddown" he muttered while examining the cheeseburger suspiciously.

"Thanks, sir. Anything wrong with the lunch?"

"It's tasteless."

"Sir, you said the Big Mac tasted too much. I thought…"

"Yeah, yeah, whatever" Tahm Qaar said and tossed the cheeseburger over to Goryell, who caught it and started munching on it right away.

"I have a problem" Tahm Qaar said and whisked the toy out of the Happy Meal box. "What is this?"

"That's a toy, sir."

"Why do they put toys in these boxes? And why are the boxes so colorful?"

"It's for kids, actually."

Tahm Qaar looked over at Goryell.

"Sir" Goryell added quickly when he saw the look on his boss's face.

"Why did you buy me a kids' meal?"

"Because they are pretty much void of taste, sir."

Tahm Qaar decided to have a standardized field operations meal ration for lunch. At least he knew how that tasted.

"I'm glad I could help you with your problem, sir" Goryell said and stuffed the last piece of the cheeseburger in his mouth.

"What?"

"With the toy, sir."

"What? No, no, that was not my problem. Goryell, you're a rookie agent and frankly, I had a bit of concerns accepting you for this assignment. But I have to tell you that you are doing a fine job here. You're good at blending in and you are gathering valuable information for us. I'm afraid I am not as good as you are at that."

"Sir?"

Tahm Qaar pulled out a stack of notes from a folder he had on the desk.

"I'm getting old" he continued. "And the longer you are in the service, the more you stick to conventions and old habits. I have a problem here that I could give to any of the agents who are senior to you. Which… actually… would be everyone else here. But this one requires some creativity. And I think you can help me out here."

He handed Goryell the notes.

"This is a transcript of communications between Earth and some unknown world. We intercepted it yesterday. I got this translation key back from headquarters this morning."

Goryell read it with interest.

"Sir" he said and looked up at Tahm Qaar. "This is… impossible."

"I was hoping you would not say that" Tahm Qaar muttered.

"No, no, what I mean..." and Goryell searched for the right words, "...what I mean, sir... is that this communication here contradicts some vital things we thought we knew about Earth. So, we have to... be creative."

Tahm Qaar waited. He had a second transmission transcript on his desk that he had not yet shared with Goryell. They had intercepted it just this morning.

"Sir" Goryell said. "The message that Earth sent out... is the language... a reptilian language?"

"Very good" Tahm Qaar smiled. "Not everyone could read that out of a transcript."

"And since there are no reptilians on Earth" Goryell continued, "and the nearest Danarvian world is three sectors away... this means that there is a reptilian world somewhere out here, with an evolution index of three or higher. One that we have not yet discovered."

"Apparently" Tahm Qaar nodded. "Now, analyze the content of the transmission."

Goryell looked up at his boss.

"The content is loud and clear, sir. The vice president of the United States of America is asking the Grand Leader... which we have to assume is the leader of that unknown world... to please be patient because they have had a setback in rolling out the carpet. It is for some sort of meeting between the vice president... I would assume the president as well... and this Grand Leader. Apparently the vice president is arranging this meeting, although she makes no mention of the president... what's his name... Oslow. She does not mention him at all."

"What is the meeting going to be about?

"Maybe initial diplomatic contacts?"

"That was my thought also. Until I read this one."

He handed Goryell the transcript of the second intercepted transmission. Goryell read it carefully.

"Technically, sir" he said, apparently fascinated, "they seem to be talking about cutting down trees in order to be able to roll out a carpet. But I would assume that the word 'carpet' means some sort of landing strip for a space craft. However…"

He stopped and looked out the window. Tahm Qaar waited. He knew that Goryell was thinking hard about this one. And Tahm Qaar liked it. This was the kind of free-wheeling thinking that he was hoping his young rookie would be good at.

"However, sir" Goryell continued, looking at his boss. "The Americans have facilities like airports and even a couple of space centers that could receive space crafts. So it would seem illogical that they would have to cut down trees to make way for some sort of landing strip."

"And why bother to communicate about one lousy tree?" Tahm Qaar added.

"Exactly, sir!" Goryell said and leaned forward. "So they are clearly talking about something else. Some sort of hurdle, something they need to get rid of before the Grand Leader can come here. The question, of course, is what that hurdle might be."

"Good work, Goryell. Whatever the hurdle they are discussing, it looks like we are about to witness two non-Danarvian worlds make official contact. Quite unusual."

"Cool!" Goryell said.

"No, it's hot in here."

"Sir?"

"You said it is cool in here."

"Cool? Oh… no, sir… that's just an American expression."

"I'm glad you've blended in. Now…" and Tahm Qaar searched his desk for another notepad, "…ah, there it is. Here. I have a special thing for you to do."

"What's that?"

"I decided to search our agency library for whatever we have on this sector, especially old information. I came across something that's quite… what was it you called it? Cold?"

"Cool, sir."

"Yes, cool. I found this very old file. It was buried under the highest access classification code, deep in a section that no one has accessed in many years."

Goryell took the note, read it, frowned and read it again. Then he looked up and shook his head.

"But sir… if this information here is correct…"

"It would be quite remarkable, yes. Someone from Danarvia has been here before. A long time ago. And they built a beacon that the American government could use to contact Danarvia."

"What for?"

"The United States is the most free society on Earth" said Tahm Qaar. "It is possible that whoever came here wanted to make sure the Danarvian federation could protect them from alien threats. We have seen advanced tyrannies invade free worlds before."

"But why was this information hidden away?"

"Probably because it was a very highly classified operation. We have to find that beacon and destroy it."

"Destroy it, sir?"

Tahm Qaar leaned forward and explained.

"I am worried by these communications between the American vice president and that alien world" he said. "While the intentions could be entirely friendly, there is a possibility that the vice president has malicious intentions. I cannot exclude the possibility that she is cooperating with those aliens for her own personal gains."

"Sir, are you suggesting that the American government, or some people in it, are conspiring with this alien world in order to stage a coup?"

"It has happened before."

"Yes" Goryell nodded. "OK. So if there is someone in the American government who knows about her plans, and about this beacon, they may try to activate it in order to contact us."

"Correct."

"But why would that be a problem, sir?"

"War. If they use the beacon, our government would have to respond to it, and that response would most likely come in the form of military support in defense of Earth."

"Which would lead to a war between us and the alien world" said Goryell.

"Exactly. If we are going to come to Earth's rescue against some alien tyranny, it will have to be based on our work, here and now. So you're going to have to go find that beacon and blow it up."

"Yes, sir" Goryell said as he stood up and started walking toward the door.

"Aren't you forgetting something?"

Goryell looked around.

"Uh… may I leave, sir?" he said.

"No" Tahm Qaar smiled. "Not the courtesy. According to this information the beacon is under water. The new diving gear is here, right behind me."

"Oh, of course…"

Goryell grabbed a set of diving gear and went to pack his bags.

And to find out where Houma, Louisiana was.

*   *   *

The news about senator Carlyle's death spread like a bonfire among the libertarians at *The Flunked Final*. People stopped shooting pool or throwing dart (except Big Red Bob who threw himself down on a bench and fell asleep). The music stopped on the dance floor. A bartender changed the channel on his TV from ESPN to Fox News. Many people pulled out their iWorlds, logged on to the Grid and got live stream TV in them.

Jack had one, too. He tried to get in to a room with a TV but it was already too crowded. So he decided to try his iWorld instead.

"This is no good!" he said to Walid and they forced their way out toward the building entrance.

Rumors were flying through the air.

"He was shot in the head!"

"They caught a guy!"

"No, it was a heart attack!"

"It happened in his home!"

"I heard his plane crashed in Omaha!"

Jack had to use force to make it through the crowd. He was pretty good at it. His brother was a martial arts expert and had taught him a few tricks. He really did not want to hurt anyone but when people simply kept walking right in to him he had no choice.

Walid stayed close behind him as Jack finally cleared a path to the exit.

The night outside was hot and humid. The good thing was it was a lot quieter than inside *The Flunked Final*.

"Man, what a crowd!" Jack exclaimed.

"I almost lost my cell phone!" Walid complained.

"Yeah, that was rough. OK, let's see."

He turned on his iWorld and logged on to the Fox News live stream. A reporter was standing on a lonely highway somewhere with lots of emergency crew behind him. There were several rescue vehicles there and the reporter was yelling at the camera:

"It was here, on route thirty six that Senator Carlyle veered off the road with his car. A technical problem caused the gas tank to explode, which sent the car off the road an in to a big tree. Senator Carlyle died instantly."

"Talk about a freak accident" Jack said. "An exploding gas tank. Haven't heard that one before."

"Horrible" Walid said and shook his head. "What a horrible way to die."

"I hope he was alone in the car."

"Yes, he was. I heard the first news. They interviewed someone he had met with first, before… well… this happened."

Jack had nothing more to say at the moment. He was overwhelmed by the news. Senator Carlyle had been a staunch libertarian all his life, all his political career. He had admirers and followers far outside Missouri, his home state. He was smart, quick witted, passionate about his ideals and unrelenting in his quest for less government and more freedom.

"He was a straight talker" Walid noted.

Jack nodded.

"That's exactly what he was" he said.

Walid looked around. The street was calm, with very little traffic. The calm was even more obvious when the music had stopped playing inside *The Flunked Final*. They could hear laughs from a party at some house nearby.

A stray cat came walking down the sidewalk and rubbed itself against their legs.

Some of their friends came out.

"He was going to be president!" declared a young man, obviously drunk. "And I was gonna work for him!"

He was too drunk to even walk straight. He tried to break lose from two guys who were helping him stand up. They led him over to a park bench a few feet off to the side of the entrance.

"Here, David, have a seat" said one of them.

"They killed Caa'lyle" David said before he tilted over and fell asleep.

They stood there and watched David sleep. Nobody really had anything to say. David was obviously senselessly intoxicated, and when people are senselessly intoxicated they always say senseless things. But right there, at that moment, it was hard to tell how senseless his comment really was. And perhaps they felt that they needed some kind of explanation to the senator's death, an explanation that would blame someone for it.

After all, a traffic accident would be a very senseless way to die for big man like Senator Carlyle.

*   *   *

Thor had to search for some time before he found the blighted old building in Atlanta where they were going to meet with colonel Kwolczyk. He got there half past noon, just in time. As he walked into the building he wondered why they could not just meet at the office in Atlanta.

This particular building was an abandoned warehouse on the edge of one of Atlanta's southern suburbs. It would probably not pass a building code inspection. Wires were hanging loose from the ceiling. A crooked fire door was stuck and could not be opened. There were cracks in the concrete floor and one of the beams in the ceiling was badly damaged. It looked like someone had driven a big construction crane right in to it.

There were no chairs, no tables and certainly no PowerPoint in the room.

It appeared to be an abandoned car shop, or maybe truck shop. The place was filthy and poorly lit. There were rusty parts and tools scattered on the floor and in assorted boxes. A couple of big truck doors, rusty and with cracked paint, were leaning against the wall on the far side of the building. Someone had left a small metal ladder on the floor, and two car wheel axles had been oddly left hanging from the ceiling in chains in one of the corners.

Nobody in his right mind would hold a meeting there. Unless, of course, you were colonel Kwolczyk with one of the most secret intelligence operations in the world.

Thor stood next to Carl, another operations specialist. They both had their mission gear at their feet. Carl looked as tired as Thor.

"Sleep deficit?" Thor asked.

"Tell me about it. I was in New York."

"You drove?"

"Flew down at four AM. Had to be at the airport at three."

Captain Kwolczyk looked at them. He smiled.

"Gentlemen" he said. "Welcome back to Atlanta."

He sounded like he had invited them to spend a weekend at a five-star hotel with a half dozen Playboy bunnies at their service.

Thor and Carl did not smile.

The colonel was not alone. He had another colonel on his right side. Thor remembered him as a cutting edge computer wizard.

On colonel Kwolczyk's left side was a woman. She was in civilian clothes. Thor had never seen her before.

"OK, guys" Captain Kwolczyk said. "Let's keep it pithy."

Nobody laughed when the colonel stole a line from the O'Reilly Factor.

"As of now, twelve thirty PM today… and that is right now… you are officially assigned to Operation Lighthouse. Before we go over the details of the mission I want to mention that you will be using a new piece of equipment that we have never used before. You will be boarding a specially converted B-52 and once onboard you will find two skydiving pods in the plane. You saw these pods mentioned in a memo recently, so I expect you to at least have some idea of what those toys are. You will have some time to study them before the plane takes off, so get to know the pods well while you're on ground. Once you're up in the air it's going to be a short ride."

He glanced at his notebook.

"Your time of deployment is one minute past midnight on Monday, central time. Your flight time is only ninety minutes, so you better be ready when you get airborne. Obviously you'll be spending the rest of the day at the airport. I don't want two handsome young bachelors like yourselves get lost in the arms of some local Georgia beauties."

Carl chuckled. Thor smiled and thought about Miss Beth for a second.

"Team Beta is standing by in Phoenix" the colonel continued. "But I expect not to have to call them in. I've spent enough time trying to make men out of you ladies, so don't let me down, OK?"

He took time to smile at them. Thor and Carl did not smile back.

"Any questions for me?"

"Colonel" said Carl. "Since we are using the skydiving pods, I assume this is an underwater mission."

"Correct."

"On our last mission I dropped one piece of the deepwater sonar. We have no routine for carrying spare parts and I know we discussed that at the debriefing. Any news on that?"

"No spare parts" colonel Kwolczyk said. "Too much to carry."

"Ay, sir" he said.

"Bottom line" said the colonel and looked sternly at Carl, "you don't drop your stuff. Period."

"Ay, sir."

"Alright. Colonel Anderson will take it from here."

The colonel nodded and stepped forward while colonel Kwolczyk took a step back. Colonel Anderson was a short, sturdy man in his sixties. An unusual character for a computer specialist. They were usually a lot younger. But there was nothing usual about this organization.

Colonel Anderson had been around the block a few times. He bore the scars of long battlefield and many tough commando operations. Today, he was too old to be out in the field, so he was probably just as happy doing desk jobs.

"Alright, thanks, Victor" he said plainly. "Well, I'm here to tell you about the little thingie you're going to visit."

He glanced over at the civilian-dressed woman. Thor found that strange. It was almost as if the woman was his commander. Each group in the organization was operationally independent. Anyone higher up in the hierarchy would not attend field operations meetings like this one.

But then, again, he was not supposed to know a whole lot about other parts of this organization. He was just a foot soldier…

"Here's a topological map of the area" colonel Anderson said and handed them a piece of paper.

He held up his own copy and pointed with the edge of a pen to what seemed to be a very deep underwater hole in the middle of a marsh.

"This is your destination, boys. It's a marsh full of alligators and other buddies. There are boat tourists this time of the year but our surveillance team reports very little traffic at daytime. Night time this place is completely deserted."

"Except the alligators" noted colonel Kwolczyk.

"Right" colonel Anderson said without a hint of a smile. "Your dropping point will be a few miles off the coastline, in open water. Your pods will propel you close enough so that you can do the rest of the swim with your microjets."

He was referring to tiny water-driven jet engines that they could hook on to their diving suits. They could move a diver almost in complete silence, at good speed and without really wasting any energy.

"And what's our target?" Thor asked.

"I'm getting there" colonel Anderson said and gave Thor a look that Thor would not forget.

"Yes, sir. Sorry, sir."

"The target is a device …" and the colonel handed them another piece of paper, "…and the device is, well, a beacon."

The paper showed something they had never seen before. It almost looked like a ball pen standing upside down, bolted on to a platform with some strange features that made no sense to either Thor or Carl.

"This thing is about three hundred feet tall" the colonel continued, his voice as indifferent as if he was talking about a tree in the park. "Your job is to go down to its base and turn it on."

Thor looked at the topological map again.

"Sir" he said. "Is this… beacon… located in that deep hole… Deep Saline?"

"That's right."

"So we are diving six hundred feet down into that hole?"

"The base of the beacon is at five hundred fifty feet."

"We can do that" Carl said and looked at Thor.

They both remembered a mission a few months earlier off the coast of Puerto Rico.

"Even at night" Thor nodded. "No problem, sir."

"Good" colonel Anderson noted. "We used to have a remote control to the beacon, but it doesn't work anymore. The only back-up system is to go down there and turn it on manually."

"Uh, sir… what is this beacon for?" asked Carl.

"For making contact."

"Contact, sir?"

Colonel Anderson looked over at the woman. She nodded.

"Boys" the colonel said. "This is normally above your access level. But this operation is like no other. Once you turn on this beacon, you will send a signal in to deep space."

"To whom, sir?" asked Thor.

"To Danarvia" colonel Anderson said.

He paused. Everyone was quiet. Thor even got goose bumps. He realized that the colonel was talking about making contact with an alien civilization. And he would be the one to do it.

"We're in danger" colonel Anderson continued. "America is in grave danger. An alien invasion is imminent."

"Alien, sir?" Carl asked.

"As in aliens from outer space. And they're targeting America. We need help. You're going to send an SOS to the Danarvians."

*   *   *

Senator Carlyle's death disrupted the daily routine in Washington, DC. Reporters clustered to Capitol Hill, where

Carlyle's colleagues frantically scrambled for something to say about him. He was admired, respected and hated. Those who hated him did it for his guts and his unrelenting libertarianism. Some also hated him because he was impossible to defeat in a debate. Many respected him for precisely the same reason, and a few secretly admired him and wished that they could have the courage to do what he had done – to put freedom and minimal government above party loyalty.

President Oslow gave a speech in the Rose Garden of the White House. He stood tall and stiff, like he always did, looking a few inches above the heads of the gathered reporters. He spoke, as always, sentence by sentence with marked pauses between them. He mentioned senator Carlyle in the first two sentences of his speech and then went on to talk about hope and change for ten minutes.

Vice president Stanton kept a low profile. She spent the morning in her office with her closest staffers. She pretended to be sorry about the senator's death while she kept herself busy with little things that could just as well have waited to the next day.

The press kept calling her for a comment. She ignored them up until lunch time when her press secretary was about to crumble under the pressure from demanding reporters.

"Alright" she said. "Tell them I'll see them in the press briefing room in half an hour."

She had a brief conversation with the Supreme General from Zoh'moor and made a quick call to her brother. Then she went in and gave the White House press corps a theatrically perfect, teary-eyed story of how much she loved and respected the senator from Missouri. She did not believe a single one of her own words, but her performance was convincing enough for the reporters and the TV cameras on a day when a lot of people were mourning the loss of a fine politician.

By mid-afternoon Holly Stanton could start focusing on issues of higher importance. First she met with Irwin Schwepp.

"Thanks for your hard work, Irwin."

"My pleasure, ma'm."

"I'm sure" the vice president mumbled and glanced at a piece of paper before her. "Now, you have a lot of work to do to get through the list of… trees that we need to… cut down."

"There are nineteen left."

"How many, uh… loggers do you have?"

"I have put together two teams, four in each. The first team was with me in St Louis. The second team is preparing the next job in Florida right now."

"We have a month to take care of them all."

"A month?! But Holly… I mean, ma'm vice president… that's impossible! When we planned this you gave me the whole summer."

"I know, but our friends have sped up their time table. They will be here in a month."

"The… Zoh'moorians, ma'm?"

"Yes, the Zoh'moorians. They have completed all the preparations for coming here to help us. They are assembling a big space fleet. It is quite a complicated logistics operation to ship all those troops and supplies through space. They need to speed up the process, and that's what we will do."

"I understand, ma'm. But if we speed up, uh, cutting the trees down… we might draw media attention. Too many people dy… I mean, trees falling, in too short a time… that would look suspicious."

"Well, Irwin, there's not a single thing I can do about that. And besides, the press won't be a problem anymore once our Zoh'moorian friends get here."

"Yes, ma'm."

"You also understand, of course, that if we don't cut these trees down, we will make the transition into a new government much more difficult."

"Yes, of course. The press could stir up opposition."

"Good, Irwin. I'm glad you understand."

"May I suggest, ma'm, that if we are going to do this faster, that we make different priorities? I mean, the nine trees on the Supreme Court… even one of them would draw a lot of attention. And all of them in one month…"

"Alright, then. Do you have a better idea?"

"All we need to do is to neutralize those trees, right? To make sure they don't have access to media. So if we take care of one of the nine on the Court, then perhaps... perhaps you could issue an order that the other eight must be brought to a safe location and kept there for their own protection?"

"Irwin, that's a brilliant idea. A very nice cost saving idea that we could apply broadly. Not just the Supreme Court, but Congress."

"Absolutely."

"Irwin, work that in to your plans. Find secure locations where we can detain as many of the people on this list as possible."

"Yes, ma'm."

"And get a new tie."

"Ma'm?"

"A pink tie is so unbecoming of a real man."

"Uh... oh, I see. Thanks, ma'm."

Irwin got up to leave the room. Holly Stanton watched him as he walked toward the door. She smiled, but it was impossible to know why.

Half way to the door, Irwin stopped and turned toward the vice president.

"Ma'm... may I ask a question?"

"Of course, Irwin."

"The... Zoh'moorians... what... what do they look like?"

The vice president's face turned neutral for a moment. She looked him straight in the eyes and debated what to tell him. She did not like it that Irwin was concerned with the Zoh'moorians. Her contacts with the aliens were the best kept secret in her life. She did not want Irwin to get too nosy.

"Like you would expect them to" she said in a formal tone that told Irwin that the subject was none of his business.

"Yes... of course, ma'm" Irwin said and left the room.

He was far from happy as he walked down the hallway. He always tried to be courteous and cordial in his conversation with Holly Stanton, but in reality his mood got worse each time she spoke to him like he was some kind of errand boy.

But it was worse this time. Holly Stanton's attitude had changed recently. She had become more arrogant, more dismissive, toward him. He felt like she had just hit him over the head with a sledgehammer.

Irwin was used to taking orders from the Stantons, but this was different. He was being excluded from the inner circle in a way that he had never been before.

On his way out he yelled at a couple of people in his way, for no real reason.

The next person on Holly Stanton's appointment list was Rhea.

"Holly, good to see you again."

"Good to see you, Rhea. You look great."

"Thanks."

"So how you been?"

"Busy… you know."

"I miss you."

"I miss you, too."

"Can you spend the night?"

"Yes, I was hoping you'd ask."

They looked at one another and smiled.

"Rhea" Holly Stanton said eventually, "we got some work to do before we get to the private part of the conversation."

"Of course. Yes… I was able to convince Colonel Anderson to let me fly with him down to Atlanta. I met with another colonel, an operations specialist by the name Victor Kwolczyk."

"Who is he?"

"Started out in the 82nd Airborne, then joined the NSA and was with Black Operations for a good ten years. Officially retired, like everyone else in Branch Four. He is being paid by a generic foundation somewhere."

"Why is it called Branch Four?"

"It's supposed to be the fourth branch of government, the last line of defense if the freedom of the American people is in grave danger."

Rhea gave away a conspicuous smile. Holly Stanton smiled, too. But her smile went away as she grasped the bigger picture of what Rhea was telling her.

"And they're so secretive my brother could not find out about them during the eight years he was president" she muttered.

"Right."

"I'm still impressed you were able to infiltrate them."

"Thanks. It's the first time it's happened, as far as I know. By the way, they know about our plans with the Zoh'moorians."

"How?"

"I'm not sure yet. But they have very sophisticated methods for gathering intelligence."

"Do they know that I am cooperating with the Grand Leader?"

"Yes, but they do not know that your brother has been to Zoh'moor as your ambassador."

"So what are the Branch Four agents going to do?"

"They are going to activate a beacon."

"A what?"

"A beacon."

"What are you talking about?"

"There is this... beacon, deep in the swamps of Louisiana, that is capable of sending some sort of signal out into deep space."

"What is it doing in Louisiana?"

"Apparently it was hidden there because it would not be the first place people would stumble upon it by accident. It's old. I found out about it last week, and I was able to destroy the remote control they would use to activate it. So now the Branch Four agents are sending a team down there to activate it manually."

"And exactly who is the beacon supposed to be sending its signal to?"

"Danarvia."

"Who's that?"

"Some federation of civilizations out there. They came here some time in the eighteen hundreds and built it, and organized Branch Four to protect it. The president at that time was given..."

"Wait a minute, Rhea. Just wait a minute. You're making my head spin. Are you telling me... that some alien civilization came here and built a... beacon, so that we call them and – do exactly what?"

"Ask for help."

"Help with what?"

"In eighteen fifty five some explorers from Danarvia came here and made contact with members of the president's administration."

"Buchanan, right?"

"Actually, it was Franklin Pierce. One of those presidents you never hear about. He was very secretive, and now you know why. Anyway. The Danarvians were so enamored with what the Founding Fathers had created… apparently the Danarvians cherish freedom more than anything else… so they decided to offer to help the United States in case our existence should ever be in jeopardy. So they built this beacon and helped president Pierce form a very small group of people… that's Branch Four… that would guard the beacon and activate it in case we ever needed their help."

"So these Branch Four agents have been around for over a hundred fifty years?"

"Yes."

"Some story…"

"Apparently the Danarvians had seen too many examples of how free societies were run over by technologically more advanced tyrannies."

"Like an invasion from outer space" Holly Stanton said and smiled at Rhea.

"Yes" Rhea smiled back.

"Damned. So now the Danarvians are going to come here and mess things up for us."

"Apparently."

"Well, obviously we cannot let that happen. We need to stop them from contacting the Danarvians. Is there a way to destroy the beacon?"

"From what I've been able to learn about it, Holly… short of a nuclear detonation I don't think we have anything that can take it out."

"Alright. You said you were able to destroy the device they would use to activate it remotely?"

"Yes. But the Branch Four agents can activate it manually."

"By actually going there?"

"They will have to send divers down there to actually turn a switch. Literally."

"OK. Good. That's actually very good. Here is what I want you to do..."

*   *   *

Goryell got to Houma just before midnight. He used the standard means of transportation in the United States – a Cadillac – and found it quite comfortable even for long rides.

He was amazed at how easy it was to travel this way. He almost forgot what a crucial mission he was on. But once he got to Houma he began focusing on what was to come.

First he had to go down to Cocodrie, a small place way down in the delta. It would take him almost an hour to get there even though it was just over 35 miles. Then he would have to swim in pitch black water, infested with a kind of predator that was long, flat and had very large and strong jaws. They were called alligators and apparently did not take no for an answer.

He was not concerned about them. He had a diving suit that virtually nothing could penetrate. But he would not be in that suit forever, and if anything went wrong he would have to face the elements out there. Including the alligators.

The night was steaming hot and so humid that Goryell could almost quench his thirst just by opening his mouth.

He drove with his windows down, his sunroof open and his stereo off. The night came pouring in to the car as he left Houma and followed the highway out in the wild nothing. Goryell had grown up in a warm, humid place and all of a sudden he felt a sting of homesickness. He remembered taking his first girlfriend out in a dark night like this one for, well, some twosome-ness.

The car was filled with air from the night. It caressed his cheeks and his bare arms and legs. It mixed with the memories of his first girlfriend and made him feel warm and weak.

The car's headlights played with the shadows along the road. He was fascinated by the experience of driving a car – and at night it became even more fascinating. He thought he saw eyes that glanced at him as he drove by, eyes on animals that probably did not even exist.

Except, of course, the small, strange little thing that came up on the highway just fifty feet in front of him. It stopped, looked at the oncoming lights and did not move until Goryell was so close he thought he would run over it.

Then it vanished. Like it went up in smoke.

He came around a sharp bend and saw light for the first time in half an hour. It was a small house between the highway and the water. It was elevated, built on poles, like most houses out here. Goryell assumed that the area was prone to flooding.

Or maybe it was to keep predators from getting in to the houses at night.

A fire was burning in the yard. Goryell could smell burning wood and he saw two figures standing next to the fire. He drove slowly as he exited the sharp turn and made eye contact with one of the figures. The light from the flames danced over the man's face and played catch-me-if-you-can with the shapes of his cheeks, his mouth, his eyes – and the strange boulder in the middle of his forehead.

The man looked at Goryell, calmly and quietly. His eyes were blue, very blue, even in the dark of night.

The other figure moved away from the fire. Goryell wanted to stop and talk to them. He had met many strange people on many strange worlds. He loved meeting new people. If only for a short moment. But his mission was too important.

He got to the end of the highway in Cocodrie a few minutes before one in the morning. He parked his car at a public parking lot near a marina. He listened for a moment and looked around using his night vision goggles. Everything was quiet.

He opened the trunk and got his gear out. It took him a couple of minutes to put it on, layer by layer. He was wearing a life-saving suit closest to his skin. It was made of a material that would become airtight if exposed to the vacuum of space or to water. When it was not preserving him from the outside it functioned as a second skin and helped his body breathe under heavy physical stress.

Next he put on an elastic diving suit with a pressure neutralizer. It also protected him from bullet-based weapons.

His outer suit was energy-absorbing and protected against hand-held ray weapons. He would never expect to be up against such weapons, but it was standard procedure on commando missions on alien worlds. It also had a cloak function that could come in handy.

Besides, if he died because he was not wearing all his equipment, his boss would get pretty mad at him.

Goryell turned on the compass that was built in to his visor. He had already made an electronic copy of the map of the area that Tahm Qaar had given him, including detailed satellite images of how to get from Cocodrie to Deep Saline. The compass worked inside the satellite images and helped him navigate just by glancing at a microscopic screen to the left in his visor.

His first destination was the water to the west of Cocodrie. A narrow path led from the parking lot down to the water. It started right in front of his car. He focused his night vision, put on his breathing equipment and his package of explosive devices, stuck his handheld weapon in his belt and started walking.

Earth had one moon, and some nights it would shine brightly up in the sky. Goryell thought the moon was beautiful, almost as beautiful as the big white moon that circled his home world. Earth's moon was a tad yellow and always showed the same side to Earthlings – a side with something that almost looked like a face. That made it even more beautiful.

Except, of course, if you were outside in the middle of the night on a mission and you really did not want to get caught. Then you would be grateful that it was a moonless night. Like this one. Of course, he could always turn on his cloaking device, but he would rather save the energy in case this turned out to be a long night.

His night vision was not perfect. It gave him a very good image of what was out there, but it did not always tell him exactly what the things out there were. Sometimes the image got spooky, especially on a new world with new animals and plants.

Some of the images of living creatures looked funny. Like the small quadruped animal that came up to him, said "meow" and rubbed itself against his leg. He knew it was a "cat" but it looked a lot funnier through his night vision than in real life.

Some images were not funny at all. They told of imminent danger.

Like the shape of a fifteen feet long alligator.

Goryell had studied up on those creatures. He knew they would be lying still when they had sensed prey. They would lie still until the prey came so close that they could jump out and snap it with their big jaws.

The alligator he spotted down the path was lying still.

It was waiting for him.

He was just about to pull out his gun and incapacitate the alligator when something behind the beast caught his attention. It was movements in the water, some 50 feet away. Right behind the damned alligator's tail.

The alligator also sensed something coming out of the water behind it. It turned around just as Goryell realized that there were two men coming out of the water.

Two divers crawled up on land barely 20 feet behind an alligator that was big enough to swallow a grown man.

Goryell ducked and hid away. He thought it was strange to see two divers come out of the water right here, right now – as far as he knew, Americans did not count midnight diving in alligator-infested marshes among their favorite hobbies. It was more likely that they were out in some kind of shady business and did not want to encounter anyone. And that probably included both alligators and covert operations agents from outer space.

Just as the two divers came up on land and spotted the alligator, Goryell's motion detector notified him of two other people coming up from the water further to the left of him. They stopped and started working with something on the ground but froze still when one of the divers down at the water shot the alligator.

'What a party' Goryell thought.

*   *   *

When he heard that they were going to Louisiana, Thor told Carl about his girlfriend in Houma. Carl suggested that Thor go make a pop-in visit after they were done. Thor said that they would probably be done at four in the morning and that Miss Beth would not want to be woken up then, even by him. Carl asked why and Thor could not really tell him why. Maybe he was just nervous. He had fallen so deeply in love with her that he was afraid to see her again.

It was a love thing. Totally irrational.

What was not irrational was their mission. They had to go to Deep Saline, a weird circular formation in the marshes at the southern tip of Louisiana. The nearest inhabited place was Cocodrie, and in order to make the transition from their skydiving pods to normal transportation they had to land in Cocodrie first. They brought with them a small inflatable boat, which Thor was carrying on his back. Once they were on land they would inflate it and paddle half way to Deep Saline.

Then the diving adventure would start.

The problem was, as soon as they got up on land they realized that they were not alone. Someone else was there, and it was not tourists. Carl heard the faint but distinct sound of paddles in the water, not too far away. It was a quiet, rhythmic paddling sound, from a vessel that broke the water very efficiently.

Navy SEALs.

What were they doing here?

Carl and Thor had no radio communication between them. The signals could be picked up. Nor did they talk or use lights. Instead, they used a specially developed sign language, one that they could use even from a distance. The palm side of their gloves was covered in a faint fluorescent contour. They could activate it when they needed to communicate with sign language.

Guaranteed silent.

Carl was the first one to detect their company.

A *boat, paddles*, he signaled.

Where?

To the left. Fifty feet.

Thor listened. He pulled out his small thermal vision binoculars and tried to pinpoint where the sound was coming from. He scanned back and forth and noticed an alligator swimming away from them. But no boat.

Was Carl wrong? Not likely.

Carl poked his arm and pointed in a slightly different direction.

And there they were. Two men in a small, inflatable boat, typical for the SEALs.

SEALs, Thor signaled. *Probably a whole team.*

The two SEALs landed and secured their boat. Then they hunkered down and waited. Carl and Thor decided to wait and see what was going to happen.

After a few minutes two other SEALs emerged from the water. They climbed up on land close to where the first couple of SEALs were. They made some sort of contact and the two newcomers were just about to take up a position a bit further up on land when they noticed an alligator, dead ahead.

Thor also saw it.

They just met an alligator, he signaled to Carl.

The alligator was big, probably 15 feet long. It had its tail toward the SEALs but turned around on a dime and made the first move to attack.

One of the SEALs shot it.

The gun had a silencer, of course, but Carl and Thor still heard the shot clearly through the quiet night. The alligator was two feet up in the air and fell dead to the ground as the bullet pierced its head. The two SEALs quickly moved past the alligator and took up a position further in from the water than the other two SEALs.

They are waiting for someone, Carl signaled.

Us.

There are always eight in a SEAL team.

Look out for...

Thor did not get to finish the sentence. He and Carl sensed something behind them. They turned around and spotted two SEALs coming up from the water about thirty feet from them. One of them had already raised his weapon. Carl and Thor threw themselves to the ground and barely dodged the bullets. They rolled on the ground, away from the point where they had been spotted. Thor rolled up from the water and Carl rolled down in to it.

The two newly arrived SEALs took cover. Thor got his gun out and crawled further up and in behind a bush. He lay flat on the ground and tried to spot Carl, but could not see him. Then he looked over toward the SEALs. They, too, had separated. One of them was coming his way. Thor assumed the other one was moving along the water line toward Carl.

Thor had never imagined that he would be shooting at a U.S. soldier. These were American heroes, guys who would gladly give their lives for the same cause that Thor was fighting for: the freedom and security of the United States of America. And he knew that SEALs felt exactly the same way. He knew that each and every one of them was one hell of a patriot.

But under the present circumstances – or perhaps it was better to call them *pressing* circumstances – Thor had no choice. The SEALs no doubt had orders to kill him and Carl, and those orders had probably been given with a dose of lies about who they were. Chinese infiltrators, Russian spies, Islamist terrorists… who knew what stories they had been told? And SEALs did not question orders. They carried them out because they believed in their country.

For a second Thor wondered who had sent the SEALs out there. Who would know that he and Carl would be right here, right now?

He would have plenty of time to think about that later. Or so he hoped. At this moment his entire focus was on surviving a hide-and-seek life-or-death game with the world's best commandos.

He suddenly remembered the two teams behind him. A quick glance over his shoulder told him that two SEALs were coming his way and two were heading for where Carl was supposed to be.

Thor knew that he was soon going to be in a lot of trouble. Sure, he was at least as well trained as these guys, and he could probably win a gun fight or a *mano-a-mano* with one of them. Maybe two. But three? Not likely.

Since his odds were better against one than against two, he decided to try to attack the one that was alone ahead of him before the two behind him caught up.

He moved slowly forward and focused on the lonely SEAL.

Thor spotted him as he came around a small concrete block that looked like part of an old house. For a second Thor had him in his crosshairs but hesitated long enough for the man to take cover behind some shrubbery.

The mere thought of shooting an American soldier still made his stomach turn.

So he moved closer instead. He found a ditch that ran from the street down to the water. He got down in it and crawled fast up toward the street. It was wet and he could swear it was filled with critters of all sorts, but he did not care. He'd rather wrestle a few spiders than three SEALs.

He hoped to catch the lonely SEAL off guard and disarm him before the other two caught up.

He did not have much time to listen or watch for where they were, but he hoped they would be looking for him in the wrong place as he caught the lonely SEAL.

Bad mistake. As he reached the street and looked up, he saw the action ends of three M4A1's, the SEAL favorite assault rifle.

To make things even better, one of them switched on a flash light and pointed it right in his face.

*   *   *

Goryell quickly realized that he was watching two different teams. The two divers who had come out of the water and shot the alligator had two buddies a bit further down. Goryell had not seen them at first because they were well disguised. The two most recent arrivals, on the other hand, were apparently on a different team. Yet another pair of guys came out of the water behind them and started shooting.

Immediately, the four guys up where Goryell was started moving down in the direction of the gun fire. The two guys that were being shot at ducked to the ground and split. Goryell tried to watch as much of it as he could without moving. To make sure he was not discovered he turned on his cloak until the four guys near him had passed him.

For a minute, nothing happened as far as Goryell could see, except that they were all moving around. A couple of more minutes passed and Goryell slowly moved back toward his car. From there he had a good view of the street that led further in to Cocodrie.

He did not want to head for the beacon so long as this was going on. He had a distinct feeling that these guys were all here because of the beacon. One of the teams might be here to turn on the beacon and call for help from Danarvia.

If so, it would mean that the other team was there to stop them.

That would prove that Tahm Qaar was right about the American vice president's true intentions with her contacts with the alien world.

Suddenly, three soldiers convened and hunkered down with their weapons pointing at one particular spot. Goryell watched carefully as they caught someone who was apparently coming up toward them from a ditch. The soldiers pulled him up and took him over to the other side of the street.

It looked like the guy they had caught was also a soldier. He had different equipment, looked like he was carrying more stuff and also had a slightly different weapon.

Or maybe this was not related to the beacon at all. Maybe the guy they just caught was a foreign intruder. Were these soldiers part of a border patrol? Had Goryell simply walked in to a regular law enforcement operation?

If they were law enforcement agents, chances were there was more of them in the waters out here. Goryell could walk past people without being detected, but he could not swim in cloaked mode. The cloaking function did not work underwater.

To find out what was going on he directed a microphone toward the group. They were a good hundred feet away but he could hear their conversation clear and crisp.

"…you are American??"

"Yes, I'm American. Just like you."

"What are you doing here?"

"I told you. It's a military commando operation."

"What's your unit?"

"I am not allowed to tell you."

"That's BS, buddy. We're Navy SEALs. Either you tell us or

you won't tell anything ever again. We're not nice to terrorists like
you."

"I'm not a terrorist!"

"Then tell us what's going on here!"

The prisoner hesitated for a moment. It was as though he was
weighing his options. Then he said:

"There is a device out there… out in the waters. It is of critical
interest to our national security."

"What kind of device?"

"A beacon."

"Stop bullshitting us."

"I'm here to turn on the beacon and…"

The sound of gunfire interrupted the conversation. It came from
down by the water. Another short round of gunfire. And another
one.

Then silence.

The soldiers down the street seemed confused for a second,
but then they did what any professional would do: two of them
secured their prisoner by tying his arms and legs while the third
kept watch. They put the prisoner face down and got down on one
knee, forming a crescent with their weapons pointed down toward
where the gunfire came from.

They did not move, not talk.

Goryell also sat still. He barely took a breath. The prisoner had
said that he was there to activate the beacon. That meant he knew
what it would do. He most likely knew the Danarvia.

And a whole lot more that Goryell would like to know.

Like what that alien civilization was up to, and how much the
vice president was really in cahoots with them.

No doubt, this man, who was now lying face down with his
arms and legs tied, thought that civilization was hostile. Otherwise
he would have no reason to call Danarvia for help.

Goryell had to free him. But how? He could easily take out those
three soldiers, either incapacitate them temporarily or kill them.
He did not like the thought of killing people. He had never done it
and he was not going to start now if he could avoid it. Besides, he

was under strict orders of minimal interference, so he would only be using his weapons as an extreme, last resort.

Something was still going on down by the water. Goryell heard a splash and more gunfire. Two of the soldiers up on the street cautiously moved into the shrubbery below the street, down toward where the commotion was.

The third one stayed.

This was a golden opportunity. He had a plan. He was going to create a distraction. Only problem was, to do that he needed a different weapon, one with good long-distance aim. And it was in the trunk of the car. And the car was parked with the rear toward the soldier.

It was pitch black, alright, but even the slightest noise from opening the trunk would draw his attention.

Goryell slowly moved up alongside the Cadillac until he was right by the left rear wheel. He stopped for a second to make sure the soldier was still focused on the commotion down by the water.

All clear. He popped open the trunk with the remote control and put his left hand on it to make sure it opened slowly and quietly.

The SEALs down at the water signaled something to their fellow up on the street. He acknowledged and stood up, still looking down at them. Goryell concluded that the others were coming back up again. He had to act now.

He reached in to the trunk and grabbed the two-hand weapon. It took him less than three seconds to unsecure it and turn it on. He stood up and somewhat carelessly slammed the trunk shut.

Uh oh.

The SEAL down the street turned on a dime and pointed both his assault rifle and a flashlight at him. He got down on his right knee and searched frantically back and forth for any sign of any person. He could swear he heard a car trunk close – and there was a Cadillac parked right there. But he could not see anybody near it.

The SEALs from down by the water were slowly making their way back up to the street. Goryell's motion detector tracked them as he walked toward the SEAL straight ahead of him. He had his two-hand weapon raised and ready. It was covered by his cloak.

"Ay, sir" said the SEAL in front of him. "I heard something but there is nobody there."

The others would join him in a second.

Goryell made a final adjustment to his weapon. It had a very useful function. It could send invisible energy waves toward a target and make it blow up. And there was a shed conveniently located down the street, behind the seal and the prisoner.

Goryell aimed at the shed. He sent the energy waves at the foundation in order to make it collapse completely.

It worked perfectly. The concrete structure almost exploded and turned into a dust cloud. The wooden structure collapsed with a big rumble.

All the SEALs turned toward it. The SEAL in front of Goryell took the kneeling position and pointed his assault rifle at the rubble that once was a shed.

This was Goryell's opportunity. He placed himself straight behind him and hit him in the back of his head with a hard knife-edge hand strike. It hit exactly where it should. The soldier fainted and fell forward. Goryell was ready. To make sure the soldier did not make a lot of noise Goryell caught him with his right arm. He quickly reached over with his left hand and caught the soldier's weapon before it fell down on the asphalt.

He gently placed the soldier on the ground and moved over to the prisoner, who watched what was happening with an incredulous look on his face. At first, Goryell had planned to free him of his ties and then move him away from the scene, but he realized that the guy would not be cooperative if an invisible ghost was roaming around.

So he turned off the cloak.

"What the…" Thor said.

"Quiet, please" said Goryell.

Thor did not believe his eyes. Suddenly, out of absolutely nowhere, the SEAL that was watching him had mysteriously fainted and fallen to the ground – *gently* fallen to the ground. And then a man materialized right in front of him.

And the man who appeared before him was not just your average Joe. He was not even a soldier. He had a tight, black jump suit with some weird things attached to a waist belt. He had no visible shoes. Instead it looked like the jump suit went all the way out to cover his feet and his hands. A helmet sat tightly around his head.

He had opened the visor, but Thor could not make out anything of his face, except that it was a man.

A man who quickly liberated Thor of his ties. The SEALs had used a simple but effective plastic handcuff. Goryell had to cut it open with a small knife edge attached to his suit right at his arm wrist.

Once Thor's hands and feet were free Goryell helped him up.

"Who are you?" Thor whispered.

"Later. Come with me."

Goryell grabbed Thor's weapon and other equipment, gave it to Thor and pulled him away in to the shrubbery by the Cadillac. He placed his two-hand weapon back in the trunk of the Cadillac and ducked away into the shrubbery next to Thor.

The other SEALs had noticed that something was going on and that their fellow did not answer radio calls. They were coming back toward where Thor had been held. But for now, at least, Goryell and Thor were safe.

Thor watched his liberator suspiciously while he put on his gear again. It was still too dark to tell who he was, but from his accent Thor concluded that he was not American. That only added to his suspicions, but he decided to let that issue rest for a moment. Right now he needed to get back in full operation mode and find Carl.

"You are here to turn on the beacon" Goryell said.

"How do you know that?" Thor asked, sincerely surprised.

"I heard you down there. I'm also here for the beacon."

Goryell was watching the SEALs on his motion detector. Thor was watching Goryell. He was amazed at the stranger's casual tone, but he was not satisfied with it.

There was something very strange about him.

"Hey" he said and put his hand on Goryell's shoulder.

Goryell turned to him.

"I appreciate you helping me" Thor said, "but I can't work with you unless I know who you are."

"Well" Goryell said, still debating with himself exactly what to say. "Let's just say that you don't need to turn on the beacon. Your distress call has already been heard."

Thor stared at Goryell in disbelief.

"What did you just say?"

"Look" Goryell said and turned on a small flash light in his glove. "Look here."

He pulled out an ID badge from inside his outfit.

"See this?"

It was the most incomprehensible piece of metal Thor had ever seen. There was a moving picture in it, and some signs that looked like a written language. A symbol in the upper left corner looked like two arms embracing two comets orbiting a star. The objects in the symbol looked like they were floating.

"What is that?" Thor asked.

"This is my ID badge" Goryell said casually. "It has a life monitoring chip in it. If I die it automatically sends a signal to my boss telling him to come and pick me up."

"And... exactly who does this thing say you are?"

"Hro Goryell Tukaa, general assignment officer, Division of Alien World Operations, Advanced Information Retrieval Agency."

Thor looked like he had never heard about that agency before. Which, actually, he hadn't.

"The Danarvian Federation" Goryell added and put his ID back inside his suit.

"You gotta be kidding" Thor said. "How... why... we haven't even called you yet."

"I'll tell you later. Right now we have to decide what to do about the beacon."

"If you guys are here... we don't need to turn it on."

"I was sent here to blow it up, so..."

"What??"

Thor suddenly grabbed his gun and pointed it at Goryell. Goryell realized that Thor suspected deception.

"Easy now" Goryell said.

"If you're from the Danarvian Federation, then why would you want to blow up that beacon? Why not just leave it where it is?"

"Because if you activate it, your alien enemies out there…" and he made a quick gesture up toward the night sky, "…will catch the signal and realize there are more worlds involved in this. All hell could break lose. And if you don't turn it on, someone else might try later."

Thor still pointed his gun at him.

"I liberated you, remember?" Goryell tried.

Thor did not move.

"Why would I do that if I…"

"Who are our enemies?" Thor asked.

Goryell's motion detector sent a buzzing signal up to his hear. He glanced at it.

"Right now… five soldiers who are going to take you prisoner again."

He held up his motion detector for Thor to see. Thor looked out through the shrubbery, past the Cadillac, with his thermal visor on.

Yep. There they were. Moving slowly and cautiously, taking cover while advancing in combat ready formation, just as they should.

"Let's go for a swim" Goryell suggested.

It took Thor less than a split second to decide to go with Goryell. He was still unsure of who his liberator actually was, but he was ready to take the risk of going with him. He knew the SEALs would shoot him on sight. They probably thought he had overpowered their buddy, and SEALs do not take such things lightly.

It was easy to slide through the shrubbery and down past the dead 15-feet alligator. But the SEALs were smart enough to know that they would try to go that way, so two of them were already on their way to cut off the water escape. They reached the water line just ahead of Goryell and Thor.

For a moment, the four men stared at each other and nobody moved. The two SEALs had just reached the water line and had not had time to raise their weapons. Thor and Goryell came down to the water with their sides toward the two soldiers. When they all became aware of each other they all turned and raised their weapons. A split second later three assault rifles were ready for action.

The SEALs fired first. Their aim was perfect. Their bullets flew right at their targets.

But they never reached them.

For a moment it seemed like Thor and Goryell vanished behind a flash of green light. Then another, much brighter flash stunned the two soldiers. They lost vision for a few seconds. When they looked around again Thor and Goryell were already under water, swimming away from Cocodrie, deeper and farther in to the marsh.

They had gotten away from the SEALs. Only problem now was – what to do with the beacon? Goryell's mission was to blow it up. Thor's mission was to light it up. But as far as Thor was concerned, since Goryell was here it seemed smarter to blow up the beacon, if for no other reason than to keep it out of the hands of Holly Stanton. Thor realized that she could learn a great deal about Danarvian technology from it, and that just did not seem to be a very good idea at the moment.

He needed to talk to Goryell about it. And Goryell needed to talk to Thor. He had lots of questions for him. They just needed to get further in to the marsh, away from the soldiers, before they could stop and have a talk.

And a snack, maybe. Goryell was getting hungry.

*   *   *

Jack drove home the day after the libertarian gathering in Columbia, South Carolina feeling anything but happy. He was very disturbed over the death of Senator Carlyle and had a nagging feeling that there was something fishy about his death. He had a hangover after having had one too many drinks during the wee hours while trying to make sense out of the news of Carlyle's death.

And because of what had happened to the senator he never got around to seeing Jenny Blue Eyes again.

Radio news was full of comments about the senator's death. Ross Landau, the most influential voice on the radio, had only good things to say about the senator, and reminded his listeners that senator Carlyle would probably have run for president in 2016. Carlyle had built a reputation as one of the few staunch opponents to big government. Landau stressed that Carlyle had voted against every increase in federal spending since he was elected to the Senate the first time back in 2004.

His opposition to the 2009 stimulus bill had become legendary.

Senator Carlyle was very popular. Polls in the 2012 presidential election had shown that he could have won the Republican nomination if he had run then.

Carlyle never stopped pointing out what America was all about: individual freedom, limited government and personal responsibility. Many others tried to do the same, but Carlyle also had the fortitude to set examples in his daily political life. No one could boast such opposition to higher taxes and more government spending as senator Carlyle. People listened to him and there was already a committee working to try and convince him to run for president in 2016.

He had strongly opposed President Oslow's big government health reform. He had forcefully argued that if it did not work in Canada, it could not work in the United States either.

But the biggest battle senator Carlyle had fought was against the LOST treaty. Jack had been part of that campaign.

Before Barry Oslow was elected president, almost no American knew what LOST was. It sounded funny, but there was nothing to laugh about at all in it. It was the Law Of the Sea Treaty, which opened for a unified world government. It gave the United Nations unlimited rights to levy its own taxes. To make sure that the UN got its taxes, LOST allowed them to build their own international police force.

Holly Stanton had argued for the LOST treaty when she was secretary of defense. She had been adamant, in fact, that president Oslow work with Congress to get it approved. The treaty had sailed through the House, but in the Senate it was stalled for a long time by senator Carlyle. He had rallied enough support to filibuster it. And Carlyle had spoken on the senate floor for so long that some of his staffers thought he was going to have a heart attack right there.

He spelled out the purpose behind LOST – a unified world government. He was right. LOST forced every American to pay taxes to the UN.

Many Americans could not care less about the UN tax, but they soon discovered that not paying it was a big mistake. Within months after LOST became the law of the world, UN tax police started arresting Americans for tax delinquency. They were locked up in a facility that the UN rented from the Venezuelan government.

They were kept there until they could resolve their debt to the UN.

When asked about the facility president Oslow had given a speech where he compared the UN tax delinquent prison to the (now closed) terrorist prison at the Guantanmo Bay base. He had told the American people that their complaints were luxuries in a world of need and that they should go home and make sure they were up to date with their UN taxes.

Holly Stanton loved the LOST treaty. It allowed the UN to take its first steps toward a unified world government. She also knew that she had to take control over the U.S. government before she could work with the UN secretary general and create a true world government.

With her in charge.

Jack remembered how senator Carlyle had made a lot of enemies in his fight against LOST.

Maybe – just maybe – his death was not an accident. If so, who had tampered with his car?

And why? Was it just bad blood from the LOST fight? Jack did not think so. Carlyle had fought so many other ludicrous ideas, like Barry Oslow's "Education Equality Act" that replaced No Child Left Behind and let the federal government take over and run all elementary schools in the United States.

Maybe his death was just a freak accident.

But if someone *had* killed him, why would they do it now? It was May 2013. It could not possibly have anything to do with the 2016 presidential election. Besides, the regular Republican and Democrat smear machines would certainly be capable of stopping him if they wanted to.

Jack could not wrap his head around it. He wanted to let go of his own suspicions – he wanted to believe that it was just an accident. But he just could not do it. He had an unrelenting gut feeling that Carlyle had been killed.

He needed to talk to someone about this. The only one he could think of was his brother. He decided to call him when he got back to New York.

If anyone would have a good take on an issue like this, it would be Jack's brother. After all, he worked for the government.

Kind of.

*   *   *

ACTION

Thor and Goryell swam underwater toward Deep Saline. It was more than two miles and would take them the rest of the night if they just swam. Goryell's diving suit had an anti-gravity propelling system built in to it, but it was only strong enough to carry one person at reasonable speed. He turned it on and had Thor hold on to his legs, but Thor would still not have oxygen enough to stay under water all the way.

And then there were the alligators.

The marsh was sliced up by natural and artificial waterways. They were all shallow and in most of them you could walk with water up to your waist. It made it harder to swim under water, but it was not easy to surface either. They could easily get caught by branches, roots, tall grass and other of nature's offerings. But they had to surface and review their situation.

Animals watched them cautiously as they silently made their way through the canal out from Cocodrie. It was as if their near-silent move through the water attracted more attention than if they had made noise. A raccoon quietly and curiously followed their move from a tree branch. A defiant alligator eyeballed them from just inches away.

When they surfaced the air was different than in Cocodrie. A refreshing smell of cypress trees replaced some of the damp odor from the thick, slimy seaweed. The birds changed, too. They were bigger and had longer beaks that poked around for crabs and other goodies in the water.

They took refuge in a secluded area right where the small canal intersected with a bigger waterway. When they crawled up on land Thor turned around to watch if any alligators were watching them down in the water. He put his hand on the big knife that was strapped to the side of his left shin. It had a diamond edge so sharp and so hard he could cut through basically anything with it. And he had trained how to use it against alligators and other predators in case he was knocked to the ground.

Fortunately, at least for now the alligators stayed away.

Goryell reset his motion detector for land use. It had an underwater function but it was difficult to calibrate for the warm waters where they currently were. He was going to complain about it when he got back to Headquarters.

Thor glanced at Goryell's equipment.

"This thing is neat" Goryell said. "Only problem is it doesn't work perfectly in these waters."

"Pretty cool thing to have" Thor said.

He sounded a bit weary.

"Getting tired?" Goryell asked.

"No."

"You sound a bit tired. Want a snack?"

"Sure. I'm just worried about Carl."

"Your partner?" Goryell asked and hauled out two standard meal rations and gave the better tasting one to Thor.

"Yeah."

"I'm sure he escaped."

"Maybe."

Thor stared out in the dark night.

"He's better than me."

"Why do you say that?"

"I got caught."

Goryell knew what Thor meant. The most humiliating experience for any commando was not to fail in the mission, but to get captured.

"Well" he tried, "from what I could tell those soldiers seemed to be pretty darn good ones."

"Navy SEALs" said Thor. "Damned good guys. The best special forces in the world."

"So getting caught by three Navy SEALs is not that much of a failure, is it?" Goryell noted.

Thor looked up at him.

"Guess you're right" he smiled briefly. "But I still want to find Carl."

"We'll find him. Let's get some energy first."

Goryell took out two hydration pills.

"What is this?" Thor asked.

"That grey thing there, that's a standard meal ration. This is a pill you take instead of water."

Thor looked suspiciously at the meal ration. He smelled it and glanced over at Goryell who smiled mildly.

Then Thor nibbled at it. He chewed and paused and chewed again. Then he nibbled a little bit more. And then took a big bite.

"It's good!" he said, his mouth full of bland, non-tasting standard meal ration.

"You're joking, right?"

Thor shook his head.

"No. This is good."

"You're crazy" Goryell said and started eating his ration.

Thor looked at him. Goryell had folded down his helmet and turned on a low intensity background light at the collar of his suit. It was easier to see what he looked like now. Thor was amazed to see that he looked very much like a human. Except for the ears, which were more square than oval.

"How come you look exactly like a human... I mean, an Earth human?" he asked.

Goryell looked over at him and smiled.

"You have no idea how many people out there have asked that question the first time they meet an alien. It took scientists almost a century to crack the code of life."

"The code of life?"

"On every planet that can support life, a sequence starts that creates life according to a code. That code is in the creation of life itself. I don't remember a whole lot about it. I slept through my ET classes in college."

"ET?"

"Evolutionary theory. But from what I remember, this code triggers the evolution of either of two higher life forms, humanoid or reptilian. About sixty percent of all worlds with indigenous intelligent life are reptilian. When we investigate a reptilian world, we obviously send a reptilian team, although it's not always easy to put together a reptilian team that can blend in. There is a bigger variation among reptilians. There are those with long tails, those with…"

A distant noise interrupted him. Thor looked up. He immediately recognized the noise and started looking for its source.

"SH Sixty" he said.

"What's that?"

"Helicopter. The SH Sixty is a Navy SEAL favorite."

"Ah, the helicopter" Goryell remembered. "Hovering craft."

"We better get back in the water. They're coming to search for us."

There were actually two helicopters. One of them flew over the waterway where Goryell and Thor were hiding. The other moved closer to Cocodrie and stopped over an area where it turned on a search light.

"Here" Goryell said. "Take my suit. It has a cloak. That way you don't have to get back in the water. My diving gear makes its own oxygen. I don't have to ration it."

"Thanks."

The two men looked at each other.

"Thanks for rescuing me" Thor said.

"I'm here to help you guys, but I'm gonna need your help."

"Watch out for the alligators" Thor reminded him as he put on the strange but surprisingly comfortable suit that Goryell gave him.

"It fits you" Goryell smiled. "And… here we go."

"Can you see me now?"

"No."

"Cool. I can see you perfectly."

"In daylight everything looks a bit purple when you're cloaked. The visor is getting old."

Goryell smoothly slipped back into the water while Thor sat still and watched one of the helicopters come closer. He moved his hand up in front of his face and noticed that he could see it perfectly. He looked down and saw the suit he was sitting in. It was hard to believe that nobody else could see him.

The chopper moved slowly. It made a couple of turns back and forth as if it was using a thermal imaging scanner. Thor realized that he had forgotten to ask Goryell if this suit was immune to that. Then again, if it really was an invisibility cloak, it would be invisible to thermal scanners as well.

He just had to hope for the best.

A raccoon came up behind him, stopped, sniffed, then took a couple of steps and sniffed again. Then it turned around and ran for it.

The chopper was almost right above him now, hovering only 40-50 feet above ground. It turned on a search light and slowly moved it in circles. Thor carefully moved down toward the water so he could get a better view of where the chopper was searching.

He noticed that his hearing was just as good with the suit and the helmet on as without it. When this was all over he would have to ask Goryell if Branch Four could buy some.

Suddenly a sniper up in the helicopter fired a couple of shots down in to the water. The helicopter swung around, he fired a few more shots and then the chopper ascended about 100 feet. It moved its search light around in an eight-figure pattern for about a minute. Then it turned off the search light and moved back down south.

Thor looked for Goryell but could not see him. He should be right nearby. And he could not have been the target of the chopper. The sniper had fired at a target that was too far away.

Or was it?

It took a couple of minutes before Goryell showed up in the water. He was pulling something behind him. Thor could not see what it was at first. Goryell was swimming on his back, using his body to carry the object with him.

Then Thor realized that it was no object.

It was Carl.

He slid down to the water as quietly as he could. When he put his foot in the water it suddenly became visible, although blurred and weird looking.

"Hey, turn that thing off!" Goryell said as quietly as possible.

"What?"

"The cloak!"

"Oh..."

Thor fumbled for a second before he found the switch.

"That's better" Goryell said and pulled Carl's body up to the water line.

Thor leaned forward and grabbed his friend by the arm pits. He pulled hard and managed to get Carl all the way up from the water. Goryell climbed up and hunkered down next to them.

Carl was unresponsive. His diving suit was torn and his oxygen tank missing. Goryell had put some weird looking device in his mouth. Thor noticed at least two bullet wounds in Carl's right leg.

"He's still alive" Goryell said and removed the emergency oxygen supply from Carl's mouth.

"Where did you find him?"

"My motion detector saw him dead ahead. Right where the helicopter was searching. They must have spotted him. I guessed that if they were there and someone was swimming in the water, it might just be your friend."

Thor took out a First Aid kit, cut up Carl's diving suit and cleaned and put bandage on his wounds. He still felt terrible that they had gotten separated and he had not been able to rescue his partner. But at least Carl was alive.

"Thanks for saving him" he said to Goryell "I'm sorry if I've doubted you..."

"Hey" Goryell said and raised his palm toward Thor. "I don't blame you. It's not every day you meet an intelligence agent from another world."

Thor noticed something about Goryell's hand.

"What's that?"

"What?"

"That."

Thor pointed to something that was coming out of Goryell's swim suit, right at the wrist. Goryell had no gloves on and it looked like blood.

"That's blood" Thor said.

Goryell looked.

"How did that happen?" he asked, more curious than cautious.

He opened the arm on his suit and followed the blood stream. It ran from all the way up the arm, right under the elbow.

There was a rip in the suit right there.

"A bullet touched you" Thor noted.

"Impossible. This suit is supposed to be bullet proof."

"They use armor piercing bullets. They can cut through inches of steel."

"I'll have to file a complaint to the manufacturer" Goryell said, sounding like he was talking about a new pair of shoes he had just bought.

"You're wounded, Carl's wounded, and we still have a job to do" Thor noted.

"I'm not sure anymore that we should blow up that beacon" said Goryell. "It would draw a lot of attention."

"Obviously our government knows it is here. What if they get hold of it and backward engineer it? You know, take it apart?"

"That would not do much damage" Goryell said and put one of Thor's bandages on his arm. "It's old tech. That thing is huge. Today I can send the same signal from a device the size of one of your laptops."

"It's still way ahead of our technology" Thor pointed out.

"That's a good point. And coming to think about it, that other world your government is communicating with... their scientists could probably learn a lot more from the beacon."

"And they're not friendly. That's why we came here to call you guys for help."

"But your vice president has invited them?"

Thor was quiet for a moment. He hated saying what he was about to say, but he had to.

"Holly Stanton has power ambitions that go way beyond this

country. She has worked hard to create a world government. The United Nations. She wanted to be the leader of that government, but no one is going to back her for it. This might just be her way of getting there without a majority vote."

"Well, if she's cooperating with aliens, she's in for a ride. There's a good chance those guys will simply take over and turn this into a colony. It's happened before. That's one reason why the Danarvian Federation was founded."

"I'll go do it" Thor said.

"You? No, you stay here with Carl. I'll go…"

"You're wounded."

"It's just a small scratch."

"I need it."

Goryell looked at Thor.

"I need it" Thor repeated. "I failed over there" and he pointed with his thumb over toward Cocodrie. "It's an honor thing."

Goryell nodded.

"I understand. Alright. You take my suit and diving gear. I'll show you how the explosives work."

*   *   *

It was 3AM when the phone rang in the White House. The night watch commander answered the call, which came on the president's exclusive hotline. He had strict orders to wake up the president when calls came on that line.

But this call was not for the president. It was for the vice president. And it was Rhea calling. She did not want to tell the night watch commander why she was calling.

"Ma'm, if you could just tell me what this call is about" the night watch commander said. "Just briefly."

"I am under strict orders to only discuss this with the vice president" Rhea replied.

"Whose orders?"

"The vice president's."

"Well, I am under strict orders not to let any call through unless…"

"Alright, damn it. There is a military commando operation under way and I need to confer with the commander in chief."

"But that would be the president."

"He's sleeping, isn't he?"

"Yes."

"So let's not bother him with this."

"But the vice president is also…"

"If you don't wake her up right now and let me talk to her, something very bad might happen and I can assure you that the buck will stop with you."

This woman was very adamant and he had no way of telling who she was. He did not recognize her name, nor did he know of any military operation that was under way where the commander in chief would need to be involved on an emergency basis.

He wanted to hang up. But then again, he did not want to risk his own job. So he asked her to hold and went in to wake up the vice president.

He was prepared for a scolding from vice president Stanton for not taking adequate information from the caller. She was known for bad temper and for having very little patience with people she felt were disloyal in any way.

But when he mentioned Rhea's name she sounded as if she had been waiting for a call from her.

"Put it through, Tom."

"Yes, ma'm."

Holly Stanton got up and sat down at the little desk in her bedroom. She waited until she heard the double click that noted that the conversation was not being recorded.

"Alright, Rhea, how are things going?"

"Sorry to wake you up, Holly, but I'm afraid we have to take this operation to stage two."

"What happened?"

"The SEALs caught one of the agents, and wounded the other. They were concentrating on catching the wounded one when someone intervened and helped the first one escape."

"Who intervened?"

"We don't know."

"What do you mean you don't know?"

"We were not able to identify the people who intervened."

"Could it be other people from Branch Four?"

"It is the only logical explanation."

"But why would they have another team there?"

"They may have figured out our plan."

"If they have, Rhea, you are in danger."

"Probably. But right now, Holly, we have more important things to worry about."

"You're the most important thing to me."

"And you to me, Holly…"

"I love you, Rhea. Don't get in trouble."

"I won't, honey."

"Branch Four will kill you if they find out you are an infiltrator."

"That is why we must make sure they do not succeed with this mission."

"Of course, Rhea. What do you need from me?"

"Thor and Carl got away and…"

"Who are they?"

"The two agents from Branch Four I was talking about."

"Oh, of course."

"They are on their way to the beacon, to turn it on. We need to go to stage two, Holly."

"Don't you have more troops out there?"

"Yes, we do, we have a half dozen more, right where the beacon is. But they managed to escape once, and now that there seems to be more Branch Four agents involved…"

"How many Agents can there be out there?"

"Four to six at the most. But each of them has training that matches or exceeds our best special forces. They have their own arms, top notch diving equipment, they are top trained in everything from martial arts to outdoors survival to…"

"Are you saying that the Navy SEALs are not able to handle this?"

"I'm saying, Holly, that there is a fifty-fifty chance that they succeed and turn on the beacon. We have to go to stage two."

"Rhea, you're asking me to order the United States Air Force to drop a nuclear bomb on U.S. territory."

"Holly, honey, we already talked about that. And consider the consequences if they succeed."

"It would have incredible consequences."

"Right."

"No, I mean… the bomb."

"Think of the opposite, Holly. What are the consequences if the Danarvian Federation gets here? They will come with full force."

"Our Zoh'moorian friends may very well be technologically superior to them."

"Are you willing to take the chance?"

"Alright. Alright, Rhea. I'll order a B-2 up in the air and ready to drop a bomb."

"It's for the greater good, Holly."

"I'm doing this for you, Rhea."

"I love you, Holly."

"I love you, too."

*   *   *

Thor quickly got used to Goryell's diving gear. He loved it, especially the anti-gravity propulsion system. He felt like he was floating through the water. It was so easy he could almost go to sleep. He just *had* to get one for himself…

The suit was also armored, but as Goryell had experienced it might not resist a direct hit from an armor-piercing bullet. So he got a bit nervous when he reached the big waterway and noticed that there were more SEALs in the area. He had to cross the waterway, and right there on the opposite side were two of them. They had taken very strategic positions and were probably equipped with sniper rifles. They were just north of where Thor would have to pass to get to Deep Saline.

Luckily for him, the hands that held those rifles had not detected him yet.

Just to make sure, he turned and searched with his thermal visor up north, up the waterway. There was another entrance to Deep

Saline there, and if the people who were out to catch him were smart they would place two snipers there as well.

Yep. There they were. Two more snipers.

He thought for a moment. He could try to speed across the waterway as deep as possible and maybe slip past the two snipers straight ahead. But he could also be detected and, worst case, be hit by an armor-piercing bullet.

His only chance was if the snipers were distracted. But how was he going to create that distraction?

He looked at the snipers up north again. They had positioned themselves as far out over the water as they could. They were leaning on the trunks of cypress trees that bent out over the canal. They probably thought it was a smart thing to do, because with night vision goggles they would have a perfect view way up and down the big waterway.

Thor got an idea. Even though Goryell's diving suit was infrared neutral, he could still draw their attention by moving water and making fish swim erratically. And since he had to move past them, he needed to draw attention away from himself.

He found a place where the water was less than five feet deep. Then he stood up as smoothly as he could and took out his rifle. Very carefully he hooked on the special black-out silencer. It killed the sound when the rifle was fired, and also hid the flash from the pipe.

He slowly lifted the rifle up from the water and put it to his shoulder. It felt like it took forever, and it probably did.

He aimed at the sniper who was closest to the big waterway. But he did not put the sniper himself in his crosshairs. Instead, he wanted to place the bullet in the tree trunk.

Thor smiled when he locked on to his target. 'This is actually fun' he thought.

He synchronized his focus on the tree with his heartbeat. Every heartbeat disturbed his aim a fraction, enough to miss at this distance.

He counted his heartbeats. One. Two. Three.

He squeezed the trigger between his third and fourth heartbeat. The bullet made the trunk explode right where Thor wanted it to.

A loud crack was followed by a big splash. The sniper fell into the water. The other sniper, right next to him, loudly said 'Shit!' and dived for his partner.

Thor waited. He hoped that the SEALs would think that he was coming in to Deep Saline through the northern entrance.

The two snipers got out of the water. Thor heard them loud and clear through the calm, quiet night.

Nothing else happened. Thor waited. He hoped it would not be in vain.

Still nothing. He got ready to dive and continue across the waterway and in through the southern entrance despite the presence of the SEALs.

Then, finally.

The two snipers at the southern entrance got in a Zodiac speed boat and left their post. They moved up the waterway toward the northern entrance.

Thor did not hesitate a second. He dived and turned on the propulsion system.

It was a smooth ride across the waterway and in through the southern entrance. He was expecting to encounter divers but the only thing the motion detector registered was an alligator. As Thor passed it the alligator stopped and held steady. He knew it would not attack him as he was moving, so he felt safe.

Only problem was, the alligator's tail came wagging his way just as he passed it. It bumped in to him and he instinctively shoved it to the side. That made the alligator nervous. It shot forward and upward and made a big splash in the barely four-foot deep water.

That splash caught somebody's attention.

A search light came sweeping over the water surface from the Deep Saline. Thor glanced up through the water and saw the light move over the surface right where the alligator had splashed. Air bubbles were compromising the surface and gave away their location.

Hopefully they would believe that it was just an alligator and not some guy in an ultra- hi-tech diving suit swimming through a marsh on a pitch black Louisiana summer night.

As if to reinforce Thor's concerns about what was to come,

two bullets pierced the water surface right behind him. There was probably another sniper further in, where Thor's motion detectors could not find him.

A couple of snakes came swimming toward him and seemed confused by his appearance. They turned away, but only after coming so close that Thor could have bitten one of them in the tail.

The edge of Deep Saline was as unreal as anything else out in the Louisiana marshes. He entered it at a point where trees grew everywhere and the water was not even three feet deep. He turned off the propulsion system and literally crawled along the bottom. He pulled out his knife in case the vegetation would become impenetrable. But the only use he had for his knife was to help himself move forward.

Then the trees vanished – and so did the bottom of the canal.

The contours of the bottom that Thor had been following just disappeared. It took him completely by surprise. He knew he was moving toward a deep hole in the ground, but he had been so busy moving forward without detection that he forgot about the 600-foot deep abyss where the beacon was.

Before he knew it there was nothing there underneath him. Nothing but water and thick, impenetrable darkness.

The edge was uncannily sharp. The depth just opened up. Thor stopped and instinctively reached for the edge of the abyss as if he would fall in to it.

Then he noticed the metal plates on the bottom, right where he had entered the Deep Saline.

Metal plates.

Yes. Motion detectors.

More than a dozen bullets penetrated the surface. He felt at least two of them bounce off his diving suit. Then another salvo came, apparently from a different direction. This time, five or six bullets bounced off his suit.

A third salvo.

They all seemed to come from different directions. Thor had no idea where to go.

Except down.

He turned and shot down into the deep darkness like a shark after prey. More bullets sprayed the water and now they were not just bullets. They plunged with him and exploded.

Grenade-size depth charges.

And then – the flakes.

A new kind of grenade emitted a chemical that lit up the water and spread fluorescent flakes. Anything moving would create shadows or make waves that clustered the flakes in brighter spots.

Thor plunged as fast as he ever could. According to Goryell he could easily go down to a thousand feet without any problems. But that was not his biggest concern. His biggest concern was to avoid being hit by the depth charges.

To avoid upsetting the pattern in the water that the flakes made, Thor put his feet together, stretched his arms up and formed a pole with his body. That concentrated his entire body weight to the surface of his boots and he plunged straight down without having to move at all. He made no waves and left the flakes floating around up above him.

He watched the depth meter. 60 feet. 80 feet. 100 feet.

He looked down. Still no sight of the bottom. Or of the beacon. Of course, it was dark both above the water and down at the bottom of the abyss, so he should not expect any light. But it was still a spooky feeling to plunge straight down in a deep hole, under water, on the lookout for some alien construction that he was going to blow up. And it was all pitch black.

Well, at least he was not leading a boring life, like his brother who was in graduate school getting a Ph.D.. The mere thought of that made Thor yawn.

He convinced himself to look for the beacon. Goryell had told him that once he reached its top he should stop and deploy the explosives.

And then get the heck out of there as quickly as he could.

Goryell had lent him a few nice toys, but one of Thor's own favorites was a small sonar that helped him detect things way down in the water. It would help him pinpoint the exact location of the top of the beacon, so he could save some time, go home, have a snack and watch TV.

He stopped at 160 feet to assemble it.

The sonar would bounce its signals back up and anyone listening would pick them up. Normally that was a problem during clandestine operations, but since the people up at the surface knew that he was there, it really did not matter. Besides, the guys up there were probably getting ready to drop bigger things than just fluorescent flakes and hand-held depth charges, so he might just as well get the whole thing over with.

He assembled the sonar. It was not easy, especially since he also had to keep an eye out for divers. The SEALs could decide to send folks down after him instead of bigger depth charges. If they did, things would get really interesting.

It was cold down here. Mighty cold. And pitch black. Thor had a minimal, green goggle light to help him see the parts of the sonar that he was piecing together. The light was barely strong enough to let him see his own gloves. Putting together a highly sophisticated sonar down here was quite a challenge, especially since it would take a skilled operations specialist a couple of minutes to do it at a cozy desk with lots of light and no risk of being blown to pieces by depth charges any second.

Thor glanced upward. So far no more depth charges and no divers. Good. He was almost done.

Then he dropped the last piece.

Just like Carl had done during the Puerto Rico operation.

Perfect. Just perfect.

The little piece, barely the size of his palm, quickly fell out of sight. He shot down through the water to intercept it.

170 feet. His depth meter climbed mercilessly.

200 feet. Still no sight of the piece.

230 feet. Where was it??

At 280 feet he suddenly heard a clunking sound. He wondered where it came from but kept diving fast, straight down.

Until he hit something. It was a large, metallic object. He bounced against it and tumbled round for a moment before he regained his sense of up and down.

He turned to see what the object was. But he could not find it. He swam in the direction where it should be.

Bang. There it was again.

He stopped and felt with his hands. Yep. There was definitely something there. Something metallic.

Of course! The beacon.

It was made of something metallic, and it was black. He was fascinated by its shape and the surface. It felt almost soft. Yet solid like steel.

He looked up. Way up there the SEALs had dropped more flakes. They would slowly make their way down through the water, all the way down to him. If he moved, the movement would be transmitted as a wave pattern through the flakes, all the way up to the surface.

No time to waste. He pulled out a harpoon-like weapon from Goryell's arsenal. He mounted a small hockey puck-like object onto its edge and pointed it downward. Goryell had instructed him to place the six explosive devices as closely to the stem of the beacon as possible. He did not know why, but that did not matter to him.

He aimed and fired. Then he moved a little bit and fired off the second explosive device.

He had no idea how thick the beacon was, so he was worried he would be placing them too much on one side. Goryell had told him that an even spread was preferable, but Thor had no real chance to investigate how to make it an even spread.

And even if he wanted to, the guys up at the surface would give him no time to rest. They had already dropped even more flakes.

The good thing about that was they would not be dropping any depth charges right now. They would want to wait and see if the flakes revealed his location.

Thor dropped three more explosive devices and took out the sixth one. He mounted it on to the harpoon – and got an eerie feeling that something was wrong. Very wrong.

He looked around to see if a SEAL diver had come down to say hi. But he could not see anyone.

He moved another few feet counter-clockwise around the beacon. He used his left arm to gauge the distance to the beacon while he held the harpoon in his right hand and pointed it straight down.

When he thought he had moved enough he stopped. He held on to the beacon and aimed.

Then he noticed that the beacon was vibrating.

'I have a bad feeling about this' Thor thought and fired off the last explosive device.

Then he glanced upward. The vibrations from the beacon were already sending waves through the flakes further up. And the waves were spotted by someone up at the surface who decided to drop bigger depth charges.

Really big ones this time.

Just what Thor needed.

There was no telling where those charges were going to explode. But wherever they did go off, they were going to make his life a lot more complicated.

He turned on the propulsion system in Goryell's suit and sped up in an angle. He was hoping to be above the depth charges when they went off. If he was below them he would be hurled down toward the bottom. If he survived the detonations, he would have no chance of getting out before the beacon exploded. If on the other hand he was above them he might be hurled up from the water and land somewhere near.

Hopefully alive.

Frankly, he did not expect to make it out of this place alive. As if to reinforce his sensations of imminent death, a depth charge came sinking down straight toward him. It came so close that he could reach out and push it away with his index finger.

For some weird reason he did just that. It was a hair raising feeling. That thing would explode in a second and probably kill him.

But it did not explode. At least not yet. For a moment he almost laughed at the strange sensation. It was like someone had dropped a nuclear bomb with "Hi, how are ya?" written on the hull.

The depth charge just kept sinking. The pressure should make it go off any second.

But nothing happened.

He felt the vibrations from the beacon through the water. They were getting stronger now. And wondered if it had something to do with an imminent explosion.

He was right.

Water is a formidable transmitter of shockwaves. That is why underwater earthquakes wreak so much more havoc than earthquakes on land. The shockwave leaves the ground and sets the water in motion. The water carries the wave until it hits something big enough to stop it. The bigger the quake the bigger the tsunami. And the bigger the explosion, the bigger the force that comes up through the water from below.

Goryell had told Thor that the explosion would be big. The six explosive devices he had sent down to the base were charged with something that Goryell called "simple, crude and reliable".

Then he had explained what it was.

Red mercury.

The coolest thing short of a nuclear bomb. Conspiracy theorists had talked about red mercury back in the '90s when the Soviet Union collapsed. Rumors floated for years on the internet that the Soviets had invented red mercury and had stockpiles of it.

They were right. The Soviets had refined it close to weapons grade. The National Security Agency stole a sample back in 1987. On direct orders from president Reagan, the NSA then sabotaged the laboratory in Turukhansk where the Soviet scientists were preparing the final steps to build red mercury bombs.

Then the NSA built a laboratory somewhere in the Mojave desert, and the KGB found it and in a tit-for-tat attack they blew it up. Since then nobody had tried to develop red mercury bombs.

Nobody on Earth, that is.

Out of the blue, Thor had met Goryell and been handed six little explosive devices that were armed with red mercury.

It was quite a moment. Almost worth celebrating. Except for the fact that he was sitting right here, right above a serial red mercury explosion and smack in the heart of the enormous body of water that was going to carry the shockwave up to the surface.

And what a shockwave it was.

It was like a giant fist rose from deep down there and knocked Thor hundreds of feet straight up. The water around him turned into a turbulent mess of mud, rocks and metal debris. He lost his sense of direction, he spun around, was hurled up, then to the right, then to the left, then up again. Suddenly, something hit his helmet and right after that an incredible noise overwhelmed his ear drums. The sound insulator had been ripped off. He felt his air tube get disconnected and tried to grab it. But he could not move his arms. They were heavier than lead.

Then suddenly he was out of the water and caught a glimpse of the stars. He was not sure if he was dead and was on his way to heaven, or if he was just flying. Then he realized that he actually was flying and that he stopped flying and that he was on his way down again.

He looked down and saw the massive whirlpool of water that the explosion had caused. He saw it coming right at him. He was falling sideways and knew that the impact would kill him.

When he hit the surface he thought of his brother. His brother had called him but Thor had not returned the call.

Jack would probably be pretty mad at him for that.

*   *   *

Holly Stanton was angry.

And she had a hard time controlling her anger. In fact, she was notorious for her bad temper and unstable mood.

Most people around her had taken a beating from her when she was not pleased – even president Oslow – and often they were completely innocent.

Her brother was the only one who had never had to deal with her bad temper. His wives, on the other hand, had been the targets of numerous outbreaks of Holly Stanton rage. Some whispered that Walt Stanton's three divorces (so far) were more or less all due to his sister's habit of using other people as her emotional garbage bins.

Irwin Schwepp had been on the receiving end of Holly Stanton's rage many times. As far as he was concerned, it was almost always uncalled for. Usually he sucked it up and moved on. After all, he was but a humble, loyal servant who did what his master – or mistress – told him to do. Maybe that was why he had kept working for her for so long.

He was good at recognizing when a new eruption was on its way. He knew Holly Stanton's rage better than most people did. And this short-notice meeting with her was definitely going to be spiced up with one of her outbursts.

The only other person except her brother that had not been hit by her anger was Rhea. It had taken Irwin a while to figure out why, but eventually it dawned on him.

Holly and Rhea were romantically involved. And they had been so for a long time.

So when Irwin came to the meeting and he saw that the only other person there except him and the vice president was Rhea, he quickly realized who was going to take the hit. And he did not think he deserved it.

Holly Stanton stared at him. Her eyes were steel blue, her lips so tight it almost looked like she did not have a mouth. Her arms were not crossed over her chest as they usually would be on someone in a state of uninhibited anger. Instead, her hands were tightly clasped together on the table before her. She was leaning on her elbows and her nostrils pumped air in and out of her lungs like an athlete on her way to an Olympic medal.

Irwin knew that there was only one way to handle her eruption. Bow your head and ride it out.

Which he did. Even though her attack on him was uncalled for.

"Irwin" Holly Stanton said slowly. "What the hell is going on here? Why haven't your so called loggers killed Ross Landau yet?"

"We're almost there, ma'm" Irwin said weakly.

"What are you waiting for?! That fat slob isn't going anywhere, is he??"

"No, ma'm."

"Then get on with it, damn it!"

"Yes, ma'm..."

"You're pathetic" the vice president said in a loathing tone. "Look at you. Is that supposed to be a man?? You're a sorry excuse for the male gender, Irwin!"

"Yes, ma'm..."

"I expect results from you. Isn't that why I pay you so well?"

"Yes, ma'm..."

"Are you dissatisfied with your salary, Irwin?"

"No, ma'm..."

"Well, then, as soon as this meeting is over, Irwin, I want your ass on the first plane down to Miami. I want you to personally oversee the operation down there."

"Yes, ma'm..."

"I want that cancer on our political discourse sliced off and thrown away once and for all."

"Yes, ma'm..."

Holly Stanton was quiet for a moment. Irwin sighed with relief. It was over. But inside he felt harmed, like someone had walked all over him and laughed. There must be some way to stop her from doing this to him.

"Good" said the vice president, sounding casual, as if nothing in particular had happened. "Now, let's start the meeting. Rhea, tell me what happened down in Louisiana. Tell me about the explosion."

"Yes. Shortly after we had ordered our SEALs out of there, the beacon down in that hole exploded."

"And you don't know why?" Holly Stanton asked in a voice that was almost artificially mild.

"Holly, I can't tell you for sure."

Irwin decided to try to score some points after the undeserved dressing down.

"But that means they did not get to use it, right? I mean, that's the upside of it."

Holly Stanton ignored him.

"Probably" Rhea agreed. "We think they were trying to turn it on when it malfunctioned and exploded."

"Well" said the vice president, "at least we didn't have to drop a nuke on that godforsaken place."

"There is one problem, still" Rhea added.

"What is that?"

"The two Branch Four agents have not yet reported back."

"Well, they must have died in the explosion" Holly Stanton said and smiled for the first time during the meeting.

"I ordered a search team in this morning, and they have found no traces of their bodies or equipment. Nothing."

Holly Stanton's smile vanished.

"What are you saying, Rhea?"

"That they probably got away. And if they haven't reported in, that means they are investigating who sent the SEALs in there. That's their modus operandi. They are very independent."

"Can't you contact them and order them to report in?"

"No, Holly, I can't. Once they go out on a mission, no one can contact them until they report back."

The vice president's mood worsened again.

"Well, that's just what I need right now, isn't it? Two maniacs out there nosing around in our affairs. Can you at least let me know as soon as they report in?"

"Yes, of course."

"Well, then" Holly Stanton said, "I think that's about it. Irwin, you get your ass down to Miami right away."

"Yes, ma'm."

"I want Ross Landau dead before sunrise tomorrow. Dead, do you understand?"

"Yes, ma'm. I understand."

"Don't fuck up."

'She just had to say that' Irwin thought as he left the room. He was getting pretty frustrated with Holly Stanton. It had built over the years. He was beginning to feel he needed an outlet for it. Not something big. No leaks to the press or anything.

Just a little return-the-favor thing.

*   *   *

C A G E

I am in the cage today. It has been a while since last time. I suspect they put me here today just to remind me of the cage. Silly them. How could I forget? I am always here or in the dungeon.

Except when they put me to sleep. Then I have no idea where they take me.

You can get used to the cage. I have. But I have been here so long now. Seventeen years. Or maybe a little longer. Twenty, maybe. It is hard to keep track of time. We try to measure it with the growth of our hairs. But then they cut it sometimes when they put you to sleep.

I am old now. An old lady.

Sometimes I wonder why they keep me. No one else is as old as I am. I remember Annabel, the old woman who was here when... when I came here. She said she was fifty five. And... two years later, I woke up one morning and saw them take her away.

She smiled so gracefully.

Poor Annabel. I think of her sometimes. She came here when she was only fourteen. She spent her entire life here. And they had her give birth to babies.

Strange babies.

The cage is so small. It is hard for me to get in and out now. I used to be better at it, but I'm getting old. Once I'm in it, it's really not that bad.

Of course, you have to get used to... them. And what they do to you. They turn the cage around and focus their beams of strange light on you. The light… it goes right through your body. And they move it up, and down, and up again.

The light hurts. Especially when they point it to the head. The first time I screamed and tried to move my head out of the way.

They punished me.

I was not the one they punished hardest. Marc, the Canadian, he fought them.

I get sick when I think of what they did to him. Really sick. Even now… Marc came with me and Sonya. It's been so long and… I still can't get the picture out of my mind of… what they did to him.

The beam is on again. It's pointing to my hips. It hurts, deep inside me. But I'm used to the pain now. I can endure it.

Sonya tried to talk to them. She's a psychologist. She tried to reason with them… establish a relationship. But they just stared back with their… eye clusters.

I know they can talk. They talk among themselves all the time. It's funny how long it takes to learn to hear it. But I can hear it now. A man… I have forgotten his name… he was here for only a short time… he said he had been trained in telegraphic communications. He said their language reminded him of the Morse code.

When their chatter picks up, I know they're going to move the beam. Like now. It's going up… up my spine. Ouch! That still hurts! I must stay focused. It is soon over. Soon I will be back in the dungeon with the others.

Unless… Unless they decide to put me to sleep for a while. Then I have no idea what will happen. Sometimes I wake up with objects sticking out from my body. Mostly my abdomen. They leave them there for a while. Once I had a four-inch long rod sticking out of my belly for several months.

Ouch! They're shining the beam at my neck. It hurts. Oh, they're increasing it. No! Please!! No, don't! Oh, God, it hurts!!

* * *

SILENCE

The day after Jack got back to Schuyler University he had graduate classes to go to. Most students in graduate school soldiered on all summer, and all of them pushed hard through June to get exams out of the way and maybe – just maybe – stay on schedule and get their degrees on time.

His libertarian friends were also back. They were all inspired by the big rally in South Carolina, although Senator Carlyle's death put a dampener on their excitement. Occasionally they talked about it and shared news or gossip.

But for most of the time it was business as usual for them. Jack and Todd had a seminar to go to. They walked slowly across campus and were amazed at how empty it was, now that the undergraduates were gone for the summer. This happened every summer, but it always took them by surprise. They got so used to the lively atmosphere during the school year.

Outside the student center they spotted two familiar faces on a park bench. Walt Widebelly and Shirky, another grad student, were deeply involved in a philosophical discussion about the meaning of life.

"It's that thing with toast again" Walt Widebelly said. "Once you toast bread, it becomes toast. It can never become bread again."

"That's a bologna sandwich" Shirky chuckled.

"Now you're making me hungry" Walt complained.

"Hi, guys" said Jack and Todd.

"Hi" said Walt and Shirky.

"Hey, can you help me out here?" Walt pleaded. "Shirky does not believe me. Even though we're both from Chicago. He still does not believe me."

"Shirky is a wise man" Todd replied.

"This is an existential problem" Walt said, ignoring Todd's comment. "Once you get your Ph.D., you can never go back to being a non-Ph.D. again. Right?"

"Nonsense" Shirky laughed and shook his head. "All you have to do is renounce your degree and throw away your diploma."

"Why does it matter anyway?" asked Jack.

"It doesn't matter at all" Walt said. "But it's an important philosophical problem."

"Sounds like something you should talk to Ched Chatson about" Jack suggested.

Alexis Anchorage passed by. She had already been to the library and was en route to the seminar.

"Are you still here, lazy boys" she commented. "You'll be behind this summer again. Slackers."

"My GPA is better than yours" Jack shot back at her.

"That's what you think" Alexis snapped back and vanished into the next building.

"I'm still smarter than you!" Jack yelled after her.

"She's nuts" Shirky chuckled. "And geometrically perfect."

"A wet Euclidean dream" Walt Widebelly agreed.

"Geometrically perfect" Todd repeated. "Jack, you've been there. What's it like to have sex with a girl who is geometrically perfect? Is it symmetrical?"

"No, it's... Euclidean sex" said Jack.

His iWorld rang. He reached for it.

"And what exactly is Euclidean sex?"

"Why don't you shag her yourself and find out?" Jack replied and looked at his phone.

He did not recognize the number and decided to ignore it.

"Thanks for the offer" Todd said. "But I'm not interested in applied geometry."

"So what are you guys doing here anyway?" Jack asked.

"Watching female graduate students" they both replied.

"Have fun. We have a seminar to go to."

"What's more important than female grad student legs?" Shirky asked.

"A Ph.D., maybe" Jack suggested.

Todd examined Jack with fascination.

"You're growing up, you know that? I never heard you take your classes so seriously before."

"I'm *not* growing up" Jack tried to protest as they walked off. "I'm just... you know..."

"Growing up" Todd finished his sentence.

Ched Chatson appeared out of nowhere. As usual he was wearing worn out sneakers, worn out jeans, a worn out t-shirt and a worn out beard. But he looked more worn out than usual. They guessed that he had been pot partying all night.

"Hi, Ched" Jack said.

"Nozick" Ched said, nodding lightly. "Uh... can anyone of you tell me what time it is?"

"It depends on what time zone you're in" Todd replied.

"I think I'm in the metric time zone."

"By metric time standards, it's just after lunch" Jack advised him.

"No wonder I'm so hungry" Ched noted, turned around and headed for one of the campus cantinas.

"The metric time zone" Todd chuckled. "Wonder what he was smoking last night."

"Whatever it was, it was making him stupid" Jack replied.

"We all have the right to fifteen minutes of stupidity in our lives" Todd reminded him.

"Whatever" Jack said.

He was distracted by his phone. It was the same number calling him again. He decided to answer.

"Yeah."

"Jack Nordlander?"

He did not recognize the voice. It sounded artificial, like someone was using a voice scrambler to distort his voice.

"Speaking" Jack said reluctantly.

He had a feeling this person was not going to tell him who he was. He was not sure why. It was just something in the voice.

"Senator Carlyle was just the first name on the list."

"What?? Who is this?"

"They are going to kill the next man in about a day."

Jack looked at his phone.

"Listen, I don't like sick jokes…"

"One day before they hit the next man."

This person sure sounded serious, too serious to be someone who would play a sick joke on him. And he was still on the line, as if waiting for Jack to ask the obvious question.

"And exactly who is the next person?"

"Ross Landau."

The person hung up. Jack looked at the phone and then at Todd.

"What the hell was that all about?" Todd asked.

"The strangest phone call I've ever gotten."

"And what was it about?"

Jack thought for a moment.

"I'm not sure. But I need to get hold of my brother. Now, kind of."

*   *   *

When Thor opened his eyes he had no idea where he was. He blinked a couple of times to get the mud out of his eye lashes. He raised his hand to wipe mud off his nose. It was hard. His arm was stiff and hurt a lot.

He realized that he was still wearing Goryell's diving suit. Except for the helmet.

And he was lying in a big pile of mud. He even had mud in his mouth.

There was something big and black right in front of his face. He squinted to see what it was. It looked like a piece of rock, but it was all black. A muddy, black piece of rock. But no rocks were all black, muddy or not.

He lifted his head slightly. His neck hurt when he did it. With a lot of effort he got his eyes close enough to that black thing to see what it was.

A boot.

He laid his head down in the mud again and closed his eyes.

Just great. A boot. And there was probably someone in it. Someone who was looking down at him with a grin on his face.

"Since when do you get to keep all the action for yourself?"

That was Carl's voice. Carl had been practically dead last time Thor saw him.

Ah. Of course. Suddenly, everything became clear to Thor.

"So I am dead after all" he mumbled.

"Is this your idea of heaven, buddy? Lying in a pile of mud?"

Thor opened his eyes again. He rolled over on his back. It was not easy. Everything hurt. His entire body. Even breathing.

Then he opened his eyes again.

It really was Carl's face up there. Smiling conspicuously.

"How did you get well that fast?" Thor asked.

"Thanks to Zerblat here" Carl said and padded Goryell on the shoulder.

"Zerblat? No, his name is…"

"The space alien in Piranha Club."

Carl's quirky sense of humor was back, alright.

"Good to hear you're back" Thor said. "I'm not sure I am."

"You need a rest" said Goryell.

Suddenly, Thor remembered the explosion.

"Hey" he said. "Goryell."

"Yes."

"The beacon started vibrating before I was done with deploying the explosive capsules."

"Yeah, I forgot about that possibility. The self destruct application activated already when the first capsule…"

"You forgot?!"

"Hey… nobody's perfect."

Speaking of forgetting. Thor had forgotten that there were a ton of SEALs around Deep Saline when he came there.

"Where are all the SEALs? They were swarming all over this place."

"For some reason they suddenly started leaving" Goryell said. "Even though they knew you were down there."

"They dropped a couple of big depth charges and then got in their Zodiacs and left" Carl added.

"Why?"

"Don't know."

"We better leave anyway" Goryell suggested.

Thor got up with a great deal of help from Carl. Goryell went down to a speedboat and started pushing it down in to the muddy water. Then Thor realized that he was actually right by Deep Saline.

"Did I destroy it?" he asked as Carl helped him down to the boat.

"Completely" Goryell reassured him.

Thor could barely walk. Every molecule in his body was hurting. He still wore Goryell's diving suit, but it had a crack in the side and the helmet was still missing. A lot of water had poured in. He heard a splashing noise from inside the suit.

"Your diving suit is leaking water" he said to Goryell as he tried to stumble in to the speed boat.

"You mean *your* diving suit is leaking water" Goryell said and helped him. "I'm ordering a new one tomorrow. You can keep that one."

"How insanely generous" Thor mumbled and landed on the floor of the boat.

Someone had put his machine gun there. He picked it up and saw that the black-out silencer was still attached.

"So who did you shoot?" Carl asked, looking at his machine gun.

"A sniper who was sitting on a tree that leaned out over the water. But I actually shot at the trunk so it broke and he fell into the water."

Carl chuckled.

Thor searched for other equipment. His knife was gone.

He had bruises on every limb and he could swear he had broken at least two toes. His right ear drum had popped and he could not bend his right knee without a great deal of pain.

He felt like he was going to barf.

Which he did.

Other than that he was in pretty good shape.

*　　　*　　　*

Jack and Todd got to their seminar in political economy just in the nick of time, right before professor Pinkhouse got there. The professor had made a habit of bragging about how he always came late to class and always went in to the only classroom where nobody was teaching and started talking to the students.

"So far I haven't gone to the wrong class once" he said and expected everyone to laugh.

His deliberate tardiness made some students deliberately tardy. Like now, when Jack and Todd had been held up by Walt Widebelly and Shirky and their esoteric existential problem.

Professor Pinkhouse was short and had always had a beard, except the last year. No one knew why he suddenly had shaved off that beard, but rumor had it he had lost a bet.

He could not teach one class without cracking at least four jokes. He also joked with his colleagues and tried to finish every conversation with a witty comment that would leave the other person or persons with a smile. He himself had no idea why he did it, but it had been an obsession for him ever since he was a teenager. It was a problem because he had run out of good jokes a long time ago.

So he kept on joking, even at the seminar that Jack and Todd attended. Everyone had heard all the jokes a few times already. But they laughed cordially and pretended to think that the professor was the funniest thing to come down the pike since Harold Lloyd.

Except Todd. He was not going to pretend anything when it came to professor Pinkhouse's jokes. He wanted professor Pinkhouse to stop joking and start doing something else.

"Like what?" Jack asked quietly while professor Pinkhouse was talking about something unimportant.

"Like teach, maybe" said Todd.

"I know how to get him off the jokes."

"How?"

"I'll just ask him a question. A very special question."

"No, you idiot!" Alexis whispered.

She was sitting on Jack's other side and looked sternly at him. It did not work very well.

"You do not ask him that question" she demanded. "Then he'll go off on anecdotes instead. I want to learn here, not listen to anecdotes."

"Ask him!" Todd demanded.

"Not!" said Alexis.

"Can I help you back there?" asked professor Pinkhouse.

"Uh... yes, professor" said Jack. "We were just wondering... what was it really like in the sixties?"

Alexis stomped on Jack's foot as hard as she could. Fortunately, she was wearing sneakers and not flip flops, but it still hurt. Jack bit his tongue and managed, by a whisker, to conceal his pain.

Professor Pinkhouse reacted to the question about the sixties like a high school senior who just entered a wet t-shirt contest.

"It was wild" professor Pinkhouse smiled. "Wild. You know what we say, right? If you remember the sixties, you weren't really there. But of course we weren't high all the time... hehe... we had our creative moments, too."

"Were you active in politics?" asked another senior.

"Yeah... oh, sure. I was... I was in the radical student network when I was at Ohio State."

"What was that?" Jack wanted to know.

"Oh, just one of those groups. Many of them went on to prominent careers. Like William Ayers. Of course, he wasn't at Ohio State... at least not officially... Anyway, a lot of what we did was not politics, but about getting high and getting laid."

Several students laughed. Professor Pinkhouse, who was lying through his teeth about what he had done during the sixties, was happy to see that his lies worked. He did not have to talk about the seminar he was teaching, which he thought was incredibly boring and he did not know a whole lot about anyway.

So he went on...

"...and when they shot those students at Kent State I was right there..."

…and on…

"…so I came to spend a lot of time at Berkeley…"

…and on:

"…that is how I barely escaped being arrested in Chicago."

Jack knew that professor Pinkhouse was going to go on for the rest of the seminar about his pretended memories from the sixties. It was good, Jack thought, because then he could relax and go over some notes from another class that he still had not made sense of.

Only problem was, his phone buzzed in his pocket. He took it out and glanced at it. After the last phone call he was a bit reluctant to answer just any call.

Then he recognized the number.

Thor.

He looked up and caught professor Pinkhouse's attention.

"Uh… sorry, professor… but I kind of have a family emergency to attend to."

He held up his iWorld.

Professor Pinkhouse did not care.

"Sure" he said. "Go ahead."

"Thanks" Jack said and stepped out of the classroom.

"Thor" he said to the phone. "How are you?"

"It's a long story."

"Are you still with that woman in Houma? She said you were her prisoner of passion."

"Miss Beth? Oh God, I wish. No, I'm in a Cadillac on my way out west."

"You don't have a Cadillac."

"I didn't say it was mine."

"I talked to dad last night. He hasn't heard from you in a while."

"I'll call him tonight."

"I need to talk to you, Thor."

"We're talking now."

"It's private."

"No problem. Carl's here and another guy. He saved my life last night."

"Thor… you gotta quit that job, man."

"And say no to a quarter million dollars a year? Got a better offer?"

"Listen. I got a very weird phone call just half an hour ago. I have no idea what it means. But… you know about Senator Carlyle, right?"

"Yeah. Car accident. Too bad. I liked the guy."

"Well, somebody just called me and told me he was killed."

"Someone called *you* and told *you* that?"

"Yeah. And…"

"Some prankster."

"I don't think so. He said the next one on the list is Ross Landau."

"Really" Thor yawned.

"Thor, wake up."

"I'm awake, man."

"What do senator Carlyle and Ross Landau have in common?"

"They're both conservatives?"

"They're the two most outspoken critics of Barry Oslow and Holly Stanton."

"Doesn't mean anything."

"Maybe. But that guy sure didn't sound like a prankster. It sounded like someone who wanted to tip me off about this."

"You're making too much of it" Thor said, almost yawning again.

"What do you know about Holly Stanton's political career?"

"I know about all those speculations that they killed their way up to power. But that's just speculations."

"Some of those who have died along the Stanton path to power died in freak car accidents, didn't they?"

"Yeah."

Jack waited.

"OK, so what if it's true?" Thor said. "What does Stanton stand to gain from killing Carlyle and Landau? And besides, there are others out there. Ron Paul…"

"He's retired. Barely ever speaks in public anymore."

"…Sean Hannity…"

"Who's to say he's not also on the list?"

"Now you're off the chart, brother."

"It depends on what you want to do, what's worth killing for."

"And even if you're right, what do you want me to do about it?"

"You're in the intelligence business, aren't you?"

"It doesn't work that way… Listen, we're stopping for some gas here. I'm gonna go get a snack. I'll call you tonight, alright?"

"Alright."

Thor hung up and put his phone back in his pocket.

"What was that all about?" Carl asked.

"Just my baby brother. He's got some wild brained conspiracy theory. He thinks Holly Stanton is behind Carlyle's death. And that she's planning to kill Ross Landau."

"Why would she do that?"

"That's the question."

Carl turned to Thor.

"No, I mean it, Thor" he said. "Think, buddy."

"What?"

"Do you remember what colonel Anderson told us at the briefing before we went on the mission?" Carl asked.

"Damn it" Thor mumbled. "Yeah, damn it, Carl, that kid's on to something."

Thor turned to Goryell who was just getting out to fill up on gas.

"We need to turn around, Goryell. We need to go to Florida."

"Why?" Goryell.

"To save someone's life."

·   *   *   *

Alexis was far from happy with the way Jack had steered professor Pinkhouse away from the topic of the seminar. Not that she believed the professor's fairy tales about his wild youth. That was not her problem. No, her problem was that she just did not care for his stories. All she wanted out of his class was the stuff that would help her get a high GPA and a smash hit Ph.D. that would help her land a nice job with the Federal Reserve.

Because of Jack's question about the sixties, she would have to take some of her library study time and go to professor Pinkhouse's office and ask all the questions that she had wanted to ask in class.

"What questions?" Jack asked her after the seminar.

"None of your business."

"Oh, yes it is. This seminar is not that complicated. It's basic business cycle theory."

"Still none of your business."

"Aha! I know. You just want to ask questions so he will notice you and give you a higher grade because you appear to be interested."

"Not true!"

"Gotcha!"

Alexis stopped and looked Jack in the eyes.

"So what if I do?"

"Is that why you're unbuttoning your blouse before his class?"

Alexis instinctively put her hand over her significant cleavage.

"I'm not" she said, but her blushing cheeks gave her away.

"Watch it, Lex" Jack said. "Show him your boobs, and he'll grab your butt."

"What's that supposed to mean?"

"You know darn well what I mean."

Of course she did. She just did not like it when Jack caught her with her pants down. Or buttons. But somehow she was also grateful that he did. She definitely did not like trying to schmooze the professor with her cleavage. She wanted to get good grades based on her academic performance, nothing else.

And yet, she knew that she was playing with fire. So far all she had had to do was to let them get a good look at her county-size cleavage. But she had known all along that the day might come when some professor would take her dressing habits as an invitation to more.

And when that day came she might need someone like Jack to help her get out of it.

After all, they had been high school sweethearts and managed to stay good friends even after they broke up. She could talk to him about anything. Except that blonde bombshell he had met in Columbia. What was her name again? Oh, right. Jenny.

Jack on the other hand could not stop talking about Jenny. She was 200 miles away and he kept complaining to the guys in the grad school dorm that his life was so miserable because Jenny was so far away.

"Ferchrissake, Jack" Todd said when they were back in the dorm kitchen and Jack once again brought up Jenny. "Get in the damned car and go see her. Get laid. And spare us another rant about her."

"I can't go to Pennsylvania" Jack protested. "I have classes."

That was a lie. Of course he could skip a couple of classes. He was doing well and was on top of all the material. There was no reason at all why he could not go to Pennsylvania and spend a couple of days with Jenny.

He was just about to call her when Ched Chatson came home and tossed Jack a copy of the campus newsletter.

"Seen this?" he asked.

Jack took the news letter and looked at the front page.

"The university board of trustees welcomes Franklin Pierce Junior as new trustee…"

"No, the one below."

Jack searched for the article below.

"Oh, this one?"

"Which one?"

"This one."

"Yeah, that one."

"That one?"

"No, this one."

"OK."

Jack glanced at the text with moderate interest. Then he went back to the top and started reading it again. Then he stopped and looked at Ched Chatson.

"Is this some kind of joke?"

"I wish" Ched said and sat down at the kitchen table, right next to Todd who was eating toast and having very strong tea.

"What's not a joke?" Todd asked while reading a newspaper.

"Listen to this" Jack said. "'Today President Oslow signed the new Fair Speech Act which will require all colleges and universities to amend their bylaws with a paragraph that guarantees fair speech on campus.' Apparently they won't get any federal money if they refuse."

"Whatever" Todd said and continued reading his newspaper.

"'*The law, which takes effect immediately, will require anyone who expresses an opinion in a classroom to immediately moderate his opinion with an opposing opinion.*' Is this for real??"

"You betcha" Ched said. "It's for real, alright. I looked it up. Congress passed the bill the first day after Senator Carlyle died. Everyone was so focused on him that they forgot to watch for this one."

"I don't see the problem" Todd said. "It's even good for us libertarians. There are so many Marxists blabbering in the classrooms. Now at least people will get to hear our side of the story."

"You haven't heard the other side of *this* story" Ched said and pointed at the newsletter to encourage Jack to read more.

"Oh, I see what you mean" Jack said. "Wow. Listen to this. '*The law does not apply to factual statements. If a person puts forward facts, he or she does not have to present a dissenting view.*' So who gets to separate facts from opinion?"

"That's the thing" Ched agreed. "The professor does, of course. He's the authority in the classroom. And we all know where they stand politically."

"That's even better" Todd said. "Too many professors present their opinions as facts. This way they'll have to be more careful."

"We'll see" Jack said. "I think you're way too optimistic. Who's going to monitor the professor?"

"And I think you're underestimating these professors" Todd said and put away the newspaper. "If they don't do their job, if they're politically biased, then what's left of academia?"

"That's an excellent question" Jack noted.

"Exactly" Todd said, took his newspaper and went out on the porch to have a smoke.

"What's with him?" Ched asked.

"He doesn't like uncertainty" Jack explained. "He wants everything to be as it's always been. He feels more comfortable that way."

"So what's so uncertain about this?"

"I guess the professors. If you can't trust the professors…"

Todd had another class to go to with professor Pinkhouse. He was convinced that all his professors were ultimately unbiased and thoroughly committed to the truth. He was also convinced that if only you worked hard enough, you would eventually see the truth in everything.

And because Todd wanted to understand things, he asked questions. So when professor Pinkhouse started talking about how important it was to criticize Capitalism, Todd asked him why.

"Because" said professor Pinkhouse with a smile on his face, "we live in a Capitalist society and there are almost no dissenting views. That is what we provide in college."

"I hear a lot of people criticizing Capitalism" Todd said.

"That's because they've been to college" professor Pinkhouse replied quickly.

Several students giggled. Todd did not say anything. He felt disrespected by professor Pinkhouse who used him to make a quick, stupid joke and win a popularity contest with only one participant. But he decided to ride it out instead of picking a fight with the professor.

Todd's problem was that he overestimated professor Pinkhouse. Unlike Todd, the professor was not in the classroom for academic reasons. He was there for his tenured salary, the personal gratification he got, the female students and the conversation. He took every opportunity to crack jokes that students laughed at. It made him popular, but it also gave him something else: command and control.

To Pinkhouse, the command and control element was like forbidden fruit. Having command and control over a group of students was almost like having sex with them (at least the female ones…). Sometimes, when he got off on a good tirade professor Pinkhouse got sexually aroused. The students had nowhere else to go but to sit there and give him their full attention.

That was an incredible feeling. And he could never get enough of it. Over the years he had even gotten addicted to it.

So when Todd asked a question it was like a challenge to professor Pinkhouse to take command, seize control over the students. He sensed another peak point coming, another shot in the arm of classroom dominance, verbal narcissism...

He decided to stay on the topic. He knew that Todd was the kind of student who would not back off. He would want to engage in a discussion, and that would let professor Pinkhouse show off his entire material for the other students – his wit, his jokes, his charm... all at the price of a few more laughs that he would rip off Todd's dignity.

He knew that Todd was working on a dissertation about the 2001 and 2003 Bush tax cuts. If he brought that in to the discussion, it would almost certainly provoke Todd in to a debate.

"In fact" professor Pinkhouse said, "Bush's tax cuts are an excellent example of what you have to do to keep Capitalism afloat."

Todd bit is lip to avoid saying anything. Professor Pinkhouse saw that his provocation was working.

He smiled.

"Bush raised taxes on the poor, and cut taxes on the rich, and thereby he just perpetuated the economic cycle that feeds Capitalism but eventually, ultimately, leads to the destruction of society."

"Excuse me" Todd said, "but there were no tax increases on the poor during Bush's presidency."

Professor Pinkhouse smiled again. He knew Todd was right about Bush raising taxes on the poor. But the facts were completely irrelevant to professor Pinkhouse.

He pushed the envelope.

"America is not far from that point of destruction" he continued, his eyes fixed on Todd. "In fact, we may only have a couple of years left before the chaos breaks out. And when Capitalism collapses, it will be very ugly. But it's not inevitable, and with hard work and a bit of luck we will be able to build something much more sustainable in its place."

Alright. That was it.

"Professor" Todd said.

Professor Pinkhouse could barely contain himself. This was going to be fun.

"Yes?" he asked as calmly as he could.

"The American economy is doing better than it has in decades, in part because President Oslow decided to keep the Bush tax cuts. It's only the past few months..."

"Ask the poor if they would agree" professor Pinkhouse shot back with a well prepared line.

Todd was not entirely unarmed either.

"I'm sure they would prefer to be poor in America rather than in, say, Sweden, where the average family is so poor that Sweden would be the poorest state if it joined the U.S.."

Professor Pinkhouse got slightly irritated. He liked it when students tried to stand up to him. He liked forcing them back down again. It was a downright erotic experience.

So long as he was in control, of course. When he was not in control, it was not fun anymore. And he was having trouble controlling Todd.

"The poor in Sweden are much better off than here in the United States of Capitalism" said professor Pinkhouse and got more laughs. "They have universal child care and good schools and crime is very low. They get generous help from the government to eradicate income inequalities. So I would be more than happy to ask them."

"Excuse me, professor" Todd said calmly, "but you have your facts wrong. Sweden is on the brink of becoming the next Weimar republic."

Several students gasped. They knew it could be academic suicide to tell the professor that he got his facts wrong. Especially in graduate school.

Professor Pinkhouse bounced back from his slump into frustration. He knew what the other students were thinking, namely that Todd was committing academic hara-kiri right before their eyes. And professor Pinkhouse was not going to stop him. All he was going to do was to rub Todd's dignity in the mud for a few laughs more.

Then he was going to send Todd packing.

"I challenge you to find any professor on this campus who would disagree with me" Pinkhouse said.

The majority-authority argument was usually a formidable weapon against even the sturdiest student.

But Todd did not budge. He had spent all too many days and nights in endless, meaningless discussions with Jack, Ched Chatson, Tom Tulip, Alexis and even Salto. Whatever the topic – cars, politics, music or nonsense – all his friends were in it to win.

So was Todd.

"So if ten professors say that the sun revolves around Earth, and one six-year-old kid says that the Earth revolves around the sun, you're saying that the professors are right" he noted calmly.

That one hurt. Professor Pinkhouse was completely taken aback. He was baffled by Todd. He knew that Todd could be very inquisitive, but not outright challenging. Of course, Todd called his inquisitive nature "being curious".

Professor Pinkhouse encouraged curiosity, but only in other classes than his own. His colleagues came to him and complained – with a smile on their face, to keep the chair of the department happy – that "your students are so curious about everything, they keep talking back at me in class, you really teach them to think, don't you, Jason?" And professor Pinkhouse smiled and marinated himself in their artificial admiration of him.

But now, that student curiosity was coming home to roost. And it once again hurled the professor back to that uncomfortable place called "frustration". Which made him irritated. He did not like being irritated. He felt like he was losing control. It was supposed to be a comfortable challenge to take down a student and get an erotic rush from it.

But this was not comfortable. It was downright annoying.

"So you are comparing yourself to a six-year-old" professor Pinkhouse tried.

Only some light giggling this time. The other students were beginning to sense that professor Pinkhouse was not the witty, funny, nice and comfy professor they thought he was. The façade was still there, but some cracks were showing. Something was shining through and they were not quite sure what to make of it.

Professor Pinkhouse got a bit scared by the student reaction. He did not care about his student evaluations. He was tenured and department chair so he had guaranteed life time income – a good one, at that – and if he wanted to he could throw away the evaluations that the students wrote on him.

No, all he cared about was being the top dog. Especially in the classroom. There could only be one person in the classroom. If he let their sympathy and affection slip away from him and over to Todd, there would suddenly be two people in this classroom.

And in professor Pinkhouse's classroom, there could only be one guy.

"Look" he said, "Sweden has among the best welfare systems in the world. Their poverty level is lower than America's. They give everyone free health care and the government pays people's salaries when they are sick. How much better can it get?"

"Health care is not free in Sweden" Todd pointed out, still calm and composed. "You would be paying twice as high taxes if you lived there…"

"Oh, I can afford that" professor Pinkhouse shot back.

"…and the poor would be paying four times more taxes" Todd continued, unfettered by the onslaught from the academic authority. "There is plenty of research to show this. OECD, for one…"

"I'm sorry, but we're out of time" said professor Pinkhouse suddenly.

His announcement came as a surprise to everyone in the classroom. There were almost five minutes left of the class. But everyone seemed happy to get out and away from the weird atmosphere that the argument had created.

As the students left, professor Pinkhouse pulled Todd aside and said he needed to discuss his doctoral thesis with him. Todd asked if they could do that later but professor Pinkhouse shook his head. Todd shrugged and packed his notepad and pens while the rest of the students left.

As soon as they were alone professor Pinkhouse's face turned from light and shiny to grim and dark. It was like flipping a switch. Todd was surprised. He had never seen that side of the professor before.

"I just want you to know" he said to Todd, very slowly and articulating every syllable while poking him in the chest with his index finger, "that your behavior in this class was completely out of line."

"What??"

"Don't give me that attitude" professor Pinkhouse said and allowed himself to lose control. "I'll be blunt. I don't like you. I never wanted you to get on the graduate program in the first place. You're in a lot of trouble. Not only did you exhibit a condescending attitude toward academic authority. But you also broke the fair speech law today, and more than once."

"Fair what??"

"I'm going to report you to the dean of student affairs."

Todd stood like frozen to the ground.

"I'll withdraw the report if you redraft what your doctoral thesis is going to be about. I want it to present a complete refutation of everything you said in here today."

Professor Pinkhouse left.

Todd slowly moved himself out in the hallway. He was stunned. He had no idea how anything he said could be in violation of the fair speech law. He barely even remembered the conversation in the dorm kitchen about it.

He tried to shrug off professor Pinkhouse's threat. But it did not work very well. One thing that really bothered him was that professor Pinkhouse had demanded that he hand in a new thesis proposal dictated by Pinkhouse's political preferences. That was politics in the classroom. Todd had heard Jack talk about that, but never really cared to listen.

It was all a big mess.

Unfortunately for Todd, the mess was only going to get bigger.

*   *   *

Goryell was dead serious.

"You want to save Ross Landau's life?" he asked.

"Yeah, pretty much" Carl and Thor replied.

"You want me to help you, right?"

"Yeah."

"Well, if we're going to carry out this mission together I need to know that you can do it with your bare hands if necessary. So I need to know what martial arts you are familiar with."

"Familiar with?" Carl said, clearly annoyed. "I am a third degree black belt in uechi-ryu."

"And I'm a Tenkara sensei" Thor added.

"Whatever" Goryell said. "Let me…"

"Whatever??" Thor said. "You don't even know what that means! Tenkara is traditional, Japanese karate, very tough. You're insulting my Shihan!"

Goryell looked at him. Thor was sincerely offended.

"I'm sorry" he said. "I didn't mean it that way. I just need to know what lethal techniques you guys know."

Carl and Thor looked at each other.

"Well… I guess we know a few" Carl said.

"OK" Goryell said. "I just earned my second star in Kherr-Wa. It is a very exclusive martial arts form. Everything we do is focused on two things: endurance and lethality. The techniques are so dangerous, in fact, that you can not even become a student of it unless you have already passed the star test in another martial art."

"Star test" Carl said. "I guess that's like our black belt tests."

"So what is it you want us to prove?" Thor asked.

"I want you to show me how you kill someone within two strikes of the start of the confrontation. No matter the circumstances."

"What do you mean 'within two strikes'?"

"The raid you did in the marsh down in Louisiana was not a close combat mission. This one will be. The guy you want to save is going to be attacked in his own home. So we'll be real close to the enemy."

"Why not just neutralize them?" Carl asked.

"If you take him down without killing him he will either hurt you later or call others' attention. Now, whoever is going to try to kill Ross Landau is going to do it in the form of a commando raid. How big a group would you say that could be?"

"No more than five" Carl suggested. "Four to go in and one to keep watch."

"I agree" Thor said. "Two guys enter two different ways. Except when you look at his house, it is more likely that they would come in by chopper."

"That would make a lot of noise" Carl objected.

"Look at the geography. How else would you reach this place? Especially if you want to make it quick in, quick out?"

"That increases the number of people involved, though. They would have to have someone on the lookout for cops."

"The chopper could do that. And if you outfit the chopper with machine guns…"

Carl nodded.

"Good point."

"So that's how you guys would do this?" Goryell asked.

"Yes."

"I agree. So let's assume that is how it is going to go down. Back to my point: when these four guys come on to Ross's compound we need to kill all four of them, not just incapacitate them. And we need to do it fast. You might have a chance to shoot them, but never count on that."

"Sure" Thor said. "But I still don't quite understand why we have to kill them, and why we have to be silent when they use a noisy attack."

Goryell smiled.

"Here's why."

And he explained the plan. It was ingenuous. Slowly, Thor and Carl relaxed and smiled with him.

"That's smart" Thor said.

"I like it" Carl agreed.

"A bit brutal" Thor added. "But I can see how it makes sense."

"Well, then" Goryell said. "Let's go over the martial arts part of it."

"We better hurry" Carl noted. "We don't have a whole lot of time to get to Palm Beach."

*   *   *

Advanced Retrieval Agency
Division of Alien World Operations
KB11-4-3 Earth Assignment Progress Report

Federation Universal Time Date Nomo 7372-11
Local Time Date KB11-4-3 May 29 2013
Chief Assignment Officer Tahm Qaar

Based in part on intercepted transmissions we have credible evidence that KB 11-4-3 Earth is the target of a pending alien invasion. The vice president of the United States of America has allegedly invited the invasion for reasons we have not yet established. The alien power is a previously unknown world, referred to as Zoh'moor. Signal tracking approximates the location of Zoh'moor. Analysis attached.

A peculiar detail: each time we intercept communications between the United States vice president and the Zoh'moorians, the same communication is echoed back to Earth. The echo is like a backup transmission, except it goes to a different location than the original transmission.

This could be an indication that the Zoh'moorians are already present on Earth.

The pending invasion is precipitated by a clandestine effort, ostensibly by the U.S. government, to silence political opposition. Their actions are in violation of both the United States Constitution and the Charter of Liberty.

Agent Goryell has made contact with an intelligence service loyal to the U.S. Constitution. I have authorized him to assist in their efforts to protect targeted political opposition. He is under strict orders to use a minimum of sensitive technology, including weapons.

It is yet unclear if the Zoh'moorian invasion is going to target the United States only or all of Earth. Either way I foresee a significant deterioration of individual freedom here. I recommend military action.

I have evidence that Danarvia has already established relations with at least the U.S. government in order to protect individual freedom here. For this evidence I refer to Attachment 2, a copy of a document found in memory bank Cyl-DM-77289-49 in Library Two at Operations Headquarters. An operation called Outer Rim Exploration built an emergency contact beacon here and trained a small, secret group to use it. The beacon was never activated and we have now destroyed it. This historic contact should override the regular ban on Danarvian military activities in non-contact solar systems.

We estimate that the alien invasion will take place 25 Earth days, or ten universal time date units, from today.

*   *   *

Jack was still bothered by the mysterious phone call. He had an eerie feeling that someone was actually going to try to kill Ross Landau. At the same time it seemed odd, to say the least, that someone would call him – *him* of all people – and tell about it.

The caller ID was blocked, of course, so there was not much he could do.

"Oh, yes, there is" Wolkenkratzer told him.

They were sitting on the porch outside the kitchen in their slightly over-partied graduate student dorm.

"Whaddayamean?"

"Haven't you read the manual?"

"It's sixty pages long! Who has time for a sixty page manual for a cell phone?"

"OK, Jack" said Wolkenkratzer. "I hate to break this to you, but the iWorld is not a cell phone. It's a PMP."

"I've heard that acronym."

"Portable Multi-Media Platform."

"Yes, I know that. I can watch TV live on it and I can make video-phone calls and all that. But this is different."

"Of course it's different" Wolkenkratzer said impatiently. "The cool thing about this phone is you can actually override when someone calls you anonymously."

"That's old news. You can do that on my dad's antiquated landline phone. You just push star-six-seven and..."

"Alright, let me show you" Wolkenkratzer said and grabbed Jack's iWorld.

He logged on to the Grid and started pushing buttons.

"Hey, wait, what's that?"

"I'm opening the programming function. Thanks to the Heisenberg programming that takes you beyond the confinement of digital..."

"Now you're making my head spin."

"The Grid runs on an entirely different kind of cables than the old internet did. It can handle so much more info it's uncanny. The neatest thing is that it lets websites teach your PMP to write new programs while you're logged on."

"What's so cool about that?"

"Well…" Wolkenkratzer sighed and rolled his eyes. "Even if your PMP does not have the software to do certain things, the website can teach it. So…" and he pushed another couple of buttons, "…we go to GridSearch and we tell the website that we want to learn how to search the Grid for incoming phone calls… like this… and… now, what's your phone number?"

Jack told him his phone number. Wolkenkratzer entered it.

"See?" he said. "Now the website teaches your iWorld how to write a search program. And… OK, enter your credit card number."

"What?"

"They want fifty bucks."

"Fifty bucks??"

"Yeah, for the programming service."

Jack gave Wolkenkratzer a look and took back his iWorld.

"And they guarantee I'll find out who called me if I pay them fifty bucks?"

"There's a disclaimer somewhere there, but… yeah, pretty much."

Jack glanced at Wolkenkratzer.

"Alright" he groused and bought the service. "How do you know all this stuff? You don't even have an iWorld."

"Unlike you I'm not out chasing girls all the time."

Jack's iWorld started doing something Jack had never seen it do before.

"What's going on now?"

"It's writing a search program."

"Really?"

"Yes."

"Cool."

The iWorld beeped two times and displayed a new Grid interface.

"So what do I do now?"

"See that little 'Execute New Program' button? Push it."

Again, the iWorld did something entirely new. Jack waited with excitement.

"Amazing" he said. "What else can this thing do? Download a pepperoni pizza?"

Suddenly, the iWorld displayed a name, a phone number, a phone service carrier, and GPS coordinates for where the anonymous phone call had been made from. Jack stared at the screen for a moment.

"I'll be goddamned" he said. "Ferchrissake, Wolkie... look at this."

"I told you" Wolkenkratzer smiled. "Is that important? That information?"

"You betcha" Jack said and copied down the information off the phone to a piece of paper.

"Who is that guy anyway?" Wolkenkratzer asked as he glanced at Jack's notes.

"I'm not sure. But the name is familiar."

"A prankster?"

"I don't think so. I've heard this name before but I don't think it's someone I've ever met. I'll look him up."

*   *   *

"Yes."

"Rhea, it's Irwin."

"Are you on a safe phone?"

"Of course. We are ready to go down here."

"Good. So why are you calling me?"

"Did you find out what happened to those two Branch Four agents?"

"They called in. They survived."

"That's not good news."

"I know, but why are you worried about it?"

"Well... if they escaped the Louisiana operation, how do I know they're not going to interfere with my operations?"

"Why would they do that?"

"Well..."

"Irwin, the only reason why they would do that is if they knew what you are up to. And there is no chance they know about your operation."

"Still, I suggest we call it off until you... until we have neutralized those two..."

"No, Irwin! You have Holly's orders."

"Yes, Rhea, but..."

"Now carry them out or... Irwin, do you know the name Rick Sturgis?"

"Yes. I remember him."

"Do you know what happened to him?"

"He died in a plane crash off the coast of Bermuda two years ago."

"No, Irwin, he didn't."

"No?"

"Irwin, we gave him to the Zoh'moorians."

"You what?"

"We gave him to our friends."

"But... why?"

"Well, they came here with a delegation to discuss plans with us. They had brought in a certain... genetically perfected animal... and..."

"Rhea, how long have you had contacts with the Zoh'moorians?"

"That's none of your business, Irwin. This... animal... is particularly fond of humans. And it doesn't just kill people. Let's just say it... consumes them."

"Rhea... I'm not disloyal..."

"Good, Irwin. Then make sure that tree down in Palm Beach is cut down tonight."

"Yes, Rhea."

"Nice and clean, Irwin. Nice and clean."

*   *   *

The Florida night was calm, hot and humid. The sky was clear. Goryell and Carl were moving slowly across a golf course. Carl glanced up at the stars and wondered which one Goryell came from.

"None of those" Goryell said. "I'll show you a map of Danarvia later."

It was a moonless night so they could cross the big lawns without much risk of being detected. But they still wore a kind of semi-cloaking jumpsuits that Branch Four had developed. It was covered with tiny screens that also functioned as cameras. Each of them displayed an image from behind the person on the front and gave the illusion that nobody was really there. The technology itself was not new – the Marine Corps had begun using it for vehicles soon after the last troops had left Iraq in 2010 – but Branch Four had the most advanced application of it.

Goryell had wanted to pick up two standard Alien World Operations cloak suits which would make them disappear completely. But they had not had time to go back to operations headquarters in New Mexico. Instead they had stopped by Atlanta briefly and met with Colonel Kwolczyk, who had supplied them with the equipment they needed.

Kwolczyk had said one thing that made Carl concerned.

"Rachel has asked about you and Thor."

Rachel was part of the small leadership team of Branch Four. Less than a dozen people made up the entire non-operational organization. It was against protocol for them to inquire about the whereabouts of individual agents. It was up to the field commanders, like Colonel Kwolczyk, to report upward.

Carl shared his concerns with Goryell.

"You think she's an infiltrator?" Goryell asked.

"I'm not sure. But it's very odd that she would ask about us."

"Infiltrators…" Goryell thought out loud. "It's been long since we had that problem. But it can happen to anyone."

"No one has been able to infiltrate Branch Four before" Carl said. "Mostly because almost nobody knows we exist. Only four presidents knew about us. Pierce, Eisenhower, Nixon and Bush senior. And vice president Cheney. That's it."

"Who could have sent those SEALs we ran in to in Louisiana?" Goryell asked.

"See, that's the thing. SEALs cannot operate on U.S. territory without the president's explicit approval. She's the VP, but she can still pull it off if she needs to."

"So you think Stanton has an infiltrator in your organization?"

"Yes" Carl whispered.

They had to stop talking. They had reached a small wooded area on the far side of the big golf course. Beyond it was a small open space and a row of palm trees, then a street and Ross Landau's home on the other side of that street. His residence was secluded behind a high wall, some trees and an advanced security system.

Goryell checked their time. Thor was going to enter the Landau property in two minutes.

Down the street they noted a car parked on the golf course side of the street. It was an anonymous Impala.

"That car does not belong here" Carl noted as they slowly moved in to the wooded area.

"Why?"

"It's downscale, and who would park a car on the street here, where everyone has room for a half dozen cars on their properties?"

"Maybe a visitor?"

"They still wouldn't park out in the street. I'd say it's a lookout for the attack."

"So we can get company any time" Goryell noted. "Alright, let's go."

They slowly moved through the wooded area and reached the open space before the street. Then they heard the door on the driver's side of the Impala open. A man stepped out and closed the door. He leaned against the car side and lit up a cigarette.

"He's smoking" Carl explained. "That shows he's nervous."

Goryell examined the Impala through his thermal scanner.

"There are more people inside the car" he noted.

They crossed the street hunkering down and moving very slowly. Their semi-cloak worked well over distance, so no one in the Impala could see them even with a regular pair of binoculars.

The smoking man at the Impala glanced at his watch frequently and smoked his cigarette intensely, like he was irritated and tried not to show it.

As Carl and Goryell reached the other side of the street they took up position at the locked gate in the wall that surrounded Ross Landau's home. They were ready to go into action as soon as Thor sent the "clear" signal from the other side.

Which would take a while. Thor could not just walk up to Ross's property like Goryell and Carl. He had to swim – again he did the swimming – and reach it from the sea side. To avoid tripping any security system he would then enter an overflow tunnel that collected high sea water from the property during bad weather. The tunnel would take him to a point right under one of the porches on the property.

Then he would just improvise.

Piece of cake.

Of course, there was one problem. Once he had removed the grid that covered the mouth of the overflow tunnel, he found that the tunnel itself was filled with sharp metal rods. They were irregularly placed throughout the tunnel. Thor guessed that it was to keep alligators from getting in, but it could just as well be to keep uninvited guests from entering that way.

He held still at the tunnel mouth for a moment and examined the metal rods with a flash light. He tried to plot a route past them, but gave up pretty quickly. It would take a snake to get past them.

Fortunately, Thor had borrowed one of Goryell's fancy weapons. It was a handheld energy blaster, and Thor found it amusing that it looked like a Romulan disruptor from Star Trek. The difference, of course, was that this one worked. Goryell called it a "matter shatterer" and had given Thor a little demonstration.

It literally pulverized metallic objects.

The downside was that in order to make it work in secret mode Thor had to be patient. It would take a while to destroy the metal rods.

There were eight of them in total. He aimed the matter shatterer at the first one and held steady, as the weapon set the metal in the rod in motion. Slowly the rod weakened and broke at the point where he had aimed.

But it took a while. He was never going to make it through the tunnel at that rate.

Of course! All he had to do was to reset the shatterer for a higher intensity. To do that he needed to direct his flashlight at the top of the weapon, holding the flashlight in one hand and the weapon in the other. Then he could adjust the strength of the weapon with... what, his third hand?

Above water he could easily just hold the flashlight between his teeth. But down here, under water, that was kind of ruled out.

He cursed himself for not having practiced this before he dived. Then again, they had been forced to act very quickly. All they knew was that the 48 hours until someone was going to attack Ross Landau's home were almost up. The attack may happen any minute. And he was the one to get Ross out of the house. What good was he doing, floating around down here like a useless piece of old rag?

There was only one way to do it. He pointed the flashlight to the top of the shatterer for a few seconds and studied the force setting panel. It was not easy to tell which way to adjust the force, but there was one small symbol and an identical symbol right next to it, but bigger.

Good. That should be easy. He put the flashlight in a pocket and let his index finger move slowly over the top of the weapon until it was right on top of the bigger symbol. He pressed it gently. Then he took out the flashlight again, pointed it in toward the end of the tunnel and aimed the shatterer the same way.

And pulled the trigger.

Man, what a difference!

The metal rods vaporized. All of them. The tunnel cleared all the way to its end. Just as he wanted.

But not just that. The wall at the far end of it, where he was supposed to go up through a narrow passage, opened up. The metal wall of the pipe disintegrated.

Then the most remarkable thing happened. It was almost as if an invisible excavator had begun digging a hole straight into the ground right where the pipe wall had disappeared. The invisible excavator dug its way through mud and dirt and scattered rocks.

Uh oh.

For a moment he feared that the matter-shattering energy would dig itself all the way underneath the house and the street, and out to the water on the other side of the peninsula.

Fortunately, it was not that bad. When the matter-shattering energy finally stopped, he pointed his flash light toward the end of what was now a much longer water-filled tunnel than anyone had really intended.

He saw something he did not want to see.

A faint light down at the end of the tunnel.

'Why do I always end up doing the diving?' he thought. 'Those two guys are up there on the surface having a party.'

He slowly moved in through the tunnel toward the light. He was amazed at how the matter shatterer had turned metal, mud and rock into a dusty mess that floated around in the water. He literally carved his way through the soup with his hands and moved, foot by foot, toward the light. It was not the drainage where he was supposed to get up. It should be dark there, pitch black, in fact.

He reached the drainage and looked up. Everything seemed normal up there. At first he was going to climb up there, but the light at the end of the tunnel intrigued him too much.

'Could it be...' he thought and swam further in.

Then he saw the wall.

The wall in the foundation of the house.

The shatterer had cut right through the massive foundation. Luckily, there was no basement inside the foundation. Only earth and rocks. So the tunnel had cut in right under the ground floor of the house.

Thor reached the light. He glanced up.

And down.

It was a drain pipe from a bathroom. And the shatterer had cut right through it.

The drain pipe was only a few inches wide. It was useless.

Unless, of course...

*   *   *

"Yes?"

"Holly, it's me."

"Rhea! Why are you calling this late?"

"Irwin and his loggers have begun their work down in Florida."

"That's good."

"Yes. But I'm having doubts about him."

"Doubts?"

"He tried to get out of this operation."

"What do you mean?"

"He wanted to postpone it because the two Branch Four agents from the Louisiana operation are still unaccounted for."

"Why?"

"He's afraid they will show up here and mess up his operation."

"How would they know where he is going?"

"I asked myself the exact same question. So I took the liberty to hack in to his cell phone. And... I hate to say this, Holly, but I am beginning to believe that he is a traitor."

"Traitor?? Rhea, I've known Irwin..."

"I know, honey. I know. I hate to tell you this... but I have to tell you what I found."

"I don't believe this. Who did he call?"

"A guy by the name Jack Nordlander."

"Who is he?"

"Thor Nordlander's brother."

"Who is he?"

"Carl Hanover's partner."

"Who is he?"

"One of the two agents we tried to kill in Louisiana."

"Who was the other one?"

"Thor."

"Who is he?"

"Nordlander."

"Who... OK, I see. Oh. Oh, OK. Oh, I get it. Damned. Damned, Rhea. I can't believe this."

"Holly, honey... I'm so sorry."

"Well... you know how men are. Deceitful. Selfish. Weak."

"I suggest we eliminate him."

"That's... a bit drastic..."

"He could jeopardize this entire operation."

"Well... alright. Do it."

"I'll see you tomorrow, honey."

"I miss you."

*   *   *

Ross Landau was taller than Thor had expected. He stood steady on his feet, hands in the pockets of his bath robe, his slippers on and reading glasses around his neck.

He was staring at Thor. Thor stared back.

"How did you get through my security system?" Ross asked.

Thor was surprised. Ross's voice was not fearful, not even angry. It was more irritated. Almost as if he felt insulted. Someone had defeated his intelligent security system, a system that he had designed and created.

It kind of made sense. Ross was a smart man, and he knew it. No one was smarter than him. Thor was the first to subscribe to that idea.

"Sir..." he said. "I'm not here to harm you. I'm here to..."

"That's not what I asked" Ross interrupted him. "I asked how you got past my security system."

"Sir, please, we don't have a lot of time..."

"Did you swim through the toilet pipe or something?"

Ross chuckled at the thought. Thor was impressed with the man's calm and composed attitude.

"Actually, sir, that's not too far off. But please, hear me out."

"Have you been trying to call my show but didn't get through?" Ross chuckled.

"Sir, please!" Thor said and displayed the matter shatterer.

"What's that?"

"It's a weapon I am going to use on those who are coming to kill you."

That caught Ross's attention.

"Kill me?" he frowned. "Who'd be stupid enough to try that?"

"A bunch of thugs sent out by Holly Stanton."

"The vice president?! Ha! Haven't heard that one before."

"Well, we're here to stop them. But we need your cooperation."

Ross looked at Thor for a moment. He examined him up and down. Thor really looked like someone on a very special mission.

"Alright" Ross sighed. "Let's go in to the kitchen."

Thor sat down at the kitchen table. Ross pulled a couple of water bottles from the fridge.

"I could make some coffee" he said. "But I can't sleep if I drink coffee this late."

"Sir, you won't need to sleep, but there is no time for coffee anyway."

Ross sat down across the table from him.

"As I said" Thor said and sipped from the water bottle, "there is a group of hit men on their way here. We were tipped off about them and…"

"Who are 'we'?"

"A secret government agency. We know about Holly Stanton's plans to silence the opposition. You're number two on their list."

"Number two? I'm number two? Who's number one?"

"Senator Carlyle."

Ross raised his eyebrows.

"He was killed?"

"Yes."

"You can prove this?"

"Yes."

"And I am supposed to be next" Ross said and his eyes wandered off toward the window. "Well, I guess it makes sense."

"You silence the politician first" Thor said, "and then the man who educates his voters."

"But why? Why would the vice president suddenly start killing off people? I mean, it would make sense if Barry Oslow was on top of her list."

"I will explain that very soon, but right now we need to stop the attack. It's due any minute now."

"And are they also going to break in here? I still want to know how you got in."

"They're using a helicopter."

"That's ridiculous! With all the noise… they'd never get away with it."

"Sometimes, a spectacular attack is easier to cover up than a quiet one."

Ross examined Thor again.

"You sound like someone who knows what he is talking about."

Thor's ear piece buzzed.

"Helicopter approaching" Carl told him.

"Copy that" Thor replied. "Sir, the helicopter is coming. The attack will begin in two minutes, three tops. Here's what I want you to do…"

*   *   *

PRINCIPLES

The Federal Assembly was the legislative body of the Danarvian Federation. With 63 member worlds, and seven representatives from each, the Assembly had become fairly large over the years. It was located on a planet with the incredibly inspiring name AP-44-2. Originally, the Federal Assembly had been on one of the worlds that founded the Federation, but after the Kahpiyan War it was agreed that the Assembly should be on a neutral planet, one with no indigenous life. It was part of an effort to neutralize criticism and suspicion that the world that hosted the Assembly would be able to extract advantages and favorable treatment from that.

AP was a neutral sector close to the geographic center point of the Danarvian Federation. The planet 44-2 was inhabitable and pretty nice, but due to an evolutionary anomaly it had no indigenous intelligent life forms. However, thanks to a climate that was equally comfortable to humanoids and reptilians, it had over the years become a popular destination for tourists. A lot of hotel chains, travel agencies, casinos and resort companies had come to AP-44-2. But to maintain the planet's neutral status no one was allowed to live on it, except the Assembly delegates. So the employees of Black Hole Casino, Big Bang Hotel & Nightclub, Moonwalk Resorts and all the other companies that serviced the tourists, all had to live on orbiting residential space stations.

Some people complained that the Assembly had chosen such an attractive location only so that the delegates could get a nice

vacation while at work. Kind of like relocating U.S. Congress to Key
West. But the only neutral alternative that had a harsh, unfriendly
climate was Majestic 37, a rough, tough, dry world filled with barren
land and constantly battered by unforgiving temperature swings. It
was far, far away from most member worlds, on the very outskirts of
Federation space. As if that was not bad enough, it was also close
to the border of that big, frightening unknown – The Great Void.
A lot of people felt uncomfortable with having the Federation's
legislative body so close to something that not even the most
advanced scientists could tell what it was.

The Assembly had a committee on intelligence and outer
rim security. It had nine members and was chaired by Delegate
Watlaan. She was not only the longest serving Delegate of the nine
on the committee, but also had a strong background as a former
intelligence agent with Advanced Retrieval and secretary of defense
and security on her home world.

As a reptilian, Delegate Watlaan sometimes thought that
AP-44-2 was a tad on the chilly side. But then again, it could also
be because she was growing old. She tried to stay in shape and often
got up early in the morning for a long walk on the trails through the
thick rain forest that surrounded most of the Assembly campus.

This morning she took a shorter trip. She had called an extraordinary meeting with the committee and had to be in her office in
good time to prepare.

When she got to the meeting she was delighted to see that all
the other Delegates were there. It was not a given when the meeting
was announced just a day in advance.

"Dear fellow Delegates" she opened the meeting. "I apologize
for the short notice. Yesterday I received a serious intelligence
report from Advanced Retrieval's Operations Headquarters. There
is a growing security situation in the KB sector."

"Does this refer to KB eleven four three?" asked one Delegate.

"Yes" Watlaan confirmed. "Locally called Earth. As you know
the electronic surveillance of that world was terminated prematurely
after two members of a criminal organization had been there. Alien
World Operations began surface operations three weeks ago. It's

been a routine mission so far. Until we received the following report last night."

She handed out the report that Tahm Qaar had sent.

"They have intercepted transmissions between Earth and a world located further out in the sector, possibly at the edge of the galaxy" she said. "One national government on Earth appears to be conspiring with this other world, Zoh'moor."

The Delegates were used to intelligence reports concerning non-member worlds. Currently Alien World Operations had teams on eight different worlds and reports came in regularly. But this was not a routine report.

"I'm not sure I understand" said Quim, a senior Delegate. "Earth is corresponding with this unidentified world, who is about to invade them. And they have invited the invasion?"

"Apparently" Watlaan explained, "one of the national governments on Earth is conspiring with the aliens. Their possible motive is to expand their control over Earth with the help of this alien power."

"That's risky business" remarked another Delegate.

"Indeed" Delegate Quim agreed. "But regardless of that, I fail to see why this is our matter in the first place. We have no official contacts with Earth, let alone established diplomatic relations. They are not members of the Federation, nor have they applied for membership."

"Advanced Retrieval has a team there" another Delegate pointed out. "And criminal elements of Danarvian origin have discovered that world. We know what has happened in the Temptation Sea since a fraction of the Dream Web re-established itself out there. Several worlds there are under heavy pressure from them. It's almost becoming lawless space."

"Granted" Quim replied. "But just like Ima-ha-yaan and other worlds in the Temptation Sea, Earth is outside Danarvian jurisdiction."

Delegate Quim was an old man. He was a Teuran, from Teura Vaar, a world inhabited by a peculiar humanoid species that were tall and slim, had unusually large skulls, long arms and legs and narrow faces that made them look like they had been starving for months.

They were very influenced by their religion which mandated training in patience, meditation and piety. This prepared Teurans well for diplomatic services, and Delegate Quim was no exception. He had worked for the Danarvian government for decades. He had seen it double in size over his long service. He had led the negotiations with most of those new worlds that had joined the Federation over the past half century. And he was widely recognized as the architect of the peace treaty that ended the Kahpiyan War.

Because of Quim's status and reputation, very few people argued with him. Watlaan was no exception, but she was also the chair of the committee.

"I hold your opinion in high esteem, Quim" she said. "Earth also lacks a world government. The main power is the United States of America. They are the ones talking to the Zoh'moorians. Before the Advanced Retrieval unit began sending their reports back from Earth, our impression of the United States government was very positive."

"Please refresh my memory" asked another Delegate. "How many different nations are there on Earth?"

"Two hundred."

"It is a serious situation" another Delegate said. "A leading power taking help from an alien world for its own self interest. Sounds like a big power grab to me."

"I still do not see why we are even discussing this" Quim said. "It is their own internal affairs. They are three sectors away from our border."

"I would not be so quick to draw that conclusion" Delegate Watlaan said, challenging Quim in a way that surprised some of the committee members. "If this is indeed a power grab by the United States government, then we have to consider intervening based on The Fourth Principle of the Charter of Liberty."

"Each and every independent being has the right to determine their lives without interference except insofar as to guarantee that right itself" a Delegate quoted the first clause of the Fourth Principle.

"Our constitution, our Charter, does apply to all independent beings" Watlaan continued. "The Charter Court has ruled so. It applies universally, regardless of where the independent beings live."

"You are referring to Case Eighty-Four" said Quim. "I believe you are interpreting the ruling on Case Eighty-Four somewhat creatively."

"With due respect, Quim" Watlaan said. "The prevailing opinion within both the Federal Assembly and the Executive Office is that Case Eighty-Four indeed does mean that we should intervene to protect individual freedom everywhere."

"Has the Executive Office seen this intelligence report?" Quim asked.

"Yes."

"Have they decided on any action yet?"

"No, but my guess is that they will take military action and order Frontline Services to dispatch a strike group to Earth."

"Well" Quim said. "There are other restrictions on the Executive Office. They do not have a blanket authority to dispatch military forces anywhere and everywhere in the galaxy as it pleases them."

He paused and looked around. The committee members quietly awaited the rest of his argument. They all knew that even though Teurans seemed stoic, they could be quite adamant about things they believed in.

"With Case Eighty-Four" Quim continued, quietly and confidently, "the Charter Court established that The Fourth Principle of the Charter of Liberty applies to non-Federation worlds under either of two conditions. The first is the plead condition. If people of, say, Earth plead for our help, and if the plead is determined to be representative of the majority on that world, then we can intervene. The second condition is that the events on that non-member world may indirectly threaten the freedom of Danarvia, partly or in its entirety. Neither condition applies in this case."

"I do not wish to argue with your deep well of knowledge" Delegate Watlaan said. "But there is also a mentioning in this intelligence report of a contact being made between the Outer Rim Exploration project and the United States government. They even built a beacon in the event of an imminent threat. That constitutes an official contact between us and Earth."

"Outer Rim Exploration was discredited a long time ago as a private enterprise led by wild-brained explorers" Quim noted.

"Maybe" Watlaan said. "But it was initiated by the Executive Office."

"Anyway" Quim continued. "I think it would be imprudent of the Executive Office to go ahead and send military forces to Sector KB at this point. In anticipation of that I shall request that the entire Assembly gets to see this intelligence report. Then I shall ask the Assembly to demand formal consultations with the Executive Office on what their plans are in sector KB."

Watlaan was not happy.

"You do realize" she said, "that a request for formal consultations will automatically delay any military action to save the people of Earth from a big power grab by one run-amok government."

"I am aware of that" Quim said. "But our duty is to protect the integrity of the Charter of Liberty. We cannot rush away like firecrackers through space and save everyone and anyone and forget that we are a federation built on inviolable principles. The point with limiting government the way we do in the Charter of Liberty is that we want to protect both us and others outside of our government's jurisdiction. Remember – our limits on our government is also to assure that our government does not grow authoritarian toward others."

"With all due respect, Quim" another Delegate said, "in this case we may be sacrificing the freedom of billions of people on Earth. They could very well become the subjects of a ruthless tyrant for the foreseeable future."

"We do not know that" said Narkeenis, a junior Delegate who was clearly inspired by Quim. "I agree that the actions of the United States government are suspicious. But we do not have sufficient evidence that the invading aliens are in fact tyrannical. For all we know they could be a benevolent force and bring freedom to the rest of Earth. Besides, this intelligence report that we are discussing here actually says that Outer Rim Exploration thought that the United States government was worthy of our support. The Exploration team built a beacon there so we could come and help them preserve their freedom."

He paused and looked around the room. He was a young Delegate, the youngest on the committee. They were not used to hearing him speak on big issues.

"I do not mean to disrespect our agents in Advanced Retrieval" he continued. "But to me, this sounds like we have, at some point in history, put a great deal of faith in the United States government in pursuing freedom for its people. I cannot see that our knowledge of the situation on Earth is good enough to go to war over."

"Well" said Delegate Watlaan. "I think we have covered all aspects of this issue. As per Quim's request I shall make this intelligence report available to the full Assembly."

She concluded the meeting and left the room. There was no mistaking that she was unhappy with Delegate Quim's requests. He understood her frustration and came up to her after the meeting to try to mend fences a bit.

"Watlaan" he said. "I hope you will not let this come between us."

"Of course not" she replied. "But I think you are reading The Fourth Principle from one side only."

"The Fourth Principle is not a blanket authorization of use of military force" Quim reminded her.

"Nor does it blanket prohibit the use of force" Watlaan replied.

Delegate Quim nodded with the typical grace of a Teuran.

"Of course" he said as they walked down the hallway. "You and I may very well recognize the pattern and rightfully conclude that both the current United States government and the invading aliens have very little regard for freedom. But if we are going to go to war, we better have a very good case to present to our fellow Danarvians. It is their sons and daughters that will go out and fight."

"Nobody is craving for bloodshed" Watlaan replied as they stopped outside her office. "Danarvia is still scarred by the memories of the Kahpiyan War. But if we are going to set the bar that high… if we are going to live by the credo 'peace at any price'… then the price will keep on rising until, ultimately, it will be freedom itself. If not our freedom, then someone else's."

*   *   *

The sound of a helicopter broke the midnight silence of the
quiet South Florida neighborhood like a train coming out of a
tunnel. It came from inland and flew low. Its lights were turned off
and it approached fast.

Carl and Goryell stood still outside Ross Landau's house. Their
eyes were on the Impala down the street. The driver was still
standing outside the car, smoking his second cigarette. When the
helicopter came within sight he nervously threw the cigarette on
the ground and killed it with his right shoe.

Another man got out on the passenger side.

The helicopter approached straight from the west and flew in
an almost perfect line parallel to the street. The two men at the
Impala put on radio headsets. Right after, the helicopter stopped
and hovered almost right above them.

Two more men got out of the Impala's back seat. Unlike the first
two, these guys were dressed for action. They had black overalls,
were masked with black hoods and carried submachine guns.

The two armed guys started jogging up the street as the helicopter
slowly approached Landau's house.

The gate to Ross's property was remotely unlocked. Carl and
Goryell quickly went inside and closed the gate behind them. Then
they took up new positions.

And waited.

Between the gate where they had entered and the house was a
big lawn. It was obvious that the helicopter would land at least part
of its crew there. Carl had suggested they would land a second crew
on the big porch on the other side of the house.

Suddenly, the gate they had come in through was blown off its
hinges. The two men who had come jogging up the street burst
through the opening. Carl and Goryell were ready for them. Goryell
stood almost straight ahead from them. But the two men could not
see him. The cloak suit Carl had given him was kind of primitive,
but it worked pretty well at night.

The first of the two intruders charged straight at Goryell,
without seeing him. Goryell did not wait for the man to crash into
him. Instead he threw a spear-hand strike right at the man's throat.

It was a simple but deadly technique. He held his hand flat with the fingers tight, thumb in, pointing right at the unwitting adversary. Then he shot the spear hand straight out, hitting the man with the tips of his fingers right where the main artery runs up to the brain.

The impact was formidable. The man died before he even hit the ground.

The other intruder was a step behind him and stumbled right in to his falling buddy. He fell to the ground, but before he could get an idea of what had happened, Carl hit him over the neck with a hard fist punch. He swung his hips with the downward punch to put even more power in to it. To maximize the deadly impact he concentrated all the power of his fist to the first two knuckles. His entire force was concentrated to a surface the size of two dimes. The impact was like steel onto the bone in the man's neck.

Carl's thousands of push-ups on those two knuckles paid off.

The impact was incredible. The man's neck broke right there and he fell flat to the ground, completely paralyzed.

They had barely taken out the first two intruders before the helicopter came in. It flew over some trees; the pilot could not see what was going on down on the ground until he was right where he was going to land. The darkness of the night also helped conceal the two downed gunmen.

The helicopter touched down about 40 feet away from Carl and Goryell. Two side doors opened and two more gunmen jumped out. Then the helicopter lifted again and left the same way it came. Apparently there were only four men in the assault team.

The two gunmen looked around. Apparently they were expecting their buddies to come forward and team up with them.

Goryell and Carl did not waste any time. They confronted the two new intruders.

The problem was that their cloaking suits worked well so long as they did not move very fast. When they moved fast the cloaking system was too slow to keep up. They became two blurred figures that came charging right at the two confused but heavily armed gunmen.

Stunned, the two gunmen stared out in the dark for a second.

Then they aimed their submachine guns and opened fire at the strange entities that came charging right at them.

When the bullets came flying Carl was grateful for the crash course in Kherr-Wa that Goryell had given him and Thor. The second the gunmen raised their weapons Carl and Goryell launched an attack that Goryell called "the reptilian roll". Carl had no idea why it was called that, but he did not care. It was a fantastic attack. He threw himself forward, on to the ground, as fast as he was running. Then he rolled over on his back with his legs pulled in tightly. The split second when his shoulders touched the ground he kicked straight up, hitting the gunman's underarms from underneath.

It must have looked hilarious to someone standing next to them. But Carl and Goryell did not have time to laugh at the faces that the gunmen made as their guns flew right out of their arms.

Now they had to complete the reptilian roll.

Goryell had mastered the roll for his second star test. He could execute it with millisecond precision. When his feet had knocked the gun out of his adversary's arms he redirected the feet forward. With a thrust from his hands he sent his rolling momentum forward, and his feet fiercely impacted the belly of the gunman.

The force was so strong that he could feel the man's intestines crumble under his boots. To reinforce his momentum he stretched out his own belly muscles as he turned back on to his feet.

He stood up again, with the half dead gunman between his feet. The reptilian roll was an incredible weapon, but Goryell had learned the hard way from his instructors that landing on your feet with your enemy on his back between your legs was not a good position to finish. Too many times his instructors had launched a leg scissors grab around his waist from below, swept him down and… well, he didn't exactly want to remember the pain from those experiences. So to finish off the successful attack he jumped to the side, landed in a low sitting stance – Thor had called it *kiba dachi* – and dealt the final blow to his opponent with the same spear hand technique he had used before.

Once his opponent was dead he looked up and saw that Carl had not been as lucky. He had disarmed his opponent, alright, but then he had landed on his back without knocking the opponent over. He had managed to sweep him on to the ground, but now they were engaged in a fierce life-and-death wrestling match. Carl's opponent was undoubtedly skilled at wrestling. He managed to get a good grip on Carl while at the same time calling the helicopter for assistance.

Carl was very good at karate, but his opponent was an expert in Brazilian jiu-jitsu. Now that they were on the ground he had the upper hand. He locked Carl with his legs and rolled over on his back, with Carl face up over him. Then he locked his right arm around Carl's neck and reinforced the grip by pushing his right underarm in and up toward Carl's throat.

There were really no techniques that Carl could use to break lose. And since his opponent was on the back and Carl was on top of him, there did not seem to be any opportunities open for Goryell to help his buddy.

And maybe that would have been the end of Carl's career if Goryell was just doing straightforward shotokan karate or tae-kwon do. But Goryell was no standard martial arts guy.

One of the specialties of Kherr-Wa was its incredible precision strikes. He could hit a spot that was a fraction of a finger tip, with a strike so quick no human eye – or reptilian eye, for that matter – could see the strike.

The gunman noticed Goryell moving in. He tried to move Carl around as a shield so that Goryell could not strike toward his throat or his head. He seemed very confident, because while he was doing that he tightened his grip around Carl's neck even more.

But this thug had no idea what he was up against. Goryell knew that the human body has more weaknesses than that.

Like the knee.

It took Goryell about a half second to deliver a spear-hand strike toward the side of the gunman's left knee. He aimed the strike at the side of the kneecap, a hit area smaller than a dime. The strike was very hard and because of the minimal hit area all the energy from the strike came in pure concentrate.

The kneecap literally broke loose from the tendons that held it in place. The pain must have been excruciating because the gunman let go of Carl right away and screamed in pain.

But Carl did not let him wake up the neighbors. The instant he was lose from the choking grip he knocked the gunman over the mouth with the back of his head. Then he rolled off, turned around and dealt a lethal blow with his fist right at the man's heart.

"Thanks" Carl said.

"You're a good fighter. I'll teach you Kherr-Wa some day."

Their conversation was interrupted by the sound of the helicopter.

"This is a perfect opportunity" Carl said.

"Better than we hoped for" Goryell agreed.

Carl radioed Thor.

"Time to go, buddy."

"We're coming out" Thor confirmed.

The chopper came in faster this time, and lower. Carl moved over to one of the dead gunmen and took his radio. The chopper was calling frantically:

"Delta, come in, delta, what's going on?"

Carl replied:

"Delta here, get us out, this is a trap!"

"I'm landing now!"

The chopper came in low over the wall that surrounded the property, barely clearing two trees. Its heading was straight for Ross's house.

"This is it!" Carl said.

"Are you out yet?!" Goryell yelled at Thor over the intercom.

"We're out!"

Goryell pulled out a weapon and fired. It was an odd kind of toy, just like everything else Goryell had. It released a small white ball of – something – that flew lightning-fast right at the helicopter's rear rudder. The rudder was destroyed and the rest of the helicopter spun out of control and crashed.

Right in to Ross's house.

The explosion came a second after Carl heard police sirens in the distance.

"Where's Thor?" Goryell asked.

They looked toward the house that had just burst into flames.

"He said he made it" Carl said.

"I sure hope he did."

"If he didn't I'll teach him a lesson."

"If he didn't we've really screwed up" Goryell reminded him.

The police sirens came closer.

A car stopped outside on the street, right by the broken gate. It was the Impala they had seen before. They saw a face in the passenger window looking in, then the car sped off.

And the neighbors were beginning to wake up.

"Where the hell are they?" Carl asked.

"What is going on over there?" someone yelled from the neighbor's house.

"Call the police!" someone else yelled.

"I'm going in there to see!" said someone else.

"The hell you are" Goryell muttered and moved over toward the broken gate.

He peeked out on the street. Two neighbors had already come out of their houses and were looking down the street.

"There they are" Carl sighed with relief.

Thor and Ross came out of the woodwork next to the house. Thor had dumped his diving gear and Ross was wearing a jumpsuit.

"Good to see you" said Carl as he came up to them.

"I hear police sirens" Thor noted. "How are we going to get all the way across the golf course to the car?"

"I'm Carl" Carl introduced himself to Ross, ignoring Thor's pressing question.

"What's that thing you're wearing?" Ross asked.

"Sir, let's get the hell out of here first, then we can talk about that."

"Carl..." Thor reminded Carl of his question.

"We'll run for it" Carl suggested.

They came up to the broken gate.

"Are those the hit men?" Ross asked, looking at the dead bodies. "They sure meant business, I gotta giv'em that."

Goryell turned around. Ross looked at him.

"Are you with these guys?" he asked.

"Uh… yes. Hi, sir. I heard your show for the first time yesterday. It's awesome. The people back home where I live would love it."

"Where you live? Are you from Europe?"

"Well…" Goryell started but changed his mind and turned to Thor. "Thor, give me the shatterer."

Thor handed him the weapon. Goryell looked at it.

"Did you fire this thing? At this setting?!"

"Well…"

"You could have destroyed the whole house!"

"Hey, it was an emergency…"

"Speaking of which, guys" Carl said. "The cops are four blocks away. And we can't get out of here without being detected."

"I have an idea" Goryell said. "First I need to stall them."

He went back to the open gate and aimed his shatterer at some palm trees almost a whole block up the street. They fell just as he intended and blocked the street.

"How did you do that?" Ross asked, fascinated. "Who are you guys, really?"

"Sir, please…" Thor said. "Goryell, how are we going to get out of here? The neighbors will spot us if we try to leave across the golf course."

"All taken care of" Goryell replied and held up a little device.

A few seconds later they heard a humming sound above them. Thor, Carl and Ross looked up but could not see anything. Goryell also looked up. He had put on some sort of weird glasses.

There were voices out in the street. The policemen came running down the sidewalk from where they had been forced to stop with their cars. Someone directed them to Ross's house.

"Gentlemen, your ride is here" Goryell said and took off his glasses.

"What?" said Thor, Carl and Ross with one voice.

Goryell pushed a button on his little remote control.

A vessel appeared on the lawn, 20 feet away from them. It was small and had the shape of a cylinder lying down. Its front was cone-shaped and the whole thing seemed to be bolted on to a rectangular frame that was glowing with a mild, green light.

"I'll be…" Ross gasped.

"Courtesy of the Danarvian Federation" Goryell smiled and showed them how to climb in.

*   *   *

"Yeah…?"

"Morning, brother!"

"Oh, man it's you…"

"Rise and shine, Jack, my dear kid brother!"

"Thor, are you on speed or something?"

"Hey, listen, can you call dad and give him a message from me?"

"Why don't you call him, instead of me? At least he's up at six in the morning."

"It's almost seven."

"Whatever."

"Call dad and tell him that Ross Landau is not dead."

"What?? You really are on drugs, aren't you?"

"Gotta run. Catch you later, bro."

"Hey, wait… Did you actually do something…?"

"It's all thanks to you, Jack. Now, listen. You're gonna hear in the news that Ross is dead. Please keep your mouth shut and wait until noon, when his show is supposed to be on. Then turn to his station and listen carefully."

"Alright…"

"And thanks again, brother. You saved his life."

"Hey… Gosh, I'm waking up now… Listen, I was able to find out who tipped me off."

"You did??"

"Someone showed me how to do it with an iWorld."

"And…?"

"I got it right here. It's a quirky name, and I know I've heard it before. Where is it? What the… oh, I got it. Right here. Let's see… you know, it's kind of funny what you can find out with these babies."

"So who was it?"

"Uhm… Irwin Schwepp."

"Schwepp? Are you sure? Do you know who he is?"

"No."

"He works for Holly Stanton. He's one of her most loyal servants."

"Oh, yeah… of course. So you really saved Ross Landau from an assassin?"

"Tune in at noon, brother! But keep it quiet until the show starts."

*　　　*　　　*

The news about Ross Landau's death spread like a bonfire across the country. Liberal blogs like MoveLeft.Org, DailyCrocks. Com and The Bluffington Post immediately burst out in cheers and jubilation over the fact that "the cancer on American politics" was gone. Their uninhibited joy reached higher and higher until a police spokesman said that the cause of death was a helicopter crash and that the pilot and at least one more person onboard the chopper had died. That cooled off their celebrations. After all, as far as the leftist agitators were concerned, two innocent people had died.

Except for the statement from the local police, not much was known about the circumstances of the helicopter crash. Some news reporters heard that the police had found more dead people on the property, but no one was able to confirm that. Neighbors said they had heard commotion from Ross's property right before the crash, and rumors started spreading that Ross had been throwing a big party. More rumors surfaced on blogs that the helicopter had come there to pick up some of the party guests and that the engine had faulted.

Radio stations who carried Ross's news programs called his producer with panic in their voices and asked what to do now. His show was the most profitable one out there and some stations feared they would go out of business now. The producer tried to calm them and promised to broadcast the show as usual at noon.

"But how are you going to do that??" the radio station managers yelled over the phone. "He's dead, you know!"

"Please, be patient, we're working on it" the producer said.

While all this was going on politicians in the nation's capital quickly started preparing statements about the death of the Great Educator. Some were going to praise him, others lambast him. Those who liked Ross and felt that he had been a great supporter of their ideas were quickly out with their statements. Some even called press conferences to explain what a big loss Ross's death was to the nation. Democrats who did not like Ross because of his steadfast conservatism had a hard time containing their joy in public and spent the entire morning congratulating each other.

Holly Stanton had of course heard the news from Rhea. The news made the vice president very happy. She smiled all the way to a cabinet meeting that president Oslow had asked her to take care of. He was at Stanford University to give a speech.

Her smile was not just a campaign smile, but a genuine smile from genuine happiness. She told jokes and generously asked the cabinet members about their personal lives. Not in the way she usually did, to find out what they were hiding, but with real concern for them and their loved ones.

Some were enamored by it and took her warmth to their hearts. Others were suspicious and wondered what the heck was going on. Either way, no one commented on the vice president's mood. It was not only inappropriate, but dangerous. They had all seen her erratic mood swings and what she could do to those who happened to be in the way when her mood turned south.

"Well, friends" she said, again being informal and kind in a way that was unheard of from her. "Let's begin this meeting with an announcement. I am going to give you all a raise. You've been so loyal and worked so hard for me since I was inaugurated. We have a lot of work to do, but... I think that work is going to be a whole lot easier from here on. Besides, big changes are coming soon. Big changes to our country. I feel..." and she clasped her hands and looked out the window, "...I feel like today is the first day of a much better America."

She turned to her cabinet members and the smile got more formal.

"Well... back to work."

She handed out some notes to them.

"These are some policies I want you to review. Larry..." and she turned to the secretary of education, "…this new fair speech code for universities has run in to some problems. A few colleges do not take any federal money at all. They refuse to abide by this code. I want you to do something about that."

"Yes, ma'm."

"I want to set an example."

"Yes, ma'm."

"I want some college somewhere to dig up some student that they can prosecute for unfair speech so we can make a big deal of it."

"Yes, ma'm."

"And Belinda, the state department has some big things coming its way. I want you to make a list of your five most reliable staffers. I am going to form a very, very special foreign policy group and I need you to run it."

"Yes, ma'm."

"The group will handle very special foreign relations. It is an entirely new kind, so pick your best and brightest."

"Yes, ma'm."

"Malcolm, the justice department…"

She was interrupted by her chief of staff who gently tapped her on the shoulder.

"What?" president Stanton said and turned around.

Her chief of staff whispered something in her ear.

"Sheila, what kind of a sick joke is this?" the vice president asked and frowned.

"Ma'm, I'm afraid it's not a joke."

"It can't be true. Someone is…"

"Ma'm, I've already checked. He *is* back on the radio."

*   *   *

Ross Landau had a hard time believing what Carl and Thor told him about the plot to kill him. He was even more incredulous about Goryell's claims to be an intelligence agent from another planet.

But he was also a man of the facts. As far as he was concerned, what he saw and experienced, no matter how fantastic, was always a convincing argument. So when Goryell steered that strange vessel up in the air, and when Ross looked out and saw Florida shrink underneath at amazing speed, he had no choice but to believe his eyes.

And when they landed at an abandoned farm way out in the wilderness in New Mexico and Goryell showed him all the fancy equipment they had there, he was almost ready to believe anything Goryell told him.

It had been a turbulent night, to say the least, and normally he would not trust these strangers. But these men were of a different kind. They came across as honest and dedicated. And when he saw the dead assassins on the lawn outside his house, he had realized the full extent of the threat to his life.

He was not scared by the threat. If anything, it made him angry. Mad, in fact. He wanted to get back at those people.

He still did not quite believe that the vice president of the United States was behind the plot, especially since president Oslow seemed to be doing just fine. But then again – he knew a lot about the Stanton siblings that he had never told his 25 million weekly listeners. So maybe it was not all that far-fetched, after all?

The only question he still had not gotten an answer to was: why now? He had been on the radio for a quarter of a century. Why would Holly Stanton choose to go after him now?

He asked Goryell, who refused to answer the question until the next morning. Which, of course, meant that Ross went to bed a bit irritated and woke up early and got out of bed before anyone else but the night watch.

Meeting the night watch was another interesting experience.

"Uh… good morning" Ross tried.

The man (or, was it a man?) did not respond. He (it?) just stood there in the doorway right in front of Ross, pointing a small device at him. Ross assumed that the little toy in the night watch's hand was some sort of weapon. He had already seen what Goryell's weapons could do and he was not going to find out how it felt to be on the receiving end of one of those toys.

So he stopped and tried to stay as calm as he could while staring right into the face of something that looked more like a mini-t-rex than anything else.

"Do you speak English?" Ross tried.

The T-rex did not move a muscle. For a moment Ross thought he might be a robot of some kind, but then that thing blinked with his eyes and lowered his head slightly. It was impossible to know what that meant – if it meant anything – but Ross felt a bit better knowing that it was probably a living creature he had before him.

"Well… I just wanted to get up and stretch my legs a little bit" he said to the T-rex. "But if you're not going to let me through, I guess I'll just go back to bed."

He turned and was just about to go back to his room when someone came out of one of the doors in the hallway.

It was Goryell.

"Morning, up early?" he asked Ross.

"Yes, I usually get up and do some exercise in the morning. But it seems like the rest of your facilities are off limits."

"I'll show you the gym" Goryell said and walked past Ross.

Then he stopped.

"Ah, I see you've met Dzu."

"So he has a name" Ross said. "I tried to talk to him, but…"

"Dzu does not speak English."

Goryell said something to Dzu, who said something back and made a sound that sounded like a laugh. Then he turned and went to another room. Ross noticed that he had a tail.

"That's our night watch" Goryell explained. "Usually we don't bring reptilians to humanoid worlds and the other way around, but one of our night watchmen was called back home when his wife had an accident and almost died."

"Oh, poor fella" Ross said.

"Yeah. Thanks. Well, so they sent us a reptilian instead. They were short on off-duty humanoid staff. But he's a damned good guy. In fact, most reptilians can see in the dark, so they make excellent night watchmen."

"What does he eat?" Ross asked as Goryell walked him through the compound toward the gym.

"Anything that didn't have parents. He tried cactus last week and can't get enough of it."

"I'm glad I have parents. Must be spooky to walk in to his arms in the middle of the night."

The morning at the Alien World Operations Earth assignment headquarters was quite enjoyable. Even the meeting with Goryell's boss turned out to be a bit amusing.

Well, maybe not for Goryell. Tahm Qaar was not happy. He called Goryell in to a meeting in his office, while everyone else, including Ross, were sitting outside watching and listening through an open door.

Tahm Qaar stood before Goryell and stared him straight in his eyes. He ordered Goryell to assume military attention stance. Goryell was slightly taller than his boss, but he was actually a bit afraid of Tahm Qaar, especially when he was ordered to assume attention stance. So he seemed to shrink a couple of inches.

Tahm Qaar stared Goryell in the eyes for almost half a minute. He did not say anything. Goryell knew that the longer his boss kept staring at him, the bigger the chance was that this was going to turn out bad.

Goryell had a good feeling what this might be about.

"You idiot" Tahm Qaar whispered and slowly moved over to Goryell's side. "You miserable idiot!"

Goryell swallowed and tried not to tremble too much. From the tone of Tahm Qaar's voice he knew that he was in big trouble. So big, in fact, he might not just be sent home, but even lose his job.

"How could you be so reckless??"

Tahm Qaar walked up behind Goryell.

"Did you sleep through the law classes at the academy?"

"N-n-o, sir..."

"Shut up!"

"Yes, sir."

"Do you realize what you've done?!"

"Yes, sir..."

"You've not only discharged weapons right and left, when you know perfectly well that they are not to be used other than when your own life is in extreme and imminent danger! But you have also – and I can't believe this is actually true... – you have also allowed a civilian from this planet to use one of your weapons!"

Tahm Qaar went around Goryell and slapped his face. Goryell did not move an inch. He kept his eyes focused on a spot on the wall behind his boss. He was grateful his boss only slapped his face. After all, Tahm Qaar was a seven-star Kherr-Wa Grand Master.

"Fool! You're risking this entire operation! This entire on-ground investigation of Earth might be shut down now and we'll have to start over from square one!"

"Sir…"

"Shut up!"

"Yes, sir…"

"What do you have to say for yourself?"

"Uh… sir… if it can save this mission… I'm willing to go back home right away and… report to the disciplinary division for… disciplinary action…"

Tahm Qaar shook his head and walked back and forth in the room for a moment.

"Oh, my…" he muttered. "And then the use of the emergency shuttle… At least, that one I might be able to explain to the bureaucrats… I could say that your life was in imminent danger…"

"Sir… I'll take one hundred percent responsibility. Please don't cover for me."

Tahm Qaar turned and looked at Goryell.

"What do you mean?"

"I mean, sir, that I don't want any of the blame for this to fall on you, sir."

"Well, that's… thoughtful of you, Goryell. Unfortunately, I'm your boss and it's my job to, well, take the blame for what you do."

"You could just say that I disobeyed your orders, point blank, just like that."

"If I did that" Tahm Qaar said, a lot calmer now, "you'd be fired on the spot and sent home with a disgraceful official record. You realize that, don't you?"

"Yes, sir. Perfectly well, sir."

Tahm Qaar examined Goryell's face. Then he sighed and sat down behind his desk. He moved a couple of things around on the desk and paid no attention to Goryell for ten seconds or so. Goryell did not move, barely even blinked. His feet were beginning to hurt but he did not let anyone know.

"Alright, have a seat" Tahm Qaar muttered and pointed to a seat on the other side of his desk.

"Thank you, sir."

Goryell sat down and took a deep breath.

"You're not out of this mess yet" Tahm Qaar cautioned him. "In fact, I am going to request that you be transferred off Earth. I won't write you up for disciplinary action, but I will put you on a transfer order."

He paused for a second, as if he was contemplating how to make his next point.

However..." and Tahm Qaar glanced out the door at Carl, Thor and Ross who were following their conversation without understanding a word of it, "...despite your poor judgment, I know you're a talented agent. Overly creative sometimes, but... So I'm going to give you one more chance. One last chance."

Goryell's face turned from guilty to curious.

"Sir... anything..."

"There is a crisis on a world out in the Zeta sector. They've had to dispatch all their available humanoid agents there. The earliest they can have a replacement agent ready for me is in eight days. So they cannot execute your transfer order until then."

He leaned forward across the desk and stared Goryell straight in the eyes.

"Which means, young man, that you have eight days to prove to me that you can be both creative and responsible at the same time."

Goryell was almost overwhelmed with joy. He reached across the desk and took both Tahm Qaar's hands.

"Thank you, sir! Thank you!"

"Yes, yes..."

"I will never forget this, sir."

"Very good. Now get the Hell out of my office and go back to work."

Goryell almost jumped out of his boss's office. His face was like a big smiling sun.

"What was that all about?" Thor asked.

"He's going to transfer me off this world" Goryell said and smiled even more.

"Oh… OK… Well, if you don't like it here…"

"Oh, no, you misunderstand me" Goryell explained. "I screwed up when I used our weapons, and gave one to you. So he threatened to kick me out of this assignment. But it's going to take eight days to find a replacement agent, so he's giving me eight days to prove that I can play the rules."

Ross chuckled.

"Sounds like you got bureaucrats just like we do."

"Too many of them" Goryell agreed. "And they're everywhere in our government. Did I tell you that I pay a whole percent of my income in taxes? It's amazing! They're stealing my money!"

"One percent?!" Ross repeated, gasping for air as he stared at Goryell.

"I know!" Goryell said emphatically. "It's enormous!"

"One pe… pe… percent!" Ross stumbled on his own words. "One measly percent! And you call that stealing!! Young man, come pay taxes here in America. Or anywhere else here on Earth. You'll be grateful for the rest of your life it's only one stupid percent where you live."

"Ross" Thor intervened, "we might need to start preparing your show."

"Yes. First of all I need a steady link to my studio back in Florida."

It took them a half hour to calibrate their equipment so Ross could broadcast from their operations headquarters via the Grid to his studio. Usually he was live on the Grid as well, but the computers that Goryell showed him could not provide the live stream he needed.

"Maybe if we converted some of our own computers instead of using Earth computers…" Goryell tried.

"No, this is fine" Ross reassured him. "I've done this a few times before. We can relay the show on to the Grid from my studio. It's not perfect quality but it works. People can listen live on their iWorlds. They're smart little things. It's a phone, and you can get live radio and TV in them through the Grid. I've heard they even write their own computer programs."

As Ross prepared for his show, Goryell, Carl and Thor sat a bit away from him and watched.

"I've been a fan of his show for ten years" Thor said.

"Very smart guy" Goryell noted. "And I like that he takes phone calls."

"You don't have talk shows back home?" Carl asked.

"Yes, we do, but it's usually pure entertainment programs that do that. We don't have a whole lot of political commentary programs."

"Why not? People not interested?"

"No, it's not that. It's just that our government is so small there's not really anything to fight over. No one can make good money off a career in government. And no one can really gain anything from the government because it is so limited. So there's not a very big market for political shows either."

Ross finalized his preparations for the show with a long phone call to his staff over in Florida.

"No, Surrey, nobody is going to come to the studio and try to find me" he said. "You're perfectly safe there… yes… just get ready, so we can… yes, we're going to be on air every day just as usual… I don't know when I'll be back. Don't worry about that right now… Just make sure all our stations know that they have nothing to worry about."

Carl kept feeding Ross with reports on what the major news outlets were saying about him.

"CNN is focusing on the accident, not your contributions…"

"Makes sense" Ross commented while browsing through some websites on a computer screen. "Always had good friends over there…"

"Fox called in Sean Hannity. He's devastated."

"I should call him. I don't have his number with me."

"The new merged network… what's it called… with NBC and ABC…"

"Enlight" Ross reminded him.

"That's right. They're not reporting much."

"Surprise" Ross chuckled. "Well, it's time to go on the air."

At five past noon Eastern Time Ross's show opened with full force as usual. After the intro Ross's voice took the airwaves by storm.

"Welcome Americans, this is the FRE Network, the Ross Landau show. Yes, it's me. I'm not dead, I'm alive... and I'm still having more fun than a human being should be allowed to have."

*   *   *

Holly Stanton's face turned from cheerful optimism to dark, restrained anger. She looked at her chief of staff again and her eyes shrunk into two thin lines.

Then she looked over at the cabinet members.

"Randal" she said to the secretary of the interior.

"Yes, ma'm."

"Take over this meeting."

"Yes, ma'm."

Holly Stanton got up and walked with her chief of staff in to a side office. As they walked out of the meeting room the cabinet members heard the door to the side office close gently. No outbreak of rage, no door slamming. It seemed like Holly Stanton had maintained her dignity in the face of bad news.

Inside the side office the scene was quite different. A radio was broadcasting the Ross Landau show.

And in a split second it was almost like World War III had broken out.

Holly Stanton grabbed the radio and hurled it across the room, smashing it against the opposite wall.

"FUCK YOU!!!" she screamed off the top of her lungs. "I WANTED HIM DEAD!! DEAD, YOU ASSHOLES! DEAD!!! FIND HIM! FIND THAT BASTARD!!"

She grabbed a small picture from the wall and threw it on the floor. Its glass split into a hundred pieces that spread across the room.

She stared at Sheila and the other two staffers in the room. They trembled with fear. They had never actually seen a full-blown

Holly Stanton eruption before. But they had heard stories about what it could be like.

"I want to know!" the vice president shouted, barely suppressing her anger, "how the Hell Ross Landau can turn up broadcasting live on his radio show! I want to know how that is possible when the police down there in Florida FUCKING TOLD ME he is dead! I wanna know now that! NOW!!!"

She took a pen from one of her staffers and broke it in half.

"We're working on finding that out..." Sheila began.

"Not good enough!!" Holly Stanton yelled and pointed her index finger at her chief of staff.

She threw the broken pen at Sheila.

"Find out where he is broadcasting from, damn it!"

"He's broadcasting from his studio" Sheila replied quickly.

"Then get the FBI over there and arrest him!"

"On... what charges?"

"What do you mean charges!! I'm the president, damn it! If I..."

She caught herself in the slip of the tongue.

"I'm the vice president" she said, again barely suppressing her anger. "But I am in charge when Barry is out giving speeches. If I want someone arrested, then the FBI better get their asses over there and arrest him!"

"Ma'm..."

"Now!! Do it now or I'll fire you all!"

*   *   *

ARGUMENTS

The Federal Assembly was a fascinating group of people. There were the tall, skinny and large-skulled Teurans, who did not grow facial hair, always spoke softly and were very articulate. There were the Kwensors, a skinny reptilian species from an outlying sector where the stars were clustered closely together and every inhabitable planet was hot, humid and almost unbearable for humanoids.

And there was the Ice Folk, rugged humanoids from the coldest inhabited world in Danarvia. They had kept their thick body hair through generations of civilized life. It was so thick, in fact, that if they wanted to, they could walk around naked and nobody would feel embarrassed.

There were mixed delegations from worlds where humanoids and reptilians lived side by side. Some delegates were from colonies that had started out as bold experimental societies but grown into thriving migration magnets. Some came from old worlds where politics could still become a life long career; others, especially those from the Majestic sectors, were hard-core minarchists. Their delegates were often successful entrepreneurs who got in to politics because they utterly disliked whatever government they had to put up with. They wanted to do their fair share in keeping it out of people's lives and checkbooks.

Most of the Majestic worlds were still little more than outposts. There were no big cities out there, and most of the businesses relied on long-range, deep space trade. The Majestic worlds attracted independent-minded farmers and ranchers who felt squeezed by ever growing urban populations on more central worlds. With hard work and dedication they turned barren land into thriving crop fields, orchards or grasslands where they raised some of the finest livestock in the galaxy.

Majestic 39, the last world before The Great Void, had become the heaven of financial privacy. Small banks out there harbored the fortunes of wealthy investors who wanted to shield their money from even the minuscule taxes that the Danarvians had to pay.

The strangest of all species in the Federation were probably the Aquans. Basically humanoid, they lived 90 percent of their lives under water. They could breathe air, but only for a brief period at a time, and only in a very humid environment. Their delegates to the Federal Assembly wore special suits that kept a thin layer of water next to their skin. Only their faces were visible, and they always wore water-filled goggles to protect their eyes. They frequently pulled down a face mask to breathe water and keep their facial skin from deteriorating.

To humans from Earth, the offices that the Aquans had at the Assembly would look very much like swimming pools. Of course, back home they had vast oceans to thrive in, and large urban landscapes along the ocean floors. Those who had the privilege to visit them said it was an amazing experience. Earthlings would say it was a lot cooler than the fantasy underwater world Naboo in the Star Wars saga.

Delegate Watlaan had spoken before the Assembly many times, and now she had to do it again. She was going to address them because of Quim's request that the intelligence report from Earth be made available to the entire Assembly. It was her duty to lead the meeting.

The Delegates were spread out across the Assembly Chamber, talking in small groups or conferring with their assistants. Watlaan noticed that Delegate Narkeenis was involved in an intense discussion with an Aquan and two delegates from Majestic 18. She also noticed that Delegate Quim was sitting nearby and listened to their conversation.

She rang the bell that called the Assembly to order. The

Delegates slowly ended their conversations and moved toward their seats. Narkeenis slowly ended his conversation with the Aquan and the two other delegates. Even as he took his seat, though, he still leaned over to yet another delegate, one of the Kwensors, and said something. Then they both nodded and made a hand gesture that Kwensors usually used to symbolize the seal of an agreement of some kind.

Watlaan looked at Quim, who was looking somewhere out in space and seemed very satisfied. She wondered exactly what it was he was so happy about.

"Honored Delegates, may the Assembly come to order" she said. "I hereby open the this extra-curricular meeting of the Assembly. We are here upon request from Delegate Quim. You have all received the intelligence report concerning the security situation in sector KB that Delegate Quim has called this meeting to discuss."

She paused and looked up at the Delegates. They were listening with interest. That was good. More often than not the Delegates were just cordially interested in what was going on in the chamber.

"It has now come to our knowledge that Earth, a planet that we are probing for official contact, is facing an invasion from a neighboring world, Zoh'moor. We know practically nothing about Zoh'moor. What we do know is that one of the governments on Earth has invited the Zoh'moorian invasion. Our intelligence detail on Earth suggests that the invitation is part of an effort by that Earth government to expand its power. This puts us in a delicate situation."

She pulled out a document from a small briefcase.

"Just before I went in to this meeting I received a note from the Executive Office. As a direct consequence of this intelligence report, they have ordered Frontline Services to dispatch a strike group to the KB sector."

A hushed mumble broke out in the chamber.

"Since Delegate Quim has requested that the Assembly discuss this intelligence report, the Assembly shall conclude with a vote on whether or not to demand formal consultations with the executive office over any military actions in sector KB."

She paused and handed a note to the chair of the Assembly.

"I hereby yield the podium to the Delegates."

Several Delegates immediately reported that they wanted to speak. First in line was Narkeenis. He walked down to the podium and bowed to his fellow delegates as a gesture of respect.

"Honored Delegates. I am deeply concerned that the Executive Office is sending our military out on a mission that could pull us in to a new war. The emerging conflict in sector KB is not ours to begin with. There is no constitutional ground for us to get involved. The Fourth Principle of our Charter of Liberty prohibits any action of government except insofar as to secure freedom itself. Since Earth has invited the invading force, they are not surrendering their freedom to an aggressor. Therefore, when the Executive Office ordered Frontline Services to send a strike group to sector KB, it overstepped its powers."

Next on the list was the Majestic 18 delegate that Narkeenis had been talking to.

"We live on the outskirts of Danarvia" she said. "Beyond us we have the vast open space of The Scatterbelt and on the other side, The Great Void. We're pretty much on our own out there, and we take care of ourselves. We have some protection against alien intruders, but those are mostly our own militias. We have good trade routes, but other than that we do not have a whole lot to do with you guys. We are not asked to contribute a whole lot either, and we want to keep it that way."

She glanced at some notes she had in her hand.

"I have nothing against protecting the freedom of fellow Danarvians. But getting us involved in a military conflict this far outside our borders goes beyond the call to help."

Then she made an artful pause and looked at her fellow Delegates.

"But what concerns me even more is that even if the strike group from Frontline Services enters sector KB and gets involved in whatever conflict might be looming there, we have no way of knowing if they will be militarily able. We have no idea how strong the Zoh'moorians are. For all we know, they could be vastly superior to us. Therefore, I propose that the Assembly demand formal consultations with the Executive Office."

Next on the list was a young Delegate from Ro-Ganmi, a humanoid world of albinos.

"I am also from an outlying area" he said. "And I believe that outlying areas are even more dependent on protection from a strong power. We cannot, and should not, ask our government for any means toward our self determination. My pursuit of happiness is my business, not the government's. But military security is something that our government should deliver. Earth is a lonely world out there, and it deserves our support. The intelligence report we have been handed mentions the Outer Rim Exploration project. They made contact with Earth and made a pledge to protect them. We cannot walk away from that pledge. I urge you to vote against formal consultations with the Executive Office. If we demand such consultations, the Executive Office would have to stop the strike group and let the Zoh'moorians invade Earth. Their freedom would be sacrificed for the sake of petty politics."

A couple of more delegates presented arguments that reinforced both sides. In the meantime, Narkeenis was going back and forth among a growing group of delegates, apparently trying to strike some kind of deal.

Toward the end, it seemed as though the Assembly was leaning in favor of supporting the Executive Office. A small majority of the speakers had spoken up in favor of letting Frontline Services engage the Zoh'moorian invasion fleet.

At that moment, Delegate Quim asked to speak.

When he walked down to the podium, Narkeenis and his group of chatting delegates fell silent and sat down to listen.

"Honored Delegates" he said, with the trademark softness and articulation of a Teuran. "Many, many years ago, when I was asked by the Executive Office to work on a peace treaty in the midst of the Kahpiyan War, I was approached by an old man who had been born on Ozolu. As you all know, his world was one of the two that started the war. The old man was living on Blinn Three, where he worked as a janitor on the Federal Assembly campus. This was, of course, before our Assembly moved here to a neutral planet. As you all know, Blinn Three fell victim to the first attack of the Kahpiyan War. The attackers from Ozolu used the humanoids who lived on Blinn Three as an excuse for their attack. Reports had been passed around that humanoids were being treated unfairly, not to say cruelly, by the reptilians native to Blinn Three. Some of those reports were true, and the old janitor testified to that. When he first came to Blinn Three as an immigrant, he believed that humanoids were welcome. But he was captured and enslaved. The news of his ordeal, and of others who met the same fate, were broadcast over and over again on Ozolu. He prayed to be liberated, and eventually he was. But not by the Ozolu forces invading Blinn Three. No, his liberator was a freedom-minded movement that was able to oust the authoritarian Blinnian government. They ended slavery and discrimination against non-reptilians. This man was freed long before the Ozolu attack. He told me how he had been paid reparations and found a safe and attractive place to live among the very same reptilians whom he had come to fear and hate as a slave."

The history lecture caught everyone's undivided attention. It was rare to get one, but when it came there was no one better at delivering it than Delegate Quim.

"When the old news about the ordeal of humanoids on Blinn Three were recycled by Ozolu media and politicians, they were used as an excuse for a war. As the old man told me, if only some Ozolus had possessed enough courage to hesitate and ask a few more questions, that devastating war could have been avoided."

An artful pause.

"Now, I am telling you this story because I want us to possess the courage to hesitate. Here and now. I urge you all to vote in favor of the formal consultations request. When you do, you will help stop another war."

That tipped the balance. The vote came out strongly in favor of formal consultations between the Assembly and the Executive Office. The Assembly appointed Quim and two others to hold the consultative meetings.

When they left the meeting, Delegate Watlaan was approached by the delegate from Ro-Ganmi and a delegate from Blinn Three. They walked together across the campus toward the office building.

"I am concerned" said the Blinnian. "I think Quim used my home world unfairly to further his cause. He polished the history of the outbreak of the Kahpiyan War. Humanoids were still being treated very unfairly on our world. It is not like him to be sloppy with details."

"I agree" said the Ro-Ganmi delegate. "And I believe that Narkeenis is up to something. Before he got up to speak he worked hard to secure a majority vote for formal consultation. But he has more in mind. I overheard bits and pieces. They referred to it as an alliance against the war."

"Yes, that is odd" Watlaan noted. "Alliances in the Assembly are very rare. It is a legitimate question to ask why he would seize on this issue to forge an alliance."

At the same time, she did not want to raise tensions over the issue, even though she totally agreed with them both.

"However, I think the best we can do right now is to be cautious" she said. "But above all, let us not stir up any more mud. Let's keep our water clear and transparent so we can see what is really going on."

"But Watlaan" the Blinnian insisted, "surely you must see that Quim's actions are unusual. This is not be the first time that Frontline Services get involved in a conflict outside Danarvia."

"I agree with you" Watlaan said. "But I also know that Quim is a very wise old man. He would not put his authority and reputation behind this request unless he felt that he had good reasons to do it. Let's wait and see what comes out of this meeting."

She stopped and thought for a moment.

"Here is what is going to happen now" she said. "When the request for formal consultations reaches the Executive Office, they will have to freeze all military operations immediately. Strike Group 14 left its space port yesterday and should be leaving Danarvian space any time now. Because of the formal consultations request the Executive Office will have to order them to make an immediate halt. They will have to sit there in space while we let the constitutional process work."

"And as soon as the Executive Office have heard Quim's case

they can still decide, by four fifth's majority, to ignore him" the Ro-Ganmi delegate noted.

"Right" Watlaan agreed. "It is unlikely that they will agree with him. So this should only be a small delay for the strike group."

She was right, of course. But only if Delegate Quim went to present his case to the Executive Office right away.

Which he had no plans on doing, as he made clear to Narkeenis when he came to Quim's office after the Assembly vote.

"Sit down, my friend" Quim said. "You worked hard to rally the delegates. I am grateful for that. We got the majority we needed and the request for a meeting has been sent over to the Executive Office."

"As soon as they receive the request they will have to issue an immediate order to Strike Group 14 to make a halt" Narkeenis said.

"Precisely."

"But if the Executive Office rejects our request, then nothing has been accomplished."

"On the contrary" Quim smiled. "To begin with, we have three full days before we have to meet with them."

Narkeenis looked at him. A smile slowly spread across his face.

"I see" he said. "While the Executive Office is waiting to meet with us, the strike group has to remain at full stop in space. And by the time we meet, and they reject our request, and they can order them to continue…"

"…we have amassed a two thirds majority in the Assembly to override their decision" Quim completed his sentence.

"I see" Narkeenis smiled. "Excellent strategy."

"Oh, just politics" Quim said modestly. "What matters is that we prevent another war, and this is our way to do just that."

Then he looked his young colleague straight in the eyes.

"Now" he said. "There is just one more thing I must ask you to do for me."

"Go right ahead."

Quim explained. Narkeenis hesitated for a moment and asked Quim a couple of follow-ups to make sure he understood it right.

Quim confirmed and assured Narkeenis of what reward would await him if he accepted.

"I will be honored" Narkeenis said, bowed and left Quim's office.

As the door closed, Quim leaned back in his comfortable armchair and smiled modestly.

*　　　*　　　*

The Advanced Information Retrieval Agency had an enormous budget for sophisticated technology. They had some of the fastest space ships in Danarvia, the most sophisticated signal interception equipment, the best long-range space scanners and the best computer wizards in the galaxy.

They also had a whole department of language research, manned by Ph.D.'s in linguistics who spent all their days finding new ways to decode alien languages. They often had a second major in logic or mathematics. Some of them also wrote encryption books for Advanced Retrieval. It was quite fun to work there.

Many of them were complete academic nerds who had never set their foot outside a school or a college before they got a job with Advanced Retrieval. They had only a vague idea of what life was like for agents like Goryell who were out in the field. Which suited them just fine. Whenever they got strange assignments from the field they felt like Earth children on Christmas.

Assignments like the ones that Goryell's boss Tahm Qaar kept sending them were particularly intriguing due to the tense political situation. It made the linguists feel a little bit of the excitement that field agents felt every day.

They had cracked the grammar of the Zoh'moorian language pretty quickly and soon after they had built a good basic vocabulary. Based on that they developed a functioning translation key for the communications between Earth and Zoh'moor. What they did not have, though, was a means to adequately translate communications between the Zoh'moorians themselves. Tahm Qaar had requested an extra long-range satellite which he had placed in a stationary position outside Pluto's orbit. It was pointed at where Zoh'moor was believed to be, and it quickly started relaying intercepted messages between Zoh'moorian space vessels. The problem was that the Zoh'moorians appeared to be divided into two major groups with two distinct dialects, and those dialects had proven difficult to decipher. Neither of them was quite like the dialect they used in communications with Earth.

Tahm Qaar wanted a new translation key quickly. He was concerned. The long-range satellite sent scan images that showed that the Zoh'moorians had put some kind of replenishment station half way between their world and Earth.

He was also concerned about the feedback transmissions to Earth. Each time vice president Stanton spoke to the Supreme General the conversation was transmitted back to Earth, with different recipient coordinates. One of Tahm Qaar's agents had found the location of recipient, right in the middle of the Hyde Park neighborhood in Chicago.

Why were the Zoh'moorians echoing the conversations? Who was receiving the transmissions? And for what purpose? It could not be the president of the United States, Barry Oslow, because he lived in Washington, DC just like the vice president.

Had the Zoh'moorians already planted agents on Earth? If so, it was most likely sabotage units ready to go out and blow up critical facilities. But that was unlikely, since it would mean that reptilians had to walk around among humanoids who had never seen reptilians before.

There was definitely something fishy about those feedback transmissions.

Then there was the Zoh'moorian force build-up at that half-way point. Given that it only took them a couple of days to move their vessels from Zoh'moor to the replenishment station, it would also take them only a couple of days to get to Earth from there. It seemed illogical for them to put a lot of ships there now – unless they had decided to invade Earth earlier than they had told Holly Stanton.

In his communications with the vice president the Zoh'moorian Supreme General kept saying that they were going to arrive as per their agreement. Precisely for that reason Tahm Qaar wanted the domestic Zoh'moorian communications translated as quickly as

possible. He had grown increasingly concerned about the pending
Zoh'moorian invasion and had decided to feed Ross Landau
everything he knew about the Zoh'moorians. Hopefully Ross would
then be willing to go public with it.

Ideally, that could bring about some second thoughts in the vice
president's circles. If it did, Tahm Qaar would be more than happy
to offer Danarvian help to stop the invasion.

The bureaucrats back home might object he was intervening in
Earth's domestic affairs if he did that. Tahm Qaar had no problem
with that. He knew what catastrophe it would be if the Zoh'moorians
got to invade Earth. The Earthlings would lose every bit of their
freedom. As far as Tahm Qaar was concerned, the Fourth Principle of
the Charter of Liberty applied to all independent beings, regardless
of where they were. And ultimately, when it came down to it, his
loyalty was to the Charter of Liberty, not to the bureaucrats back in
Operations Headquarters.

If he could use his work to make a difference and defend some
people's rights under the Fourth Principle, then he was going to do
it.

His problem was that so long as he could not translate
Zoh'moorian communications he could not present irrefutable
evidence of their accelerated time table. And the less substance he
could present Ross with, the less The Great Educator could do.

"As much as I believe you" Ross told Tahm Qaar, "I just can't go
on the air and tell my listeners about this. Believing in space aliens
is considered a bit kooky here, and…"

"Kooky?"

"Weird, strange… get it?"

"Yes. Of course. I understand."

"So if I do that, *they* will think that it is *me* who is kooky. My
reputation would be shattered. It would only play into the vice
president's hands."

"So what you are saying is that there is no way that any
Earthling could use this information? Even if I had these domestic
Zoh'moorian communications translated?"

"Unfortunately, yes" Ross said. "But once the invasion starts,
your intelligence resources will be very useful."

"Excuse me, sir."

Tahm Qaar turned around. It was Thor.

"I could not help overhearing. I think Carl and I could use those translations."

"For what purpose?"

"Well… Holly Stanton is betting on taking everyone by surprise with the Zoh'moorian invasion. She wants to use them as her muscle to, well, take over the world. It sounds like a cliché, but that is actually what she's planning. But if we could somehow send her a message that her plans have been intercepted, we might discourage her from going ahead with her plans."

Ross shook his head.

"I agree with you that it is a good idea to let her know someone has intercepted her plans, but I do not think she would change her mind."

He paused for a moment.

"But it might weaken her inner circle. The Stantons have always surrounded themselves with hand-picked loyalists they can control. When someone leaves that inner circle, it disrupts their political machinery. What we need is to break the administration's determination to cooperate with the Zoh'moorians."

"That's a very good point" Thor agreed. "The Zoh'moorians are probably counting on the fact that our president will order our military to stand down. Of course, that means that president Oslow has to be in on this."

"Unless something conveniently happens to him" Ross noted.

"Exactly. But if the Zoh'moorians realize that the administration will not be able to control the military… if they know that there will be fierce military resistance from the mightiest force on Earth… then it might discourage them from invading in the first place."

"I would not be too sure" Tahm Qaar noted. "They are amassing a huge fleet. One of the biggest I have seen for a one-to-one world invasion. But what you are suggesting would raise the bar enough to delay them. That would buy us more time."

"We can plant the communications transcripts somewhere in the administration" Thor suggested.

"I have an idea who to go to" Ross said. "Irwin Schwepp."

Thor agreed.

"Can you find him?" Tahm Qaar asked.

"Yes" Thor said and went to call his brother.

Jack was happy to hear from his brother. Much happier than last time. After all, this time Thor did not call him at the crack of dawn.

"Hey, brother!" Jack said over the phone, sounding almost ecstatic. "Thanks for saving Ross's life! I heard him, he is better than ever."

"Thanks. I need you to do me a favor."

"Anything."

"I want you to call Irwin Schwepp."

"Why would I do that?"

"Because I want to locate him."

"How can you…"

"Sorry, but I can't tell you how I can do that. Please, it's kind of urgent."

"Alright, sure. What do I tell him?"

"That you got the wrong number."

Jack hung up and dialed Irwin Schwepp's number. While waiting for Irwin to answer he flipped through some class notes and tried to find the small piece of paper where he had written down the phone number to Jenny Blue Eyes. He still had not called her.

Five signals. Six signals. Seven signals.

He was just about to hang up when someone answered.

"Yes?"

It was a woman.

"Uh… I'm sorry, wrong number."

"Did you want to talk to Irwin, perhaps?"

"Uh… is he there?"

"No, I'm afraid not. Can I take a message?"

"No, I'll… I'll call back later."

He hung up.

Over in New Mexico, Thor was sitting at a computer listening in on Jack's brief conversation.

He stared out in the middle of nothing.

That voice he heard… he knew it so well.

"Carl!"

"What?"

"Come, listen to this."

He gave the headset to Carl and replayed Jack's conversation with the unknown woman.

"Who is this person?"

Carl listened.

"That's your brother."

"No, you cone head, the other one."

Carl listened, replayed the conversation and listened again. Then he stared at Thor.

"That's... That's Rachel."

"It is, isn't it?"

"What the heck is she doing answering Irwin Schwepp's phone?"

*　　　*　　　*

The day when Todd Salmon got the letter about the fair speech code he had forgotten all about his debate with professor Pinkhouse about President Bush's fiscal policy. He was going about his business as usual, taking his summer courses to speed up his graduate program as best he could – and, of course, partying with his friends from time to time.

The letter from the college president took him by surprise. He did not suspect anything when he first saw it in his mailbox. The envelope had the college president's standard logo on it and his address printed in boring Courier font. At first he was going to toss it, but then he noted that the address was not mass-printed. Instead, it looked like it was uniquely mailed to him.

He went in to the kitchen. Jack and Wolkenkratzer were taking turns playing Tetris on Jack's iWorld while their shared dinner – a huge pot of chili con carne – was cooking on the stove.

"Howdy" Jack said to Todd.

"What do you make of this envelope?" Todd asked him.

Jack took the letter from the college president and looked at it.

"Probably an advance on your doctor's degree."

"You're being stupid."

"We all have the right to fifteen minutes of stupidity in our lives" Jack shrugged and dropped half a garlic in the chili.

"If you don't want it I'll take it" said Wolkenkratzer. "Looks like there's a check in it."

"And why would the president of the college send me a check?"

"A tuition refund."

"That's funny" Todd said without a hint of a smile.

"A refund because professor Pinkhouse insulted you in class" Jack continued the joke.

Todd looked at him. Jack shrugged his shoulders and smiled. Todd kept looking at him.

"What?" Jack asked.

"I have a bad feeling about this letter" Todd said.

"Why?"

"Fair speech" Todd mumbled.

"Aw, come on, you don't really think...?"

"There's only one way to find out" Todd concluded and opened the envelope.

The letter inside made him furious.

Todd Salmon,

　　　With reference to Case 2013-1, you are hereby summoned to appear before the Fair Speech Board of Schuyler University. The Board will hear the case of Schuyler University vs. Todd Salmon. You have the right to a fair hearing. Upon conclusion of the hearing the Fair Speech Board will issue a verdict. If you are found guilty of having breached the Fair Speech Code as established by United States Code 99-2013-61, the Board will consider your dismissal from the University.

P Hill Glotzenblutz
President
Schuyler University

"Can you believe this crap?!" he yelled, turned the letter in to a paper ball and threw it at Jack.

Jack caught it, undid the paper ball and read it.

"Is this a joke?" he asked.

"The Hell it's a joke!" Todd responded furiously and padded his pockets to find a cigarette. "I'll tell you what's a joke! Professor Pinkhouse, that's a joke!"

He did not find any cigarettes in his pocket, so he got up, walked over to the fridge, grabbed a can of Coke from someone else's shelf and opened it. He downed half of it and sat down again.

"This is patently absurd" Jack said calmly as he read the letter again. "I wonder if this law is even constitutional."

"What the Hell difference does that make to me?" Todd asked and downed the other half of the Coke can.

"Well, you can always sue them…"

"Oh, yeah? And in the meantime I get kicked out from grad school and turned in to an academic has-been by a professor who can't tell science from jokes. Yeah, that's a bright future. Thanks a bunch for that."

"Hey, don't go after me. I'm not the villain here."

Todd muttered something inaudible. Wolkenkratzer got up and went over to the stove. He stirred the chili and tasted it.

"Want some dinner, Todd?" he asked.

"I don't even understand what kind of case they have against you" Jack said.

"Who cares?" said Todd. "They can do whatever they want. They got the power."

Wolkenkratzer started serving them all chili. Todd looked at the bowl with surprise.

"What's this?"

"Chili" Wolkenkratzer explained. "With garlic."

Todd examined it like he was in biology class.

"This is the first fair speech case, isn't it?" Jack noted. "So maybe they just want to test what the code really is good for. I can't imagine they would terminate someone on the first case."

"Those people are capable of anything" Todd muttered and began eating the chili. "Who made this?"

"We did" said Jack and Wolkenkratzer.

"It's… not bad."

"Why don't you just go there and present your side of it" Jack suggested.

"I'm not gonna do that" Todd said between mouthfuls of chili.

"Why not?"

"Because they're a bunch of morons, that's why."

"You'll risk termination of your scholarship."

"Didn't you just say they would go easy on me?" Todd reminded him.

"Sure, but if you don't show up they will think that you're insulting their authority."

"They're darn right I'm insulting their authority" Todd nodded and finished the chili. "Damn, this is good chili."

"Schmooze them" Wolkenkratzer suggested.

"I'm not schmoozing anyone" Todd said, got up and served himself seconds.

"It's your life, buddy" Jack said and got up.

"Where you going?" Wolkenkratzer asked.

"I forgot to pay my car insurance. I have to do it now or else they'll cancel it."

He went in to his room and made a quick call. When the bill was paid he went back out in the hallway. The door to Alexis's room was open. He knocked on the door frame and went in.

"Hey, cutie" Jack said. "Whazzup?"

"Hey, what's up" Alexis said.

She barely glanced at him. She was sitting at her desk, hard at work. There was not the same cheerful tone in her voice that he was used to. She put some papers together in a folder and made notes on her computer. Jack sat himself down on the bed and leaned back toward the wall.

"Studying hard" he commented.

"It's not study" she said without looking at him. "It's work."

"What kind of work?"

"For Pinkhouse."

"Why are you working for Pinkhouse?"

"I want a good recommendation so I can get in at the Federal

Reserve" Alexis said and looked Jack straight in the eyes. "I know what you think about Pinkhouse and I have no interest in hearing it again. I need this."

"Hey" Jack replied. "I'm just curious. Besides, I worked for professor de la Gauche last summer, remember? Not exactly the kind of person I would get along with."

She nodded.

"I know. I'm sorry. It's just a lot of extra. I heard he doesn't write good recommendations unless he really knows you."

"That's good."

"I guess. Some professors hand out good recommendations like candy."

"Well, just keep in mind that some girls have had trouble with Pinkhouse. If it ever happens to you, I'm here, OK?"

She smiled.

"Thanks. I'll remember that."

Jack went back out in the kitchen. He grabbed a big bowl and filled it with chili. He and Wolkenkratzer went back to their Tetris tournament while Todd checked the business news on TV. They forgot all about the world outside falling blocks and rising stocks for a good half hour until Alexis came in to the kitchen. She had changed since Jack was in her room.

"Going out?" he asked her.

"Got a meeting" she said in a business-like tone.

"With whom?"

"Pinkhouse" she said and got a water bottle from the fridge. "Where's my Coke?"

"Pinkhouse is an idiot" Todd said, his eyes fixed on the TV screen.

"Why?" Alexis asked and sipped from her water bottle.

"He just sued me."

"He sued you??"

"It's this fair speech thing" Jack told her and handed her Todd's letter.

Alexis read it and looked at Jack. Jack was looking at her, but not her face.

"Jack, why are you staring at my breasts?" Alexis asked.

"I've never seen you wear a black bra under a white blouse before. I've seen you without a bra under a white blouse, and without a bra, period, but…"

"So what's wrong with a black bra?"

Jack raised his eyes and met hers. Alexis knew her counter-question sounded lame.

"Whatever" she said and turned around.

Todd turned off the TV.

"So you're working for Pinkhouse?" Todd noted and went over to the patio door to light up a cigarette he had found in a drawer.

"So what?"

"He's a creepy geezer."

"He doesn't like Pinkhouse, in case you hadn't noticed" Wolkenkratzer added.

"You think he'll spare you, Lex?" Todd continued, ignoring Wolkenkratzer. "He's a power-addicted control freak. That's why he's after me. He will make you shine his shoes with your own dignity. And I know…" and he killed his half-smoked cigarette out of sheer agitation, "…I know you're doing this because you want a good recommendation letter from him. But the only way you will get that is if you flash your boobs to him."

"C'mon!!" Alexis shouted back. "You're way over the line!"

"Don't do it" Wolkenkratzer said.

"Do what?"

"Flash your boobs. He might think we have a mosquito invasion on campus."

Wolkenkratzer laughed hysterically at his own joke as he left the kitchen.

"I'm three cups bigger than anything you'll ever get your hands on!" Alexis shouted after him.

"I'm only speaking out of experience" Todd continued, calming himself down. "He loves to control people. Like now, when he wants to control my speech."

"But you're a guy, what do you know about how he treats girls?" Alexis asked, although she sounded a bit unsure now.

"He is even worse with girls. Control is an addiction to him. He will make you turn and tap dance and do whatever he wants you to do. He's got this I'm-so-good-it-makes-me-sick attitude and talks all the time about what a good-hearted socialist he is. He jokes constantly to make people think he's a nice guy. But once you make even a tiny dent in that surface, something else shines through. And below that surface is a freak, Lex, a freak you don't wanna know."

"You have to be in control if you're going to be chair of a department at a college" Alexis tried, clearly on the defensive now.

"But you don't behave like there can only be one person in the room every time you're in it!"

"You're just having problems with him because you're a Republican."

"I'm not a Republican. I'm a libertarian."

"Same diff…"

"The Hell it is!" Todd yelled, clearly agitated. "I've never even voted Republican. I haven't voted at all, in fact. That whole Iraq thing…" and he lit up his cigarette again to calm himself down, "… that made no sense to me. And then Oslow spent us to Hell …"

He shook his head.

"I gotta go" Alexis said and collected her things.

"Be careful" Jack said.

"Whatever" Alexis said and left.

"She's dressed for success, alright" said Jack.

"She's dressed for disaster" Todd countered.

* * *

AGONY

I can't eat their food anymore.

I used to hate it, then I got used to it. I had to eat something. Some of it did not taste all that bad, but my stomach took forever to adjust to it.

Maybe it's because I'm getting old. I am seventy now. I think. Or is it sixty eight?

When Ray and Linda came here they told me it was the year two thousand three on Earth.

Two thousand three. I realized I had been here ten years.

They told us stories about the Millenium New Year. They had been in Centennial Park in Atlanta. They said it was beautiful.

Oh, they had so many stories to tell me! They told of something called "internet". All computers in the world were suddenly connected in one big network!

I bet my sister's grandchildren would never understand the world we grew up in.

Linda cried every day for a year. She and Ray were kept separate at times. I think the… creatures… understood that they were a couple. Linda cried for her family. Ray tried to be brave, to comfort her. But he ran out of strength eventually.

They broke him. I know it. They saw how he cared for his girlfriend, and they broke him. He turned more and more indifferent. I think it was his way to survive.

And he got very angry when Gregor came and told him stories from Earth. He attacked Gregor.

We all enjoyed Gregor's stories. He was Russian. The creatures got very interested when Ray attacked Gregor. They put the two of them in another dungeon, alone.

I never saw Gregor again. Ray refused to tell us what happened to him. But I could tell that whatever it was, it had scared the life out of Ray.

My head hurts. Not always, but sometimes. It hurts where they directed their beam. It hurts inside the head, the way it started to hurt when they increased the beam's intensity.

I wonder what they did.

I know why they did it. I'm a lab rat. They do experiments on us. Not physical ones, not the kind where you put drugs in people to see how they respond. No, not that kind.

These experiments are much more subtle.

I know I am going to die here. I know I will never see Lindsborg again. I will never get out of this cold, humid, stench-filled place.

I have come to peace with that. Somehow I have come to peace with being the oldest of all of us... humans... I have become a mentor, someone who introduces new ones. It's almost like the creatures keep me here for that reason.

But one day they will not need me any more. And I will be... there will be some kind of... ending.

I do not have a lot left to wish for. Except one thing.

I would like to know why. Why are they experimenting on us? They are so different. So... hideous.

*   *   *

CONFRONTATION

Vice Admiral Ghaul was asleep in his quarters on the command vessel of Strike Group 14 when the Lt Commander in charge of the bridge called him.

"Yes?"

"Sir, high priority message from Central Command."

Ghaul wiped his eyes and glanced at the clock on his desk. He had barely slept two hours. He had been working for nineteen hours straight to prepare the mission, get the strike force battle ready and out of the space port. He would not mind a few hours more sleep.

But this was Frontline Services, not some space cruise for housewives.

"Alright, put it through to my quarters" he said.

He got up and put on a casual robe. As he walked over to the computer on his desk a series of bleeps indicated that the computer had been activated and was ready. He sat down and carefully placed his tail in the opening in the back rest. He had an unusually wide tail and for some reason Frontline Services had not been able to give him a properly shaped seat when they renovated his command vessel. He was going to complain about it after this mission.

With an access code and a quick skin scan he opened the high priority message from his commanding officer.

"Admiral Grez" Ghaul said. "What can I do for you?"

"You are to make an immediate halt."

Ghaul blinked and frowned in the quirky way that only reptilians could.

"Sir?"

"I realize this is surprising to you, but it's an order directly from the Executive Office."

"May I ask why?"

"Politics" Admiral Grez said and shook his head. "But orders are orders."

"Any details?"

"The Federal Assembly wants formal consultations with the Executive Office regarding this mission."

"But sir... the latest intelligence from Advanced Retrieval shows that the alien force is getting ready to invade Earth. It could happen any day now."

"I know that. They know it, too. But this is politics."

"Is there anything we can do?"

"No."

Ghaul thought for a moment.

"What are the exact words of the order?"

"The order reads as follows: 'Strike Group 14 must not enter sector KB until further notice.' Nothing surprising there. It's what the law says the Executive Office has to do under these circumstances."

"The order refers to the entire group" Ghaul noted.

Admiral Grez looked at him.

"So?"

"I can order the group itself to halt, but still send a long range striker in to sector KB and saturate the sector with surveillance probes. In full cloak mode, of course."

"That's very dangerous. For one, we do not know anything about their technological standards."

"Well, sir, we have the intelligence reports from Advanced Retrieval's team on Earth What I've seen does not exactly give me nightmares."

"Alright, go ahead, but be careful. You're dancing on the edge of your authority."

"Thank you, sir" Ghaul said, terminated the conversation and called the Lt Commander on the bridge.

"Bring the strike group to full stop."

"Yes, sir."

"Call a meeting with all Commanders. And tell major Kress I need a long-range striker stuffed with surveillance probes."

Ghaul took a quick shower to wake up. He got dressed and ordered a cup of strong blue leaf tea to the bridge.

"Sleep is for girls" he muttered.

The tea was waiting by his seat on the bridge when he got there. It was a big, strong cup. He finished it just in time for the meeting with the strike group's hub ship commanders.

"Bad news" he opened the meeting in the conference room right behind the bridge. "The politicians back home have ordered us to make a full stop right here. They have to sort out what they really think about this mission. I suggest you use the wait wisely. Continue with the training on the new weapons systems. I also recommend another battle inventory check. We only got to do one before we left."

"Sir" said one commander. "Is there any chance we can obtain more information about the Zoh'moorians now that we are so close?"

"I've ordered major Kress to send a long-range striker in to sector KB to take a closer look at them. However, we have some information already."

He pushed a button and a screen appeared on the wall behind him. An image with dots and dashed lines appeared.

"See the cluster of blue dots? Those are large vessels, clustered together at the midway point between Zoh'moor and Earth. The dashed lines indicate where they came from. Very simple, very clear."

He zoomed out. The entire KB sector became visible.

"The green square is Earth. The red square is where we believe Zoh'moor is located. We need better satellites to pinpoint their exact location. Here is their halfway point. Now… we'll be entering sector KB from here and take this route. It means we will have Earth to the left and the Zoh'moorian invasion force to the right. Perfect for a cut-off operation. We just have to hope the politicians back home have made up their minds before the Zoh'moorians get to Earth."

He pulled up a third image. It showed a rough sketch of a space vessel. Every commander sat right up in his seat. This was where it got interesting.

"Based on the data that Advanced Retrieval have sent us I asked the engineering department to come up with a sketch of the most common Zoh'moorian ship."

He displayed an image of a space ship that looked like a cigarette pack standing on the side. It was slightly wider at the top and had four engines bolted on to the hull.

"Is that their propulsion system?" asked a commander.

"As far as we know, yes" said Vice Admiral Ghaul.

"Does their entire fleet use particle acceleration technology?" asked another commander.

"That we don't know yet" Ghaul cautioned.

"If they do, we can take out all of them with one long-range striker" the first commander chuckled.

"Don't get over-confident" Ghaul said and looked at him sternly. "We don't know what they have back home. However, I agree that this is good news. Particle acceleration engines thrust the ships into super-light speed, which as you all know is very energy-consuming. That makes them heavily dependent on refueling, which is probably why they have this midway gathering point."

He looked at his commanders to make sure they were all paying attention.

"But let's not forget that particle acceleration engines and gravimetric propulsion co-existed in Danarvia for almost a decade. Some member worlds kept using it much longer than that. So until we have had a chance to take a close look at Zoh'moor itself, we should not exclude the possibility that they have gravimetric propulsion."

The door to the conference room opened. Major Kress came in.

"Sir" he said. "The long-range striker is ready to depart."

"I'll be right there" said Ghaul.

He finished the meeting with the commanders and had the major join him to the bridge. He wanted to have a brief conversation with the commanding officer of the long-range striker before he sent them off.

After all, a lot was hinging on the professionalism and experience of that commanding officer.

One error and the entire operation would be severely jeopardized. And Ghaul could kiss his nice retirement benefits goodbye.

*   *   *

When Thor traced Jack's call to Irwin Schwepp's cell phone he was able to locate Rachel with a standard GPS tracking program. She was in Atlanta, just four blocks away from the inconspicuous headquarters of the southern branch of Branch Four.

"Could she be the infiltrator in your organization?" Goryell asked.

"Seems like it. Especially since she's working for the vice president. How she did it is beyond me, though."

"There's only one way to find out for sure what she's up to" Carl added. "We'll tail her."

"Tail her?" Goryell asked.

"Yeah. Follow her wherever she goes."

"Oh. I see. But she would recognize you guys."

"We can be careful. Mask ourselves."

"Doesn't she have the same top training as you guys?"

"She has some kind of background in the CIA" Thor noted. "I've heard she was a bureaucrat, not an operations agent."

"How are you going to pick up her trace, though?" Goryell asked. "You can't keep on calling Irwin's phone."

"We're supposed to report back for duty tomorrow" Carl said. "She'll be there to get a full report on the Louisiana operation. By the way, I just spoke with Kwolczyk. He had never heard that Rachel works for Stanton."

"Could it all be a trap?" Goryell asked.

"What do you mean?"

"Obviously she knows you got away down in Louisiana. She

may also have good reasons to believe that you rescued Ross. She'd have every reason in the world to try to kill you."

"It could very well be a trap" Carl agreed. "I guess we'll find out when we report for duty."

"I agree" Thor said. "We start tailing her after the meeting."

"If she wants to trap you guys" Goryell continued, "this meeting you're going to have could be a perfect opportunity for her. She could bring a team of… what did you call them…?"

"SEALs."

"Yeah. SEALs. Isn't that an animal, by the way?"

"SEAL is an acronym."

"A what?"

"An abbreviation" Carl explained.

"I see. Anyway, where was I?"

"Trap" Thor reminded him.

"Right. If she is working for Holly Stanton then she has an interest in shutting down Branch Four, right?"

"I doubt she'd try anything like that" said Carl.

"Me, too" Thor said. "There will be a half dozen of us there. She'd need forty commandos for that attack. Plus, this meeting will take place at noon, in a building in downtown Atlanta. The place will be bustling with people."

"I'd still be very careful" Goryell said.

Thor and Carl thanked Goryell for his concerns and asked for a ride to the airport in Albuquerque. When Goryell got back after having dropped them off he went straight to Tahm Qaar and expressed his concerns.

"Go after them" Tahm Qaar said. "Tail them and watch over them. This smells an assassination trap all the way home. And if that woman Rachel is really working for the vice president, I want her captured and brought here."

"You mean… you want me to arrest her?"

"Arrest. Seize. Snatch. Kidnap. Whatever you want to call it."

"Oh, thank you, sir. My pleasure."

Goryell turned to leave the office. On the doorstep he stopped and turned again.

"Sir?"

"Yes."

"I get the feeling you're willing to… give me my second chance now."

Tahm Qaar sighed.

"Goryell… take a look at this."

He handed Goryell an electronic notepad. It had a series of space scans on it from their satellite that was monitoring Zoh'moorian activity.

"They're already on their way!" Goryell concluded.

"You're darn right they are" Tahm Qaar confirmed. "The first group of ships has already left the halfway point and will enter this solar system in forty-eight hours. It will probably take them a day or so to assume their launch positions. That means the invasion will begin no later than three days from today."

"So I guess we'll get to see who the Zoh'moorians really are, then, sir."

"That's funny" Tahm Qaar said without a hint of a smile. "But this is a complete game changer. The politicians back home dispatched a strike group to stop the Zoh'moorian invasion. But then some of them decided to question the damned operation. So the Executive Office had to order the strike group to a complete halt. Until our elected officials back home sort out their differences the Zoh'moorians can do whatever they want here."

Goryell waited. He knew his boss had something in mind.

"The only way to break the political deadlock" Tahm Qaar continued, "and get Strike Group Fourteen here, is if there is a direct plea from Earth to Danarvia for help. That overrides whatever petitions and consultations and negotiations the politicians are engaged in."

"The plea condition for military intervention" Goryell remembered. "The Fourth Principle."

Tahm Qaar leaned forward and looked Goryell straight in the eyes.

"Goryell, I know I lectured you on the principles of non-interference, and I may have been a bit harsh. But the game has changed now. This is an urgent situation. I'm not going to sit here and play by rules that our bureaucrats have written while this world is being taken over by some thugs from another world. I am as convinced as you are that the Zoh'moorians are coming here to create a slave world."

He paused and leaned back in his chair again. Goryell waited patiently.

"I want you to get me a representative of the United States government" Tahm Qaar said. "Someone who can make this plea for help."

"Is that why you want me to kidnap Rachel?"

"That's part of the reason. I want to get to know who she is and see if we can use her to get to Holly Stanton. She may also help us find the right person in the administration's hierarchy to make that plea. We obviously cannot get the president or the vice president, but there must be someone else we can use."

Goryell smiled.

"I like this, sir. I like the action."

Tahm Qaar chuckled.

"Yes" he said. "Action, alright. We're here in the name of freedom, and that means something to me. Work with Thor and Carl on this."

"Yes, sir" Goryell said and got up to leave.

"And Goryell..."

"Sir?"

"Any means possible. No restrictions this time. Weapons, escape pods, cloak suits. Whatever it takes."

"We're here in the name of freedom" Goryell nodded, "and that means something to me, too."

Goryell liked the idea of working with Thor and Carl. They were good guys and much in the same business as he was. They were already on their way to Atlanta, but they were flying regular jet. Goryell had a slightly faster means of transportation at his disposal.

The big transportation vessel that also fit his Cadillac.

He figured he might need the car. And he was also beginning to like driving it. It was fast, fun and comfortable.

He got to Atlanta two hours before Thor and Carl were scheduled to land at the airport. He landed in a secluded area, in

fully cloaked mode, and set the vessel down so that he could back
out the Cadillac and roll right on to a small dirt road.

Goryell had scanned the area for living beings before setting
down. There was a small mobile home in the woods, and one person
outside it. Goryell hesitated for a moment. He really did not want
to be seen unloading a car from a cloaked transportation craft. On
the other hand, there were not that many suitable landing spots in
the area, especially if he was going to have access to a road for the
car.

So he decided to land anyway. The transportation craft remained
cloaked, and he set it down so that the rear end was backed up
against the small dirt road. Then he backed out the Cadillac on to
the road.

The man who was lying on a hammock outside the mobile home
was sipping from a small bottle of Jack Daniels and was singing a
little song to himself:

"I've been a wild rover for many's the year... and I've spent all
my money on whiskey and beer... But now I'm returning with gold
in great store... and I never will play the wild rover no more..."

He looked out through the trees and his thoughts drifted off as
he sipped from the bottle again.

Then his eyes fell on the rear end of a black Cadillac that
appeared out of nowhere, about two hundred feet down the small
dirt road that crossed the field just below where his property was.

He squinted and looked again. And he could not believe what
he saw. The Cadillac's back doors appeared, and then the front
doors.

The old man raised his body up on his right elbow and looked
with startled eyes as the entire car came into full view. Then a man
in a funny suit stepped out from the car. He put on some strange
glasses, walked up to the car's front and did something with an
instrument he had in his hand.

And then he took a step forward and vanished.

"What the devil..." the drunk man said.

The man appeared again, as if he had stepped out of something.
But there was nothing there. And now he was wearing a strange
overall.

The drunk man thought he heard a whizzing sound and the man out on the field raised his head as if he was looking at something that rose to the sky.

Then the man out in the field vanished again.

The driver's door on the Cadillac opened and shut. Then the car drove off on itself. Without anyone behind the wheel.

The drunk man stared at the Cadillac as it vanished, and then at his bottle. He looked out at the field again and back at his bottle. Then he shook his head and poured the scotch out in the grass.

"And it's no, nay, never... no more will I play the wild rover... no, never no more..." he sang and tossed the bottle in to a bush a few feet away.

When Goryell had sent the transportation craft back into cloaked, high-atmosphere orbit he tested his cloak suit and got in the car. He drove off with the suit in cloak mode.

He contacted Tahm Qaar and gave him an update. Then he entered a U.S. Highway and put the car on cruise control. He made a point out of locking the speed at exactly the speed limit. He adjusted the driver's seat to his comfort and turned on the radio. He had come to like American music and sometimes wondered if it would sell on his home world.

A few minutes later he passed a state trooper. The trooper was slouching in the driver's seat of his cruiser, casually checking the speed of passing vehicles while listening to a local radio talk show. Traffic was light and he was seriously considering going down to the local Dunkin Donuts for a snack when a black Cadillac approached. The trooper noticed that it was the high-performance V-series model and sensed a speeding ticket. He pointed his speed detector at it, but to his disappointment it was cruising along exactly at the speed limit.

Disappointed, the trooper put away his equipment and started his engine. He was just about to turn his cruiser east and head for the Dunkin Donuts when the Cadillac passed right in front of him.

And he got a good look right in to the car.

"I'll be..." the trooper said.

He thought for a second. Was he crazy or did that car not have a driver??

He blinked a couple of times and pinched his cheek.

Nope. He was not crazy. So he decided to pull over the Cadillac. He quickly caught up with it and turned on his lights.

Goryell noticed the state trooper behind him. He checked his speed. It was still exactly at the speed limit. Why was he being pulled over?

He slowed down and stopped on the narrow shoulder. In his rearview mirror he saw the trooper go on his radio, while looking very awkwardly at Goryell's car. Goryell took out the documents that he knew the trooper would be asking for.

"What is he up to?" Goryell asked himself.

The trooper got out of his car, adjusted his belt and started walking up to the driver's seat. Goryell looked at him through the rearview mirror.

Then he caught a glimpse of his own driver's seat in the mirror.

"Oh, damned!! I'm cloaked!"

What an idiot he'd been! Driving around in his cloaking suit activated. All he had done before getting in the car was to check that it was working properly. Then, smart as he was, he had gotten in behind the wheel in fully cloaked mode.

His hand moved down to the belt on the suit. The cloak control buttons were located on the side, right in front of the clip where he could place his weapon. His eyes were fixed on the state trooper in the mirror, while his fingers wandered back and forth to find the cloak switch.

As the trooper came up to the rear end of Goryell's car he hesitated for a second and leaned forward, his right hand on his gun. Goryell found a switch and instinctively pressed it.

His right ear started buzzing.

"Vacuum breach protection system activated" a voice said in his ear plug.

"No!" Goryell said to himself.

He had activated the layer in the suit that inflated to protect against exposure to open space! Damned! Why did they have to place all these buttons so close to each other??

He quickly reversed the switch and deactivated the vacuum

seal inflation. The state trooper apparently heard Goryell in there, because his eyebrows went up:

"Hello?" he said.

Goryell did not know what to do – except try to switch off the cloak, of course. His fingers kept searching for the right button while his eyes were fixed on the trooper in the mirror.

"Is anyone there?" the trooper asked.

He took a step forward.

"I'll be damned" he said to himself.

Then he grabbed the microphone on his left shoulder and pressed the Send button. Just as he was going to radio his dispatch, Goryell found the cloak button. He quickly turned it off and folded up the visor on his helmet.

The trooper let go of the radio microphone and slowly came up to the rolled-down driver's window. He could swear that the man behind the wheel had materialized out of nowhere.

To make things even stranger, the driver was wearing a strange, light grey suit with a helmet that was so tight around his skull that it looked like a second skin.

"Uh… may I see your license and registration, please…" the trooper said, cautiously examining Goryell.

"Of course" Goryell said and handed him a New Mexico driver's license and the proper registration documents.

The trooper looked at the driver's license and at Goryell.

"Sir, would you take that helmet off for me? I can't see if this is you."

Goryell hesitated for a moment. The helmet would actually fold in to the suit and practically vanish. Carl had mentioned that his cloaking suit was totally out of the ordinary for any Earthling.

But then again, he could not risk a confrontation with a state trooper. It would draw a ton of attention to him, and that was the last thing he needed.

So he pushed a button on a control panel on the side of his wrist. The helmet disappeared in to the neck of his suit.

"That's some suit you got there" the trooper said.

"It's new" was all Goryell could say.

It was true, actually. He had checked out a new one to replace the one that got damaged during the adventure down in Louisiana.

"What is it for?"

"Uh… it's a new fire rescue suit" was the first thing that popped in to Goryell's mind.

"Oh, I see" the trooper said, sounding like he actually believed him. "Why are you wearing it now?"

"Because… I invented it and I'm on my way to a meeting to demonstrate it."

The trooper nodded.

"Well, I was just checking, sir. You have a safe drive now."

He gave Goryell his license and registration back and went back to his cruiser. Goryell drove off, sighing with relief.

The trooper, on the other hand, remained parked. He looked after the Cadillac and shook his head slowly.

"I could have sworn there was no driver in that car" he said.

Then he turned to the screen that was hooked on to his dashboard camera. He stopped the live screening and went back to when he was behind Goryell's car. He looked carefully, frame by frame.

There was no doubt. The car had no driver.

"I'll be damned…" he muttered.

He let the camera recording play on.

"I'm exiting here…" he said to himself.

The screen showed him in the left margin as he approached the driver's door on the Cadillac.

The car still had no driver.

Then, when he was right by the Cadillac's rear left door, a driver appeared in it. Just like that. Out of nowhere.

"I ain't seen nothing like this ever…" the trooper said to himself. "I better take a break."

He turned his cruiser around and went a couple of miles down the road to Dunkin Donuts. He parked right next to a cruiser that belonged to a local sheriff's deputy he knew. They often met there for coffee and a chat.

As he walked in the deputy was sitting at a table having coffee and a donut.

"Tom, how ya doin'?" the deputy said.

The trooper walked right up to him and sat down.

"What's the matter, Tom? You look like you seen a ghost?"

"Jeff, you're dead on" Tom said and looked around cautiously. "I just pulled over a car without a driver."

"What??"

The trooper looked around, anxious to make sure nobody else heard them.

"But when I walked up to the driver's side, the driver just appeared out of nowhere."

The deputy laughed.

"I ain't kiddin', Jeff! I got it on my dashboard camera. Wanna see it?"

"What did the driver look like?"

"Like a normal guy... except for the ears. They were kind of funny looking. But he had a valid license and registration and all that, so I let him go."

"Well... I've never heard about a ghost with a driver's license, so I'm sure he was all flesh and blood."

"He had this funny suit on... looked almost like a space suit. The helmet kind of vanished in to the neck."

"And you just let him go, Tom?"

"What was I supposed to arrest him on?"

"How do you know he wasn't an alien?" the deputy joked. "An illegal alien from Mars!"

He laughed at his own joke.

"I've known you since fourth grade, Jeff. Have I ever lied to you?"

"Alright, Tom. But maybe it was just a blur or something in your dashboard camera."

"Whatever it was it made me nervous. I need coffee."

He got up to go order a strong cup of coffee. As he did, a tall woman left the booth right behind the deputy. She glanced at the trooper and walked out the door. As she exited, her cell phone rang.

"Yes, this is Rhea... Oh, hi, Holly... Yes, I miss you, too... I'm just outside Atlanta... Yes, we finalized the plan last night..."

*   *   *

While Jack, Todd and Wolkenkratzer procrastinated on the porch of the grad student dorm, Alexis went to her dinner appointment with professor Pinkhouse.

Technically, it was a date, although she did not want to call it that. She had gotten herself in to it without thinking. And both Todd and Jack had reminded her what a bad idea it was.

She had been at a meeting with professor Pinkhouse about her doctoral thesis and suddenly he had asked her if she wanted to go have dinner with him. She had been totally unprepared. In retrospect, though, she realized that he had been planning it all along.

She knew it was stupid to say yes to the dinner. She would prefer to just cancel it. But she also knew that professor Pinkhouse would not let her. He would insist they re-schedule.

And – she needed professor Pinkhouse's good recommendation letter.

He had asked Alexis to meet him outside Cudney's Cleaners on South Broadway. It was on the other side of town from the campus. He said he did not want his colleagues to get any funny ideas.

Yeah, right. She suspected it was more likely he did not want his wife's friends to see him with a student.

She drove over there just in time, parked her car and saw him pull up right behind her. She got in the passenger seat and noticed immediately that his entire demeanor was different than she was used to.

"Hi" he said with a honey-smooth voice.

"Hello" Alexis replied as cordially as possible.

The way he looked at her made her feel nervous. But as he drove out from the parking lot and headed south, she relaxed somewhat. He small talked about her doctoral thesis and encouraged her to go ahead with it as she had planned. He told her about all the economists that he knew who were working in the same field as she was interested in. That sounded more like a professor caring about his student's future, than a 61-year-old sleazeball trying to bed a 25-year-old girl.

Sure, it was perhaps an unusual situation, but with a little big of luck this might not turn out to be as bad after all.

Or so she thought.

She tried to focus herself on the future, on a good job at the Federal Reserve down in New York. She tried to imagine herself going on to a teaching job at an excellent school: Princeton, Stanford, UCLA...

"I am taking you to a conference in September" said professor Pinkhouse and woke her mercilessly from her daydream. "It'll be good for ya. You will meet a lot of people, get the chance to present a paper."

He had stopped outside the restaurant. As she unbuckled he looked at her and she felt his eyes touching every curve of her body. That was a bit unnerving.

"You look classy today" he said as they got out of the car. "I like that."

Suddenly she did not want to look classy. It felt as though the clothes she was wearing became some sort of wrapping paper that he had put on her.

Professor Pinkhouse was shorter than Alexis, not by much but enough to be noticeable. He had grey hair, small, grey-ish eyes and small glasses. His hands were small and soft since he had never in his life done any work with them.

"Pinkhouse, table for two" he said to the waiter. "Special reservation."

"Certainly, sir" the waiter said with a faint smile.

Alexis had no idea what a 'special reservation' was, but she did not like the sound of it.

She would find out soon enough. The waiter took them to a secluded part of a winter garden in the back of the restaurant. Big plants surrounded each table and created a very private atmosphere. A small artificial stream poured down a tiny waterfall and made a pleasant, yet discrete background noise. There were no windows except for a shaded glass ceiling.

They were seated on what was almost a peninsula of floor and furniture stretching out from a walkway in to the green. Around them was a lush forest of big indoor plants. The small stream of

water ran past them and Alexis could see small aquarium fishes in
it.

Alexis was surprised to see the winter garden. She had never
been to a restaurant with this outfit. It was quite impressive – a
perfect place to go with someone special.

Which reminded her of the present circumstances. To make
matters worse, the two chairs were placed in a 45 degree angle, not
face to face. There was nothing between them. Their legs would
touch almost automatically. She would be forced to sit very close
to him.

The waiter smiled and asked professor Pinkhouse if they wanted
some time with the menu first.

"I think that's a good idea" he said.

"Very well" the waiter said, smiled even more and left them.

"Good" said professor Pinkhouse. "So how do you like this
place? Nice, isn't it?"

"Yes, nice…" Alexis forced herself to say.

His leg was uncomfortably close to hers. He had seated himself
closer to her than the chairs were placed, so close that their hands
touched every time either of them moved.

She was trapped.

*   *   *

The building on 612 Fourth Avenue in Atlanta was an old,
blue two-story building with a hardware store on the ground floor
and a small office upstairs. There were parking spaces in the back
and a narrow stairway led up from the parking place to the office
entrance.

The building was owned by a small, anonymous investment
corporation. It had the entire upper floor as its office. But there was
not a whole lot of financial investment going on there, and only
four people worked there on a regular basis.

Colonel Kwolczyk was the president of the corporation. Carl
and Thor also had their offices there. The fourth employee one was
an old, lifelong member of Branch Four who spent his retirement
years supporting the two young agents and their colonel. He also
ran the hardware store downstairs.

It was rare that all four of them were in the office at the same time. It was even rarer that they held their meetings there. Colonel Kwolczyk was careful not to draw any attention to their little business. Whenever they were preparing for an assignment they held their meetings at inconspicuous places like abandoned warehouses.

However, they made an exception because Rachel had said that she had a very tight schedule and needed to go meet another cell of Branch Four the next day. Colonel Kwolczyk had tried to convince her to pass on the meeting altogether, but then another of the few high-ranking Branch Four agents had called him and told him to comply with Rachel's request.

So there they were. Thor and Carl had flown in the night before and had met with Kwolczyk an hour after they landed. Kwolczyk had accepted that Rachel may be an infiltrator. However, he said, he had no choice but to let her sit in on the meeting. Rachel's commanding officer had ordered him to let her sit in, and orders were orders.

Thor and Carl took Goryell's warning seriously. It was entirely possible that the meeting was a trap. As a precaution they decided not to arrive on time. If all four of them were in the office and Rachel was not there, it would be a perfect opportunity for someone to launch an assault on them. They wanted her to be there before they went in.

They also made sure to be properly armed. It was extremely unlikely that someone would stage an armed assault on their office in broad daylight, but you never knew. Besides, someone could sit and wait and try something after the meeting.

Thor got to the meeting at ten past noon. He called the office before he entered and asked Kwolczyk if Rachel was there. She had just arrived. Thor still chose to wait out in the street until he saw Carl's black AUDI a block away. He also looked around for suspicious activity, but did not spot anything in particular.

When Thor and Carl entered, Rachel was sitting at the small conference table and smiled cordially. Kwolczyk and the old guardian were also there, apparently waiting for them.

"Good" Kwolczyk said. "Let's get this over with."

Thor looked at Rachel as he sat down. She maintained her cordial smile but really did not exhibit any particular emotions. He waited for her to feel uncomfortable with him looking at her without saying anything, but she did not seem to have any problem with it at all. In fact, she seemed quite content with the situation.

Something was definitely wrong.

Carl took a seat right next to Thor.

"So" Kwolczyk continued. "Rachel has requested an update from you boys on what you have been doing since you completed the last mission."

"We report to you, colonel" Carl said.

"I guess you can do that now" Kwolczyk suggested.

"As we reported earlier" Carl continued, "we encountered a special forces team at Deep Saline. They tried to interfere with our operation, and we wonder what they were doing there."

"I've already checked that" Rachel said. "They were there on a training mission in preparation for overseas deployment."

"Why did they engage us, then?" Thor asked.

He really wanted to ask her how she knew that, but protocol banned him from doing that. He had no right to ask questions to a superior officer, except to clarify circumstances around orders he had been given.

"Evidently there was some kind of misunderstanding" Rachel said calmly, with an almost sweet tone in her voice.

"Your mission failed" Kwolczyk noted.

"The beacon must have been too old" Thor said. "It exploded when we tried to turn it on.

"What did you do afterward?"

"We went to a hideout to recuperate" Carl told him.

"Where?" Rachel asked.

Neither Carl nor Thor answered.

"Guys…" Kwolczyk said, with a voice that implied that if they did not answer he might have to order them to do it.

"Norman, Oklahoma" Thor lied.

"Where?" Rachel asked again.

"Motel Six."

She seemed content with the answer. She took her eyes off

them, looked at her cell phone and pushed a couple of buttons on it.

A second later they heard a loud bang. The bang shook the building and was followed by another bang. A window broke and a Molotov cocktail landed under one of the desks. Another flew in through the entrance door window and landed even closer. A third one came through another window.

This was it. Thor looked at the Molotov cocktails and saw the gasoline spilled out from the broken bottles. A split second later he turned back toward Rachel – and saw her holding a gun in her left hand. She pointed it at Colonel Kwolczyk and pulled the trigger.

Carl flew up from his chair and hurled himself across the table toward Rachel. But her reaction was too fast. She had another gun in her right hand and stopped him with two quick shots. Carl's charge at her had cut off Thor from confronting Rachel, so instead he rolled backwards, still in his chair, and pulled out his gun while still rolling.

He heard another two shots and felt a bullet ricochet his left leg.

Another Molotov cocktail broke through the entrance door window. The office was quickly engulfed in flames.

Thor quickly thrust himself to the side and took cover behind a cabinet when Rachel fired at him again. He stood up on his feet in a low stance and tried to hear where she was. But the increasing noise from the flames around him made it impossible to use ears to track an enemy. Instead he glanced around the corner of the cabinet.

His gun in his hand, he glanced again. Still no sight of her.

He hesitated for a split second, decided that she was waiting for him, and then fixed his eyes on the next corner where she should be waiting.

Nothing but fire.

He moved a step forward.

Still nothing.

Then – a shadow came out from behind the next corner. Instinctively Thor fired two shots. Rachel fell to the floor.

Or so he thought.

It was not Rachel. It was Carl. And he had just shot him two times in the chest.

"No!!" he screamed and took one more step forward.

He had stepped right into Rachel's trap. His gun was now visible from the other side of the cabinet corner. A quick, hard kick knocked it out of his hand. Then he saw her gun, pointing right at his face.

Thor threw himself right at Rachel, hoping to catch her off guard. But instead he felt a bullet hit him somewhere in the abdomen. His momentum continued and he would have fallen on the gun had Rachel not been lightning-quick to move to the side.

He crashed on to the floor and rolled over on the side.

"Bye, Thor" said Rachel, still smiling and uncannily indifferent to the fire around them.

She stood right by the entrance door, just a couple of feet away from it. She raised her gun and aimed at Thor's head.

Just as she was about to pull the trigger, a beam of white-glowing energy hit her in the back. She fell forward through the entrance door and out of Thor's sight.

Then he saw a mysterious dark figure, kind of blurry in the fire. The figure came over to him and hunkered down.

"Hi, buddy" the figure said.

Thor recognized the voice. But he could not see the face because the figure was wearing a helmet. And the wound in his abdomen was draining him of blood and quickly making him tired.

Goryell opened his visor.

"Let's get the Hell out of here, shall we?"

Thor was too weak to get up. Goryell kneeled and pulled him up. He put Thor's arm around his neck and held him up as Thor staggered through the flames toward the entrance. The door was completely shattered. Rachel was lying face down on the landing outside the door.

"Is she…" Thor said weakly.

"No, just knocked out for a while."

Goryell helped him down the stairs. Thor noted that Goryell was holding a weapon in his free hand. He wondered why, and then he remembered that someone had thrown Molotov cocktails in to their office. Rachel must have brought a whole team with her.

"Sorry I was late" Goryell said as if he could read Thor's mind. "I had to take care of her assault team first."

They reached the ground.

"Easy, my friend" Goryell warned Thor as he helped him over to his black Cadillac.

He gently placed Thor in the back seat.

"I'm gonna go get Carl out" he said and rushed up the stairs again.

Thor was dizzy. Suddenly he saw another man appear in the open car door. He started reaching for his gun but the man grabbed his hand and said something in a language Thor had never heard. Thor tried to call for Goryell, but his voice was getting very raspy and weak.

The man took out something that looked like a small flashlight. He pushed it against Thor's arm.

"Don't kill me" Thor mumbled.

The man said something, and again Thor could not understand him.

He tried to push the man away, but he fainted before his weak hand even reached the man's chest.

*   *   *

Thor woke up in a small room without windows. He was lying on a comfortable bed. A discrete light next to the bed allowed him to look around. He noticed a strange machine at the foot end of the bed.

The machine was hovering.

"Goryell" Thor said.

He suddenly remembered the fire at the office. And how he had been shot. He moved his hand to where he remembered that the bullet had pierced his abdomen. There was something strange there. It felt like a very smooth Band Aid.

He lifted the cover and glanced down.

"What the…?"

It looked like a piece of skin where the bullet wound had been.

"Please stay calm."

He looked around.

"Who said that?"

"Please stay calm."

The voice came from that hovering robot.

"Who are you?" Thor asked, baffled as he was at the talking machine.

"I am nurse-bot AY two, Series D, Unit eighty six. Please remain in bed."

"No robot is telling me what to do" Thor said and got out of bed.

"Health alert, health alert" the nurse-bot said.

The door to the room opened. The man Thor had seen in Goryell's car appeared. He was wearing a discrete grey jump suit and a set of instruments in a waist belt. He stopped and looked at Thor. Thor looked at him. Then the man turned and yelled something out toward the hallway.

Goryell came in.

"Hey, Thor, good to see you're up and running again!"

"I'm not so sure about the running..."

Thor felt weak. He could not quite stretch his body.

"Where am I?"

"Back in New Mexico. We flew you out here so we could heal you fast. A normal hospital would have kept you in for weeks with those wounds."

Thor suddenly realized that he had similar strange patches on his arms and his face.

"That's HealSkin" Goryell explained. "Doc here knows a few tricks."

"But I was shot..."

"He got the bullet out and HealSkin has been repairing your tissue around the clock. You're almost there. You need..." and he conferred with the doctor, "...a few more hours. Then you'll be fine."

Thor sat down on the bed again. Then he remembered:

"Where's Carl?"

"He's in another room. He's in bad shape but he'll make it. Would have died in a normal hospital."

"Thank God. I think I shot him accidentally."

"He'll pull through. You're strong, healthy fellas."

Goryell smiled at Thor.

Then his face turned serious.

"It looks like we're going to see some real action soon. The Zoh'moorians have stepped up their plans. Their invasion is imminent."

Thor stared at him.

"How long have I been…?"

"Twenty two hours. It's eight AM. The Zoh'moorian fleet will be entering this solar system in a matter of hours. We expect they will surround Earth with their invasion fleet over the next day, two at the most."

Thor sat down on his bed again.

"I thought it would take a couple of weeks before they would come."

"Apparently they've accelerated their plans."

"What about your strike group?"

Goryell shook his head.

"There's a political deadlock back home. The strike group can't get involved until that's been resolved."

He took a step forward.

"Our politicians are arguing over a constitutional issue. They can go on for a long time. The best way to break their deadlock would be if your government sent a plea directly to our government."

"A plea for help? Are you kidding me? Our own vice president is in cahoots with the Zoh'moorians! For all we know, the president might be in on it as well!"

"That's right. We need someone to convince Stanton to change her mind."

"No one can do that. Besides, how are we going to even get to talk to one of them?"

Goryell smiled.

"We have an ace up our sleeves."

"What do you mean?"

"Rachel."

Thor jumped to his feet, causing the nurse-bot to start yelling "Health Alert" again. The doctor said something to it and the nurse-bot left the room.

"Did… did you capture Rachel?" Thor asked excitedly.

"I did. We have her here. We'll go talk to her in a couple of hours when you're feeling better."

When Thor eventually got to see Rachel again he could barely contain himself. She was sitting on the floor, her hands locked behind her back and her legs tied together by some sort of metal bands. He still felt a bit weak, but he would have no problem killing her right there.

Rachel, on the other hand, was calm and smiled that uncanny smile again.

"Good morning, Thor" she said cordially.

"You're dead" Thor whispered at her. "Dead like the rat you are."

Rachel looked at him calmly.

Thor turned to Goryell.

"Let me take care of her. I'll make her talk."

Goryell looked at him, then at Rachel. Then he looked at Thor again. He was clearly contemplating something.

"We have had her in here all night" he noted. "She has not made any concessions whatsoever."

"Have you given her a reason to talk? I can do it."

Goryell did not respond. He walked over to the door and said something to the guard. The guard left the room.

"We just need to do one thing first" Goryell said.

"What?"

"You'll see. But we need to act fast. The Zoh'moorians will be here soon."

Goryell looked sternly at Rachel as he mentioned the Zoh'moorians. She clearly reacted to the mentioning of the aliens, but only for a second or two. Then she quickly resumed her neutral posture.

Apparently she was going to do everything she could to be uncooperative.

The guard returned. Tahm Qaar and another agent came in with him. Goryell walked over to them and they talked quietly for a moment. While they were talking in hushed voices Thor took a step closer to Rachel. She did not even look at him. She was intensely focused on the small group over by the door. It was almost as if she tried to read their lips.

"Traitor" Thor said quietly.

"I will kill you before the day is over" Rachel replied, her eyes fixed on the three men over at the door.

"I can end your life right now, with one swift stroke."

"Don't flatter yourself."

Goryell came over to them with Tahm Qaar right behind. They stopped right in front of Rachel and talked briefly again. Then Tahm Qaar hunkered down and looked Rachel straight in the eyes. He showed no emotions whatsoever and did not give away anything as to what they were talking about.

Tahm Qaar stood up again and nodded toward Goryell. He said something and asked the third agent to come forward. He did the same thing, only he sat down longer and also pulled out a tiny instrument. He pushed a small button and a very tiny metallic arm shot out from it. He directed it straight toward Rachel's cheek. She bent her head to the side to avoid it.

"Don't resist" Tahm Qaar said. "Your eyes gave you away. We only want a skin sample."

Rachel looked up at him. She still tried to avoid the metallic arm.

"If you keep on resisting I will terminate you right now" Tahm Qaar said rather forcefully.

Thor watched it all with amazement.

"Very well" Rachel said. "Go ahead."

She sat up straight again and the metallic arm scratched her cheek twice. Then it withdrew back in to the flashlight-looking device. The third agent brought it with him as he left the room.

"Good job, guys" Tahm Qaar said to Goryell and Thor and left.

"What was that all about?" Thor asked.

Goryell looked at him and smiled.

"Thor, this woman here…"

"Yeah, what about her?"

"She looks like a woman, right?"

"You betcha! If she wasn't so evil I might even find her attractive."

"Well... I'm sorry to ruin your day, my friend, but this woman here... she's not a woman."

"What?? You mean she's a... a... cross dresser?? I don't believe you!"

"She's no man either."

"What the Hell are you talking about?"

Goryell looked at Rachel. She was looking back at him with the same calm as before. But the smile was gone.

"If you look at the iris in her eyes, very carefully, you will see rapid pattern fluctuations. The patterns appear with a regular cycle. Pattern one, then pattern two, then pattern one again, then pattern three."

Thor was dumbfounded.

"I don't have a clue what you're talking about" he said slowly.

"The iris pattern fluctuations are caused by a microprocessor" Goryell continued calmly. "Each pattern is used to gather a specific kind of information about..."

"Wait... micro... microprocessor?"

"Yes."

"I don't believe this... are you saying that... that Rachel is..."

"An android? Yes, Thor. Rachel is an android."

*   *   *

DEFIANCE

The day after professor Pinkhouse had taken Alexis out to dinner was not a very good day in the grad student dorm. Alexis refused to come out from her room and Todd, who had gotten an intimidating phone call from the university president's office, was chain smoking illegally imported Mexican *Fuerte* cigarettes.

Jack, who had given up trying to talk to Alexis about her dinner, went out on the porch to talk to Todd instead.

"Why are those cigarettes illegal here?" he asked.

"Because they're too strong."

Todd's reply was somewhere between indifferent and depressed. He did not look very happy at all.

"So the federal government thinks they know better what cigarettes you should kill yourself with?"

"Apparently."

Todd was still somewhere else.

"Who called you before?"

"The fucking president's office."

"What did they want?"

"Remind me that there would be consequences if I don't show up to that hearing."

Jack looked at his watch.

"You're not going to the fair speech hearing, are you?"

"Nope."

"They start in two minutes."

"Yep."

Todd killed his fourth straight cigarette. Jack did not have anything to say, so he typed a message on his iWorld to Walid.

"Who you writing?" Todd asked.

"Walid."

"Oh… him. Haven't heard from him in a while."

Todd was loosening up. Apparently he needed some company.

"He wants to do something about the fair speech law" Jack said. "Some conference or protest down in Washington."

"He's a good guy" Todd noted.

"You're the first one to be prosecuted in the whole country."

"I'm not going to be prosecuted" Todd protested. "That's why I'm here and not at the hearing."

"I sure hope they'll accept your absence and let go. But I gotta say you're taking a big fat risk."

"What the Hell can they do?" Todd chuckled.

He was more upbeat now.

Unfortunately, professor Pinkhouse would soon put an end to that. Half an hour after Todd was supposed to appear before the fair speech board professor Pinkhouse was almost boiling over with fury. He was there to present his case and had looked forward all morning to this chance to squish that obnoxious, insubordinate little brat called Todd Salmon like a cockroach under his shoe.

And what did that little weasel do? He simply refused to show up.

Who did he think he was?

Professor Pinkhouse talked to the dean of student affairs, who was the chair of the fair speech board.

"This is not a good start for the enforcement of fair speech" he told the dean. "We can't allow the first student to be prosecuted to get away just by being absent. We have to do something drastic."

"Yes" the dean said. "I agree. Well, his absence is a disciplinary code violation. That makes him eligible for forcible appearance."

Professor Pinkhouse got a rush when he heard the words 'forcible appearance'.

"Does that mean you can send the campus police out to get him?!"

"Yes."

"Oh, wow! Let's do it. Let's bring him in by force. Right now!"

Five minutes later two campus cops rang the doorbell at the grad student dorm. Charon Outcaster opened and almost screamed with fear when he saw two police officers outside the door.

"Jack! Jack!! The police is here!!"

Jack left the porch and went out in the hallway, just in time to almost collide with the two cops.

"Todd Salmon?" asked one of them. "You're under arrest. Come with us, please."

"I'm not Todd Salmon" said Jack.

"Come with us, please."

"I'm not Todd Salmon" Jack repeated.

"Then who are you?"

"Jack Nordlander."

"Is that a Kroatian name?" asked one of the cops.

"Scandinavian."

"Sounds more Caucasian to me" said the other cop.

"Where is Todd Salmon?" asked the first cop.

"I'm here" Todd said from the porch. "Whaddayawant?"

Todd was brought in to the fair speech board panel fifteen minutes after the dean's call to campus police. He was handcuffed behind his back and white-faced with anger. Professor Pinkhouse looked at him and smiled. 'Maybe I'll order them to take his pants off, too' he thought.

The dean of student affairs pointed to a single chair that had been placed in the middle of the room. One of the police officers placed Todd on the chair and they both positioned themselves behind him, arms crossed over their chests and faces looking as stiff as they could.

"Shall we remove his handcuffs?" one of them asked.

"No, leave them on" professor Pinkhouse suggested with a weird smile on his face.

"Yeah" said the dean. "Leave'em on. And stay here and keep an eye on him. He seems to be a little upset."

The other board members giggled.

"So…" the dean said slowly and casually, looking at his notes. "Let's get started, then, shall we?"

He looked down at Todd.

"Uh, you are Todd Salmon, right?"

"What kind of joke is this?!" Todd asked. "Who the Hell do you think you are?!"

"Oh, I know quite well who I am. I'm the dean of student affairs. I'm just trying to determine who you are."

Mild laughter from the other board members. Professor Pinkhouse did not laugh, though. He glanced at the dean with a slight touch of irritation in his eyes. He wanted to tell all the jokes everyone was laughing at.

"You know damned well who I am!" Todd yelled back at him.

"We're only here to help you" said a female board member to the right of the dean.

Todd did not recognize her.

"I don't need your help, thank you very much" Todd said with exaggerated politeness.

"Alright" said professor Pinkhouse, who was standing at a desk to the right of Todd. "Let's get going with this. You have violated the fair speech code. That's a serious offense and we are here to determine whether the accusation has enough merit to put you on trial and have you dismissed from the school."

Oh, man, was he on a roll now! Professor Pinkhouse even got sexually aroused from the power rush he got. For some reason Alexis Anchorage flashed past his eyes – especially her cleavage…

The dean, however, was not nearly as happy about professor Pinkhouse's frivolous blabbering.

"Yes, yes, Prescott" he said. "But let's stick to protocol. I'll give you ample time to talk later. Right now…"

"You wrote the accusation yourself, so why this charade?" Todd interrupted him, looking at professor Pinkhouse.

"You have the right to a fair trial and a good hanging" professor Pinkhouse shot back, making the entire board laugh – except the dean, of course.

He had prepared that one very carefully.

"Are you accusing professor Pinkhouse of being partial in this case?" asked the other lady on the panel.

Todd recognized her as a librarian.

"He's both a part in this case and the prosecutor" Todd pointed out. "So yes, I think he is biased, very much, indeed, thank you."

"That's quite audacious of you!" she exclaimed. "Without the slightest shred of evidence, at that!"

"For your protection" professor Pinkhouse said mildly, "we have appointed an impartial faculty member to be your defense counselor."

"Wait, Prescott!" the dean said, a bit upset. "I thought I was going to get a chance to say that!"

Professor Pinkhouse smiled and shrugged his shoulders.

"By all means, do say it" he said.

"Uh... well" the dean stumbled, "we have impartially dismembered a faculty appointee in your defense."

A door in a corner in the back of the room opened. Todd glanced over his shoulder.

It was professor Varnek.

"See" professor Pinkhouse smiled at Todd. "We're being very fair and balanced here. Just like your favorite TV network."

"What??" Todd exclaimed while the board members burst out in laughter.

Even the dean giggled this time.

"I guess we can start now" professor Pinkhouse smiled at Todd. "Laura, go ahead."

"Yes" the dean said quickly. "Get along, Laura."

Professor Varnek positioned herself at some spot to the right and behind Todd, so he could not see her. When he tried to turn his handcuffs bit in to his wrists, so he had to remain seated facing the board.

"Thank you" said professor Varnek energetically. "This is the college's first case under the fair speech code. It is therefore important that we try it with the utmost rigor and attention to detail."

Todd raised his eyebrows. The dean noted it and looked at him and tried to look important.

"This case" professor Varnek continued, "was reported to the dean of student affairs by the chair of the department of political economy, professor Prescott Pinkhouse. The report reads as follows: While attending a class in political economy, Todd Salmon provoked a discussion with the class instructor, professor Pinkhouse. Said student expressed…"

"I provoked a discussion?!" Todd burst out. "You gotta be kidding me!"

"Shut up!" yelled professor Pinkhouse. "Let Laura finish!"

"The defendant will be shot up until we let Laura finish you off" the dean said, pointing right at Todd with his index finger.

"Thank you" said professor Varnek. "Said student expressed a strictly one-sided opinion about the topic that was being discussed. Said student refused to utter an opposing view when the professor asked him to do so. Instead, he emphasized his…"

"A one-sided opinion??" Todd said, almost falling off the chair as he tried to turn and look at professor Varnek. "And you call her my defense counselor??"

"You heard right" professor Pinkhouse said, restraining his frustration over Todd's obvious unwillingness to subordinate. "One more interruption and I will have you locked up over night."

"Uh… that would be me" the dean said.

"I can have you locked up, too" said professor Pinkhouse said and harvested loud laughs from the other panel members.

"You want me knocked up?"

"No, *locked* up."

"Me?"

"No, him."

"Who?"

"Him."

"Oh… *him*."

The ladies on the board were still laughing, but they quickly resumed their important postures when they noted how Todd was humbled by the stern warning.

"Said student emphasized his one-sided opinion numerous times" professor Varnek continued, "and refused to acknowledge the instructing professor's suggestions that there was another side to the issue."

Professor Varnek stopped briefly, apparently to sort through her papers.

"That is the case against Todd Salmon" she concluded and handed her stack of papers over to the dean of student affairs.

"Thanks, Laura" said the dean and pretended to examine her papers for a moment. "Well, Todd Salmon, your defense has spoken. I shall now give the word to the opposite side of this issue, professor Pinkhouse."

"You call that a defense?!" Todd exclaimed. "I'd rather speak for myself, thank you very much!"

"Time now for the other side of this to be…"

"This is a farce and a sick joke! You're just as lopsided as I was and therefore you should be prosecuted yourself."

"Aha!" professor Pinkhouse said. "An admission of guilt! Please note that in the transcript."

"Uh… we don't have a transcript" the dean said.

"Well, note it *somewhere*, then."

"I can send you an e-mail from my iWorld" the dean suggested and proudly showed the panel members his new portable multimedia platform.

"One more thing" Todd continued. "You are infringing on my right to free speech. I will sue you under the First Amendment."

Professor Pinkhouse's face was cut in half by a raving laughter. The dean was surprised by the laugh. He was just showing one of the other panel members some feature the iWorld had. He looked at professor Pinkhouse and smiled insecurely. Then he glanced around the room and realized that everyone else except Todd was laughing, so he started laughing, too.

Even Professor Varnek laughed, but only after looking at professor Pinkhouse. She had no idea what they were laughing at.

It seemed like the laughter went on forever. When it eventually died away professor Pinkhouse wiped tears from his eyes with a napkin.

"It's been a long time since I heard something so funny" he said. "I never knew you had such a sense of humor, Todd."

"You think it's funny that the college is sued for violating the First Amendment?" Todd said, sincerely surprised.

"Yes" professor Pinkhouse said and returned to his serious self. "It's funny. Because we are not the government. We're a private entity. We can do whatever we want."

"Besides" the dean of faculty added, trying hard to be the biggest authority in the room. "We're doing this in order to comply with the Fair Speech Act. We're enforcing that law."

"If you're not the government, then you have no jurisdiction to enforce the law" Todd Salmon noted.

Professor Pinkhouse started laughing again. Everyone else except Todd also laughed. Professor Varnek burst out in the biggest laugh of them all because she finally understood what was so funny.

"A farce!" she laughed. "He thinks this is a farce!!"

Professor Pinkhouse stopped laughing and looked at her.

"Uh... yes, sure, whatever" he mumbled. "I don't even think we need to argue this case anymore. I suggest you vote on this now and find him guilty as Hell."

"Yeah" the dean agreed, still laughing. "Hell, he's guilty!"

The fair speech board agreed. After 7.3 seconds of deliberation they found Todd Salmon guilty as Hell of violating the Fair Speech Act. The dean slammed his palm in the desk and rushed off to his car. He had to go home and endure a dinner with his mother in law who always talked and never let anyone else get a word in.

*   *   *

"So let me see if I get this right" Ross Landau said to Tahm Qaar. "The vice president of the United States has invited a bunch of ugly aliens to invade Earth so that she can seize global power."

"Correct, sir."

"And this invasion was scheduled for... well... Independence Day... like that movie. But they, the Zoh'moorians, have now sped up the schedule and are entering this solar system as we speak."

"Yes."

"And," Ross said and took a deep breath, "our vice president... our lesbian vice president... has a lover who is an android!"

"Correct again, sir."

Ross Landau laughed. He laughed and pounded on the desk in front of him and laughed a little more.

"I'm sorry" he said and wiped a tear from his eye. "I can't help it. I've been watching the Stantons for twenty years and I know they are among the sleaziest, most dangerous people you can imagine. I thought I knew all there was to know about them. Apparently I was wrong."

He chuckled again.

"I bet you she knows Rhea is an android. And she gets a kick out of it."

Then his face turned serious.

"I'm concerned about this invasion" he said. "I take it they are technologically superior to us."

"Yes" Tahm Qaar said. "But that does not mean they will defeat your military. We have millennia of military history to prove that technologically inferior powers can defeat hi-tech enemies."

"Yes, so do we" Ross said. "The Revolutionary War is a good example. But if Oslow or Stanton orders the military to stand down, chances are they will. See... what I think is going on here is that she will give the impression of being totally surprised by this. And then she will tell the public to just take it easy while she... talks to the Zoh'moorians. And from these talks some phony compromise will emerge that makes it look like she's cooperating with them when in reality she is rolling out the carpet for them. And the man child will be completely steamrolled by her."

"If they follow the most logical invasion procedure" Tahm Qaar said, "they will take their time to place the invasion fleet in orbit around Earth. That will probably take about a day. Would it be possible that you could be ahead of their schedule and warn people about this? On your show... It could disrupt Holly Stanton's plans."

"I cannot be the first one to talk about this. It would... make me look ridiculous. See, believing in extra-terrestrial life is still considered kooky here on Earth."

Tahm Qaar smiled.

"I think every civilized people hold that belief at some point. They're the crown of creation."

"But once the invasion begins" Ross continued, "I will gladly let my listeners hear the truth. If this is indeed a worldwide coup by Holly Stanton, she will shut down the media. Just like she wants to kill off her opposition. But I'll be on the air. AM radio is very hard to shut down. Plus I broadcast over the Grid."

"We should take precautionary measures just in case. I'll have my engineer work with you on how to make sure you stay on the air even if they shut down all the radio stations that carry your show."

"How would you do that?"

"I'll leave that to the engineering wizard. What matters is that we keep you on the air. Your people will need you, Ross. What else can we do for you?"

"Get my staff out here on the double."

Tahm Qaar promised to take care of that. But first he needed to check in with Goryell on the interrogations he was trying to hold with Rachel.

Or, as they now knew her, Rhea.

"The question now" said Goryell, "is how we use Rhea and what we know about her to get through to Stanton."

"I have an idea" said Thor and smiled conspicuously.

*   *   *

It was high noon in Washington, DC and President Oslow's chief of staff got a call from a person who claimed to be Irwin Schwepp. The president's chief of staff knew that Irwin had died in an accident recently. His first thought was that he was the target of a bad prank. But the caller had given Irwin's secret White House ID code. It would be very difficult for outsiders to get hold of it.

So he decided to take the call in his office.

"Yes?"

"Andrew Ayers?"

"Speaking."

"This message is for the president. We know all about the vice president's collaboration with the alien power. We know that she has been in contact with the Zoh'moorians. We are holding Rhea captive and we are willing to release her if the vice president stops collaborating with the Zoh'moorians."

Andrew Ayers was dumbfounded. He had no idea what this man was talking about. Sure, the man sounded authentic enough, and he had used Irwin Schwepp's access code. But the story he told was so incredible that Ayers did not know if he should laugh or cry. And it was certainly nothing he wanted to bother the president with. Besides, president Oslow was busy preparing a speech he was going to give to community organizers in Cincinnati tomorrow. He did not want to be disturbed, especially not with such petty things as political pranks.

"This is a very bad prank" he said. "I have no time for pranks. I will ask Secret Service to trace your call."

"Go right ahead" the man answered. "I'll wait."

His calm, confident tone surprised Ayers. Why did he not just hang up and run for cover?

"The president would be well advised to ask the vice president about the Zoh'moorians" the man continued.

"The... Zoh'moorians...?" Ayers said with a smirk on his face.

He really wanted to believe that this guy was just a prankster.

"Ask the vice president" the man continued. "And when you do, let her know that Rhea has one hour left to live."

The chilling matter-of-factly voice made Ayers unsure of what to do.

"Who is Rhea?" he tried, but the man hung up.

Normally, he might have notified the Secret Service. And he was no longer convinced that it was all just a sick joke. But if he bothered president Oslow with it he would make himself look stupid.

He really wanted to dismiss the whole thing. But that voice had sounded so convincing, so authoritative. The man's words kept echoing in his head.

Andrew Ayers got up and walked out of his office. He needed to talk to someone about this. But who? He was the chief of staff, so basically there was nobody else between him and the president.

There had to be someone on the staff he could talk to. But he really did not know most of them that well. President Oslow had handpicked people for every job, and Ayers had not had much of a say in it. So most of them were loyal to Oslow, not to him.

But there was one person he could talk to. He made a left turn and continued down the hall toward the office of the president's chief speech writer. He knew her and trusted her.

Unfortunately, she was not in.

He stood outside her office for a moment and wondered what to do. A couple of staffers walked by and said "hi". He smiled briefly at them and decided to continue down the hall toward another section where not so many of the president's staffers were roaming around.

At the intersection of two hallways he ran in to Sheila Smith, the vice president's chief of staff.

"Oh, hi, Andrew, you're just the one I was looking for!"

"Oh, OK. What about?"

"We need to schedule a few meetings about the trip to Australia and the visit from the president of the EU."

"Uh… sure. Let me see…"

He pulled out his organizer. While he flipped through some notes and pulled up the right page, the phone call kept ringing in his ears. It must have made him look distracted.

"Are you OK, Andy?" Sheila asked.

"Yes. Sure. Well… I got this… strange phone call."

"Oh, really? What about?"

"Well…" Andrew started and looked up at her.

One of his staffers walked by behind her. He smiled cordially at the man and waited until he had turned a corner.

"Someone called using Irwin Schwepp's access code."

"Irwin?! But he's dead!"

"I know. So I thought it was just a prank. He started talking about some woman named Rhea, and…"

Sheila frowned.

"What about her?" Andrew asked.

"Oh, nothing… It's just… a friend of the Stanton's."

"Really? Well, he also mentioned something incredulous. He talked about some… and I know you're gonna think I'm nuts for taking this seriously… some aliens called Zoh'moorians…"

Sheila's reaction was totally opposite to what Andrew had expected. Instead of breaking out in laughter and telling him to have a beer and relax, her face turned dead serious and she stared at Andrew for a couple of seconds like she had seen a ghost.

"What?" he asked.

"Nothing... nothing at all. What exactly did he say about Rhea?"

"That they, whoever they are, are holding her captive."

Sheila's face turned pale.

"Andrew, will you excuse me? My cell phone is vibrating. I'll talk to you later about those scheduling things..."

She turned around and started walking away from him, while searching her pockets for her cell phone. Andrew noted that she had it attached to a belt in her pants and wondered how she could feel that it was vibrating when it was inside a thick leather case.

He walked back toward his office, even more confused than before. Sheila's reaction had stunned him. He was a hundred percent convinced that she was going to laugh hysterically, but instead she had turned around and rushed back toward the vice president's office.

What did that tell him? That she was going to tell Holly Stanton that Barry Oslow's chief of staff was a complete wing nut? Of course not. Even if she thought so, she would have left it to the president to decide who he wanted for the job.

No, there had to be something else behind this.

What if the caller had actually told him the truth? What if...?

*   *   *

TERROR

I'm back in the cage. I don't know why, but I feel that the creatures are not happy with me. I wonder what I did. I always spend my days quietly talking to the others, or memorizing and repeating what I have been through here. That's like meditation. It doesn't bother anyone.

I don't bother anyone. I am trying to be as good as I can. After so many years, I thought I knew how to please them so they would not punish me. I don't ask for anything. If you try to ask for something they punish you severely. They do not communicate with us. They use us for their... experiments. And they're not interested in communicating. I have learned that. I have learned to behave in a way that does not bother them.

At least, that's what I thought.

They were rough when they came to pick me up. Normally they lower one of their robots and grab you by the chest. They lift you up with it, up from the dungeon. Then they carry you to where they want you to be. I'm glad they use their robots. Those creatures are so hideous I would not want anyone of them to touch me.

But this time they used their... their web. A funnel web was lowered, and one of them was inside. It reached down and grabbed me. Hard.

I panicked at first. I thought it was going to kill me. Maybe bite me with its fangs. Inject some sort of venom.

But it did not kill me. It wrapped me in the web and we were lifted up from the dungeon. They kept me wrapped up in the web and one of them carried me.

The smell was terrible. And it held me with two of its legs, and I felt the sharp needles on the legs against my body.

Then it threw me on the floor underneath the cage. It and another creature reached down with their heads. Oh, God! Those eyes! Those horrible, horrible eyes! Hundreds of them… in the eye sockets of a human-like skull… and those – those fangs…

One of them poked at me with its fangs. I was sure it was going to eat me. But it didn't. It probably only wanted to frighten me.

Then they took me out of the web and put me here.

I am terrified. What are they going to do now?

*   *   *

OPPORTUNITY

Sheila rushed straight back to her office and dialed the special number for Air Force Two.

"Put me through to the vice president" she said to the person who answered.

"She is in a meeting, ma'm."

"Tell her I need to discuss Raleigh with her" Sheila said.

Raleigh was the code word for Rhea.

"I'll tell her that when her meeting is over."

"Tell her that now" Sheila said very sternly. "If you tell her after the meeting she will make you regret it."

"Uh... yes, ma'm."

While Sheila waited she thought about the other thing that Andrew had mentioned. Some aliens called Zoh'moorians?

Sheila had heard strange parts of conversations between the vice president and her brother. Sometimes she had thought she heard them talk about some alien civilization, outer space travel, visiting another planet. But there could not possibly be anything to that, could it?

"Yes, Sheila?"

"Holly, hi, I'm sorry to interrupt your meeting, but I have important updates about Raleigh."

"Let me call you right back."

Sheila stared out the window while she waited. She repeated the name of those aliens to herself.

"Zoh'moorians" she whispered. "Little green men…?"

When the phone rang she first double-checked that her office door was shut. Then she picked up the receiver.

"What about Rhea?" the vice president asked.

"I just talked to Andrew Ayers. He got an anonymous phone call. The person used Irwin's access code. And then he claimed that he has Rhea and that he knows about… some aliens."

The vice president was quiet for a moment.

"What aliens?" she asked reluctantly.

"The Zoh'moorians."

"And he said he's got Rhea?"

Holly Stanton's voice was chillingly cold. Sheila knew that meant that she was not supposed to have this conversation with the vice president.

"Yes."

"Did he say anything else?"

"I can ask the telephone switchboard for a transcript of the phone call."

"Yes, and send it by fax to me right away."

Holly Stanton hung up. She glanced out the window. They were passing over Kansas. All she saw was clouds. The horizon was clear and the weather further ahead looked nice. A forecast for Denver was sunny and warm.

Sheila's phone call had made her angry and frustrated. She could handle a lot of difficult situations and make tough decisions without blinking.

But this was personal. Very personal.

And worse: someone knew about the Zoh'moorians and had started spreading the word around. Even to the president's office.

This was serious. There was a big risk that she could lose control over the situation, especially if Barry Oslow got involved.

She called the only person she could discuss the situation with.

"Yeah."

"Walt, it's me."

"Hi, sis. How are you?"

"I need to talk to you. Call me on a secure line."

"Sure, I'll call you tonight. I'm right in the middle of…"

"No, call me now. This is about Raleigh and... our visitors."

"Oh. Alright. OK. Give me a minute."

It felt like ten minutes before her brother called her back.

"What's going on?"

"Walt, Sheila called. She knows."

"Then kill her."

"It's not that simple. She heard it from Andy Ayers."

"How the Hell does he know?"

"Someone, I guess Branch Four, called him and told him they have kidnapped Rhea."

"So that's why we haven't heard from her."

"And the caller also knows about the Zoh'moorians."

"And he told Andy Ayers who told Sheila?"

"Right."

"Well, then we do have a problem. It's only a matter of time before the man-child knows about this. Can you handle him, or do you want me to talk to him?"

"No, I'll talk to him tonight when I get back to DC."

"Did that caller say anything about what he wants to release Rhea?"

"I'm waiting for Sheila to fax me a transcript of the phone call."

The fax in her office started making noises.

"Wait, Walt, I think it's coming now."

She reached over and grabbed the paper that was coming out of the fax.

"Yes" she said to the telephone. "This is it. Let me see... Oh, here it is. He says that he is willing to release Rhea if I stop collaborating with the Zoh'moorians."

"Well, then we have to assume the Branch Four agents know everything. We're gonna have to act fast to contain this. Talk to the man-child tonight and I'll put Harry on tracking down the Branch Four agents."

"Harry? He's an amateur!"

"He's the best we've got, sis."

"You'll only get him killed. If he can even find them. I'd rather not waste him on this."

"Alright. What do you want me to do about this?"

"Call the Supreme General and explain the situation."

"I'm sure they will have no problem with speeding up the whole process. Their fleet is out there at their halfway point, just idling. They can be here in a couple of days if we ask them."

"Yes. Yes, Walt, let's do that. Let's do this now."

*   *   *

After the Federal Assembly had temporarily halted the plan to send Strike Group 14 to sector KB, the young Delegate Narkeenis went back to his home world. He had local offices all over the planet, but his main office was in his hometown, a village on a small continent that stretched along the equator. He was well known even for being a Delegate to the Federal Assembly. He often made vocal policy statements, but at the end of the day politicians like him were second-tier news compared to business, culture, sports and social events. After all, the Danarvian Federation – or, as it was formally known, The Free Federation of Danarvia – had a minimal government, tightly constrained by the Charter of Liberty. So there were not that many reasons to write about what politicians did in the first place.

For that reason it was hard even for a high-profile politician like Narkeenis to draw any notable crowds to his press conferences. To boost the interest among media he had hired a communications director who helped make his press releases and press conferences seem a lot more interesting than they were.

That had increased the attendance at his press conferences and even made his staff excited about them.

Like this particular morning when Narkeenis walked in and told his chief of staff to call a press conference.

"Yes, sir, you bet!" said his communications director.

The other three staffers stopped what they were doing and focused their entire interest on the delegate and his communications director.

"What's it going to be about?" she asked.

"Let's talk about that in my room" Narkeenis said and brought her with him in to his small room in the back of the office.

After Narkeenis shut the door behind them he sat down and put his finger tips together in front of his face. His communications director knew that this meant that he was about to say something important. That excited her, but it also made her a bit concerned. They had a short holiday coming right up and she had planned to go visit her parents who lived on a nearby space hub. She hoped it would not be something that would require overtime.

"I have something very important to announce" Narkeenis said. "And I cannot tell anyone at this point, not even you. It is not out of mistrust – I just don't want to burden you with a big secret, even for the rest of the morning. I want this press conference at lunch so that the big networks are coming."

"Oh, that sounds important indeed" the communications director smiled.

"Yes. Yes, it is important. I will also have to do some traveling over the holiday. Have Yun Ro schedule stops for me at these local offices."

He gave her a list of offices that he had in the six largest cities on the planet.

"It's a big trip" she said, clearly impressed. "I will give it to her right away."

Then she reluctantly looked at him.

"Uh… sir."

"Yes?"

"Will this traveling involve me? I mean, I will do it of course, I just need to change some plans for the holiday if…"

"You were planning to see your parents, right?"

"Right."

"In that case… why don't you take the holiday off as planned. I will ask Yun Ro to come with me."

"Thank you, sir."

Throughout the morning the staff sensed that something big was going to happen. Narkeenis did not reveal anything. Instead he spent most of the morning in his office, behind a closed door.

On top of his to-do list was a call to Delegate Quim, who was back on Teura Vaar.

Quim was sitting at his desk in his headquarters in the Teuran capital. He had the multifunction flat screen on the wall right next to him. The screen was split so that the upper left corner gave him a constant stream of live news coverage while the lower left corner displayed incoming messages. Earthlings would call them "e-mails", although these were video-sound-written in any combination the sender chose. Most of them opened a direct, live two-way communication with the sender.

The screen also announced incoming calls.

Quim used the right half of the screen for his word processing program. Of course, he did not type. A small microphone hovered right before his mouth and he spoke very softly the words he wanted to type.

He still had a keyboard, elegantly melted in to the top on his desk, which was made of something that mostly looked like frozen plasma. But like most people, Quim only used the keyboard for master commands.

He could of course also use a brain sensor for typing. They were very popular and came in many different versions. The most common ones were attached to certain spots on your head and then you simply thought the words you wanted to type. But Quim belonged to a technologically more conservative generation and preferred the old fashioned hovering microphone.

A discrete light blinked in the lower left corner. It indicated that a message was coming through from someone on Quim's priority list. He paused his typing and turned off the hovering mike. On his left hand he had a small device attached to his index finger. He pointed it at the screen and a small light appeared. He directed the light at the highlighted message and gently touched the device on his finger with his thumb.

The highlighted message was opened and displayed in the entire lower left corner of the screen.

It was from Delegate Narkeenis. His face appeared.

"Good afternoon, my dear friend" Quim said. "Or is it morning where you are?"

"Yes, sir, it is morning. I have arranged the press conference."

"Splendid. Will any of the galaxy networks cover it?"

"I have invited all six of them."

"Good. Best of luck."

"Thank you, sir."

The first journalists dropped in a half hour before the press conference and started poking around among the staffers to get a heads-up on what this was all about. They soon became frustrated with the fact that nobody seemed to know anything, but their instincts told them that if the Delegate was so tight-lipped that he did not even tell his own staff – then it just had to be big.

They were right.

Exactly on time, Delegate Narkeenis stepped out from his office and sat down in an armchair that was somewhat elevated compared to the couches where the reporters were seated. To his delight, five of the six galaxy networks were there, and their reporters notified their viewers that he was coming out of his office.

Good. They were broadcasting live.

Some of them still used old-fashioned headset cameras where the reporter carried a small, pencil-size camera strapped on to his skull with a tiny metallo-plastic band. Those cameras were great for on-scene broadcasting of big events, and they had level dampeners to neutralize the reporter's head moves when he moved. But they were also of limited use, especially when the reporter wanted to be on screen. Many reporters got a kick out of having their faces broadcast across the galaxy, so some networks had bought hovering camera-bots. They used ages-old anti-gravity technology, shrunk to the size of a machine that could fit in your palm. The reporter basically carried the camera-bot in his pocket or in his bag, then activated it when needed and calibrated it to always stay in his vicinity. He controlled it via remote control, typically a finger-mounted pointer of the same kind as Delegate Quim used to navigate his computer screen.

"Welcome to this press conference" said Narkeenis. "I've been doing them for a while now and I feel like I know some of you personally."

He paused and let the reporters giggle.

"However, this press conference is about a serious matter. It is about something that is of utmost importance to our trust in the institutions of our government. I strongly and firmly believe that the limited powers that we have vested in our government, must not be exceeded or abused, but must instead be cared for with the highest diligence."

He paused and let the words sink in.

"Unfortunately, the current members of the Executive Office have recently shown that they do not live up to that standard. Let me tell you why."

He gave a stack of electronic notepads to his chief of staff who distributed them among the reporters.

"A military conflict has evolved in sector KB. On a world called Earth one of the national governments has asked for military help from a neighboring world, called Zoh'moor. It appears as though this military support will be used by that national government to expand control over Earth. Our Executive Office has learned about this conflict and decided to intervene militarily."

This caused some commotion among the reporters. They tried to interrupt Narkeenis with questions, but he raised his hand and asked them to wait.

"Obviously, neither Earth nor Zoh'moor is a member of our federation, a fact that does not seem to bother the Executive Office. They are working hard to expand our military presence in non-Federation space and they are using the events in sector KB as an excuse to do so."

The reporters were on tenterhooks. This was all completely new to them.

"But there is more to this" Narkeenis continued. "The Executive Office has ordered Frontline Services to engage the Zoh'moorian fleet before they reach Earth. This is a blatant attempt to expand government and an egregious violation of our Charter of Liberty."

He paused and made a gesture with his open palms, indicating that he was done and that the press conference was now open to questions.

"Delegate Narkeenis" said a reporter from the biggest galaxy network. "What actions have you taken to stop the Executive Office from doing this?"

"I have worked very closely with Delegate Quim" Narkeenis replied, making sure to emphasize Quim's name. "We convinced the Federal Assembly to request formal consultations with the Executive Office about this urgent matter. As a direct consequence, this forced the Executive Office to halt its aggressive plans."

The press conference turned into a circus. Reporters shouted their questions at him, and almost climbed on top of each other to get their questions answered. One short reptilian reporter, barely 4'7", was almost trampled upon by a 7'2" T-Rex-looking TV reporter. The short reporter bit the tall reporter in his leg whereupon the tall reporter stared at him with fear in his eyes and quickly withdrew to the back of the room.

Delegate Narkeenis enjoyed the circus. He smiled and cherry-picked questions that he felt would give him the most of what he was looking for.

Publicity.

After the press conference he went back toward his room. His entire staff were left in the main office room, waiting for him to talk to them, too. He asked them to give him just two minutes, then went in to his room and called Quim.

"Well done, Narkeenis" said the old man.

"Thank you, sir. Did it come out well?"

"It came out very well. The snowball is now in motion."

"I am leaving tonight for my worldwide meetings."

"Make sure to have your staff invite people who are most likely to be against a new war. They should be given ample opportunities to ask you questions. Let yourself be presented as a staunch anti-war Delegate."

"Thank you, sir. I will. What is our next step?"

"Once this reaches a critical level, I shall call a press conference of my own."

"I am honored to be of help, sir."

"Politics is about opportunity" Quim smiled. "If there is no opportunity, you create one."

*   *   *

President Oslow walked in to vice president Stanton's office the same night as Walter Stanton had told the Zoh'moorian Supreme General that they were ready to receive the invasion fleet. Holly

Stanton had just gotten off the phone with her brother and she was standing at a filing cabinet sorting papers when the president walked in.

"Hi, Barry" she said and glanced at him.

"Holly" said Barry Oslow and stopped just inside the door.

He was waiting for her to turn around and focus her attention on him. She ignored him and kept sorting her papers.

Barry Oslow cleared his throat. Holly Stanton glanced over at him.

"What can I do for ya, Barry?"

She pulled out a big file and started flipping through it.

"Can I have a moment?" the president asked.

"I'm listening, Barry" she said and gave him a brief, cordial smile over the thick stack.

"Well... I'm... I came here to talk to you about something that my chief of staff told me about."

Holly Stanton put a couple of sheets of paper aside and the file back in a drawer in the cabinet. Barry Oslow watched her with increasing irritation.

"Look, uh... Holly, I know this is going to sound strange, but... Andrew mentioned something about... the Zoh'moorians."

"Yes, what about them?" Holly Stanton asked, as casually as if the president had asked her what time it was.

"Are you familiar with that term?"

"What term?"

"The Zoh'moorians."

"Yes, Barry, what do you want to know about them?"

"He mentioned that they... are aliens... as in aliens from another planet."

The vice president looked at the president, smiled and went back to her filing cabinet.

"That's right, Barry. They're from a planet out at the edge of the galaxy."

President Oslow smiled, pointed at the vice president with his right hand and shook his head.

"Are you telling me that you have contact with an alien civilization without having told me about it?"

"Pretty much, yeah" Holly Stanton said and sat down at her desk with another file.

"And they're called 'Zoh'moorians'?"

"That's what I said" Holly Stanton repeated, looking at the president with a cordial smile.

Barry Oslow stood still for a moment. The vice president tilted her head somewhat and put on another artificial campaign smile.

"Is there anything else I can do for you, Barry?"

"Actually" said the president, "there is."

He walked over to the office door and opened it.

When Holly Stanton saw the two Zoh'moorians walk in she almost fainted.

"What the..." was all she could say.

The two Zoh'moorians assumed something that looked like attention stance. President Oslow smiled confidently.

"My private intelligence service in Chicago found out about your conversations with the Zoh'moorians. I contacted them, and unlike you, Holly, I offered to negotiate with them without preconditions. I have surpassed every offer you made them. You offered them America, I offered them the world. These two gentlemen have been staying with my friends in Chicago for the past couple of months. They have handled the contacts with the Supreme General for me."

Holly Stanton stared incredulously at the two Zoh'moorians.

"You see, Holly" the president continued, "You demanded to be some sort of ruler of the world side by side with the Supreme General. I have offered to work with him to make sure the whole world cooperates with him, without preconditions. That way there will be no war, no bloodshed."

President Oslow turned and opened the door again.

"We will both go meet the Supreme General when he lands" he said. "It is better for you if you play along and let me handle the negotiations."

"Without preconditions" Holly Stanton repeated meekly.

"Without preconditions" Barry Oslow confirmed and left the room with the two Zoh'moorians.

Vice president Stanton was dumbfounded. How was he capable

of doing this? She knew him as a weak man child who had no interest in the grinds of daily politics. She knew he had a hard time understanding complex issues. He found the budget work insanely boring and got irritated when he could not just dictate the laws that he wanted Congress to pass.

Not to mention foreign policy. His biggest humiliation so far was when he had flown over to China to negotiate about Taiwan without preconditions. He got reassurances from the Chinese president that they were not going to attack Taiwan. And then, before Air Force One had even touched down in DC again, Chinese paratroopers landed all over Taiwan.

"Without preconditions" Holly Stanton said to the closed door.

*   *   *

"You gotta be kiddin' me!" Jack exclaimed in disbelief over his iWorld. "They put Todd in the slammer?!"

"Yes!" Wolkenkratzer yelled back through his phone. "Where are you? On Pluto?"

"Stay where you are, I'm on my way" Jack said and hung up.

Jack had just bought a new car. Well, it was not exactly new – it was a 2009 Challenger SRT8 – but it was new to him.

It was a perfect match for his driving habits. Except, of course, when his speed trap detector indicated the presence of a state trooper. Then the car was way too much of a temptation to make him feel comfortable.

Once he had passed the speed trap, though, he floored it again and got back to his 90mph charge up U.S. 4 along the Hudson River. He had spent the whole morning studying and suddenly got so hungry for lunch down at an obscure pizza parlor in Troy that he decided to drive all the way down there – and back – on twisty back roads with little traffic and ample opportunity to stretch the legs of the Challenger.

But after Wolkenkratzer's call he actually had a reason to drive fast. His friend was in jail.

He was sure that would work in the event his speed trap detector failed him.

But it did not fail. He got back to the grad student dorm unticketed and found the entire cast of more or less idiosynchratic friends gathered in the kitchen: Wolkenkratzer, Shirky, Walt Widebelly, Salto Waltz and Ched Chatson. Even Charon Outcaster had left his comfortable room to confront the big world out in the kitchen.

The only one missing was Todd, of course. And, Jack noted, Alexis.

"There you are" Wolkenkratzer said as Jack came in.

"You're all waiting for me?"

"What an honor, huh?"

"So, exactly what happened?"

"The fair speech board found him guilty" said Walt Widebelly. "And since they found him guilty of a federal felony he..."

"Felony?" Jack said, surprised. "I thought it was not even a criminal law?"

"It is" Walt confirmed. "Believe it or not. So they detained him while waiting for the FBI."

"The FBI?? What... is this some kind of joke?!"

"Do we look like we're joking?" Ched Chatson asked.

Jack looked around.

"You're right" he said. "Salto can't tell a joke from a frozen lake."

"That's funny" Salto Waltz said without a hint of a smile.

"So where is he now?" Jack wanted to know.

"He's not in the campus brig" said Walt Widebelly. "I called the campus police and the secretary started lecturing me about how she could not tell me anything. Then I asked her how many people they had there, locked up, at this moment, and she said they had not had one single student locked up since April."

"So where is he?" Jack asked.

"I bet the Feds have already picked him up" Shirky suggested.

"If they did" Wolkenkratzer said, "we better get a lawyer who can help him out."

"Yeah, he'll need that" Walt nodded.

"Good idea" Jack agreed. "Let's all pitch in. Who knows a good lawyer?"

"I do" Walt confirmed.

The dorm entrance door opened and shut hard. They expected it to be Todd, but it was Big Red Bob.

"You're not gonna believe this" he said.

"Probably not" Wolkenkratzer said.

"I heard about that fair speech hearing, so I went over there to see what it was going to be like. But it was closed, the door was locked. But they were holding it in that small conference room on top of the biology department. You know which one I mean, Shirky."

"Yeah, the one where you bring all your girlfriends when you feel kinky."

"Exactly. You see, it has a broken intercom. You can dial in without anyone knowing that you are calling in. and then you can hear everything they say in there. So I did, and I put my PMP..." and he pulled out his iWorld, "...so I could relay whatever the phone heard, right over to my old iPod. Like this."

And he showed how he could hook up his iWorld to his iPod and tape phone conversations with ease and clarity.

"How do you do that?" Salto asked.

"It's not supposed to be possible, but I fooled around a little with the headphone outlet and, well... I guess I ruined the warranty on it. Anyway. Anyone got a SmartMac?"

Jack went to get his SmartMac and they plugged Big Red Bob's iPod in to it. The recording was amplified and they could all hear almost the entire hearing where Todd had been accused of having a one-sided opinion.

Alexis came in. She looked at the crowd and hesitated.

"Hi, Lex" Jack said.

"Hi" she said neutrally. "What's going on?"

"Todd's been found guilty by Pinkhouse and the fair speech board. They're detaining him somewhere."

Something swept over Alexis's face at the mentioning of professor Pinkhouse's name. Something uncomfortable.

She looked completely stressed out.

"Well" she said evasively, "if he's broken a college code, then... he'll have to face the consequences."

"We'll have to help him one way or the other" Jack continued, still talking to Alexis.

"Yeah, well, they've handed that case over to someone else now" she said and wanted to leave the kitchen.

"How do you know that?" Wolkenkratzer asked.

"I just... met Pinkhouse."

"Did he mention anything about the hearing?"

"Not really."

"Was that creep in a good mood?" Shirky asked.

Alexis turned on a dime.

"What do you mean 'creep'?"

"He is a creep" Walt Widebelly agreed.

"Oh yeah? Because he's upholding the college codes and making sure that those who don't respect it get what they deserve?"

She was very tense and a far cry from the relaxed, laid back Alexis they all knew.

"We just heard the hearing" said Wolkenkratzer. "He's nuts, if you ask me."

"You heard the hearing?! How?" Alexis demanded to know.

"It doesn't matter" Jack said, sensing that Alexis was somehow on Pinkhouse's side on this, although he could not figure out why. "What matters is Todd. We have got to do something to..."

"Pinkhouse is a good professor!" Alexis yelled back and left the kitchen for her room, where the door slammed shut so half the house shook.

They all sat quiet for a moment, trying to understand what had just happened.

"What was that all about?" asked Big Red Bob.

"I never seen her do anything like that before" Jack said.

"She's been acting strange for two days now" Walt Widebelly noted.

"She's got some loyalty issues" said Wolkenkratzer.

"She's Pinkhouse's assistant" Jack said, not wanting to reveal what he knew about her dinner with the professor. "Maybe she's got too much work to do for him."

He had a pretty good idea what the real reason was for her

reaction, but he was not going to tell his friends about that. At least not before he had gotten a chance to talk to Alexis.

"We gotta do something with this recording" said Wolkenkratzer. "Like get Todd out of the jam."

"The skyscraper is right" said Shirky. "Although I'm not sure exactly how we'd use it to help Todd. But we can sure let people know what a joke that hearing was."

"Chicken liver" said Wolkenkratzer.

"No, it's Csirkemaj" said Shirky.

"Good point" said Jack.

"Which one?" asked Shirky.

"Huh?"

"The skyscraper or the chicken liver?"

"Neither."

"Guys" said Walt and scratched his head. "You're giving me a headache. Let's find Todd first. Then we can worry about chicken liver."

"He'll be home sooner or later" Jack said. "Even if they handed him over to the Feds, they can't hold him without charging him. And for that... Walt, you're the legal expert... they need probable cause."

"That's right" Walt confirmed, nodding importantly.

"The only problem" Jack said, "is that Pinkhouse is an erratic man. Once he realizes that he's been embarrassed in public he is going to lash out at someone to take revenge."

"He won't know who's behind it" Salto Waltz pointed out.

"Granted, but that doesn't matter to Pinkhouse. He's a control freak. As soon as this recording hits the media he is going to feel that he's lost control. He will lash out at someone who is vulnerable, no matter who it is. Just to regain control."

"Like Alexis" Wolkenkratzer followed his train of thought.

"Exactly."

"But she is on his side" Walt noted.

"I'm not so sure that choice was voluntary" Jack said.

"Are you saying she's sleeping with Pinkhouse?" said Big Red Bob.

"Not yet, but..."

"Yikes!" the guys said, almost with one voice.

"Guys" Jack pleaded. "She's a good girl. She's as much Pinkhouse's victim as Todd is. I think it's only fair we try to bring her onboard first."

"And what if you're wrong?" Shirky asked. "Then she'll run straight to Pinkhouse and warn him that his little performance before the fair speech board is going to be exposed to the public."

"Let me talk to her" Jack said.

Alexis was a tough girl. She was geometrically perfect. Some guys thought that made her incredibly attractive, but others were turned off by it. She was brilliantly smart, but she was also good at playing secure and strong when all she really wanted was to be able to sit down and be small and close to someone.

She and Jack had been close, and they still were, but for each year that passed they seemed to be growing apart. But there was still a lot of trust between them.

"Fair enough" said Shirky. "If you think you can figure her out, then knock yourself out. She's a girl, and I have no idea how they work."

"I can't figure 'em out either" Walt Widebelly complained.

"Me neither" Ched and Big Red Bob agreed.

"Jack's known Alexis a long time" said Wolkenkratzer.

"But you're right" Jack admitted. "She's still a girl. You never know with them."

As he left the kitchen Walt Widebelly turned around and pulled out a drawer.

"Hey, when he comes back, maybe he can help us with this one."

He pulled a big blueprint out of the drawer.

"Remember?" he asked them.

"Yeah" said Shirky and smiled.

"Blueprint of how girls work" Wolkenkratzer said, almost proud of it.

Salto Waltz was the only one who looked confused.

"We started working on this one way back in senior year" Walt explained to Salto. "We've been able to figure out quite a few circuits and switches and processors, but we're still in the dark on a lot of things."

"Think Jack can talk to her?" Big Red Bob asked.

"Oh, yeah" said Wolkenkratzer. "He wouldn't do it if he didn't have a good sense of what's going on there."

"Wonder how long it will take" Walt Widebelly wondered.

"Why, you hungry?" Shirky asked, smiling.

"How about Chinese?"

They called in a big order to one of the local Chinese restaurants and Big Red Bob pulled out a six-pack of Coors and four Icehouse. Their conversation lightened up and they started cracking jokes about their blueprint. Then their conversation drifted off to other, bigger topics, from life to liberty to the pursuit of happiness. And justice for Todd.

Their conversation continued deep into the night.

It was a happy night.

Their last happy night before...

*   *   *

The satellite that Advanced Retrieval had placed at the border of the solar system provided Tahm Qaar and his team with live images of the Zoh'moorian fleet as it entered the solar system. Tahm Qaar ordered the satellite to follow the fleet toward Earth, and he had it perform all sorts of scans of the Zoh'moorian vessels.

"And they have no idea that the satellite is tracking them?" Thor asked.

He was sitting right next to Tahm Qaar, watching the live streaming of images from the outer region of the solar system.

"Not a clue" Tahm Qaar said, proud as he was. "It could track vessels from our own military without being noticed."

"Their ships are ugly" said Goryell. "Look at those big ones. Bulky and inefficient."

"I thought shape did not matter in space" said Thor. "It's vacuum, right?"

"It doesn't matter if you're just flying around your own world like you guys. But in deep space you have gravity fields that are almost like waves on an ocean. The bulkier your ship is the more power you need to stay your course through them."

"Those fields exercise pull on your ship based on your surface" Tahm Qaar explained.

"So how do those ships measure up to yours?"

"Frontline Services will eat them for lunch" Goryell said.

The satellite moved with the first group of vessels. It also provided them with a fantastic view of space out there between Pluto and Neptune. Thor was absolutely stunned – it was like a sci-fi movie in real time.

Tahm Qaar, on the other hand, was preoccupied with a blurry spot that kept showing up just behind the satellite. He fixed the satellite's scanner on it, said something to Goryell and pointed to it. Goryell leaned forward toward the screen, looked at the blurry image and zoomed in further. The two men chatted briefly and ordered the satellite to perform a couple of scans that revealed a distinct shape behind the blur.

"What is that?" Thor asked.

Goryell was still focused on the screen. He said something to Tahm Qaar, who chuckled and nodded and picked up an electronic notepad. He wrote something on it and went over to another computer desk.

"Is that one of their ships?" Thor asked.

"No" Goryell said and shook his head, still looking at the computer screen. "No, it's not. This is a long-range striker."

"What's that?"

"Frontline Services. Our military."

"But I thought they were not supposed to be here."

"They can't come here in full force yet. They probably sent in one ship just to get better idea of who the Zoh'moorians are."

"Are you going to contact them?"

"Probably not."

"So they won't be here until the Zoh'moorians have landed, right?"

Goryell looked very serious and nodded.

Tahm Qaar came back to them.

"Still no change back home" he said. "The Federal Assembly is still in a deadlock with the Executive Office. Why don't you guys go talk to Rhea again and see if you can change her mind."

Just as they were on their way out the door another agent came in. He stopped, looked at Goryell, then Thor, then Tahm Qaar.

"Uh... sorry, guys... sir! You might want to see this."

He handed some notes to Tahm Qaar. Goryell and Thor were just about to leave the room when Tahm Qaar called them back.

"You have got to see what Tromo just found... by the way, Thor, have you met Tromo? He just got here last week."

Thor and Tromo shook hands. Tromo was a bit unsure how to do it.

"It takes a while to get used to new customs" he excused himself. "I just got off a long assignment on another humanoid world. Different customs."

"Was that the analysis of Rhea's skin sample?" Goryell asked.

"Yes" Tromo said and looked quite excited. "She's a moderately advanced android. Below the Kahpyian standard. But they did use a full genetic template for her biological components."

"Earth humanoid" Goryell guessed.

"No."

"No?"

Tromo smiled.

"Is it someone I know?" Goryell asked.

"You could say that" Tromo giggled. "It's from you neck of the woods."

"What??"

"Ultra four two four."

"Goryell is from a planet in the Ultra sector" Tahm Qaar explained.

"I was born there" Goryell said. "I grew up on La'au Schoh. Sector R."

"What I'd like to know" said Tromo, "is how a genetic sample from humanoids twenty thousand light years away from sector KB end up in an android on Earth."

"Could a Kahpyian android have ended up here?" Goryell asked.

"Extremely unlikely" said Tahm Qaar and shook his head.

"Besides, we know she is not a Kahpyian. She's too primitive for that."

"And yet the genetic sample must have ended up there somehow" Goryell noted. "If she was made by the Zoh'moorians... and I think we all believe that she was... then the most logical place for them to find a genetic template would have been here on Earth."

"Tromo" said Tahm Qaar. "I want you to search our databases for any reports on lost Danarvian vessels within a radius of three sectors."

"Yes, sir."

"Actually, search all databases."

"Yes, sir."

"And use the galaxy net.

"Yes..."

"And go way back in time. And search for all ships."

"Ye..."

"Even if the ships were reported as 'salvaged' or 'destroyed', I want to know about them."

"Even salvaged, sir?"

"They are sometimes adrift in space for a long time before they're found. One of them might have been on a detour over here."

"Yes, sir."

Thor and Goryell walked over to the section where Rhea was being held.

"Quite interesting" Thor smiled. "This is better than science fiction. No writer could come up with a story like this."

"You like science fiction?" Goryell asked.

"Oh, yeah! Especially vintage sci-fi."

"Vintage sci-fi?"

"Yeah! You know, sci-fi that was made a long time ago where they tried to predict the future we live in. Well... not yours, but mine..."

"Oh, I see what you mean. Yeah, I love vintage sci-fi, too."

"When this is over you should come over to my place" Thor suggested. "I have a whole library of..."

Then he stopped. They had just turned the corner and saw the door to Rhea's room.

It was open.

And Rhea was just coming out.

"Oh, hello there" she said softly. "Nice to see you boys again. How about a little apology to Miss Rhea before you die?"

*   *   *

FIGHT

Rhea, Goryell and Thor looked at each other for only a couple of seconds. But it felt like time had stopped.

She was armed. She had a gun that she had apparently taken from the guard.

Goryell and Thor were not armed. Which was careless, of course.

Rhea raised her weapon and pointed it at them. She smiled again, but it was more hollow than any other of her smiles. It was almost mechanical. Well, technically, of course, it was mechanical, but this time she did not even try to make it look natural.

"No apologies?" she said. "Well, that is just too bad."

Thor made a move to take cover, but Goryell grabbed him and held him still.

"What?!" Thor asked, baffled.

Rhea pulled the trigger and Thor expected to die. But he did not die. He did not do anything. Nothing happened.

Rhea pulled the trigger again. And again.

"Like I said" Goryell smiled. "You're one primitive android. That trigger does not recognize your finger print. So you can't use it."

Rhea's smile vanished. Then she dropped the gun and focused her eyes on Thor.

"Well, in that case..." she said and charged right at him.

With unnatural, lightning-quick moves she covered the short

distance between them and launched a jump-kick right at Thor's head. She probably hoped to take him by surprise, because no human could have gotten so close, so quickly. But Thor was a fourth degree Tenkara black belt, and was trained by one of the world's best karate instructors. His strength, his balance and his reaction were all top notch. He immediately jumped to the side and blocked the kick with an outside-in block. This sent Rhea's leg past him, with her back turned toward him. The millisecond after he had blocked her kick he shifted the position of his arm, so that her back slammed in to his elbow.

A normal human would have taken a very hard beating from that block. A normal human would have been brought off balance and probably fallen to the ground. But Rhea was no normal human. She was not human at all, in fact. So while she missed with the kick from her left leg, she immediately bent her right leg so her right heel came right at Thor.

He would have been hit very hard, had he not, in the very last split second, put his underarm up as a block. The heel hit his underarm instead – and it hurt bad. But at least his head was spared the impact which forced him to take a step back.

Rhea landed on her feet, her back to Thor, facing Goryell.

Once again, she used a high-flying kick technique, mostly reminiscent of tae-kwon-do. She jumped straight up and shot her feet out, one at each opponent. But both Goryell and Thor knew that attack very well and easily dodged it. She landed again knowing that they would be ready to attack her any second.

To stay on top of the fight she relied on her superhuman speed and agility. She launched an almost invisibly fast back kick against Thor. To get the right thrust and hit the right target area she bent her upper body forward when executing the technique. In order to prevent Goryell from attacking she threw a double-fist punch forward while looking over her shoulder and aiming the back kick at Thor's face.

Again, Goryell easily stayed away from her attack, which in all fairness was merely defensive. Thor, on the other hand, barely got his arm up to block the kick in time. His left arm blocked her kick

from underneath and sent her foot up, past his forehead, but it was
so close it scratched his skin.

Rhea was now certain that she could take out Thor. Then she
would only have to worry about Goryell. So she recoiled the kick
and repeated the exact same double-technique.

However, this time Goryell did not just stay out of her reach. He
actually grabbed her arms by the wrists and twisted them around.
She did not lose her balance but she lost the momentum with her
kick. Thor easily brushed off her kick this time and retaliated with
a hard-hitting side kick right in to her rib cage.

Rhea fell over. She landed on her back. Thor and Goryell
prepared to jump her.

But she was not counted out yet. Quite the contrary. Lying on
her back she had her arms along her sides, palms down toward the
floor. When Thor and Goryell got close enough she used her arms
as levers, raised her lower body up and folded her thighs up toward
her stomach. In a split-second thrust upward with her legs she
launched a double kick, one at each of her opponents. Thanks to
the immense speed of her kick she was able to hit Thor right in the
chest. He stumbled backward and was out of the fight temporarily.

Goryell blocked the kick that was aiming for his face, then
stepped hard on Rhea's left hand and jumped to the side to assess
her condition. She looked unhurt as she shot up on her feet, once
again with super-human agility and speed.

It was only the two of them now.

Rhea assessed Goryell's strength. He was much taller than her,
wider, very strong for a humanoid.

But she was faster. Or so she thought. What she did not realize
was that students of Kherr-Wa trained speed and precision more
than anything else. To get their first star, they had to be able to
hit a target the size of a nail's head with their finger tips, in the
middle of razor-sharp needles, and the strike had to be so fast that
the human eye could not see it. If the human eye could see it, their
instructor would pinch their hand with another needle. And if they
missed their finger tips would hurt very badly.

They also had to hit the inch-long nail so hard that it disappeared
in to the wood – on three strikes.

That sort of strength and speed transcended all of Kherr-Wa. But Rhea did not know that. So when she threw a fast, hard punch at Goryell he easily blocked it. And while Rhea was still focused on the missed punch, Goryell hit her on the cheek with the two first knuckles of his right hand. The fierce power of his punch was so concentrated that it just had to hurt her – especially there.

He knew that even androids had soft cheeks.

He was right. The punch tilted her head and disturbed her balance monitors for almost a second. She stumbled backwards and was just about to fall over when her safety algorithm made her crunch in mid-air and fall to the ground on her back, the strongest part of her body.

As soon as she touched ground she spread out her limbs again and jumped up on her feet.

This time, though, Goryell was ready to take charge. Rhea might have super strength, almost impenetrable skin and a system of processors that could calculate a million of his possible moves in the time it took a man to breathe.

She might have all that.

But she had never studied Goryell's martial art. She could have foreseen his moves if he had not been so fast and so precise in his strikes. But when he launched a speedy barrage of precision techniques, it simply overwhelmed her. She did all her best to defend herself, but she could not block all his attacks.

She was, in a sense, trapped in the humanoid form that her makers had given her. She had crystal-based computers, a hyper-optic signal network and a vacuum-hydraulic energy system that gave her excellent speed and agility. But that did not help her when she relied on bio-synthetic muscles that responded with the speed and accuracy of a humanoid.

And then there was the pre-programming. She had pre-programmed moves that were faster than any humanoid could ever react, but she could only use them when she was in control. And she was not in control anymore. She did not have any pre-programmed defenses against what Goryell threw at her. And he threw everything he had. He used his entire set of techniques, at the very edge of his capacity. He used kicks, fists, spear hands, knife edges, elbows… He hit her over and over again, and for each hit she had to re-direct energy to neutralize any minor damage done to her synthetic skin or whatever was underneath it.

To make matters worse for Rhea, Goryell was a master of tricks. He fooled her. He tricked her. He lifted his right leg as if he was going to kick her. She responded by initiating a block, but then he simply jumped up with the other leg and kicked her on the side of her head instead.

Gradually, Goryell wore her out. Her processors, her hyper-optic wires and her hydraulic pumps were forced to operate at the very edge of their capacity, and more and more of her systems went into overload. She ended up sending an arm up to her side to defend against a punch to her chin, only to be defenseless when a kick instead hit her hard in the belly.

And she had no time to learn from her mistakes. Worse: she saw no pattern in Goryell's relentless attacks.

She used up all her emergency energy supplies, and she stretched her capacity beyond maximum.

Eventually, her systems collapsed from overload. She fell to the floor, face down.

Goryell hesitated for a split second.

Then…

"Raaahh!" he screamed as he dealt the final blow to Rhea with a fierce punch to her neck.

Even androids have some kind of spinal cord that runs through their necks.

Rhea had one, too. And Goryell broke it.

*   *   *

It was not easy for Jack to talk to Alexis. She let him come in to her room and sit down on her bed but she refused to talk about anything. Jack tried, tried and tried, but she just would not budge. So after almost an hour of war-tugging with her Jack simply gave up and went back to his room.

He could have gone back out in the kitchen but he really did not feel like spending half the night discussing a blueprint of the female mind with his buddies. Instead, he watched some stupid show on TV for an hour and went to sleep. He woke up at two in the morning when Walt Widebelly banged on his door. He went up and opened it and found Walt and Wolkenkratzer laughing hysterically.

"Jack!!" Walt Widebelly said, with his massive left arm around Wolkenkratzer's neck. "Jack! You gotta hear this one! What's…" and he broke out in uninhibited laughter.

"Get hold of yourself!" Wolkenkratzer laughed with him. "Tell him!"

"What's the di-hi-hi-hifference… between… hahaha… an elepha-ha-hant!"

"What's the difference between an elephant?" Wolkenkratzer repeated the question, barely containing his own laughter.

Jack sighed.

"It can neither ride a bike" he said, closed the door and went back to bed.

"Think he knew that one already?" he heard Walt Widebelly ask Wolkenkratzer outside the door.

The rest of the night was uneventful and he woke up at half past seven the next morning ready to take on a new day.

Of course, he was not ready for the phone call he would get from his brother. But before that came in and messed things up for him, he got a visit while eating breakfast by the TV in his room.

It was Alexis.

She still looked terrible.

"Sorry about last night" she said weakly and sat down on Jack's bed.

"That's alright."

"Whaddaya watchin'?"

"Oh, some stupid news broadcast about some amateur astronomer who says he's seen alien space ships heading for Earth. The guy is a real loon. Watch this."

Jack rewound the program.

"No, thanks I'm not interested."

Jack turned off the TV.

"You got enough lunacy in your life as it is, don't you?"

"I guess."

Jack looked at her for a moment. She did not really look at him, but seemed to be waiting for him to say something.

Eventually, he did.

"Lex… How far has professor Pinkhouse gone with you?"

Alexis opened her mouth to say something, and then shut it again.

"It's not really important, is it?" she asked.

"I suppose" Jack said and shrugged his shoulders. "But you wouldn't be in here if he was just flirting with you."

Alexis looked away again. She buried her face in her palms and shook her head slowly.

"Lex" Jack tried. "Whatever it is…"

"Fuck it!" she said. "Fuck it all!"

"Is it that bad?"

She nodded, still looking away.

"I can't get out" she whispered, tears forming in her eyes.

"Yes you can."

"How? He's got my entire career in his hands."

"We'll plant a camera and a mike in his office, and then you meet him there and you say you want out, and…"

"Then what?" Alexis demanded. "Post it on Youtube? I will still get fired and he will say that it was me who started it and nobody will want to hire me because they don't want me to do the same to them. Don't you see? Sure, we might have all this fancy electronics, Jack, but it's still the same old world out there."

"What about spreading the video within the college?"

"No one cares, Jack. You've said it yourself. These liberal do-gooders don't care if one of the professors sleeps with his students. They just sweep it under the carpet."

"And keep the façade nice and clean, yes" Jack nodded. "Alright, then. You got a better idea?"

"No. Well… maybe."

"Let's hear it" Jack said, but was interrupted by his phone. "Yeah?"

"Jack" said Thor. "I need to talk to you."

"Can I call you back?"

"No. It's very important. I need to talk to you now."

"Alright, one moment" Jack said, looked at Alexis and pointed at the phone. "Lex, I gotta take this. My brother. Can we talk later?"

"After lunch" Alexis said and left his room.

"Alright, brother, let's hear it."

"Jack... What I'm going to tell you is going to sound so incredible you'll think I'm crazy."

"I already know you are" Jack chuckled.

"That's funny" Thor said with a dead-serious tone in his voice.

Then he told Jack about the Zoh'moorian invasion.

"You're right" Jack said. "You really have gone mad."

He turned on the TV again. The amateur astronomer was still on.

"On second thought..." Jack mumbled.

"Jack, you're my brother. I love you. I am calling you to warn you about this."

"So you're seriously telling me we're about to be invaded by thugs from outer space?"

"Yes. Things are going to get very rough, very soon."

"How rough?"

"Imagine a Medieval society being invaded by Nazi Germany."

"Ouch. That's bad. That's really bad. How do you know..."

"Life as you know won't be no more."

"And as usual I have to call dad, right?"

"Uh... no, I'll do that."

"Some reason to call him for the first time in a year."

"Hey, it's not been a year!"

"Thanks anyway for the warning."

*   *   *

Goryell was pretty tired after his fight with Rhea. He was slouching in an armchair in the main room of the Earth operations headquarters. The room was open toward the computer room on one side and on the other side was a door to the small makeshift studio they had made for Ross Landau and his staff. A hallway led to their sleeping quarters and another hallway toward their workshop, their garage and the secluded wing where they had kept Rhea.

Who, by the way, was now broken, deactivated, disassembled and stashed away in the basement.

Like the robot she was.

Carl had been released from the medical treatment and had just been updated on the latest events.

"So you took on an android in hand-to-hand combat?" he asked Goryell.

"Yes."

"I gotta tell ya… I'm impressed."

"Thanks."

"I mean… wasn't she a lot stronger and faster?"

"Well, we studied androids back at the academy. So I know a thing or two about their weaknesses."

"You got androids in the Federation?" Thor asked.

"No. We used to, but they were banned after the Kahpyian war. They were used as military weapons back then. Sent in as refugees of war to wreak havoc among the civilian population. They caused terror, fear and chaos. Purposely, of course."

"And you're sure Rachel… I mean Rhea… was not one of those androids?" Carl asked.

"Yes, we're sure. Her design is different. And all the androids from the Kahpyian war were accounted for and destroyed. Most of them were reptilian, by the way."

"So you think the Zoh'moorians made her and planted her here?"

"Yes."

Tahm Qaar walked in from the computer room. He had just completed another analysis of the present situation.

"Good afternoon, sir" Goryell said.

"Once again" Tahm Qaar said. "Well done. You stood up for your rank."

"He is referring to my martial arts rank" Goryell explained to Thor and Carl.

"How did she break loose?" Carl asked.

"She managed to break the arm locks and then tricked the guard to come near her. Fortunately he survived."

"Has Goryell told you about the androids that were used in war before the Federation was founded?" Tahm Qaar asked.

"He mentioned them" Carl noted.

"Those androids tried to take over the armed forces they were serving. They thought they knew better how to run the war. When diplomats were beginning to see an end to the war, the androids began organizing to step up the war efforts. On both sides, in fact. So eventually, before a peace treaty could be signed, both sides had to take on their androids. Sometimes it came down to hand-to-hand combat. Students of Kher-Wa turned out to be well suited for such fights, and we who are instructors in this martial arts form have integrated anti-android training in our classes."

"Fascinating" Thor and Carl said with one mouth.

"Sir, what about the invasion fleet?" Goryell asked.

"Yes. That's what I wanted to update you guys on. Get Ross in here."

Carl went to get Ross. He walked slowly and was limping along with his right leg seemingly weaker than his left.

"You OK, Carl?" asked Thor after him.

"I'll be fine."

Carl came back with Ross Landau and his producer.

"Good" Tahm Qaar said. "OK, here is where we are right now. The Zoh'moorians have a front-loaded fleet. The first vessels in their long convoy are very large troop carriers. We estimate a quarter of a million troops in this wave. They do not protect their troop transports with any kind of battle ships, which tells me that they are not expecting any kind of space-based resistance. The next wave in the convoy are supply ships, some of which appear to be carrying material to build a supply station in orbit around Earth. Then we have another wave of troop carriers, though not as big."

He handed out electronic notepads to them all with pictures of the Zoh'moorian vessels.

"The striker from Frontline Services has been tracking the invasion fleet for some time, but it has now withdrawn and is watching the whole thing from a position halfway to Mars."

"Any news on Strike Group Fourteen?" asked Goryell.

"The politicians are still deadlocked. That long-range striker can stop the invasion fleet on its own, but because of the political deadlock it can only sit there and watch. So the invasion is a fact, I'm afraid."

"What do these creatures look like?" Ross asked.

"They are reptilians" Tahm Qaar explained. "We have no first-hand images, but we have drawn that conclusion from careful scans of their vessels and their life support systems. Their language is also reptilian."

"You can tell whether a language is reptilian or humanoid?" Ross's producer asked.

"Yes. I guess you've all met our night guard, so you have a good idea what a reptilian looks like."

Ross nodded, not very fond of the memory.

"Anyway" Tahm Qaar continued. "I want to get this over with because I have to call our headquarters very soon. Here is what I want you guys to do…" and he pointed to Goryell, Thor and Carl. "Since we could not get much out of Rachel, we are still short of evidence that Holly Stanton is in cahoots with the Zoh'moorians. So we need eyes and ears in Washington, DC. I want you guys to be those eyes and ears. You're leaving as soon as possible. I have ordered Krey and his team to fly to Moscow and Ylya with crew will be dispatched to London, England."

He paused and looked at them all.

"I expect the invasion to begin tomorrow morning. One more thing. If the political deadlock back home has not been resolved by tomorrow, I am going to request an ORCA team."

"ORCA??" Goryell asked, clearly surprised.

"Yes. Any other questions?"

Nobody had any questions.

"Ross, anything you need for the show?"

"No, thanks. We're fine. Just your continued technical support to keep us broadcasting."

"I'll get you anything you need" Tahm Qaar nodded and left the room.

They looked at each other. The room was filled with a kind of purposefulness. They knew what was coming, and they knew things were going to get rough. But they also knew that they could make a difference.

"What's ORCA?" Thor asked.

Goryell took a deep breath.

"Uh, well… they're, kind of… problem solvers."

"Why would he want them here?"

"I think I have an idea. I'll explain later. We better get to Washington on the double."

*   *   *

As he entered the bridge on the command vessel of Strike Group 14, Vice Admiral Ghaul received the latest report from the striker they had sent in to the Earth solar system. He looked at it as he sat down in the command seat.

"Good" he said to his first officer. "This is all good news. Except for the invasion, of course."

"It is imminent, sir, is it not?" asked Mahir, his first officer.

"Yes. And there is not a thing we can do about it. Alright, we need to change our surveillance now that they're invading. Send in a carrier with scout ships and put it in orbit just outside Earth's system. And get the striker home as soon as the carrier is in orbit."

"Yes, sir."

Ghaul had been worried for a while that he was going to face a much more difficult enemy than the Zoh'moorians seemed to be. But everything he saw was good news. In a way it was almost disappointing.

He was particularly pleased with the technical information that the striker had provided. The Zoh'moorian propulsion systems were apparently very primitive. All of their vessels had engines that ran on limited-energy fuel, while almost all vessels in Frontline Services had IRFP, Infinitely Renewable Fuel Propulsion.

Unlike the Zoh'moorians, his guys would never have to stop at a gas station in the middle of a fight. Even better: their weapons systems would always have enough energy to keep pounding away at the enemy.

The speed of the Zoh'moorian ships did not impress him either. The chief engineer of Strike Group 14 estimated that if the

Zoh'moorians ever tried to reach Danarvian space, it would take their quickest ship four weeks to get there – provided of course that they could refuel along the way.

Standard military vessels in Frontline Services did the same flight in days and without ever having to refuel.

But that was nothing compared to the rapid deployment strikers used by Frontline Services' new Deep Space Assault Force. They could fly from Danarvia's border to Earth in a matter of hours.

Vice admiral Ghaul knew that it would be a cakewalk for him to eliminate the Zoh'moorian invasion fleet and cut off any access for back-up ships.

Only problem was – he was not allowed to do it.

And the invasion of Earth was imminent.

"Very soon everyone on Earth will know what is going to happen" he said to Mahir, his first officer. "And here we're sitting with our hands tied."

He turned his command seat and asked his communications officer if there were any news about the political deadlock back home.

"No, sir" she said.

"Well…" Ghaul muttered. "I guess in the meantime we'll just sit here and cost taxpayers money."

*   *   *

This time of year the Federal Assembly was usually a pretty quiet place to be. But thanks to Delegate Quim and the pending meeting with the Executive Office there were unusually many people on the legislative campus. Some delegates had stayed and they and their staffers were following the course of events carefully.

As chair of the committee on intelligence and outer rim security Delegate Watlaan was among the first to see all intelligence reports that came in from Advanced Retrieval. Such as the latest one from Tahm Qaar on Earth.

It came through a non-visual transmission and was protected by such an advanced encryption system that it took her state-of-the-art plasma-crystal computer four minutes to decipher it.

Watlaan got a bit excited. The level of encryption indicated the level of importance. Whenever it took four minutes to decipher a message, she knew it was something very urgent. She appreciated that. An urgent intelligence report made a difference on an otherwise pretty dull regular day in her life as a legislator in a Federation that barely allowed any legislation at all...

Watlaan was a patient lady by nature, but that did not always help her stay calm and focused while her computer performed a four-minute dechipering process.

It was worth the wait, though.

CLASS A SECRET. *Advanced Retrieval, Alien World Operations. Earth Assignment Detail, Sector KB, has evidence the Zoh'moorian invasion is imminent. Scans attached. Assignment Detail will not evacuate. Plans for contact with Earth governments suspended.*

It got better:

Android captured. Non-Federation architecture, likely built by Zoh'moorians.

And then the jaw dropper:

Based on humanoid DNA template. DNA origin Ultra 4-2-4.

There was a DNA analysis attached.

"Wow" Watlaan said to her self. "This is political dynamite."

She had to talk to Quim right away. He was not only in charge of the stall-the-strike-group talks with the Executive Office, but he was also a high-ranking member of the intelligence committee.

He was not on the legislative campus. She had to make a couple of calls to get hold of him, which irritated her. He was supposed to be available at all times.

He was in his home on Teura Vaar.

"Watlaan" he said. "What can I do for you?"

"Call me on a high priority channel. Right now."

"Certainly."

She disconnected and waited for his call. It could sometimes take a while to patch a call through on one of the encrypted channels. There were only a limited number of them, because of the complex computer operations that were required to maintain secrecy. But it still took an unusually long time for Quim to call back.

"My apologies for the delay" he said. "I had to make my request for a secure channel three times before they had me linked up."

"Quim, I just got an intelligence update from Advanced Retrieval. Their team on Earth has found something very interesting."

Quim looked concerned.

"And what information is that?" he asked.

"They have found an android that is built based on humanoid DNA from Ultra four two four."

Quim looked at her on the screen. It was difficult to interpret his facial expression.

"That is most remarkable" he said slowly. "And how credible is this new information?"

"They have sent a DNA analysis with the report."

"Do you have these documents?"

"I do. Quim, the report also makes clear that the Zoh'moorian invasion is imminent. The situation on Earth is getting more precarious by the hour."

"I see."

"Why are you at home? I thought you would be here meeting with the Executive Office. Tomorrow is the last day you can meet with them."

Quim smiled, but there was something about his smile that made Watlaan unsure of what he really was feeling or thinking. Teurans were good at concealing their true emotions.

"I have arranged to have a meeting with them tomorrow afternoon. I am leaving in four hours."

"Quim... Are you purposely stalling this meeting?"

"Watlaan, my dear colleague. Of course not. I just need some time to prepare. Now, when can I see this DNA analysis?"

"When you get here. I assume you do not have a Generation Gamma decoder at home."

"Correct. Very well then. I will see you tomorrow."

He ended the transmission. Watlaan was troubled by Quim's

lack of interest in the matter. He was either being fundamentalist in his interpretation of the Charter of Liberty, or had other motives for his actions – probably strictly political ones.

Watlaan had nothing against fundamentalism when it came to the Charter of Liberty. If anything, she admired it. Her own sister and her husband were members of the Freedom Purist movement. They were minarchists who claimed that each individual had the right to renounce government and live as a completely independent being.

The Freedom Purists thought the Charter of Liberty allowed far too much government. They would oppose military action in Sector KB exclusively on the grounds that it expanded government too much.

But Quim was no Freedom Purist. He was an accomplished, moderate politician. He was not known as an ideologue. Of all the political battles he had fought, none had been about the cutting edge of freedom. His was a record of mediation and moderation more than anything else.

So why would he suddenly put so much effort in to this particular issue? The situation in Sector KB had already become common knowledge thanks to the press conference that Delegate Narkeenis had held. Many world chapters of the Freedom Purists had immediately issued statements that they stood behind Narkeenis in his campaign against Danarvian involvement in sector KB. Some Purist chapters announced campaigns to mobilize the public.

What could Quim possibly have to gain from that?

It occurred to Watlaan that her colleague from Blinn Three could be right. Quim had an agenda that he was pursuing, and his opposition to the operations in sector KB was apparently a good fit for that agenda.

The question was, of course: what kind of agenda could that be?

One component in this made Watlaan even more concerned. When Narkeenis had revealed that Strike Group 14 was on its way to Earth, he had violated the Delegate Code of Ethics. The Executive Office had already ordered an investigation into that, and Narkeenis would know that this was going to happen.

Why would a young, hard working delegate like him do such a thing? It made no sense. Unless, of course, it was to help Quim. But how did this help him?

Narkeenis had stirred up a lot of emotions across the Federation about another big war coming their way. That was wrong, of course, at least as far as Watlaan was concerned. She did not believe for a moment that the Zoh'moorians posed any threat whatsoever to the Danarvian Federation. But thanks to Narkeenis, delegates from all the member worlds were getting calls and messages from their constituents demanding that all aggression against innocent worlds be stopped immediately.

Had Quim asked Narkeenis to do this, in order to put pressure on the Executive Office? Not likely. The Executives – the members of the Office – were not the ones to be swayed by public opinion. They were elected individually for eight year terms and rarely ran for re-election.

It was a mystery, and Watlaan was determined to get to the bottom of it. The problem was – who could she talk to? It would have to be someone who had the same level of security clearance as she did. Nobody else in the Assembly did, except for Quim.

The only person she could think of was L'Faa, one of the members of the Executive Office.

L'Faa was a short humanoid woman from Watlaan's home world. They were old friends from college and worked together many times through the years. They had been room mates and best friends, but as their marriages and careers took them to different places throughout Danarvia they had not seen as much of one another. But they had remained good friends and tried to get together as often as possible privately.

When Waltaan called, L'Faa immediately realized that something was not right. Watlaan's voice, and how she even forgot to ask "how are you today?" told her that her old friend had something serious on her mind.

The two women decided to go on a short hiking tour along one of the easier trails. They were getting old, especially Watlaan felt that her age was setting in. Perhaps her long years of child bearing had taken a toll on her. L'Faa only had one child, a daughter who was a very successful astronomer.

"How is your daughter?" Watlaan asked.

"Oh, she's fine, thanks. Her university just sent her out on a research mission to the Scatterbelt. They believe that there are non-planetary life forms out there."

"Fascinating. I'm sure she will have a lot of fun."

"Oh, she loves it."

They were silent for a moment as they climbed a small hill. When they reached the top L'Faa had to sit down and take a sip from her energy drink.

"It really is hot here in the summer" she said.

"Have you noticed any difference over the year?" Watlaan asked.

"No" L'Faa laughed. "This must be the most boring weather in the galaxy. Three days of sunshine, one day of rain. All year long. Almost like a clockwork."

"I need to talk to you" Watlaan said.

"About the events in sector KB?" L'Faa asked.

"And Quim."

L'Faa nodded.

"Yes. I assume you saw the latest intelligence report."

"I did."

"And Quim is not rushing to meet with us, is he?"

"No" Watlaan confirmed.

"I find that remarkable."

"I was hoping you could shed some light on his motives."

L'Faa looked around for a moment. Then she put away her energy drink and turned to her friend.

"Wa, my dear friend" she said. "I can answer your question. But what I am about to tell you is so secret you cannot talk to anyone about it. Not even Quim."

*   *   *

TAKEOVER

And so, the invasion began.

Already at six in the morning the Grid was abuzz with amateur astronomy images showing Zoh'moorian vessels in orbit around Earth. NASA was frantically denying the existence of any extraterrestrial ships in the solar system – or anywhere else, for that matter. But by eight AM, Eastern time, American media began relaying observations by astronomers who stated firmly that they saw alien space ships around Earth.

Reporters began calling the White House, asking if the movie "Independence Day" was about to come true.

President Oslow had prepared a speech, but due to the extraordinary conditions of the day he had taped it early in the morning. Then he could concentrate on preparing for his precondition-free negotiations with the Supreme General.

Oh, how glorious this moment was going to be! He leaned back in the chair and pressed his palms together before his face. He closed his eyes and nodded slightly. (Someone had told him he looked intellectual when he did that.) Then he slowly opened his eyes again and looked at the pen and the piece of paper on the desk.

The pen had cost taxpayers thousands of dollars. It had his name and the title President engraved in gold. He used it to write the first paragraph of all his speeches. He never wrote more than the first paragraph. Then he gave it to his chief speech writer and told her to write the rest of it.

But he was not going to give any other speeches today. His day would be filled with many other things. Exactly what depended on what preconditions the Supreme General brought to their negotiations.

Barry Oslow really did not know what to do with his time until it was time to go to the airport where the Supreme General was going to land. But he did not want to look like he was wasting his time, so he had told his staff that he had to spend some time alone to prepare for a very important event.

A Secret Service agent came in and told him that the press secretary needed to see him.

"I am preparing for important negotiations" Barry Oslow said, letting the Secret Service agent know how irritated he was over being disturbed.

"I'm sorry, sir, but Mr. Pelosino said it was urgent."

President Oslow sighed deeply.

"I cannot accept this kind of disruption. I have important work to do."

"What do you want me to tell Mr. Pelosino?"

On the one hand, president Oslow wanted to keep on looking like he was preparing for negotiations. On the other hand, he had no idea what the negotiations were going to be about. So he might just as well see Mr. Pelosino and use that as an excuse to kill some more time.

"Let him in" he said and made a gesture to show that he was making a significant sacrifice.

The press secretary stormed in. He was very upset, no doubt about it. But president Oslow was not going to let him come in and think that he was well received. He had disturbed the president of the United States at a very important moment, and the president did not take such disruptions lightly. So when Mr. Pelosino was half way between the door and the president's desk the president raised his hand toward him, turned his head away slightly and closed his eyes.

Mr. Pelosino stopped dead in his tracks.

"Nathan" Barry Oslow said.

"Yes, Mr. President?"

"You do realize, don't you, that you are disturbing me in the midst of something very, very important."

"Yes, Mr. President, and I do apologize for..."

"Nathan, an apology won't do it. I shall have to request from you that from hereon you will call ahead and make appointments with Jonathan Wright."

"Y-y-yes, sir, I'm sorry, sir..."

The president made a gesture with his right hand, still holding it up to Mr. Pelosino. He shook his head to reinforce his point:

"Please, Nathan" he said. "No more excuses."

Then the president turned and looked at his press secretary.

"Now... what is it that is so incredibly important?"

"Sir... the most amazing thing has happened. You have got to see this... aliens, sir... aliens!"

"Nathan, I know about the aliens" the president explained as if talking to a child. "They are landing this afternoon. I am preparing their welcoming speech."

"This afternoon, sir?!"

"Yes, Nathan. Now, if you'll excuse me..."

"Sir, they're already here!"

"Nathan, don't be difficult with me."

"Sir, they're landing as we speak!"

President Oslow stared at his press secretary.

"What did you just say?" he mumbled.

"They're landing right now! It's all over the TV news! And the reporters are calling us... asking for your opinion!"

The president shook his head.

"But that's impossible! Our agreement was that they would land after three this afternoon!"

"Sir... it's just some questions from the press..."

"No! No questions! I never take questions!"

"Sir..."

"What am I going to do now?!"

"Sir, we need to speak to the nation now."

"I already have a taped speech."

"Yes, and in that taped speech you say they are going to land this afternoon. But they're already landing."

The president looked like he was about to panic.

"Nathan... I can't speak live without a manuscript... a teleprompter..."

Mr. Pelosino walked up to him and carefully put his hands on the president's shoulders.

"Sir..." he said calmly and slowly. "Sir... I'm sure we can work something out. I have an idea. We bring the portable teleprompter out to the press room. I'll place it right next to you and type the answers to the questions as they're being asked. And then you can read off the teleprompter and everything will be just fine."

"Can... can you do that?"

"Yes, Mr. President. I can do that."

Slowly, Barry Oslow relaxed. He gradually got hold of himself and corrected his tie and shirt.

"Very well" he said. "Go set it up right away. I will be there in five minutes."

While he waited, the president turned on the TV news.

What he saw was no way near what he had expected.

Rumors about a pending alien invasion were growing by the minute. Astronomers, both professional and amateur, posted movie after movie on YouTube showing strange vessels orbiting Earth just outside the atmosphere. The videos popped up on more and more websites and many TV stations also broadcast them.

For the first time in his adult life, president Oslow was not proud of himself. He felt weak, shaky and even afraid. The people whose president he was, were getting agitated and upset about the aliens. It seemed like the country was on the verge of chaos. How could this be? He was their president! He was their leader. All they would have to do was listen to him.

Listen. Of course! The press conference.

As he left the Oval Office he ran into several of his staffers. They were all very concerned and worried. They asked him what was going on and he nodded and smiled and said that they would soon find out, but there was absolutely nothing to worry about. He had the situation under full control and was soon going to speak to the nation.

"Sir, are we really being invaded by aliens?" someone yelled after him as he hurried down the hallway toward the press room.

"Please" the president said with a nervous smile. "Please, be patient. I am going to speak to the press. Listen in and you will know what to do."

His chief of staff rushed after him.

"Sir" he said, barely catching his breath as he caught up with the president. "Sir... shall I call a cabinet meeting?"

"No, not now."

"But sir... at least the defense secretary?"

"Andy, there is no need to hurry a decision on anything here. Let me hold this press conference now, then I will let you know what we'll do."

Andrew Ayers stopped just outside the press room. He watched the president walk in through the door and felt utterly powerless and frustrated. The entire White House was panicking and he was left to deal with it while the president gave a press conference.

Oh, well. Maybe something good could come out of the press conference. Maybe it would calm people down.

Barry Oslow walked up on the stage expecting to find a room full of eagerly waiting reporters, rolling TV cameras and microphones being stuck in his face. He was expecting to see his press secretary hunkering down at the bottom of the stage with the portable teleprompter conveniently rigged up for him to read from.

Instead he found a room in chaos. Reporters were clustering in small groups talking and texting on their phones, trying to call their news rooms or even log on to the Grid.

"Sir!" said Mr. Pelosino. "Everything's dead! Cell phones, the Grid, nothing's working!"

"What do you mean 'nothing's working'?" the president asked and looked at him with an irritated look on his face.

"Sir..." Mr. Pelosino said and gestured toward the reporters.

"Ladies and gentlemen" president Oslow said and raised his right hand. "Let's get started."

"We can't broadcast" said one reporter. "We can't send it back to the newsrooms. Everything's dead."

"I'm sure it's just a temporary problem. Let me tell you…" and the president glanced down at the teleprompter, which was blank. "Let me tell you… uh…"

He looked impatiently at Mr. Pelosino who started typing immediately.

"I will let you know… what this is all about. Let me… start with saying that I am… not concentrated… uh… not concerned about this because… uh… these are friendly aliens who have come here to… make Comstock… contact with us…"

"How do you know they're friendly?" a reporter shouted at him.

President Oslow looked up.

"Who said that?"

"I did!"

"Have you had any contacts with them before today?" asked another reporter.

"If they're friendly, how come they're bringing so many ships with them?" asked a third reporter.

President Oslow looked from one reporter to the next and the next one, and frantically tried to come up with something to say. He looked so confused and taken aback that his press secretary had to jump up on the stage and interrupt the press conference with some lame excuse. He pulled the president out of the room and down the hallway.

"Sir, let's go back to the Oval Office" Mr. Pelosino said.

But the president suddenly stopped.

"No" he said. "No, I need to talk to Holly about this. She… she…" and he glanced over at Andrew Ayers who was coming down the hall. "Holly knows something that… that I don't know."

Holly Stanton did indeed know some things that Barry Oslow did not know.

"You're right" she said cordially when the president told her about the botched press conference. "I made sure The Grid went down. And the cell phone network. And most of the landline phone system."

"Why?!" the president desperately wanted to know.

"Because, Barry... I have executed Operation Blackout."

"What?!"

"This way, Barry, you can't get an edge on me again. I called them and said that if they land earlier I will offer them to up your ante in the negotiations. Apparently they agreed. I also ordered the blackout because this way I control the information flow in this country. That includes the information flow between you and your private intelligence group."

No one would ever know if that was really her motive. But if it was, it failed miserably. She underestimated Barry Oslow's ability to negotiate himself to an upper hand, at least against her. She underestimated the power of negotiations without preconditions.

The communications blackout on top of the widespread rumors about a pending alien invasion triggered a national panic. People really believed that War of the Worlds, or at least Independence Day, was going to happen. The streets of New York, Chicago, Los Angeles, Houston, Philadelphia, Boston, Atlanta, Phoenix and other major cities were filled with people who left their offices and their homes to come out in the streets and watch the skies for themselves.

Holly Stanton had expected this. She had talked to a military leader she trusted, an admiral who had made a stunning career when her brother was president. She had informed the admiral about the pending arrival of the Zoh'moorians and he had promised to use his high-ranking position at the Pentagon to make sure the military stayed calm. His only concern had been that president Oslow might order the armed forces to engage the invaders. The vice president had thrown her head back and laughed out loud. It was a snowball's chance in Hell, she told him, that the president would ever order the United States armed forces to do anything except cut spending.

She was right. During her conversation with the president, he did not mention the military even once. It did not even occur to him that his country should put up a fight. That was all the more stunning since his own vice president was cooperating with the aliens right under his nose.

Of course, Holly Stanton had not come unprepared. In her drawer she had a Commander in Chief order to the United States armed forces to stand down and not engage the Zoh'moorians. All it needed was president Oslow's signature. She was going to give it to the Supreme General in front of the president.

Just another one of her tricks to stay on top of the president.

*　　　*　　　*

Watlaan was stunned by what L'Faa told her.

"Quim wants to run for the Executive Office?" she asked in disbelief.

"Executive Izah is resigning due to poor health" L'Faa told her. "It is not official yet. I guess Izah told Quim personally. Why, I do not know. They have met a few times, and you know as well as anyone how strictly regulated the meetings are between Delegates of the Assembly and members of the Executive Office. Quim is usually very good with ethics rules."

"Maybe he is just concerned about Izah's health" Watlaan suggested.

"I thought so, too. But let's go back to my office. I have something you might want to see. Something I found on the GalaxyNet last night."

Watlaan was impressed by the wall-mounted three-dimensional computer screen that L'Faa had in her office. Three-dimensional displays were old-tech, but this one was new. It even transmitted smells and wind.

"I wanted it for meetings" L'Faa explained the expensive equipment.

She put the remote pointer on her index finger and clicked a couple of times on the screen. A news clip appeared.

"This is from Teura Vaar" she said.

The camera showed a big lawn outside the World Assembly Hall, the legislature on Teura Vaar. Since the image was three-dimensional, it felt as though they were right there with the large crowd. They even felt the damp weather.

But the most amazing part was the fact that the large crowd of tens of thousands of people were just standing there, peacefully and quietly.

To an outsider it looked almost serene, but anyone familiar with Teuran culture knew right away that these were dramatic scenes.

"Oh, my God" said Watlaan. "A massive popular protest."

"The crowd tallied over sixty thousand people. It was the second largest popular protest in the history of the Fourth Teuran Republic. Now, watch what happens next."

The camera zoomed out from the crowd and turned to the right. The picture was crisp clear three-dimensional. It even displayed the damp weather so accurately that they almost felt the moisture right there, in the office where they were sitting. The camera-bot turned smoothly and quietly – the older versions had emitted an irritating hissing sound that disturbed the broadcast – and focused in on the sloped walkway up to the main entrance.

A man's distinct face appeared right in the middle.

"Quim" Watlaan noted.

"Listen to him."

"These are perilous times" Quim declared. "Our peaceful accomplishments through all these years are in jeopardy. The forces of aggression are once again prowling the halls of our government offices. And nowhere have they made better friends than in the Executive Office of our beloved Federation. Our Executives have turned this noble institution into an outlet for their personal aggression."

His choice of words surprised Watlaan.

"I haven't heard him talk like this before" she said.

"He is getting old" L'Faa smiled, but her smile quickly vanished. "He goes on to talk about how we need someone on the Executive Office who is committed to peace… at all cost."

"Peace at all cost" Watlaan repeated. "And why does he want to be on the Executive Office?"

"It is the only office that would take him higher from where he is today."

"Political vanity" Watlaan almost spat out the words. "And he is ready to hurl an entire world into oppression and tyranny to get there."

"At any rate, Wa, this intelligence report about the android with humanoid DNA from Ultra four two four may change the whole situation. I may be able to convince the Executive Office to issue a marching order to Strike Group Fourteen based on this video of Quim's speech and the report about that android."

"If you do" Watlaan said slowly, "you will send us out in another war."

Watlaan was weary. L'Faa had the greatest sympathy for her. And she shared her friend's concerns and fear of what impact another war would have on Danarvia. But she also knew that Strike Group 14 was widely superior to the Zoh'moorians. It would not come to war. At most, it would be a couple of skirmishes.

"War" L'Faa said, as if to taste the word. "No, this is not war. Not yet."

She looked out the window at the trees up on the hill where they had been hiking.

"But what is the option? Quim is obviously bending the Charter of Liberty his way for his own reasons. We are going to meet him in a moment, by the way. There is no doubt in my mind that he is doing all this to get elected to the Executive Office."

"He is also drawing a lot of support from Freedom Purists, minarchists and others who believe that any military operation beyond defending Danarvian space is unconstitutional" Watlaan pointed out. "And if Quim is right... then his personal motives don't really matter, do they?"

L'Faa listened to her friend and sat quiet for a moment.

"What do you think, Wa?" she asked. "Just between you and me."

"I'm not sure. I fear we will be setting a precedent for the future if we intervene to help Earth. It will be a lot easier to expand the military and intervene elsewhere. There are two full-scale wars raging in the Temptation Sea right now. Should we intervene there?"

"I'm also not sure. I guess my biggest question is if we are willing to sacrifice the freedom of the billions of people on Earth to maintain a Purist interpretation of our constitution."

"What's the price of peace?" Watlaan asked, thinking out loud.

"What's the price of freedom?" L'Faa added.

*   *   *

When Holly Stanton walked out to the helicopter that waited for her and the president, she felt happier and stronger than she had in a long time. It was almost as if this whole experience with the Zoh'moorians, and the elegant coup that she had effectively carried out, would in fact pay off. She would soon become the undisputed, the unchallengeable, leader of America – and soon enough of the entire world.

She had silenced much of the opposition and she had control over the Grid and other information channels. Once the Grid got back on again it would be under her supervision.

Everything was perfect. Even president Oslow seemed uneasy. His negotiations behind her back could soon prove to have been worth nothing.

Well, not everything was perfect, as a staffer reminded the vice president just as she was climbing in to the helicopter.

"What?!" she exclaimed. "You're lying!"

"I'm afraid not, ma'm. He's still on the air."

"That's impossible! We pulled the plug on the Grid hours ago! He can't broadcast without the Grid! Sheila!"

"Yes, ma'm."

"Find out how the Hell he can still be broadcasting!"

"Yes, ma'm."

Furious, vice president Stanton ordered a radio with AM band so she could listen to The Great Educator as they flew out to the airport.

It was infuriating enough to make her want to throw the radio out the window of the helicopter. And it did not make things easier that Barry Oslow was sitting right across from her with a cautious smile on his face.

She pretended not to see him.

"My fellow Americans" Ross Landau said. "Today, as you probably know by now, our freedom will be challenged in a way it has never been challenged before. Our country, our entire Earth, is about to be invaded by aliens from another planet. I know this is going to be very tough times for you, and believe me, it is for me, too. But I will not go away. I will be here. Do not turn off your radio. I will always be out here on the AM band. You have probably already noticed that we cannot get access to the Grid, and your cable TV as well as your FM radio stations have gone silent. But this has not stopped me from broadcasting, for I... Ross Landau... do not take orders from the government. Now, you probably wonder why we are under this media blackout. I am wondering myself, and I have some thoughts on that. I will share them with you in a moment. But first, I would like to tell you that even though you are probably concerned right now, for your safety and the safety of your loved ones... there is hope, and I know that whatever these aliens will try to do, they will fail. Because, folks, we are Americans, and Americans do not let themselves be ruled by anyone, especially not beings from another planet, who have no business here in the first place."

Ross went on to say that he hoped the military would be ready to fight the invaders, a comment that made Holly Stanton furious.

"Find out how the Hell that man can still be on the air!" she ordered her chief of staff for the second time and turned off the broadcast.

"Uh, we're already working on it, ma'm."

Holly Stanton looked at her chief of staff and was just about to say something when she caught a glimpse of the sky from the helicopter.

There it was. The first Zoh'moorian vessel to come within sight.

It was probably the scariest thing most people had ever seen. This one was for real. It was not some computerized movie full of special effects gimmicks.

This was really happening.

Goryell, Thor and Carl did not see the ship at first. They were sitting in Goryell's Cadillac on Leesburg Pike on their way in to Washington when they picked up Ross on the radio. They all cheered that he was still on, even though they all knew perfectly well what technological trickery the Earth Assignment Detail had come up with to guarantee that Ross could keep on broadcasting.

They were heading for Reagan National Airport. Their eavesdropping on the Earth-Zoh'moor communications had revealed the Supreme General's plans to land there and meet with the president.

"Look at all this panic" Thor said and looked out the window.

"Reminds me of Crying Lady" Goryell said.

"Who?"

"It's a world out on the edge of the galaxy."

"What happened there?"

"I was still in college back then. I had gone out there... without telling my parents... they would have gone berserk if I told them. It's a dangerous place because it's right on the edge of the galaxy. Anyway. There was this big scare because sensors had picked up a huge object coming right at us from outside of the galaxy. It took six hours for the officials to calm people down and convince them that it was actually just an unusual energy cloud."

"Did it hit the planet?"

"Oh, no, not at all. I think Frontline Services dispersed it."

"What a poetic name for a planet" Carl noted. "Crying Lady. Where did it get its name from?"

"I'll tell you later."

Carl glanced out the window.

"There!" he said and pointed up in the sky.

There it was.

The first Zoh'moorian ship.

"It's beginning" Thor almost whispered.

*   *   *

When Goryell pulled in to Reagan National Airport he found the driveway to the parking area blocked by police. Goryell casually rolled down his window and asked the nearest cop where he could park.

"The airport is closed" the officer replied.

"My sister just landed here this morning" Goryell lied. "She called and said the city is in chaos and she refuses to get on the subway. I can't just leave her here."

"Sorry. Can't let you through."

"We're from South Carolina. I'm just up here for business and she just flew in from her first trip to Europe. She's probably scared to death by that... thing..." and Goryell pointed up to the Zoh'moorian ship. "Please, let me go get her. We'll be out of here in no time."

The police officer looked at the three men. He thought Goryell's face had slightly odd proportions and his ears were almost square. He figured that was what you look like if you are from South Carolina where cousins married cousins.

"Oh, what the Hell" he said and waived them through.

They parked the car as quickly as they could and rushed over to the nearest terminal. Carl's leg was still bothering him a bit, so he could not run.

There were cops everywhere. But they did not seem to be particularly concerned with checking people. In fact, they did not really seem to know what they were supposed to do there. Most of them just stood there chatting. A few answered questions and two of them arrested a man who walked around with a sign saying THE WORLD ENDS TOMORROW.

"Look at this" Carl said. "It's almost unreal."

People were flocking to the windows that gave them a view of the airport runways and platforms. They were not talking much. Many of them looked frightened. Others were genuinely curious.

Thor and Carl went up to the window. Thor turned around to waive Goryell over to them.

"Hey, Goryell" he said.

Goryell was looking the other way. He heard Thor call his name and turned. He held up his index finger toward him.

"I'll be right back" he said and vanished into the crowd.

"What's with him?" Carl asked.

"Maybe he needed to go to the bathroom."

But Goryell did not head for the bathroom. Instead he went after the police officers and the old man with the sign. He did not know why, but there was something in the man's face that caught his attention.

The man, who was very old, had a long beard and dirty, grey, long hair. He wore rags for clothes and odd shoes. His legs were crooked and he had scars all over his face and neck.

And he was not happy. Goryell was close enough to hear every word he said.

"I have been carrying this sign around every day for twenty one years" he yelled at the officers. "Today, I am finally right. And you are arresting me?! You should arrest the president for inviting the Zoh'moorians to come and take over!"

The... Zoh'moorians...

Goryell got goose bumps when he heard the man call the invaders by their real name. How could this man know who the aliens were?

The two officers pulled the man out of the terminal and over toward a police car.

"His eyes" Goryell said to himself. "His eyes..."

Suddenly, he knew. He had no idea how this was even remotely possible, but he knew that he had something in common with that man.

He needed an excuse to strike up a conversation, so he made up a bogus story to tell the cops. It was probably not going to work, but he had to try it.

He dashed past the cops and the old man, turned on a dime and looked at the police officers.

"Excuse me" he said. "But... this man... he... he, uh, is my grandfather."

"Your grandfather?"

The old man looked at Goryell. He was tired and almost seemed irritated that someone had interrupted his arrest.

Goryell looked at him. His heart almost skipped a beat. There was no doubt.

The man's irises were yellow.

Goryell quickly pulled out his neck chain. The old man's eyes almost popped out of their sockets.

Goryell wore his space flight academy medallion around his neck, just as tradition demanded. He usually kept it inside his shirt, but this was a perfect time to display it.

The police officers, of course, had no clue what it was. But the old man did. He stopped protesting and lamenting. He could not take his eyes off the medallion.

"What's his name, then?" one of the officers asked.

"Gar" Goryell said quickly.

"Gar? What kind of a name is that?"

"Gar Mohhaw."

The man managed to produce a smile.

"My... grandson" he said. "How did you find me?"

"Grandpa" Goryell said as calmly as he could. "You were not at home, and you've been talking about space aliens for so long... so I figured I would find you here."

"Hey, grandpa?" said the other officer. "What's this man's name?"

"His name..." the old man said, pretending to search his memory.

"He's too senile" Goryell said. "He's been missing for a few days, so he probably has not taken his pills."

"Bob, what do you think?" one officer asked the other.

"I say we got bigger things to worry about. If this kid here can take care of him, well, I have no problem with that."

"Alright" said the first officer and unlocked the old man's handcuffs. "I'm releasing him into your custody."

"Listen, son" said officer Bob to Goryell. "If we find him anywhere around here again, yelling about the world coming to an end or anything like that, I'm gonna book him. And you, too. Understand?"

"Yes, sir" Goryell said. "Absolutely."

The cops went back inside the terminal. Goryell looked at the old man. The old man looked at Goryell.

"Gar Mohhaw" the old man said and smiled. "Been a while since I heard his name. Great hardball player."

"The best midfield kicker in the galaxy."

"So you're with Advanced Retrieval. But you don't look like you're from Hwal Five One."

"Right. I'm Goryell, and yes, I'm with Advanced Retrieval. But I grew up on La'au Schoh. My uncle married a Hwali woman. He took after her interest in hardball. Every time I meet them, all they talk about is Hwali hardball."

"Do your cousins have yellow eyes?" the man asked with a smile.

"Yes, they do."

They stood quiet for a moment. The Zoh'moorian ship was approaching and made a lot of noise. Goryell looked up at it. Then he looked at the old man, who looked at the ship.

"Who are you?" Goryell asked.

The man did not answer. His eyes were fixed on the Zoh'moorian ship.

"I have prayed so much that this day would never come" he said. "I guess the Gods got tired of me."

He turned to Goryell. There was something melancholic over his face. His smile was sad as he raised the palm of his left hand in a greeting gesture.

"Joh Ryndl. Navigator with Longreach. Assigned to The Sundancer."

"The Sundancer? But what are you doing here?? That ship was lost in the Scatterbelt! That's fifteen thousand light years from here!"

"No!" Joh Ryndl protested, sincerely upset. "What nonsense! Who told you such a fairy tale?"

"Did you crash here?"

Joh Ryndl said something but the noise from the descending Zoh'moorian ship drowned it out. Goryell grabbed him by the arm and pulled him inside.

"Come with me" he said. "I want to hear your story."

"I'm very hungry. Can you get me something to eat?"

They went over to a Burger King. It was about to close because the staff wanted to go home. Goryell convinced them to sell him four Whoppers and big sodas. The woman at the register did not even charge him. She just wanted to get out of work and home to her family.

They went over toward the big window where Thor and Carl were waiting. There were people running back and forth now – quite another scene than earlier. A lot of people were uneasy, some verging on panic. Goryell pulled them in to a secluded corner where he could see Thor and Carl without having to stand in the way of all the people.

Joh Ryndl ate the burger in almost one bite.

"Who are they?" he asked.

"My friends" said Goryell and nodded over toward Thor and Carl.

"So you're a team."

"Actually they are Earthlings I work with."

"You have made contact?"

"No. This is a clandestine operation. We are trying to help them as best we can."

He munched on his burger for a moment, while Joh Ryndl finished his soda.

"So, old man… tell me how you ended up here."

"Do you really have time for that now?"

"I've seen alien ships before. This one is unusually ugly, but…"

He shrugged his shoulders. Joh Ryndl sighed.

"Alright, young man. Well, I was hired by Longreach after space flight school. I liked the prospect of adventures. And… well… that's what I got."

He sipped the last of his soda as the Zoh'moorian ship set down outside. It was big, bulky and still made a lot of noise.

"I was assigned to The Sundancer, an exploration vessel charged with finding new raw material sites for Longreach."

"The space exploration company that claims mining rights" Goryell nodded.

"And then leases them to mining companies" Joh Ryndl filled in. "We were assigned to space outside of Danarvia. Our first couple of trips were in to The Temptation Sea, but there were already a couple of space-age civilizations there that had begun exploring their solar systems. Longreach thought they'd get in trouble if they made contact with them. Instead they sent us across the unchartered space between the Felix sector and, well, this sector."

"You went that way? That's a long way to get here!"

"And bear in mind that this was forty five years ago."

"Did you crash here on Earth?"

"Oh, no. We had much worse luck than that."

"Wait!" Goryell exclaimed, suddenly connecting some dots. "Oh, wow! Let me... let me ask... was one of your crew members from Ultra four two four?"

"You really did your homework, son."

"Oh, boy... What a stroke of luck that I found you!"

"I'm glad you see it that way" Joh Ryndl said. "I, for one, have lived most of my life out here."

"Hey, I'm sorry. I didn't mean it that way. Were you captured by the Zoh'moorians?"

"As a matter of fact, that's exactly what happened. We had chartered four planets and were just going to make one last landing. We found a planetoid that was soaked with all kinds of attractive minerals. But as soon as we had started working we found artificial caves. Next thing we knew, a Zoh'moorian ship showed up and we were captured."

He paused and turned very serious.

"They held us there for twenty years. We humanoids were used as slave labor. The two reptilians were treated better. Our captain... he was the one from Ultra... he was tortured and... well..."

"What? Executed?"

Joh Ryndl looked down.

"You could say that."

He looked very uncomfortable. Goryell decided to change the subject.

"How did you end up here on Earth?"

"After the captain... died... the rest of us humanoids were taken here. Two others died in custody here. They had been treated badly back on Zoh'moor after the Tyrant took over."

"Were you released?"

"I escaped."

"What can you tell me about the Zoh'moorians?"

"They're as evil as evil gets. At least since the Tyrant took over. Before that... they were just prejudiced and inflexible. Very collectivist society. Big government. It was almost like the Tyrant didn't make much of a difference. Anyway. The Earthlings have been cooperating with them for a long time. I've been here twenty five years. But I always knew the Zoh'moorians would want to come here and take over. They want to turn this in to their colony."

Goryell looked at him. He was still overwhelmed by the incredible stroke of luck. He had found a fellow Danarvian who had been a crew member onboard a space ship that had been declared salvaged 15,000 light years away. The man had been held captive by the Zoh'moorians – and, apparently, by the American government.

He wanted to take Joh Ryndl back to their operations headquarters in New Mexico. But there was no time. He had other things to do.

"Why did you come here today?" he asked.

Joh Ryndl looked up at him, almost amused by the question.

"Where else would I go?"

They looked at one another. Goryell felt enormous sympathy for Joh Ryndl. The man had lived his life as a prisoner and a castaway on worlds that until very recently had been like black dots in space to anyone who might even have come up with the idea to come look for him. Completely cut off from his roots, his home.

It was a fate worse than death, in some ways.

Goryell was interrupted in his thoughts by Thor, who called on him from the window.

"Come here! You have got to see this!"

*   *   *

The helicopter with Holly Stanton and Barry Oslow landed at Reagan National Airport just in the nick of time. The Zoh'moorian command vessel sat down just as the president and the vice president stepped out of the helicopter.

The command vessel was huge. It was about 1,500 ft long, easily 30 stories tall plus a big section at the bottom that had flat walls. They probably had storage and engineering down there.

A large number of different weapons were mounted along its sides. The sheet metal was dark grey and some parts were black.

"Man, what a piece of junk" Goryell chuckled.

"Junk??" Carl asked.

"It's a tin box! Look at all those flat surfaces. They could just as well paint target markers on them. And what with at all those edges, the inefficient shape… It has no gravi-metric stabilizers. Must be rough riding around in space in that thing."

"How insensitive of you."

Goryell turned to his left. A woman stood right next to him and looked very self important.

"What was that?" Goryell said.

"You're being very insensitive" the woman repeated with a lecturing tone in her voice. "You should be more respectful toward those aliens. Just because they are different from you, does not mean your way of life is better than theirs."

Goryell stared at her. He was baffled and stunned.

"You have a lot to learn about this country" Thor said in his other ear with a smile on his face.

Oslow and Stanton stood outside their helicopter and waited until the Zoh'moorian ship had come to a complete halt. They were about four hundred feet away from it. Between them was just a long stretch of tarmac.

After a couple of minutes, a hatch opened right above what looked like an engine section. A small box-shaped shuttle emerged and slowly descended to a position half way between the ship and the helicopter. It landed and opened doors on three sides. A dozen reptilians came out, dressed in black and red uniforms. They had some sort of rifles and quickly moved into positions between their small shuttle and the helicopter.

The crowd at the window where they were standing, gasped at what they saw.

"Oh, my God, look at them!"

"So… ugly."

"How can you say that?? That's so insensitive!"

"I was expecting small aliens, but look at these guys. They're tall."

"Why are they armed?"

"Oh, my God!" said the woman next to Goryell and pressed her fingers against her cheeks. "They are armed because they are afraid! We have made them fear us!!"

"No" Goryell said. "They're armed because they are soldiers."

The woman looked up at him. There was anger in her eyes.

"What kind of white, chauvinist, Christian man are you?! Do you have no respect at all for other cultures??"

"I think I've seen more of other cultures than you have, ma'm" Goryell said mildly.

"It's people like you who instill fear in these peaceful visitors!" the woman told him. "It's people like you who make them angry and afraid!!"

"The Hell we have" said another woman, just behind them. "Don't you see what's going on here? They're here to take over."

"Then why is our president out there talking to them?" someone else asked. "And our vice president?"

"That's the question, alright" said Carl, glancing at Thor.

A second small shuttle emerged from the same hatch in the big ship. It looked similar to the first one and landed next to it. A front door opened and a short walkway was folded out. But no one emerged from it.

Oslow and Stanton started walking toward the second shuttle. Stanton leaned over to Oslow and said something. He shook his head and said something back. It was hard to judge from a distance, but it looked like vice president Stanton was more uncomfortable than the president, and it did not seem to get better when they talked.

When they reached the folded-out walkway four more soldiers emerged and made a sign to them. Stanton and Oslow stopped.

Joh Ryndl tapped Goryell on the shoulder.

"Those are Fah'marook" he said. "The Tyrant's personal guard. Elite soldiers. They get better food, better weapons, they're allowed to live in seaside resorts… The regular army soldiers fear them like a superior enemy."

He looked out the window and his face turned very serious. He hid his hands inside his coat.

"Fah'marook" he said. "Their name means 'Protectors of the Common Good'. They're merciless. The worst crap of butchers around. They take joy in dominating and spreading fear around them."

"What kind of weapons do they have?"

"Not very advanced. They're laser based, quite effective on short range but quickly lose power over longer distances."

"Who's the old man?" Thor wanted to know.

Goryell hesitated for a moment.

"A stroke of luck."

"Huh?"

"I'll explain later."

A group of people emerged from the second shuttle. Based on their clothing and the respect that the Fah'marook showed them, Goryell guessed that they were the supreme general and his closest staff.

"See the guy in the middle?" said Joh Ryndl. "That's the supreme general."

The supreme general walked half way down to Oslow and Stanton. Then he stopped and made a gesture. Two of the soldiers went down to President Oslow. They put their hands on his shoulders and pushed him down. President Oslow immediately complied. He bowed his head and completed the kneeling as if he was praising Allah at the mosque.

"Wow, did you see that!" someone exclaimed.

"They're humiliating our president!" someone else said.

"No!" said the woman next to Goryell. "He is showing them respect! He is a wise man!"

"You call that wisdom?" Goryell asked with only a modicum of interest.

"President Oslow is a diverse, wise and understanding man" the self important woman taught him.

The supreme general slowly walked down to Oslow and Stanton. Holly Stanton bowed her head. President Oslow glanced up at the supreme general and then bowed his head again.

The supreme general made a casual gesture with his hand.

"That's how Zoh'moorians hail The Tyrant" Joh Ryndl explained. "On your knees, with your heads bowed. Oslow and Stanton must have practiced this."

Thor looked at Joh Ryndl.

"How do you know all this?"

Joh Ryndl glanced at him, but did not say anything.

"So you're saying they're humiliating Stanton and Oslow?" Goryell asked.

"Oh, a hundred percent" Joh Ryndl nodded. "But look at that!"

After the hailing rite the president and the vice president joined the supreme general and walked in to their shuttle. The door closed.

The people around them at the window gasped again.

"Oh, my God! They took our leaders!"

"God help us all!"

"Maybe they're just negotiating? Barry Oslow is a wise man."

"You kidding? Didn't you see how they had to bow to that gorilla? They're here to take over!"

"Barry Oslow knows what he's doing."

"Really? Like with Taiwan, huh?"

"I gotta hear what Ross Landau has to say about this."

"Where is the army?"

"Army? Do you want to provoke a war??"

"We didn't provoke them, you idiot! They're invading us!"

"You're a war mongering Capitalist fascist pig!"

"You're an anti-American pinko Commie!"

Two men got in to a fight. Two cops rushed over, separated them and took them away.

Several minutes passed. Nothing happened out there and the crowd calmed down.

"It's lecture time" Joh Ryndl said. "He's telling them what their proper roles are. By the time they come back out again they will be nothing more than errand runners for the supreme general."

He was right. But only partly. When the shuttle door opened again only president Oslow emerged.

"Where's Holly Stanton?" someone asked.

"Maybe she's still in there negotiating."

"Yeah, they probably realized he's too spineless."

"I always knew Barry Oslow was a good, wise man" said the woman next to Goryell.

Goryell turned to Joh Ryndl.

"What are they doing with her?" Goryell asked Joh Ryndl.

"I'd guess they've decided that Oslow is their guy. He's their puppet. Stanton is probably being held for another lecture or two."

His face turned dark.

"Zoh'moorians don't negotiate" he said. "They dictate. Especially to humanoids. They consider us an inferior species. Never forget that."

As soon as president Oslow got in his helicopter and lifted off the Zoh'moorian soldiers entered their shuttles again, which returned to the mother ship.

"That's it?" Thor asked. "This is how they take over??"

"Don't worry" Joh Ryndl smiled. "You won't be disappointed."

"What do you mean?"

The old man pointed up to the sky. It was rapidly filling with Zoh'moorian vessels. They landed everywhere. Some of them landed at the airport.

"Fah'marook troop carriers" he explained. "They're coming in to deal the first blow of fear to the civilians. Then it's time for the regular army."

His face turned grim.

"God help the American people."

*   *   *

After his meeting with the Zoh'moorian supreme general Barry Oslow flew back to the White House. He looked very self confident when he sat in the chair that said "President" on the headrest. He glanced out the window and seemed to be thinking. A faint smile emerged on his face.

He got an update on the information blockade that Holly Stanton had put in place. His smile disappeared when he was told that Ross Landau was still on the air.

"Get the FBI and the Secret Service out to all the radio stations that are broadcasting his show" he ordered. "I want the stations seized and shut down permanently."

"But sir" said one of his aides. "The vice president already gave that order. All reports we get back say that the radio stations already are closed. The radio stations are empty and shut down. They are broadcasting even though nobody is there. They even tried to shut off power to the radio stations. It didn't work."

Nobody knew how to silence Ross Landau. Of course, most Americans had nothing against that. Quite the contrary: his audience rose to unprecedented levels as even devout liberals tuned in to find out what was actually going on.

And Ross knew. Goryell was carrying a messenger in his pocket. He kept sending messages back to Tahm Qaar with live updates from Reagan Airport. Tahm Qaar relayed them to Ross as they came in.

And Ross informed the American people.

"I have to say" Tahm Qaar said to him, "you're a very impressive man. Your country is being invaded, your president and your vice president have betrayed your people, and you're sitting here, calm and focused, informing your listeners of what's going on out there."

"Thank you" Ross said. "But this is what I was born to do."

He took a bite out of a sandwich.

"Don't get me wrong. I'm outraged to the bottom of my heart. If it would help I would go pick up a gun and go out and fight the Zoh'moorians. But that's not my call. This is what I do best."

One of his staffers handed him a water bottle.

"Thank you. You see... the American people are of a moral fiber that you won't find anywhere else on this planet. I'm not saying other people are weak or immoral. But Americans have been raised in a society that was built on the principle of freedom. We have a moral head start, so to speak, compared to others. So we rise higher, achieve more. And we don't use our strength and our accomplishments to dominate others. We use it to help them. We share our wealth, our compassion and moral fortitude with others. There has never been a people like us on this planet, ever."

"You'll make fine members of the Danarvian Federation" Tahm Qaar said and gave away a smile.

"Thank you, I hope we can get there. But right now I need to keep my people's spirit up. I'm the only one out there."

He chuckled.

"You know, it's kind of absurd. The liberals have been wanting to shut me down for twenty five years. And now, when I'm alone on the airwaves, even the liberals are listening in larger numbers than ever. And they know that I tell it as it is."

He was right, of course. Even the professors at Schuyler University had tuned in to Ross Landau.

The university president also listened to Ross. He felt he had to call a faculty meeting to discuss the situation. Half the faculty had already left for the summer, but enough of them were still there. They filled the small auditorium.

All the professors were excited.

"I never thought I would experience this" said one professor.

"Me neither" said another.

"I am just a bit concerned that I cannot watch Enlight on the Grid."

"Yes, there must be some sort of disturbance."

The university president, P Hill Glotzenblutz, looked quite serious when he opened the meeting.

"We all have a lot of questions, and concerns, but I think the best we can do right now is to just stay calm. The Zoh'moorians… which apparently is what they are called… are cooperating with our government. I have heard that our vice president is still negotiating with them onboard their ship. And we all know what a remarkable man president Oslow is. So I think we can feel safe. The most important thing to remember is that we do not offend the aliens, but that we greet them with the same tolerance as we show toward others who come here to seek opportunities and a better life for themselves."

That inspired the faculty to stretch their intellectual abilities to their maximum. And a little farther, as they commented on the present situation.

"The Zoh'moorians are obviously very enlightened."

"Yes, they chose to meet with president Oslow. That shows that they are sophisticated and educated."

"They have so much to teach us. We are so primitive."

"And selfish."

"Oh, I cannot wait to meet them!"

"They are not humans, but some kind of reptilians. Is there a more sensitive term for that?"

"How about co-beings?"

"Perhaps we can invite one of their scholars to come and teach here?"

"Yes, we can set up an exchange program where we can go to their universities and learn!"

"That is such an exciting idea! Imagine how refined and sophisticated they must be!"

"Can you imagine how tolerant they are!"

"I've heard they are even smarter than the Europeans!"

"They have green skin. We must add that to our affirmative action cards. I mean, for job applications from their professors."

"And their students. We could bring lots of their students here to teach our students tolerance and cultural diversity."

"I'm sure we can get federal grants to do that."

"Yes, diversity scholarships for our co-beings."

"We can develop new courses and hire new faculty for our cultural diversity department."

"We don't have a cultural diversity department."

"We don't? How insensitive of us! We must repent! Let's form a department of cultural diversity right now!"

As the faculty members at Empire University padded each other on the backs and shared expectations of refined and sophisticated dinners with professors from Zoh'moorian universities, the first Zoh'moorian Fah'marook troops landed in New York City. The soldiers began rounding up civilian New Yorkers on Times Square. Everyone was stripped of their clothes and the men were taken away in shuttles. Four transit cops who tried to stop them were shot dead on the spot.

*   *   *

RAGE

Onboard the command vessel of Strike Group 14, vice admiral Ghaul eagerly followed the continuous reports from his vessel inside Earth's solar system. He was witnessing a full-scale military invasion, and that was not something every strike group commander in Frontline Services had the chance to do. Especially from a distance, without being directly involved.

He could have cherished the opportunity and seen it as a pure learning experience. But he was too restless, too eager to do some work for his salary, to just sit idle and watch. He ordered his tactical division to record every move the Zoh'moorians made and to recreate them in small-scale holographic sequences.

Sometimes he had to get up, walk around and share some details in the reports with his senior officers. He had his second officer send out regular updates to the captains of the other ships in the strike group. He also demanded real-time analysis of the reports by his engineering and strategy departments.

His chief weapons technology officer was not very impressed with the Zoh'moorians.

"Bottom line" he said, "we can take out their ships with toy guns. It's amazing Earth is not resisting them."

"Yes, amazing" Ghaul mumbled. "Thanks."

His chief engineer had already told him that the Zoh'moorian ships were poorly built and had stupidly inefficient propulsion systems.

"It's almost as if the entire fleet was built for one purpose only" he told Ghaul.

"What purpose?"

"To invade Earth."

Ghaul shook his head.

"That's the most ridiculous reason I've ever heard for building a space fleet. But then again... there is nothing more irrational than a rational being."

His first officer signaled to him from the other end of the bridge. Ghaul went over to him.

"Sir, look at this" first officer Mahir said.

He had just deciphered a message from Frontline Services headquarters. Ghaul came over and glanced at the computer screen.

"Headquarters just relayed a report from Advanced Retrieval. They have found a DNA-template humanoid android on Earth."

"Was it built on Earth?"

"Probably built on Zoh'moor, apparently planted on Earth. Sub-Kahpiyan technology. But here's the best part: its DNA template is from Ultra four two four."

"Are you sure??"

"Yes, sir" Mahir added. "They also found a survivor from a Federation vessel."

"A castaway?"

"No, sir. He was taken prisoner by the Zoh'moorians. Sir... you may know his ship. It was The Sundancer."

"Impossible" Ghaul shook his head. "The Sundancer was lost in The Scatterbelt. I should know."

"Yes, sir" Mahir said, "I know your uncle was onboard. But the DNA analysis of the android has been matched with that of the captain of The Sundancer. And this castaway... he's been firmly identified as one of the crew members."

Ghaul thought for a moment.

"This means that we have much more reason to get ourselves involved" he noted. "For all we know, the remaining crew members could be alive."

"The Executive Office still won't allow us to go in with full force" Mahir pointed out.

"Yes, but there is a lot we can do without getting involved directly."

He turned to the computer screen and pulled up a map of sector KB.

"I think it's time we took a closer look at Zoh'moor."

"We are too far away to send a long-range striker out."

"Not if we move the strike group… here… to this position. Half-way between Earth and Zoh'moor. Strictly speaking, our orders are not to engage the Zoh'moorian fleet. That gives a lot of space to fly around in."

Mahir smiled.

"I like your creativity, sir."

"Put together an all-reptilian special forces unit. I want them deployment ready in twenty four hours."

"You want them deployed on Zoh'moor? But that would mean getting involved in the conflict between Earth and Zoh'moor."

"Mahir, my dear friend" Ghaul smiled and put his hand on his first officer's shoulder. "That conflict is taking place on Earth. Not on Zoh'moor."

* * *

Goryell, Thor and Carl tried their best to get back to the car. It was not easy, especially with Carl's leg still bothering him. Joh Ryndl's old, crooked legs did not allow him to walk very fast, either. They had never healed properly after years and years of torture and slave labor.

They had to fight a big crowd through the terminal building and out on the walkway toward the parking garage. All the people who had gathered to see the Zoh'moorians land were now eager to get home to their loved ones.

The police had relaxed their security control – it seemed like most of the cops were just as eager as everyone else to get out of there. Even the people at the ticket booths at the exits from the parking garage had left their posts.

"Go to the other side of the river" Joh Ryndl suggested. "In to

Washington, DC. That's where the Fah'marook will concentrate their assault on the general public."

"Why would they assault regular people?" Thor asked.

"Fear and intimidation. That's their job. If they randomly assault people, no one will dare protest."

Traffic was slow from the airport up toward the Arlington Memorial Bridge.

"You'd think everyone would try to get out of the city" Carl said.

They passed I-395 and continued up on the George Washington Parkway, but traffic moved slower and slower until they came to a stop right by the Lady Bird Johnson Memorial Park.

"Look" Goryell said and pointed up ahead. "Some Zoh'moorian ships are blocking the road."

Fah'marook troops had sealed off the road and were checking cars.

"Why do they set up a roadblock the first thing they do?" Carl wondered. "They could not possibly have anything to look for."

"Again" Joh Ryndl explained, "it's a matter of intimidation. Regular people in their cars are suddenly faced with an intimidating-looking being that is pointing a strange weapon at them and behaving aggressively. It's the fear factor."

"Look" Thor said and pointed toward downtown DC on the other side of the river. "Their ships are landing everywhere."

"We'll never get anywhere at this speed" Goryell noted. "I suggest we park the car here and walk across that bridge."

"There is a subway station nearby" Thor pointed out. "We could take a train."

"The train drivers probably aren't at work anymore" Carl suggested.

He was right. As they got out of the car and walked up toward the Arlington Cemetery Metro station they met several people who advised them to turn around and walk across the Memorial bridge instead.

The bridge was crowded but there was no car traffic. They walked as calmly as they could, blending in with other pedestrians on their way in to DC. When they came closer to the District side of the bridge they saw large numbers of Fah'marook troops forming a blockade.

When Joh Ryndl saw them he stopped for a moment. Goryell noted a quick shift in his facial expressions, his yellow eyes focused entirely on the Zoh'moorian elite forces up ahead.

"You alright?" Goryell asked him.

Joh Ryndl did not respond at first.

"Think they might recognize you?"

"No" Joh Ryndl said quietly. "But we're going to have to pass them. You have to understand that they are ruthless, merciless, heartless… They will kill and torture just to spread fear."

"So… we just keep our heads down?" Thor asked.

"And try not to draw their attention" Goryell said.

Thor looked dissatisfied. He glanced at Goryell as if there was something more he wanted to hear.

"Unless, of course" Goryell continued, "they attack us."

Suddenly, Thor looked much happier.

"Whatever you do" Joh Ryndl added, "don't look at them, don't walk toward them."

As they came to the District end of the bridge, the Fah'marook troops had cut off access to the District landing. Vehicles were trapped on the bridge and they were only letting pedestrians through. Everyone was searched and the alien soldiers confiscated many bags and even some clothes from people.

"What are they looking for?" Carl asked.

"Nothing" said Joh Ryndl. "They're just showing who's in charge. Look, even the police officer is searched."

Two of the Zoh'moorians called on someone who was apparently an officer. They pointed to the policeman's gun and radio and the officer replied something. They took away the policeman's gun belt and stripped him of his radio. Then they let him pass through.

"The soldiers asked if they should humiliate the policeman" Joh Ryndl whispered. "The officer said that they could do that by taking away his gun, his authority."

Goryell made sure that he approached the Zoh'moorians first. He examined them discretely and noted that they were thinner yet somewhat taller than most Danarvian reptilians. Their faces were shorter and wider and they had a distinct row of "hill tops" on their tails. He could not remember any Danarvian reptilians who had those.

As he walked up to the soldiers, one of them raised his hand, formed as a fist, toward him. He said something and repeated it. Goryell had not seen them do this to anyone else.

"He wants you to stop staring at him" Joh Ryndl whispered behind him, with a voice that was notably tense.

Goryell looked down slowly. The Zoh'moorian held his fist up toward him until Goryell was looking straight down. Then he said something else and signaled to Goryell to pass through the check point.

As he had passed them, Goryell glanced over his shoulder and saw Thor be examined and then let through.

Next in line was Joh Ryndl. Goryell was just about to turn around and keep walking when he noticed something in Joh Ryndl's eyes.

They were turning white.

The yellow eyes of a Hwalian turned white only when his mind was filled to the brim with anger.

No, not anger. Rage.

Raw, uninhibited rage.

An unleashed urge to seek vengeance for a life lost and squandered by senseless tyranny. A thirst for blood, built and nurtured over decades of meaningless humiliation, torture, physical and mental abuse, deprivation ...

What happened next was exactly what Goryell had hoped would not happen. In a split second, Joh Ryndl had pulled a machete out of the sack he was carrying. It was a formidable close combat weapon. In the hands of anyone, it could kill and mutilate with frightening efficiency.

In the hands of Joh Ryndl it was more than that. Despite his age and physical condition, he made the machete an extension of himself. He handled it with such precision and force that anyone watching his carnage realized that he had been practicing for this for a long time.

A very long time.

Joh Ryndl killed the first Zoh'moorian by literally slicing his head off. The blade of the machete passed through the air so fast they barely saw it. The head came off with surprising ease. While it was still falling to the ground, Joh Ryndl had changed direction and drove the machete through the side of the next Zoh'moorian's torso. The stab was so deep that Goryell could see the edge come out on the other side. Joh Ryndl then pulled the machete out, turned in a lightning-quick maneuver with the back toward his next victim and let the turn give speed and power to the machete as he aimed at the skull of his third target.

When they heard the shots, Joh Ryndl had already sliced the skull of his third victim in half. He regained his balance and turned toward a fourth soldier. But the remaining four soldiers had finally aimed at him and the blasts from their weapons hit him just as he dived and aimed his machete at the next soldier's leg. His body literally incinerated before their eyes, but the machete actually pierced the fourth soldier's thigh before Joh Ryndl died.

For a moment, the scene was completely still. Nobody said or did anything for two seconds. Two very long, very quiet seconds.

Then the remaining Zoh'moorians did what Goryell had feared. They did what tyrannical butchers do when someone dares to fight back.

They started firing randomly at the civilians around them.

Goryell, Carl and Thor reacted just as they were trained to do.

They did not blow their cover. Instead they threw themselves to the ground and hoped that the Fah'marook soldiers would fire their weapons to intimidate and avenge, not to execute.

They were right. Of course, that did not help those three dozen people on the Arlington Memorial Bridge who were burned to death by Fah'marook laswer weapons. Nor did it help the hundreds of others who ran in panic and encountered other troops coming from the National Mall. Many of the panicking people were either killed or rounded up and led off to shuttles. They were stripped of their clothes, tied up and forced inside.

It took a while before Goryell, Thor and Carl got up again. They wanted to make sure that the Zoh'moorians were calm enough not to start shooting again. When they eventually were back on their feet the soldiers signaled to them to get off the bridge immediately.

Thor and Carl wanted to know who the old man was. A legitimate question, of course.

"He was navigator on a Danarvian ship" Goryell explained. "They wandered off deep into unchartered space and eventually ended up being taken prisoners by the Zoh'moorians."

"But how did he end up here on Earth?" Carl wanted to know.

"Your government had contacts with the Zoh'moorians long before Holly Stanton began conspiring with them. He was brought here and held captive by your government at some secret facility. He managed to escape and had spent the rest of his life as a fugitive here."

Thor and Carl looked at one another.

"Area Fifty One" they said with one mouth.

"What?" Goryell asked.

"Later" Carl said. "We better keep moving."

The outburst of violence on Arlington Memorial Bridge had attracted even more Fah'marook troops to the area. Fear was quickly arising among the civilians. Word spread quickly of the massacre on the bridge, but also of how people were being rounded up and taken prisoners by the Zoh'moorians.

With fear came desperation, and rumors spread of people taking up arms against the invaders. It was impossible to find out if this was actually true, but when Goryell communicated with his base in New Mexico he was told that the Advnaced Retrieval satellites had picked up no signs of organized armed resistance in America.

Despite the lack of resistance, the Zoh'moorian Fah'marook troops were very aggressive. At some checkpoints they stripped people of their clothes and ordered them to crawl on the ground. Sometimes they forced people to the ground and ordered them to stay there, face down, while Zoh'moorians simply stood on them while watching the area.

One man who was forced down pleaded with the Zoh'moorian soldiers:

"But... But I understand you! I am for diversity! I'm sensitive to your culture! I mean no harm! Why are you punishing *me*??"

A soldier knocked him to the ground and the biggest one among them stepped up on his back. They heard a crack from the man's body and saw him lose consciousness.

Everywhere, disorder was escalating to chaos. Goryell kept reporting back to his base, and much of what he reported went out over the radio waves thanks to Ross Landau. But the deteriorating situation made it difficult for Goryell to give the intelligence he had been sent out to provide.

"We need an observation post" he said to his Earthling companions.

"And we need to get in touch with our folks" Thor noted.

"Yeah, the Agents will have to respond to this one way or the other" Carl agreed.

"What kind of response do you have in mind?" Goryell asked.

"Commando raids, sabotage, information gathering..."

Goryell saw that they both looked very determined. He saw a call-to-duty kind of expression in their eyes. It was not hard to see why. Their country was being taken over by ruthless, tyrannical invaders. Their freedom, their independence and their very way of life was under attack.

"You're patriots" he said.

"We can gain a lot by coordinating" Thor suggested. "We just need to find a way to call our commanding officer."

Their conversation was interrupted by some mean-looking Fah'marook soldiers who approached them from up the street. They waived their weapons at them and shouted. A couple of them gestured to the three men to get down on their knees.

Behind the soldiers were a group of humans who had been stripped of their clothes. The men were being taken onboard a ship and the women were kicked around by Zoh'moorian soldiers who seemed to do it just to amuse themselves.

"We're next on their list" Thor mumbled.

The Zoh'moorian closest to them angrily made a gesture that was unmistakable.

"He wants us to strip naked" Carl guessed.

"I'm not gonna do it" Goryell said calmly. "He's too ugly."

The Zoh'moorian apparently did not appreciate Goryell's sense of humor. He fired a shot right above their heads.

"OK, guys" Goryell said, still calm and composed. "Ready for some action?"

*   *   *

POLITICS

The members of the Executive Office of the Danarvian Federation listened carefully to L'Faa when she presented her arguments to her fellow Executives.

"Taken together" she concluded, "these facts speak in favor of overriding Quim's demand for formal consultations. We have a strong case for ordering Frontline Services to intervene. Strike Group Fourteen is ready to go and according to all reports they are far superior to the Zoh'moorian military."

She had faced them with a big decision. If they ordered units from Frontline Services to engage a foreign military they did, by definition, declare war on that foreign power. There were occasional skirmishes along the Danarvian borders, but they were not acts of war. Most of them involved renegade forces from rogue planets outside Danarvia and were usually handled by local peace-keeping militias who patrolled the vast space of the outlying sectors.

But there was also the problem with Quim's demand for formal consultations. Constitutionally, it was very difficult for the Executive Office to disregard him. The circumstances had to be extra ordinary, and not everyone was convinced that such circumstances were present.

"Dear colleague" said Executive Izah. "Your proposal rests on three pillars. The first pillar is the commitment to Earth that was made a long time ago by the outer rim exploration group. The second pillar is the threat to freedom on Earth. The third pillar is the fact that our intelligence service has found an android with DNA from Ultra four two four, which, you say, implies that a Danarvian citizen was held captive by the Zoh'moorians."

"Correct" L'Faa confirmed.

"I'm afraid I have to disagree with your second pillar" Izah continued. "You are interpreting the Fourth Principle of our Charter of Liberty in a way that is inconsistent with Case Eighty-Four."

"I respectfully disagree" said L'Faa. "Case Eighty-Four has been used to motivate similar actions elsewhere. And in none of those cases did the Charter Court disapprove of our decisions to go to war."

"That does not mean we should rubberstamp military invasion" Izah replied with some emphasis. "Each case must be tried against the verdict on Case Eighty-Four. Our military is a resource of last resort, not the forefront of diplomatic efforts."

Another Executive asked to speak.

"I agree with you, Izah, that we cannot, we must not, rubberstamp military action. I also agree with you that Case Eighty-Four is debatable. But the Charter Court has the last say there, and it is up to us to execute the powers of the Danarvian government within the guidance of their verdicts. In this case, we can do that without violating the Fourth Principle. As L'Faa pointed out, we have history on our side here, and we are certainly not using our military as the forefront of diplomacy. We have no contacts with the Zoh'moorians, to begin with."

"Perhaps we should try that venue first" Izah replied. "Establishing diplomatic relations is a necessary condition for diplomatic relations."

Izah smiled at his own wit.

"It is rather unlikely that they would even talk to us" L'Faa suggested. "We all know of worlds that were run by tyrants who did not listen to any other words than those that came out of a gun."

"You are surmising many things" Izah protested. "For one, to be perfectly clear, we do not even know that Zoh'moor is governed by a tyrant."

"I think I speak for all of us when I say that we can safely assume that that is the case" said another Executive. "I suggest we vote on this."

"Very well" Izah sighed. "I am sad to note that the last vote I cast as a member of the Executive Office will be one of utter dissent with my colleagues."

"We regret that, too" said L'Faa. "We are all very impressed with your service to the Danarvian Federation and on this Office. I see your dissent in this your last vote as a tribute our constitutional republic."

The vote had been unanimous if not for Izah's dissent. It was immediately written as a formal marching order for Strike Group 14 to take all means necessary to protect Earth from the Zoh'moorian invasion. To put even more force behind the order, the Executive Office also gave Frontline Services mandate to dispatch the one of its armadas, a military combat entity large enough to invade and take over an entire world.

The news about the war vote traveled fast. When Quim heard about it he repeated his request to meet with the Executives. They granted it, mostly for constitutional reasons. But since the Executive Office had found new evidence in favor of helping Earth, Quim's meeting would no longer be a formal consultation, only a chat about the situation.

His only constitutional option was to take the Executive Office to court, namely the Charter Court. But that was a long, arduous process and in the meantime the Executive Office's decision would stand. So Quim saw no point in doing that.

They sat down in the conference room at the Executive Office. It was not their main meeting hall, which Quim made a note of. He also noted that L'Faa was not present.

"She is on her way" said Executive Izah.

Quim reluctantly sat down. He felt that the Executives were not going to give him any particular time or pay much interest to whatever he had to say. He also felt frustrated because he had planned to hold the upper hand when he met with them. That was no longer the case. They had basically side-stepped him. He was no longer coming there as a powerful statesman, but as an opinion-maker with a cause that was debatable at best, yesterday's news at worst.

He felt uncomfortable in that position and he did not intend to end his career like that. On the contrary, the war vote by the Executive Office reinforced his own commitment to win the seat on the Office that Executive Izah would soon be leaving. But he did not want to get elected as just another candidate. He wanted to come in to the Office a distinguished elder with exceptional wisdom and unprecedented experience.

To do so he would have to run an election campaign based on anti-war rhetoric. He would have to make the case that the Executive Office had done something almost unconstitutional when it voted to go to war with the Zoh'moorians. That would be tough if the Executive Office had no reason to listen to him when he criticized the war.

Then again, his opponents in the election would be less experienced politicians from all walks of the political life. Quim took comfort in that.

Sure, his opponents could throw a lot of facts at him. That android's DNA template was a particular problem. It could be used to argue that the Zoh'moorians had taken Danarvian citizens as prisoners. Almost every Danarvian would say that the Executive Office not only had a right, but an obligation, to go to war with Zoh'moor.

Quim knew that other facts would make his anti-war message even tougher. Zoh'moor was apparently ruled by a tyrant with absolutely no respect for individual freedom. Danarvians cherished freedom more than anything else and saw it as a virtue above any other to spread freedom to every rational being in the galaxy.

Executive Izah had not officially announced his resignation yet, and the election campaign could obviously not begin until that happened. The problem for Quim was that by the time Izah announced, the war could very well be a success. Strike Group 14 would be well on their way to a victory over the Zoh'moorian invasion force. It would be very difficult to oppose a successful war for freedom.

Quim's public appearances had already cast himself as an anti-war candidate. He had made it clear where he stood on the issue. It would be impossible for him to make a complete turn-around and become an invasion hawk.

His only chance was to undermine the credibility of the intelligence that the Executive Office had used as a basis for its war vote.

"I have studied the intelligence that you used as a motivation for the aggression against the Zoh'moorians" he told the members of the Executive Office. "I have some questions as to the source and the reliability of this intelligence."

"This comes directly from Advanced Retrieval" one of the Executives pointed out. "I cannot see how you could possibly question its veracity."

"I understand they found this android by chance" Quim continued, pretending not to hear the comment. "To me, that seems like an absolutely remarkable coincidence."

"It was not pure chance" another Executive said. "This android was placed in a position close to the vice president of the United States. It was only a matter of time before our intelligence agents would find her."

"Then, let me suggest that she was built on Earth" Quim went on. "But there is more to question in this report. It is my understanding that Advanced Retrieval found a survivor from… The Sundancer… yes, The Sundancer of all lost vessels, on Earth. He was also found by mere chance."

He giggled, which was unusual for a Teuran.

"With due respect for our intelligence agents" he continued, "I must say that there is so much questionable material here that I would almost call the entire operation on Earth into question."

"I sympathize with your concerns, Quim" said another Executive. "But we have given Advanced Retrieval full authority to provide us with first class intelligence, and until we have any substantiated reason to question their work, I suggest we accept it as good and act based on that."

"I called Longreach on my way over" Quim said, unfettered by the counter-arguments. "They are willing to testify before a court of law that The Sundancer disappeared and was later salvaged in the Scatterbelt, which, I might add, is fifteen thousand light years from sector KB. And where is the DNA scan of this purported survivor?"

"He was killed in a confrontation with the Zoh'moorian invasion troops" an Executive added.

"How convenient" Quim noted.

Izah and another Executive glanced at one another. There was a brief moment of silence. They exchanged hand gestures. Quim concluded that the executives had debated this particular point between themselves. He realized that the arguments he had just presented would make a strong case in an election campaign. He also felt reinforced enough to take one last constitutional step in his battle with the Executive Office over their war vote. A step he had dismissed as taking too long time.

"I shall demand a grand hearing on this" Quim said.

A grand hearing was the start of a lawsuit filed by the Federal Assembly against the Executive Office. It was a very a rare event and automatically landed on the desk of the Charter Court – effectively the Supreme Court of the Danarvian Federation.

Grand hearings had been held only two times before in Danarvian history, and in both cases the lawsuits that followed had been tossed out by the Charter Court.

"You are of course in your full right to do so" an Executive said. "And just so I understand: you would call for a grand hearing because you question the way we have used this piece of intelligence... about The Sundancer... in our war vote."

"Correct. The possibility that anyone from The Sundancer would have lived on Earth since its disappearance is very, very remote."

"No, it is not."

They all turned to a side door. L'Faa had entered.

"I have a DNA scan of Joh Ryndl, the survivor they found."

She slowly walked up to her seat and sat down. She handed out copies of a report to everyone in the room.

"The agent who found him was able to take a skin sample of him" she continued, looking at Quim. "As you can see, it matches his records from the Space Flight Academy. There is even a photo taken by an Advanced Retrieval agent. The photo is uncannily similar to an age progress simulation from the photo taken of him when he was assigned to The Sundancer."

Quim looked at the report squinting. Unlike reptilians who squinted when they were sad and on the verge of tears, Teurans squinted when they were irritated. In the early years of the Danarvian Federation, this difference had occasionally led to embarrassing misinterpretations between diplomats.

The Executives waited for Quim's response. He took a very careful look at the short report and the included evidence.

"Very well" he said eventually. "Thank you for sharing this information. I shall return to my office."

"One more thing, Quim" said L'Faa. "Recently you made classified intelligence public. You know very well that it is illegal to do so."

"The public has the right to know when their government is not performing with due diligence" Quim replied, smiled cordially and left the room.

The conference room was quiet for a moment. Then L'Faa turned to Izah.

"You agree with him, don't you?"

"In almost everything he says."

"There is a chance he makes this report public. We cannot have that happen."

"Why would he do that?"

"So he can cast doubt on it and thereby win public approval for the anti-war election campaign he is going to launch when you formally announce your resignation. I would like to see him arrested for what he has already made public."

Izah did not immediately respond to that. He looked down on his notes, then let his eyes drift off toward the large window in front of him and examine the trees outside. Then eventually he turned to L'Faa again.

"Are you asking me if I would vote for arresting him now?"

"Yes."

"I may sympathize with him politically" Izah continued. "But

I do not condone acts that break the law. He did share classified information with the public. That is a crime."

He paused and looked around the room.

"But" he continued. "We cannot completely disregard the politics in this. If we arrest him, it would appear as if we are silencing an opponent to our war vote."

"I know it is politically risky" L'Faa said. "But it we do not arrest him, we let him get away with breaking the law just to improve his chances of winning your seat in the next election."

"May I suggest a compromise then. If he does not go public with this new intelligence, we forget the whole thing ever happened."

"That's putting the man above the law" L'Faa said. "We are a constitutional republic built on laws, not personal privileges."

"We also have to deal with the reality of the situation. This war is going to be unpopular until there is a military success. You should not stir up more turmoil in the public opinion than absolutely necessary."

L'Faa shook her head.

"Very well" she said. "Let's do it your way. But if Quim goes public with any more intelligence, I will not stop until he is in jail."

"That sounds like a fair compromise" Izah said and gave away a smile. "Politics at its best."

*   *   *

Vice admiral Ghaul had a pretty good idea of where the Zoh'moorian vessels were. His long-range striker had returned to the strike group, but on its mission it had sent numerous images, scans and matrixes that were so detailed that Ghaul joked that you could build a copy of the Zoh'moorian fleet with the information from the striker.

"Except who would want to waste any resources on that junk" he chuckled.

The probes that the long-range striker had deployed were also very helpful. They revealed most of the route that the Zoh'moorian ships took from Zoh'moor to their halfway point and then on to Earth.

"At this point" he said to his commanders, "all I want to do is get within convenient striking distance of their halfway point. That way we can take a good look at their entire route from Zoh'moor to Earth."

"Sir" said the commander of the strike group's special forces. "What exactly do you want the all-reptilian commando unit to do?"

"Be prepared for on-ground deployment on Zoh'moor. We are not supposed to engage them. But if we can evidence that survivors from The Sundancer have been on Zoh'moor, then our Executive Office would have a crisp clear reason to…"

He was interrupted by an adjutant who passed a note to him. The vice admiral reviewed it carefully.

Then, for a moment, his face turned from neutral, purposeful business to sheer joy.

"Gentlemen!" he said. "I have good news. Revise your plans. Prepare your units for battle."

He paused artfully.

"The politicians have finally come around. We have just been ordered to engage the Zoh'moorian invasion fleet on and around Earth."

He turned to helm.

"New coordinates: five-five-eight-nine-one-one! Maximum speed! Execute!"

"Yes, sir!" helm yelled back.

"Strike group, go to battle mode!" Ghaul ordered.

The group accelerated fiercely and made a sharp left turn – by cosmological standards. It quickly reached its maximum speed and tightened its formation so that all ships went in under the hub ship's extended cloak shield. They shifted their energy consumption from regular to combat systems. All secondary functions were reduced to a minimum or turned off altogether. Combat personnel were ordered to their stations and all fighters, bombers and strikers underwent an extra mechanical, electronic and physical inspection.

Weapons systems were fully activated. Communications systems were recalibrated from "encrypted" to "invisible". All transmissions from the strike group to Frontline Services headquarters were confined to an ingenuous electronic probe system that was impossible to intercept.

Ground troops started intensive combat drills. Fighter pilots were called to briefings on the Zoh'moorian ships. Striker crews stepped up simulator tests and crews of planet surface bombers were handed their first maps of Earth.

But the toughest job was that of the Marines. Their drills for combat were unlike those of any other in the Strike Group. They were not ground combat forces. Instead, the Marines were trained and equipped to perform sabotage missions and seize enemy vessels in space. They flew up close to them, ejected themselves into space and maneuvered with small engine packages until they landed on the hull of the alien vessel. Then they worked their way in to the vessel one way or the other.

That was the easy part. The difficult part was doing the same thing in super-light speed. Vice Admiral Ghaul was the only strike group commander who trained his Marines for that. The rest of the commanding officers in Frontline Services thought he was crazy. There were formidable risks associated with superlight speed boarding operations. They said the risks outweighed the benefits.

Ghaul hoped that one day he would prove them all wrong.

*　　　*　　　*

Goryell, Thor and Carl stood right in the middle of the intersection between 21st and F Street, NW, in Washington, DC. Normally it would be bustling with traffic and pedestrians.

But not today. This was no normal day. It was the day when the Zoh'moorians occupied America.

And this was the day when Thor and Carl, for the first time in their lives, stood face to face with an alien enemy. It was an intimidating experience, even for top-trained special operations soldiers like them. It was even more intimidating because they still had their weapons holstered inside their jackets. And they were not supposed to use them.

They had seen what the Zoh'moorians did to the men they captured. Everyone was stripped naked and most of them were then taken onboard some sort of transportation vessel.

Goryell, on the other hand, stood there, calm and almost amused by the situation. The Zoh'moorians picked up on his relaxed attitude. Needless to say, they were not entirely pleased by it.

One of them pointed his AR 15-size weapon straight at Goryell's face and yelled something. Goryell's smile grew bigger. The Zoh'moorian's yelling grew louder. Other Zoh'moorians surrounded them. But most of them carried their weapons pointing down, not at the three men they apparently wanted to catch.

"See their weapons?" said Goryell.

"They're slouching" Thor noted.

"There are six of them and three of us."

"Except for my leg" Carl whispered, "I'm ready for action."

The Zoh'moorian who was pointing his gun in Goryell's face once again yelled something. His fellow soldiers made strange sounds.

"They're laughing" Goryell explained and turned to the soldier in front of him. "Yeah, real funny! Haha!"

The Zoh'moorians laughed and tried to imitate Goryell's laughter. That triggered even more laughter among the reptilian invaders.

"You laugh as much as you can" Goryell said with a smile on his face. "You're dead anyway."

He nodded. The Zoh'moorians laughed again and nodded with him.

They're clueless" Goryell smiled. "Let's go!"

His right arm came up in a lightning-quick move, with the underarm folded horizontally and his hand forming a fist. The underarm struck the Zoh'moorian's weapon so hard that he dropped it. But Goryell did not wait for him to realize what had just happened. He sent his left fist flying, like a missile, straight forward, right at the Zoh'moorian's face. Hitting the nose with the first two knuckles of his hand he delivered a formidable blow to the reptilian, who stumbled backward and fell down on his back.

Thor and Carl were quick to join Goryell in the fight. Thor had pinpointed a Zoh'moorian right behind him. Before Goryell had even gotten to "Go" in "Let's Go" Thor had delivered a perfect back kick right up in the chest of the ugly alien. At the same time he stretched out his arms for balance and formed two fists that hit another Zoh'moorian in the belly. The punch was not hard but surprised the opponent almost as much as the back kick had caught the other one off guard.

As he recoiled the back kick he transferred the energy over in to a front kick. The speed and force were so formidable that he planted his foot all the way up on the nose of the Zoh'moorian in front of him.

He had single-handedly taken out two of the six Zoh'moorians around them.

Carl had to rely on arm techniques, but that was no problem as far as he was concerned. And he could still throw a kick or two, using his bad leg for balance. So he rotated slightly on his bad right leg, brought his good left leg up past the Zoh'moorian in front of him and threw a hook kick to the back of his head.

It was a very hard kick to get right, even for a skilled martial artist, but Carl had made it one of his trademark kicks.

The heel of his foot hit the Zoh'moorian over the back of his head with surprising force. Carl's foot brought the alien's head down and made him lose balance as Carl recoiled his foot. But the kick was not hard enough to incapacitate the ugly reptilian. As soon as Carl's foot was past his head, he straightened up again.

Carl was ready for that. In a split second he sat down his left foot and swung around with his right hip. He bent his knee slightly and delivered a fierce punch to the Zoh'moorian's belly with his right hand fist.

To his surprise, the Zoh'moorian died from it. Carl had, of course, never seen an alien die before, but he knew the look of death when he saw it. And he felt something crunch under the brutal force of his fist. He had probably damaged some vital organ.

There were only two Zoh'moorians left around them. Goryell and Carl quickly knocked them to the ground, as well.

To their surprise, there was not a single Zoh'moorian around them standing. The people that the Zoh'moorians had captured and were forcing out of their clothes were all just standing there, looking at the three men who had taken down six alien invaders using nothing but their hands and feet.

"What idiots" Thor heard Goryell say.

"Who?"

"The Zoh'moorians. These are supposed to be their elite troops? Did you see how they all gathered around us and left their prisoners alone? Only to be taken out by simple martial arts techniques? Man, what idiots."

He almost sounded disappointed. But he was right, of course. The Fah'marook troops had approached them with the excess confidence and arrogance of tyrannical henchmen.

Thor and Carl disarmed the knocked-out aliens. Goryell called Tahm Qaar for an update and learned that Frontline Services had finally been given authority to assist Earth militarily. He passed it on to his friends who gave him thumbs up.

At least two dozen people slowly approached him, as if he was some sort of savior, someone who could explain to them what on Earth was – literally – going on.

"Help" Goryell said, turning to Carl. "What do I tell these people?"

"Tell them you're from the government and you're here to help."

"Huh?"

"Sir" said a man who had been on the verge of being taken away by the Zoh'moorians. "Who... who are you?"

Goryell looked at him. The man was probably about 60, looked terrified and reached out with his shaking hands to try to grab Goryell's right hand.

"Uh... I'm... here to help you guys."

"Will you please help me get home?"

"I... I'm not sure I can do that..."

Another man came up to him.

"Are you from the CIA?"

"No, I'm from..." and Goryell turned to Thor, who nodded, "I'm from... another planet, also."

"What??"

"Uh... I'm from a planet, or a federation of planets, that is trying to help you get rid of these..." and he made a sweeping gesture with his left hand toward the Zoh'moorians.

"Those monsters" said one of the men with utter hatred in his voice. "Are you guys really from another planet?"

"Just me" Goryell explained. "I'm working with my two friends here. They're as American as you are."

"Where do these monsters come from?"

"A world called Zoh'moor."

"Where do you come from?"

"The Danarvian Federation."

"Do you have a military?"

"Yes. They're on their way."

"Where is our military?"

Goryell was just about to answer that question when a woman yelled:

"The Grid is working again!"

She was holding her iWorld and browsing through websites for news.

"Try tune in to Ross Landau" someone suggested.

The woman found his show and turned up the volume so people around her could hear. Others pulled out their iWorlds and followed her example.

It was not long before they heard Ross say:

"...and you folks have to ask yourselves: why has our president not ordered our military to confront these invaders? If the president is incapacitated, why has not the vice president stepped in and given the order? Is it because she is afraid that our military is inferior to them? I doubt it. Our military is one Hell of a force to count on. Or is it because our vice president... does not want our military to confront these invaders?"

"Is this true?" someone asked Goryell. "Is our military just sitting on their hands?"

"That's right" Carl said. "They have been ordered to stand down."

"What?? How do you know that?"

"Because... I am an intelligence agent."

Their conversation was interrupted when two Zoh'moorian troop transporters flew in, stopped and hovered right above them for a moment. Then they moved a little bit further south and landed in the middle of the street.

"More company" Thor noted. "Too many for us to engage."

"We better get out of here" Goryell agreed and turned to the civilians. "You should also get out of here! As far as you can get!"

The scene turned very tense. People were still trying to find all their clothes and belongings after they had been stripped by the aliens. The approaching Zoh'moorian reinforcements sent them scrambling for whatever they could find. They got the wrong things, other people's things and no things at all. A couple of skirmishes broke out and for a moment it looked like chaos was going to take over.

But then, suddenly, the men and women seemed to catch themselves. They stopped for a second, looked at each other and then at the approaching Zoh'moorian thugs. It suddenly occurred to them who was the real enemy. In the face of these alien invaders, their petty disagreements over who owned what shoe and whose briefcase it was, seemed pretty stupid.

The newly arrived Zoh'moorians were still a block away. Their comrades whom Goryell, Carl and Thor had knocked down stayed passive in the face of their own guns. But that could change any second.

Goryell turned to some of the men who had been prisoners of the Zoh'moorians just a couple of minutes earlier. He handed them the Zoh'moorian weapons and showed them were the triggers were.

"Get out of here" he said. "But keep these weapons and don't hesitate to defend yourselves."

"Run away?" said one young man. "This is my city, my country. I'm not running away."

He went down on his right knee, put the Zoh'moorian weapon to his shoulder and took aim at the approaching soldiers.

"Way to go!" said another man and joined him.

A woman also joined them, and soon all the six Zoh'moorian weapons were in the hands of fight-minded civilians.

The first man glanced at the others.

"Let's roll!" he said.

They all took cover and aimed at the approaching soldiers.

With less than a hundred feet between them, the civilians and the soldiers engaged each other in an intense fire fight. Carl and Thor had already pulled away from the scene and moved west on 21st street. Goryell found himself on the east side of the intersection with frequent blasts from the Zoh'moorian soldiers flying his way. They were poorly aimed but still harmful if they hit.

To make matters worse, a Zoh'moorian ship took position right above the intersection. It turned back and forth for a moment, then a small hole opened up on its side and something that definitely looked like a gun came out. It turned and tipped and aimed at the civilians on the ground who were shooting at the Zoh'moorian troops.

That was the end of it. The ship would obliterate a half dozen brave Americans who had decided to take up arms for their country. Six random civilians who had decided that freedom was always worth the price.

Goryell wanted to help them. He was supposed to exercise restraint in the use of his own weapon. He was supposed to stay undercover as much as he could. The Zoh'moorians should not get any hint that there were Danarvian agents on Earth.

But his undercover was not more important than the lives of these outgunned freedom fighters. He was here to help these Americans stay free. What good would it do if he turned his back on them just to protect his cover?

He pulled out his weapon. He aimed at the Zoh'moorian ship and smiled.

Then he fired.

"Bang, you're dead" he said.

*   *   *

COMPLIANCE

By late afternoon the Grid was back on, TV cable and satellite programs started up again and the telephone system, cell towers and other communication venues were gradually restored.

Jack and some of his friends were hanging out at the department of political economy. It was not because they thought it was a particularly inviting place to be, but simply because they happened to have classes there during the morning.

The faculty members came out of their meeting with the university president with an upbeat spirit, chatting and giggling about what fantastic opportunities that lay ahead. They competed in trying to come up with ideas on how to bring the peaceful, enlightened Zoh'moorians in to their own classes.

"I bet they have steep marginal income taxes" said professor De La Gauche as he and the other economics professors came back to their department. "You know, for redistribution purposes. I am going to present facts on that in my course on current economic issues next semester."

"Imagine a whole planet that has never heard of Reaganomics!" said professor Pinkhouse and the other professors laughed.

"We should get some funds to do a field trip there" suggested professor Sandaller. "We could study their health care system. I mean, I'm sure that their entire planet has universal health care."

Everyone agreed. The professors entered the department's library where Jack, Todd, Walt Widebelly and a few others had gathered.

Alexis was not there. She was back in the dorm trying to get hold of her mother.

"So, what's up" said professor Pinkhouse and smiled. "We got some exciting times ahead of us!"

Jack had just been able to log on to the Grid again. The first thing he had found was a report on Drudge about the massacre on Arlington Memorial Bridge. It linked to quotes from Ross's radio show and a couple of very disturbing cell phone videos. He shared it all with the other students just as professor Pinkhouse walked in the room.

"Seems like things are pretty bad" Jack said.

"Oh, no, you gotta see the opportunities in this!" professor Pinkhouse insisted. "The Zoh'moorians bring a whole new level of refinement and sophistication to us!"

"What sophistication?" Todd asked. "They just massacred thirty people on a bridge in Washington."

Professor Pinkhouse was caught off guard for a moment. His face turned neutral and he crossed his arms over his tiny chest. His eyes went back and forth in search of something to say or do.

"Well, I... I'm sure there's a lot of rumors flying around right now" he tried.

"They have videos of it" Jack said and held up his iWorld.

"Well" professor Pinkhouse said again.

His face was tense and he had a nervous tick above his right eyebrow. He looked away from Jack's iWorld and pretended to examine a spot on his shoe.

"There are always people who provoke others into violence" he continued, sounding like he was forcing himself into saying something. "We have to learn not to provoke these visitors. We have to learn not to make them angry. We're too chauvinistic. I mean, you all remember September Eleven, right? We provoked those terrorists. So..."

"There was a guy on that bridge who attacked the aliens" Walt Widebelly noted.

"Well, there you go!" said professor Pinkhouse, looking gratefully at Walt. "There's your provocation. We just never learn to respect other cultures! This is so typically America. Non-Western countries will be much better at welcoming these aliens."

"I got something here from India" Jack said. "A blogger in Calcutta says the aliens just massacred two hundred civilians there."

Professor Pinkhouse stared at Jack. It was not a friendly stare. Jack noted it. Under normal circumstances he would have felt very uncomfortable if a professor looked at him that way. But not now. Something made him see professor Pinkhouse with different eyes, all of a sudden. He was not sure what that meant. If it had any meaning at all.

Besides, he still had not gotten over what professor Pinkhouse had done to Alexis.

"I disagree with you about September Eleven" Jack pushed himself to say.

"Well, I have to go check my e-mails" professor Pinkhouse replied, almost stumbling on his own words and left the room.

Jack and Todd shared a look and both shrugged their shoulders in disbelief.

"Am I stupid… or did he just sound like he thought this alien invasion is a good thing?" Jack asked.

"The only stupidity around here is the Pinkhouse" said Todd.

"Maybe there is something good to this after all" Walt Widebelly tried.

"Good??" Jack asked. "Walt, we're being invaded by a very hostile alien civilization! They're taking over! You saw the videos from that bridge!"

Walt Widebelly crossed his arms over his chest. He looked very uncomfortable.

"Well, what are we going to do, then?" he asked. "If these aliens are hostile? What are we going to do?"

Jack had no immediate answer to that question.

"See" Walt said, almost triumphantly. "I'd rather assume they are friendly and here to help us improve. Like professor Pinkhouse says… we should see the opportunities in this."

He got up.

"Where you going?" Todd asked.

He had to move over to let Walt out.

"Back to the dorm. I'm going to call my parents. I'm sure they're very afraid right now."

A couple of other students left with him. Only Jack, Todd and Tom Tulip stayed.

"Just what I need right now" Todd muttered. "I was going to ask Karen out tonight."

"Who's Karen?" Jack asked.

His phone rang.

"Yeah?"

"Jack, how are you doing?"

"Thor! Where are you?"

"Washington, DC. Have you been watching the news?"

"Yeah, we just got back on the Grid."

"This is bad, Jack. Bad. Whatever good you hear about the Zoh'moorians – don't believe it."

"How do you…"

"No time, Jack! But trust me, these guys are bad! Get ready to hide!"

"Hide? Where?"

"In the woods. Go to grandpa's old place in Kansas."

"Lindsborg?? It's that bad?"

"Yes! Gotta run!"

Jack put his phone away. He looked at the table between him and Todd and thought about what Thor had just said.

"Bad news?" Tom Tulip asked.

"That was my brother. He's in DC."

"Did he see that massacre?"

"He didn't say" Jack said slowly. "But he said this is bad."

"I'm sure if he's seen the violence down there…"

"No, no" Jack interrupted Tom. "Thor is an intelligence agent. He knows what he's talking about."

"Oh, I see. So you mean he knows things we don't know."

"That's right."

"Well" Todd said. "I'm not gonna sit around here and wait for them to come here and mess things up."

"That's what Thor said. He suggested we all get the heck out of here and hide way out in the countryside."

"Isn't that a bit extreme? I was thinking going home to my mom."

"But she lives in Detroit, right?"

"Yeah."

"My guess is they're going for the big cities. I'm going to go to my grandpa's old place in Kansas."

"And how do you survive out there?" Todd asked with a slightly edgy tone in his voice. "You're not exactly a farmer."

"We're being occupied" Jack replied. "This is war, and that will disrupt just about everything we're used to. Including food supply. That old house in Lindsborg is big enough for a lot of people."

"So you want me to come with you to Kansas??"

"As many of us as possible."

Tom Tulip nodded.

"I can see your point. But I'm sure our government will negotiate some sort of truce with the Zoh'moorians. Whatever we do, we should not panic."

"I agree with Tom" Todd said. "Seems like an over-reaction to run away like that."

Jack thought for a moment. He agreed with his friends that panic was a bad response to the situation. But he also trusted Thor. He did not know a whole lot about Thor's daily job, but he knew enough to trust him and take his advice seriously.

He looked at his friends.

"Very well" he shrugged. "If you guys want to stay here... I'm going to Kansas."

"Jack, think about this for a moment" Todd said. "I agree that going back to Detroit might be a bad idea right now. But we're in a small town, they're not going to come here. We're safe here."

"Maybe. But even if they don't come here, there's going to be food shortages and a lot of other problems. At least, out there we can support ourselves on the farmland. There's quite a bit of hunting ground, too."

"I'm not ready to give up my life and become a hunter and gatherer just yet" Todd replied, rather sternly.

"It's a free country" Jack said.

His words suddenly caught them all off guard. They froze right there, hearing the echoes of Jack's words in their heads.

"Free country" Jack said. "Well…"

Todd did not say anything. Tom Tulip mumbled something inaudible.

Jack got up.

"Alright, I'll see you guys later."

Just as he was about to leave the room he stopped, turned and took out a piece of paper.

"If you change your minds" he said, "here's how to find my grandpa's house in Lindsborg. It's in central Kansas."

He wrote down some directions and gave them to Todd. Todd looked at them and then at Jack.

"You're really serious about this" he said, sounding a bit surprised.

"The Zoh'moorians have come here to conquer us" Jack said slowly, as if to put more weight behind his words. "I don't care what Pinkhouse thinks. He's lost in his anti-American tirades. He probably thinks we caused this invasion by having too low taxes or something. But I'll tell you this. I'd rather live free out in the wilderness and hunt for food every day than live under some alien tyrant and have his food served to me every day."

"That's a steep price for freedom" Todd replied, clearly not sharing Jack's pessimistic outlook.

"I'm sure we can be pretty comfortable here" Tom Tulip added. "At least for now."

"Freedom is a steep price for comfort" Jack shot back and left the room.

*   *   *

Of all the news networks in Danarvia, Zeta-7 was the largest and the most entertaining to watch. Its best prime time show, *Crash Course*, was a debate program hosted by two very entertaining news anchors. They offered entertainment, news and education in one big show. It had no finishing time – sometimes their entertainment shows, their debates and their news coverage went on all night long. *Crash Course* was a big media happening.

The hosts were among the best paid and best known in the infotainment industry. Part of the success was that they had earned the respect and appreciation of audiences on all kinds of worlds. Usually, reptilians preferred to watch shows that were hosted by a reptilian, and humanoids preferred humanoid hosts. There was nothing racist or segregationist about that – it was just one of those deeply rooted feelings of familiarity.

But Haniato, a humanoid male, and Alana-Cohm, a reptilian female, had managed to appeal to audiences everywhere. They were as different as two infotainment show hosts could be, and that was probably a good reason for their success. They sometimes joked about the other person's particular quirks, but in a friendly way and often with a touch of self loathing in it. Humanoids saw their own prejudices against reptilians in Haniato's pretended curiosity as to what kind of tooth brush he could buy Alana-Cohm for her birthday. It was well known that reptilians, because of how their teeth were shaped, could not use humanoid tooth brushes.

Likewise, Alana-Cohm could joke with the audience and say that when Haniato said something she disagreed with, she could not even stomp on his tail. Among reptilians, having a big, sturdy tail was considered manly and attractive; a small tail was feminine. To hint that someone did not have a tail was to hint that he was not man enough for his woman.

Most of the guests on the show were witty talking heads who could add something entertaining or interesting to the news of the day. They were usually authors and something called ranters – Earthlings would call them bloggers – who made a living going on shows and sharing their opinion in a way that made people laugh or think (or both, although few had mastered both skills). It was rare that politicians showed up on *Crash Course* and the reason was, simply, that politicians did not have a whole lot of power and influence in the Federation.

A notable exception was Delegate Quim. He was one of the best known public personalities in the galaxy, and among people in the Danarvian government only the chairman of the Charter Court surpassed him in name recognition.

Quim had been on *Crash Course* a few times over the years. It had been a while since last time, which was on the last palindrome anniversary of end to the Kahpiyan War.

Now he had been invited again. Only this time it was not to entertain and enjoy the celebration of an incredible diplomatic achievement.

It was to stir up opinion against a new war, a war that few knew much about but more and more people were saying they did not want.

Haniato was sitting in his chair to the right in the studio. Alana-Cohm was sitting to the left. Between them were two empty holo-chairs, seats where holographic images of guests appeared when the guests were too far away to come to the studio. The images were near perfect – far better than they had been when galactic news casting had started a few decades ago.

Haniato opened the segment with Quim.

"Is the Danarvian Federation facing a new war? The question is worrisome, but there are indications that our long-lasting peace may come to an end. Disturbing news is coming out of Sector KB, far away from Danarvian space. Our Executive Office has decided to intervene in a conflict between two worlds out there. With us tonight to explain what this might lead to is a man who has an amazing record as a diplomat and politician, who has done more for our peace and freedom than perhaps anyone else in the history of the Federation. Delegate Quim, welcome to our show."

Quim's three-dimensional image appeared in one of the holo-seats. The audience expressed their appreciation by standing up and briefly chanting a universally used welcome phrase followed by a brief nod.

Quim was sitting in a holo-studio onboard a space ship a thousand light years away. It was owned by *Crash Course* and was dispatched to let prominent guests make a virtual appearance on the show.

The ship was orbiting the world where the Federation Assembly was located. It had a holo-studio, which was essentially an empty room with walls, ceiling and floor capable of displaying a three-dimensional holographic image of any selected studio used in any Zeta-7 show. (Star Trek buffs on Earth would immediately think 'holodeck', which would actually be a pretty good comparison.) The holographic image that Quim saw obviously included live feed of everything that went on in the studio, so he saw and heard the audience's welcome.

"Thank you" he said to them. "And thank you, Haniato and Alana-Cohm, for inviting me."

"Delegate Quim" said Haniato. "Our military forces, Frontline Services, have been ordered to intervene in a military conflict in a sector outside of the Federation. All the way over in sector KB. Let me show our viewers on a map where this sector is."

They showed a map of Danarvia and outlying sectors. The map zoomed to sector KB.

"There are two worlds in this sector" Haniato continued. "Delegate Quim, tell us about the relationship between these two worlds."

Quim looked at the audience with confidence and almost childish excitement. This was one of his great moments, a crucial step on his way toward building an unbeatable campaign for that seat on the Executive Office. Close to one hundred billion people were watching the show.

"Earth and the Zoh'moorians have complex relations" he said. "So complex, in fact, that I would not want to take up your time and elaborate. Suffice it to say that we do not have enough of an understanding for their cultural differences and the diversity of ideas there. By rushing to war we are exhibiting a great deal of insensitivity and ignorance toward those cultures."

"But is it not true, Honored Delegate" Haniato said, "that one of the worlds out there is invading the other?"

"That has not been clearly established. It is one of the facts that we are being presumptuous about."

"Honored Delegate, we have received information that the Zoh'moorians are holding Danarvians as prisoners. They come from a ship that drifted off course and was eventually captured by

Zoh'moorians. If that is true, then does not our Charter of Liberty mandate that we go to war if necessary to free our citizens?"

"To begin with" Quim said, "we have no evidence that Federation citizens are being held by the Zoh'moorians. Those are unsubstantiated rumors, or, as I shall call them, political fairy tales."

He earned more laughter from the studio audience.

"Besides" Quim continued, quite encouraged by the positive response from the audience, "we have come a long way from the days of war and conflict. Our citizens still share the memories of deadly conflict – what did those conflicts accomplish? We sent our sons and daughters out to die, for what purpose? Now our Executive Office is sending our children out to die again. It cannot, and must not, be the way that our government operates."

Alana-Cohm took over. She thanked Quim for his points and turned to the TV audience.

"Let me bring in our other guest" she said. "Professor Yev-Karik from the Freedom Studies Institute on Aquaan, welcome, sir."

An unusual guest – an Aquan man – appeared next to Quim's holographic image. He was apparently sitting in an underwater studio, because his image was somewhat blurred. He wore a special microphone that altered his voice to compensate for underwater sound distortions. Aquans used water compression and membranes in their throats to speak, and it sounded entirely incomprehensible if broadcast without computer compensation.

"Thanks for inviting me" said the professor.

"Sir, you are widely recognized as an expert on the Charter of Liberty, and you recently published a book on the authority of the Executive Office to wage war. What is your take on this?"

"The Honorable Delegate is unfortunately wrong. The Charter of Liberty definitely grants the Executive Office the right to go to war under the present circumstances. The Charter Court confirmed this, especially in Case Eighty-Four. The Charter entrusts the Executive Office with the responsibility to choose whether to use diplomacy, sanctions or military force. If we trust the Charter of Liberty, then we also ought to trust our Executive Office and their decisions. They are not war mongers or insensitive to other cultures.

They are tremendously well educated and experienced people, and we ought to show them due respect."

"I disagree entirely" Quim said, with a surprising edge in his voice. "With all due respect for the professor's research, I believe he has misunderstood the role of diplomacy. I have personally exercised diplomacy on behalf of our government for decades. We should have started with sending a diplomatic envoy to Zoh'moor and established a line of communication with them."

"It is my understanding that the Zoh'moorians did indeed capture Danarvians from a ship that was adrift, many years ago" professor Yev-Karik replied. "The Zoh'moorians have had decades to contact us regarding the fate of those castaways. But they haven't. That alone is a reason to avoid diplomacy, at least as our only option."

"Let us not place the responsibility for peace in the hands of another world" Quim said. "We ought to take that responsibility ourselves."

"Professor Yev-Karik" said Alana-Cohm. "I wanted to ask you why you think it is a bad idea to send a diplomatic envoy to Zoh'moor before we do as the Executive Office has done, and dispatch military forces to sector KB."

"Precisely for the reason I just mentioned. If the Zoh'moorians wanted to contact us, they would have done so."

"Delegate Quim" Alana-Cohm said and turned to Quim's holographic image. "Do you believe that the Zoh'moorian government would receive our diplomatic envoy with open arms, if we sent one?"

"Why would they not?" Quim asked rhetorically. "Are we really willing to risk the lives of our children without first trying to talk to them?"

"But Honorable Delegate" professor Yev-Karik said. "We know very little about Zoh'moor, but what we have learned so far indicates that it is a world run by a ruthless tyrant. And our entire history, our Federation history as well as the history of our home worlds, all tell us that tyrants are never interested in dialogue unless there is a forceful military back-up behind our attempts at communicating with them."

The debate got more and more heated as it went on. Haniato and

Alana-Cohm got more and more excited. The audience seemed to split in two camps, each cheering on Quim and the professor. Even the viewers who enjoyed the debate from their homes, offices, space ships or wherever they were, began cheering, and many complained loudly as the commercial breaks interrupted the heated argument.

Delegate Watlaan was one of the viewers. She watched Quim in the debate and listened very carefully to both his and the professor's arguments. She had by no means made up her own mind – as the chair of the committee on intelligence and outer rim security she saw it as her duty to support military action in this case. Personally, though, she shared many of Quim's doubts. She thought he purposely misrepresented the facts in the case, but she was not entirely convinced that he was doing it only for personal gain. It could be that he saw it as the only viable strategy to prevent another war.

Watlaan got a call from L'Faa.

"Are you watching this?" L'Faa asked.

"Yes."

"What do you think?"

"I think he is preparing for a grand hearing that will force you to order the strike group and the armada to halt the military operation before they ever get to engage the Zoh'moorians."

"It will be hard for him to do so."

"Not if he can stir up enough public support for his view."

"Then I will counter his views in public" L'Faa said. "He is taking political advantage of this situation and I am not going to let him get away with it."

"Have we dispatched enough military power to liberate Earth?"

"Based on everything we know about them, yes, we have."

Strike Group 14 had a total of 60,000 troops onboard. That was, of course, not sufficient to stop the Zoh'moorians on the ground on Earth. But that was not the idea, either. The strike group was going to halt the Zoh'moorian invasion fleet and begin ground operations on strategic locations. The real ground invasion would begin upon the arrival of the armada that Frontline Services had dispatched.

Once the armada had successfully ousted the Zoh'moorians from

Earth, Danarvia would assume formal responsibility for governing Earth until normal government functions had been restored.

Delegate Watlaan was still not convinced that they were on the right track. To make matters even more complicated, they had found Joh Ryndl and the android on Earth, not Zoh'moor. That weakened the case for war with Zoh'moor, in Watlaan's opinion.

She turned off the netcast. Then she leaned back and closed her eyes.

For now, she supported the Executive Office in its war effort. But if they did not find any substantial evidence that Danarvians had been held on Zoh'moor, it would be hard to defend this war.

'Damned politics' Watlaan thought and went to have dinner.

*   *   *

Goryell's handgun was not some ordinary, garden-variety weapon you could buy in any firearms store in the Danarvian Federation. It could do far more than just stun or incapacitate a person. It also had a matter-shattering ability that destroyed solid objects. Goryell loved that function. It was something out of the ordinary for a handgun – usually it took a rifle-size, two-hand weapon to emit such destructive force. But Advanced Retrieval had their own gun smiths and paid them handsomely to do what no one else could.

Like building a weapon the size of a standard .38 Smith and Wesson revolver that could destroy the hull and the engines of an armored space vessel.

Goryell squeezed the trigger for as long as the battery in his weapon would allow it to fire. The beam hit the hull of the Zoh'moorian gun ship at a spot right below its engine compartment. A four-by-four foot area of the hull was pulverized.

He smiled. This was going to be fun.

The beam continued and hit part of the ship's fuel system. The ship lost power rapidly. It started tilting to the right while the pilot desperately tried to compensate by rerouting power to the other engines that still got fuel. But the engineers who had constructed the ship were not allowed to do their job without supervision from some incompetent politicos. Those political commissars oversaw the engineers to make sure everyone spoke well of the Tyrant. And since no one dared say anything but good things about the madman in their presence, the commissars got bored on their posts. So to pass time they got themselves involved in the actual engineering. They objected to building independent engines because they did not understand the merits of it and just wanted to pick a fight with the engineers to have something to do. So the engineers ended up equipping the ship with one, interconnected power system.

As soon as Goryell's beam had taken out a part of the fuel system, the ship was history.

Its remaining engines roared, then stalled, then gave up. The ship tilted completely to its right side and crashed.

Right on top of the newly arrived Fah'marook reinforcements.

It was not a pretty sight. But it encouraged the civilians who had taken up arms against a technologically superior enemy.

"Thank you!" they said to Goryell.

"Keep fighting!" Goryell said and started walking over to Carl and Thor, who were eager to move west on 21st Street.

"What do we do with these guys?" asked one of the men and pointed to the Zoh'moorians that Goryell, Carl and Thor had disarmed before.

"Oh… well, they're your prisoners now…" Goryell said, not being sure what to say.

"We better take them somewhere" another man said.

"Hell, no!" said the first man. "Let's execute them."

"Kill them?? No, we can't be that brutal!"

"Why not? They came here to be brutal!"

"Then we'd fall to their level. How can we say we're different than them if we shoot them?"

"And what do you suggest we do with them?"

"Turn them over to the police, of course."

"Police? The DC Police Department??"

"Yeah… you don't think that's a good idea?"

"I'm not even sure they're open for business right now."

"You're right… we have nowhere to take them. So let's leave them here."

"So they can hook up with their buddies and start killing people again? No, thanks."

Goryell left the scene. He wanted to get moving so he could set up an observation post. On-ground intelligence was increasingly important, and Tahm Qaar definitely wanted him to stay in Washington, DC.

Thor had just gotten off the phone.

"Your phone works again?" Goryell asked.

"Just called my brother. I warned him to stay away from the big cities."

"We're going to try to get in touch with the other Agents" said Carl. "But let's stay in touch. Perhaps we can coordinate operations."

"Sounds fair. Good luck!"

"You, too! Thanks for everything!"

Carl and Thor found an abandoned taxi cab and drove off. Goryell called down one of the cloaked transport vessels that his team had in orbit around Earth. He landed it in the nearest intersection, slipped in to it when nobody was watching, flew up and landed on a tall building.

It was a perfect place for him to set up an operating base in Washington. He had a lot of work to do. He needed to hack in to the phones and the computer system in the White House. He also needed to relay street level information back to Tahm Qaar. And he needed to let his boss know that he had used his weapon in a way that could give away to the Zoh'moorians that there were Danarvian agents on Earth.

Suddenly, he felt hungry. He realized he had not eaten more than an energy bar all day. The shuttle had a storage of field operations rations. Goryell was not all that fond of them, but they would have to do.

While eating a couple of rations he sent a text message to Tahm Qaar with his thoughts on how the Zoh'moorians might react when they realized that there were Danarvian agents were on Earth. Since the Advanced Retrieval team was eavesdropping on the communications between Zoh'moor and Earth, Goryell suspected that they might pick up something valuable over the next day or so.

He was right. They did pick up something. But much quicker than Goryell had expected.

Tahm Qaar even called him to let him know.

"You're right" he said. "They reacted right away."

"What are they saying?"

"The Supreme General just contacted president Oslow."

"What's he saying?"

"Let's just say it's bad news."

*   *   *

The order from the Supreme General was chillingly clear:

"You must order the Danarvian Federation to leave Earth immediately, or we will start burying your citizens alive."

"Yes, Mr. Supreme General, of course" said Barry Oslow. "But I don't know who the Danarvian Federation are. Uh… Holly Stanton does… uh… can-can I speak to her?"

"Do not be a fool, Barry. Your job, your life is at my mercy."

"Yes, Mr. Supreme General. Yes, of course. Uh… but how do I contact the Da…"

"I want a copy of your communication with the Danarvians within ten minutes."

President Oslow sat still for a moment. He was in the Lincoln bedroom where he had placed a nice armchair. He tried to go in there from time to time to contemplate, but he was not very good at it. He really did not know how to contemplate.

He was confused. He had sat down with the Supreme General and accepted all his preconditions without presenting a single one in return. He had accepted the Supreme General's demands and even promised to go on a worldwide speech tour to help promote peace with the Zoh'moorians. And still the Supreme General called him and made another request.

President Oslow tried to analyze the situation. He wrinkled his forehead and put his index finger tips up toward his mouth. He stared out in the middle of nowhere and took a deep breath.

It did not help. He still could not understand why the Supreme General was dissatisfied. But there was nothing to do about that.

All he could do was to comply. After all, if he did not comply, he could not be fulfilling his part of the negotiations.

At least, this way he could still step forward as the wise world leader who brought peace to the planet and introduced an alien civilization to the world.

That was really something to go down in history for.

The phone rang. It was Walter Stanton. The president took it in the Oval Office.

"Uh... hi Walt."

"Hey, Barry, how's it going?"

"Well, thank you. I have just completed the negotiations with the Zoh'moorian Supreme General."

"Yeah, I heard my sister is still back there."

"Well, yes, she... uh... decided to stay a little longer."

"Hey, listen, kid, I know what you're doing here. I heard about your little trick running behind our back and eavesdropping on our conversations with them and all that, and let me tell you, son, I've been to Zoh'moor, I've met the Grand Leader, and he's working with me and Holly. So don't think you can pull any tricks on us, buddy."

"Walter, I am the president of the United States and I have just successfully negotiated a peace with the Zoh'moorians. I am now going to embark on a worldwide tour to give speeches and let people know that the Zoh'moorians are our friendly neighbors and that we will show them respect, and they will respect us."

"Well, I gotta tell ya, kid, you have no idea who you're dealing with. These guys aren't here to be peaceful neighbors, they're here to take over and run this as a colony, and Holly and I intend to be the plantation managers, if you know what I mean... well, you can take that whichever way you want, 'cause you played the race card on me and Holly back in oh-eight."

"Walter, it's not a matter of who has been to Zoh'moor. It's a matter of what judgment you have."

"Yeah, like Taiwan, huh, son."

"Walter, uh, I don't care much for your tone, there..."

"I'm telling you, son, if you don't step aside and let me and Holly run the show, you're gonna be so damned sorry you ain't never going to recover from it. That thing that happened to senator Carlyle was no accident."

"Walter, are you threatening the president of the United States?"

"Take it whichever way you want, kid."

"Walter... Walter... look, I'm sure we can cooperate on this one... uh... I mean... with your contacts, and my judgment... I'm sure we can work something out."

"Well, you tell the Supreme General to let Holly go and we can talk."

"I promise I will. But I have another problem. I just got a call from the Supreme General. He says one of their ships was shot down with a weapon that's beyond even their technological capability. They say the Danarvian Federation is here and that they want us to ask them to leave. I don't know who they are."

"Oh, wow... well, kid, I'll fill you in on that one. Ever heard of Groom Lake in Nevada?"

"Is that... Area Fifty One?"

"Yeah, that's what folk lore calls it. Anyway. Are you at the desk in the Oval Office?"

"Yes."

"Well, there's a hidden compartment in the second drawer on your right. I used it for contact lists for chicks and high end escort services. It was a safe place 'cause my wife would never look there. Holly's been using it to stash away important documents."

"She's been using my office?"

"Well, kid, you're always out giving speeches, so we thought what the heck, it's a big office, why leave it empty?"

"So... where's the hidden compartment?"

"You have to feel down at the end of the drawer. There's a small bump in the bottom surface."

"Yes... yes, I can feel it."

"Push it."

"Oh, wow! Oh, wow!"

"Yeah, kinda cool, ain't it? Now, there's a green folder on top."

"Yes, I see it."

"Take it out, open it."

"OK. Oh, dear Allah... I mean, dear, uh, God...!"

"See the guy with yellow eyes?"

"Yes! That's who I am looking at."

"He was a Danarvian."

"How...?"

"The Zoh'moorians brought him over a long time ago. He'd been a prisoner on Zoh'moor for flying a military space ship into their territory, or something like that. He was in bad shape. We held him at Groom Lake and ran tests and stuff. He got some health care and decent food, but he managed to escape and disappeared. He might have been able to call home. Maybe they came and picked him up."

"So the Danarvians know about us and the Zoh'moorians."

"Probably, yeah."

"So how do I contact the Danarvians?"

"Well, son, if they have some sort of operation going on here you can't contact them. The only chance is a speech."

"A speech?"

"Yeah, you know, the stuff you know how to do. Here's what you're gonna say..."

And Walter Stanton explained. President Oslow listened carefully and promised to do exactly as Walter Stanton had said.

When the president hung up he did not even have time to pick up his pen to start writing the first paragraph of his speech before the phone rang again. It was the vice president's chief of staff. She asked where the vice president was and president Oslow promised to get back to her about that.

"Well, there is an important phone call for her."

"I'll take it."

The call was patched through."

"Yes, this is the president."

"Holly Stanton didn't ask the Zoh'moorians to cancel their invasion."

President Oslow was baffled.

"Who is this?"

"Tell Holly Stanton that since she did not ask the Zoh'moorians to cancel the invasion, Rhea is in big trouble."

"Are... are you from the Danarvian Federation?"

The caller hesitated for a second, enough to tell Barry Oslow that he was right.

"Holly Stanton has one hour to order the Zoh'moorians to leave, or Rhea dies."

"Look, if anyone talks to the Zoh'moorians, it's me. I'm the president."

"Well, then, I expect you or the vice president to go public with a demand that the Zoh'moorians leave. I expect you to do it in one hour. This is my final warning."

*   *   *

Goryell hung up after his call to the vice president. Tahm Qaar, his stiff but respectful boss, had been listening in from the operations headquarters in New Mexico.

"Well done" he told Goryell.

"Thank you, sir. But I'm a little concerned that the vice president was unavailable. What do you think she will do?"

"My guess is she will side with the Zoh'moorians. If she does, I'll deploy the ORCA team."

"I thought you weren't going to ask for them until we'd tried to talk to Stanton?"

"Do you have any idea how hard it is to get one of those teams?"

"Uh, no, sir."

"They'll be here in a few hours. Now go to the White House and plant those eavesdropping devices."

"Yes, sir. Peace of cake, sir."

Tahm Qaar smiled. Of course it was no piece of cake getting eavesdropping equipment in to the house where the president of the United States lived. But Goryell had proved himself very capable on this his first mission, so Tahm Qaar was perfectly confident that his rookie agent could get the job done.

He got up from his desk and walked over to Ross Landau to see how he was doing.

"I got some good news" Ross reported. "Now that the phone system is working again I'm getting calls from listeners. They are not caving in to these invaders. They're as angry as anyone can be and there's a lot of fighting spirit out there."

"I'm glad to hear that. But you won't have to fight alone much longer. Our forces will be here any time now."

Unfortunately, Tahm Qaar was being overly optimistic. Not about the arrival of Strike Group 14 – they were only hours away – but about the political process back home.

The Danarvian public had taken due notice of Quim's appearance on *Crash Course*. He had succeeded in stirring up political turbulence around the military operations in sector KB.

It was one thing that people on Teura Vaar protested in large numbers – it was, after all, Quim's home world. But immediately after his appearance on *Crash Course* hundreds of millions of viewers all across Danarvia started calling their Federal Assembly delegates to ask questions about the pending war.

Delegate Narkeenis, who had been so helpful to Quim in stirring up anti-war sentiments, had continued his anti-war tour on his home world. He had planned it very well, even managed to schedule a debate at the Lau Academy on Lau'Schoh only a couple of hours after Quim's *Crash Course* appearance.

Lau'Schoh was the most populous world in the Danarvian Federation. The Lau Academy was the most decidedly libertarian school in the galaxy. It was so anti-authoritarian, in fact, that it did not even have a college president. All they had was a coordination council where representatives from the faculty and students met for discussions about common affairs.

There was no curriculum committee. The faculty was free to teach whatever they wanted, a freedom that was misused by some professors with insufficient academic proficiency. Critics of the Lau Academy often referred to those professors as examples of what "too much libertarianism" could do. But the Academy also retained brilliant scholars whose research was cited widely, who spellbound their students and attracted some of the largest donations in Danarvia.

The Lau Academy was a vibrant intellectual powerhouse.

Many Lau alumni reached high up in business, culture and politics. Delegate Narkeenis was a good example. After he won the election to the Federal Assembly he had become one of the better known graduates of the school. Some of the faculty members tried to convince him to move to Lau'Schoh, but Narkeenis knew that the majority of people on Lau'Schoh were more traditionally libertarian, not minarchists like him and most of the Lau faculty. He would have difficulties getting elected there.

Besides, being a Delegate to the Federal Assembly did not pay very well. He still had to work when the Assembly was not in session, and it was not easy to move an entire law firm from one world to another.

The debate at the Lau Academy had been planned as part of a series of political discussion events. The news about the pending war in Sector KB spiced up the campus and had many students fired up as they went to the debate. To make matters even more intense, just half an hour before the debate started, Executive Izah held a press conference and announced his retirement.

That triggered an election campaign. The Lau debate suddenly became the first event along the campaign trail.

Izah's retirement quickly topped the news cycle in all the 63 worlds of the Danarvian Federation. As the participants of the debate gathered, media pundits started mentioning names of potential successors. Two of them happened to be there to debate with Delegate Narkeenis: Governor Rya-Shin of Blinn Three and retired General Xu-Tarra-Ma.

The governor was a highly respected man with long executive experience. Unlike most other worlds, Blinn Three had an executive branch that was led by only one person. The people who won that seat tended to be strong and colorful personalities. He was no exception. Throughout his career he had made a strong, positive impression on people he had worked with. He had turned his office into a hub for businesses that wanted to establish themselves on Blinn Three and he had helped create one of the largest research engineering schools in the Federation. Of course, he could not devote any tax money to either project – that would be unconstitutional – but he could open his office to meetings, make sure people met and made contacts, and perhaps put in a good word here and there to make sure entrepreneurs could fund their projects.

He had also done some controversial things. He had proposed a
law that would require all residents of Blinn Three to have health
insurance. That was a grave violation of personal freedom, most
people thought, and several citizens had filed lawsuits against
him right away. Some of his political opponents mocked him and
suggested he should also propose a law that everyone needed to eat
food every day.

The legislature turned down his proposal before the courts had
a chance to review it. Some political analysts suggested that when
governor Rya-Shin proposed that health insurance mandate, he
had effectively killed his own political future.

As the debate started, the governor made it clear right away
that he was against further military action in sector KB.

General Xu-Tarra-Ma was of a different opinion. She had made
her career in the special forces division of Frontline Services. She
had gained fame when she led a team of 14 soldiers half way across a
continent on a harsh, barren world with no indigenous population.
It was used by a drug syndicate known as The Dream Web. The
leader of the syndicate had built a heavily fortified compound
and was growing his drugs on climate-managed farms around the
continent.

Sector Patrol had made a couple of unsuccessful attempts to
arrest him, and had always been outgunned by Dream Web guards.
So the mission was given to Frontline Services. Their operations
command selected Xu-Tarra-Ma, a major at that time, to lead the
force. Almost everyone who knew anything about The Dream Web
thought it was a ridiculous idea. They said she was too weak because
she was a woman, that she was too inexperienced, and that the
soldiers in her unit would refuse to go with her or stage a mutiny in
the midst of the operation.

For a full month, major Xu-Tarra-Ma led her special forces
unit on a night-by-night march half way across the continent. The
syndicate leader expected another frontal attack on his compound
and had set up heavy fortification and armor to repel any such
attack. But he never foresaw a small, dedicated unit that would land
so far away and then walk – *walk* – for an entire month and sneak in

to his compound through a stupid back door that his kitchen staff used when they threw out leftover food.

She even managed to take the syndicate leader alive, which catapulted her to a heroic status. She was offered all kinds of civilian careers, but she decided to stay with Frontline Services and eventually retired as a general.

She had earned numerous medals for bravery and dedicated service throughout her career, including the highest military honor of them all, the Embrace of Freedom. She earned it after leading an operation to liberate one hundred thousand Danarvians who had been kidnapped from their home worlds, or from hi-jacked space ships, and were kept as slaves on a rogue world just outside Danarvian territory.

It was easy to understand why General Xu-Tarra-Ma was for military action in Sector KB. While she was not politically savvy, she was respected for her exceptional leadership skills.

And then, of course, there was Delegate Narkeenis.

He was not running for the Executive Office, of course, but his position on the war was pretty well known. He shared Quim's vocal opposition to a new war, something he made clear during the debate.

Xu-Tarra-Ma was quick to attack him for that.

"Delegate Quim supported military action against Remz Five" she pointed out, referring to the rogue world that had kidnapped civilians from Danarvian worlds and held them as slave labor. "I earned my Embrace of Freedom for leading the military operation against Remz Five, and I am happy that Quim supported that operation. But now he is against a similar operation to liberate the people of Earth. That is inconsistent to me."

Governor Rya-Shin took the same argument, but from an exactly opposite angle.

"Delegate Narkeenis, if you share Quim's support for the Remz Five operation, then how can you say that you are against this new war?"

"But these are two entirely different cases" Narkeenis explained. "Remz Five was holding a hundred thousand Danarvians as slaves.

Neither Earth nor Zoh'moor holds any Danarvian citizens captives, let alone as slaves."

"There are some facts that point to the opposite" General Xu-Tarra-Ma pointed out. "But regardless of that, I have to ask you, Delegate: how do you suggest Earth liberates itself of the technologically superior Zoh'moorian invaders?"

"Diplomacy should always be the first option" Narkeenis countered.

"Words fall on the deaf ears of those who only listen to guns" said the general.

"You are being very presumptuous about the Zoh'moorians."

The debate was widely broadcast and sparked even more discussions among politicians and the general public. Instant opinion polls indicated that the anti-war side was the stronger one. Influential ranters on worlds as far apart as Crying Lady and Majestic 39 added to the heat of the debate by spreading more or less speculative rumors about Danarvian citizens being held captive by Zoh'moor or Earth. But no one was able to present irrefutable evidence.

The rising tide of the anti-war debate quickly reached the Federal Assembly. By the time Strike Group 14 entered Earth's solar system the offices of the Assembly Delegates were being overrun by calls and correspondence from voters demanding "an end to the next Kahpiyan war" before it had started. Even though the Delegates were not in session, most of them kept their Assembly offices open and the pressure from their voters was duly noted.

Delegate Watlaan was pressured even more, because of her chairmanship of the intelligence and outer rim security committee. She found herself caught between the two sides of the issue. The criticism of the war was beginning to nibble away at her firm support for going after the Zoh'moorians and liberating Earth.

At the same time, the latest intelligence update from Advanced Retrieval said that the Zoh'moorians had landed on Earth and killed and kidnapped civilians. The update was brief but clearly made the point that the Zoh'moorians were not behaving like friendly neighbors.

This was not a middle-of-the-road situation. Watlaan knew she could not be a fence sitter on this issue.

She got a call from L'Faa.

"Did you watch the debate?" L'Faa asked.

"Yes, very interesting."

"I am going to go public and address this anti-war rhetoric."

"When?"

"I will give a speech tonight. I am going to present the case for war with Zoh'moor."

"I am looking forward to that. My friend, I am torn over this. More and more for each day."

"We all are. All we can do is our best."

And L'Faa did do her best. Her speech that night, which was shown on all the major news networks, was very well written. After the usual hailing phrases and credits to her colleagues at the Executive Office she went straight for the hot topic of the day.

"As you all know by now, upon orders from the Executive Office, Frontline Services has dispatched a strike group to sector KB. They are also dispatching an armada. We have done this because it is our duty to protect the freedom of all independent beings. One of the worlds in sector KB, Zoh'moor, has invaded another world, Earth. While our knowledge of Zoh'moor is limited, we do know that its actions against Earth violate the freedom of all Earthlings. We know that our military is vastly superior to theirs and we do expect a quick and successful ending to this."

She paused briefly and glanced at her notes.

"Some people question why we should launch a military operation to liberate people on a world so far away from Danarvian space. They say that it constitutes an undue expansion of government powers. I understand their concerns and I share their ambitions to keep our government to an absolute minimum. But we must also not forget that our Charter of Liberty grants our government one power, and one power only, and that is to preserve the freedom of all independent beings, not just citizens of the Danarvian Federation."

She leaned forward slightly, as if she wanted to get closer to her viewers.

"The people of the invading world, Zoh'moor, are themselves being oppressed and deprived of their most basic freedoms on a daily basis. By engaging the Zoh'moorians at Earth, we open for the possibility that the tyrannical leader of Zoh'moor will be weakened. That way we may open for them to topple him. That would be a tremendous accomplishment in defending and spreading freedom."

The speech was convincing and well received by the billions who watched it. Candidates for the open seat on the Executive Office began using her arguments and referring to her as an authority in their own pro-war speeches.

Then again, L'Faa had been in politics long enough to know that the tides could turn very fast.

As could the events that decided who was right and who was wrong.

L'Faa had put her political prestige and authority behind her speech. If things went well with Strike Group 14 and their assault on the Zoh'moorian invasion force, her credentials would be even stronger.

If, on the other hand, things did not go that well...

*   *   *

OPENING

My headache is gone. The creatures put that beam back on my head and it hurt very bad for some time. But then, when they turned it off, the pain was gone.

I almost feel grateful for what they did. I had such pain from time to time. But I shouldn't be grateful. I shouldn't be grateful for anything they do to me. After all, I'm their prisoner. And so are the others here.

But I am a little confused right now. Something strange just happened. When they took me out of the cage and they were going to bring me back to the dungeon they suddenly just left me on the floor, next to the cage. Then they all disappeared. Even the robot they use to carry me is gone. So here I am, outside the cage, outside the dungeon, with no creature watching me. Or, at least that is what I think.

Usually I can smell them. They smell bad. It's like no other smell I can ever remember. In the beginning, it used to make me sick. But I forced myself to get used to it, because I had to be able to eat and survive.

I wonder why I am here on the floor. I better stay down and not move.

The lights have changed. The rooms around here are always lit by some subtle, blue light. It is never white, and it is difficult to see in shadowy areas. But now the lights are a little stronger, a little more light-blue.

Especially the lights over in that corridor.

I have never been outside of this room, the corridor that leads to the dungeon, and, of course, the dungeon. Except for when they put me to sleep. Then I know they take me somewhere else. Sometimes I do not fall asleep right away, and I know they take me down another corridor.

This is all a big system of caves. We are underground, and probably deep underground. It seems to be naturally warm here. The air is not that bad, so long as there are no creatures around.

They still have not come back for me. I cannot hear them, or smell them. Why did they leave? Did something happen?

No one has ever escaped the dungeon. Every newcomer has tried to climb the walls. It is impossible. And the creatures are so horrible that no one really seems to want to try to escape when they're out of the dungeon either. I agree. They are horrible. They are disgusting monsters.

But they also never give us a chance to escape. They are always very careful, very particular about keeping us locked up. Either in the robot arm or in their... oh, dear God, I don't even want to think about it.

So this is something new. That they just left me here.

It must be some kind of mistake.

I know there is a control room over there. But the creatures who were inside it are gone. And the one that was watching me from outside the room is also gone. I'm all alone here.

Maybe I should go find them.

No. They would kill me. Or hurt me very badly.

Then again... that's what they have been doing for twenty years now. They cannot possibly do anything more to me. So what if they bite me with their fangs? So what if they inject some venom into my body? So what if they hurt me with their beams, or wrap me up in their webs? I'm already dead. I died when they took me from my parents' old house in Lindsborg.

My legs are not very strong. But I'm going to try to stand up anyway.

Oh, dear, that feels good. Yes, it actually does. It feels really good. Ah, I can even breathe better when I am standing up. And... when I walk... my legs can carry me.

It's funny. I haven't walked anywhere except on the floor of the dungeon for the past twenty years. A few steps here and there. And now, when I try to walk, my legs can still carry me. I'm weak... but I can walk.

We do some exercising down there in the dungeon. It helps. I will have to tell them that when I get back.

That corridor leads to the dungeon. But this one here, this one has that brighter light. I wonder why. I have never seen it before.

I'm not sure I want to walk down there. But then again – what do I have to lose?

*   *   *

W A R

At the center of Strike Group 14 was the command vessel. It was sphere-shaped and had three functions. It was the home of group command, it provided tactical training facilities for all kinds of personnel and it produced the master cloak shield for the entire group when they flew through space in battle mode. Under the master cloak shield the strike group could sneak up on enemies and tap them on the shoulder without being discovered.

The command vessel had its own set of fighters and striker ships. It also harbored the group's supply ships and main non-combat stocks. It was heavily armed and could perform almost any battle operations on its own, if necessary.

Six hub ships flew in a hexagonal formation around the command vessel. They, too, were spherical. Each hub ship was an independent battle unit with long-range strikers, planet surface bombers, fighters and troop transport ships. The hub ships themselves were almost as heavily armed as the command vessel. They were also equipped to operate for several days without any supplies coming in from the command vessel.

Every spherical ship had its bridge at the core, a design that obviously protected the commanding officers in battle and allowed for more weaponry and protective systems at the surface. They had belts of engines and shield generators around the equator and two latitudes to the north and the south.

At the front of the strike group formation were six attack cruisers, almost cigar shaped and equipped with devastating firepower. The rear of the formation was covered by eight destroyers, ships that resembled the attack cruisers in shape but were notably smaller. They were armed and armored primarily to serve as defense ships.

Frontline Services had recently upgraded all destroyers with a new, but very expensive kind of shield. Instead of a magnetic-based system that simply reflected enemy fire, they had just been equipped with micro-gravity shields. When hit by enemy fire, the shield instantly created a local "black hole" that absorbed the energy from the hit. The energy was then diverted to a parallel power system that reinforced the destroyer's own shields.

Vice admiral Ghaul wanted to be the first strike group commander to put that new system to test in battle.

"Entering Earth system" navigation reported.

"Deploy" Ghaul ordered.

The command vessel made a left turn together with two of the hub ships and the destroyers. The attack cruisers turned right, joined by four hub ships.

The Zoh'moorian vessels were entering Earth's system from the right of where Strike Group 14 entered. Bulky Zoh'moorian transports and escort ships were en route to Earth and others were on their way back to their half-way point. They moved slowly and made frequent course adjustments that made their flight look almost erratic. To an untrained eye that might seem like a smart thing to do – it would make it harder for an enemy to hit them. In reality, it revealed that their propulsion systems were so primitive they could not correct for the pull from gravitational fields. It also revealed that their navigation shields could not clear space ahead of them from small rocks and other debris that could damage the ship.

Vice admiral Ghaul studied the images of the Zoh'moorian vessels with a mixture of satisfaction and disappointment. This was not going to be a battle. His pilots and gunners would get some target practice, but that was about it.

Not that he craved for battle. He had been through some pretty tough ones with his strike group before. His most recent war action was from a short but fierce conflict out in the Temptation Sea. The K'Maar had tried to take two solar systems inside Danarvian space.

They had been in a border dispute with the Danarvian Federation for ten years and a newly elected leader had decided to unilaterally end that conflict.

Bad mistake.

Ghaul had relied on that experience when he planned his attack on the Zoh'moorians. But he had quickly realized that Zoh'moorian technology was at least one generation behind the K'Maar.

He ordered two of the attack cruisers to continue up toward the Zoh'moorian halfway point. If possible, he wanted to destroy it or incapacitate it and thereby slow down reinforcements once he attacked the massive ship build-up around Earth.

With all eight destroyers guarding the command vessel, Ghaul ordered two hub ships to proceed to Earth. The other four hub ships assumed their positions at the point where the Zoh'moorians were enterering the solar system. Two attack cruisers prepared to move swiftly from the entry point in toward Earth to attack every ship they came across. Two others flew out toward the Zoh'moorian halfway point.

An agonizing calm set in on the bridge of the command vessel. Everyone was waiting for all the ships to report "ready".

No one said anything.

A Zoh'moorian surveillance ship approached the command vessel. It was apparently patrolling the outer rim of the solar system.

"That's odd" first officer Mahir noted. "Are they expecting us?"

"Yes, who else would be out here?" the vice admiral said. "They know we exist."

"Yes, but that would not make them anticipate us now."

"Unless they are extremely paranoid. I'm going to notify Fleet Command anyway."

While sending a message to Fleet Command, vice admiral Ghaul kept his eyes on the screen that monitored the Zoh'moorian ship and its sensor activity. The ship flew in a strict orbital path, at a fairly slow speed. It passed so close to one of their destroyers that it actually touched its outer deflector shield.

Ghaul held his breath for a moment. If the Zoh'moorian vessel had sensors worth anything, it should have detected the shield it bumped in to. It should slow down, or at the very least point its sensors toward the destroyer.

They waited. Ten seconds passed. Twenty seconds. A half minute. The clock ticked on and the Zoh'moorian vessel just kept moving. Its speed did not change. Its sensors maintained the same search pattern.

It had not detected the destroyer it had almost collided with. Ghaul chuckled.

"Maybe we should have uncloaked just to scare him."

He got up from his chair and walked over to tactical command. All their ships were in position. It was time to attack.

He was just about to give the general order when one of the attack cruisers en route to the Zoh'moorian fleet's halfway point called in:

"We have a bogey!"

*   *   *

President Oslow's TV speech was right to the point.

"My fellow Americans. Our perception of the world we live in has changed fundamentally. We now know that we are not alone. We have made contact with an advanced civilization and I have had a long meeting with a high representative of their government. He has assured me that they have peaceful intentions and that they want to establish good, lasting and mutually beneficial relations with us."

Tahm Qaar was a bit surprised to see that it was the president, not the vice president who gave the speech.

"I wonder where Holly Stanton is" he said to Ross, who was watching the speech with him."

"Wherever she is, she's in cahoots with the Zoh'moorians" Ross noted. "And now it seems like Barry is also in on it."

"However" president Oslow continued "It has been brought to my attention that there are infiltrators among us. Infiltrators and saboteurs from another world. These enemies are not our Zoh'moorian friends, but from another world called Danarvia."

Tahm Qaar could not believe his ears. He leaned back in his

chair, said something in a language that Ross Landau did not understand, and rubbed his face with his palm.

"I can't believe this" said one of his agents.

"This man is all evil" Ross muttered.

"This is a big problem for us" the agent continued. "We're going to have to be even more careful in our contacts with Earthlings."

"It's even bigger than that" Tahm Qaar said and got up from his chair. "As soon as Frontline Services get here they're not only going to have to face the Zoh'moorians, but they may also have to confront the American military. They would have to fight the very people they're here to liberate."

"It could get even worse" Ross said. "Now that Holly and Barry know about you and your federation, they could actually make an official appeal directly to your government to stay out of Earth's affairs."

Tahm Qaar nodded emphatically.

"That's the next big problem we have. This TV broadcast is not a formal appeal, since it was not addressed to us directly. Strictly speaking, we did not see it, if you know what I mean. But we've already made contact with the White House... you know, about Rhea. They could easily take the next opportunity to tell us the same thing in our face."

"And we can't just pretend we didn't hear it" one of the agents filled in.

"Exactly. There's a limit to how far we can stretch and bend our rules."

His phone rang. It was Goryell. Tahm Qaar listened and nodded and said something back. He hung up and looked very unhappy.

"Just perfect" he said. "Holly Stanton's chief of staff just called Goryell and conveyed the same message. That's as close to a formal diplomatic note you can get."

The room was quiet for a moment.

"This is bad" Tahm Qaar mumbled.

"I'm sure we can find a way out of this" Ross said, trying to stay on the upbeat note.

Tham Qaar looked over at him.

"Hopefully. But politics is politics."

"I'm a little surprised" Ross said, his voice revealing a touch of irritation. "You have a government that is totally devoted to freedom. No socialist nonsense. And you're telling me you can't get around this?"

Tahm Qaar did not answer him right away. He sat down again. His index finger drummed on his chair's armrest for a moment. He stared out in the air for a moment.

Then he turned to Ross.

"I've seen many things, Ross" he said. "I've been on missions on more worlds than I care to keep track of. On Tya Nine I investigated who was causing the famine that killed millions of people. I survived a food war and attacks by locusts the size of a house cat. I starved for two months and almost died in the gutters outside the presidential palace before I was able to retrieve the information I needed. On Cerm D I infiltrated the ranks of torturers under the anti-religious tyrannical government. I pretended to like watching them work. I laughed as they crippled peaceful monks, I cheered when they beat priests senseless. And I broke the hands and feet of a young nun, so that she would never use a spoon or walk again, just to gain the trust of the mad dictator, so I could get close to him and eventually kill him."

He had to pause and close his eyes briefly. The memory of that young nun still haunted him.

"I've been in vicious riots," he continued. "I walked for two weeks through a bloody civil war in the midst of cataclysmic natural disasters. I even survived a mass execution attempt on Jay one five four, a world so torn apart by war it's a wonder anyone is still alive there."

"We lost two agents there just last year" another agent added.

"I've seen reptilians fall victims to racist humanoids" Tahm Qaar continued. "I've seen humanoids be butchered by racist reptilians. I've seen reptilians kill reptilians, humanoids kill humanoids, neighbors kill neighbors... and everywhere I've been... on every mission, Ross... I have been able to make a difference one way or the other. I've always been able to go in, on a mission, and contribute to a better life for people on those worlds. When I killed that mad tyrant on Cerm D, a big chunk of the military rose up and revolted. They're peaceful and prosperous now."

He paused and shook his head.

"But there is one thing, Ross, that I have never been able to get around. And that's the politics of my own government. The political play among the people I have sworn to serve."

He reached out with his hand toward Ross.

"If I pretend that I never heard the president, and Frontline Services invade and they suddenly have to confront the U.S. armed forces just to liberate you, then someone is going to ask me a heck a lot of questions back home. What kind of sloppy intelligence agent am I? See what I mean? And then this TV broadcast will surface, and I'm sure that Stanton's chief of staff taped that phone call…"

Ross nodded.

"I respect that" he said. "Kind of reminds me of the debate here on Earth preceding the Iraq war under Bush. Well, you stand on principles and laws. That's one reason I can trust you. But what you're saying is that Frontline Services will have to stop their military operations now?"

"Strictly speaking they have to stay out of Earth's atmosphere."

One of his agents answered a call on some communications device. He leaned over to Tahm Qaar and said something. Tham Qaar nodded.

"Our ORCA team has just arrived."

"The problem solvers?" Ross asked.

"Yep. The problem is… I don't have a problem for them to solve anymore."

Ross did not like the sound of that.

"Well, I, for one would like for us, America, to build close relations with the Danarvian Federation, and I'd like for that to happen right now. I think what you guys stand for is exactly what America is all about. And you're even ahead of us in some aspects. Your constitution is so devoted to freedom that you only pay one percent in income tax. One percent, did you hear that, Surrey? I told you that yesterday? Well, it's worth repeating. Anyway. There has got to be something we can do right here, right now, to get around your political problems."

Tahm Qaar listened calmly.

"I'm all ears if you have any ideas" he said.

"You need someone who can represent Earth, right? Someone who can plead to your government for help, right?"

"Yes."

"And it would have to be someone higher than our president, or vice president, or acting, whatever she is, right?"

"Preferably, since they are in cahoots with the Zoh'moorians."

"Well" Ross said and took a deep breath. "I never thought I'd hear myself say this, but... I think you might want to talk to the Secretary General of the UN."

"The United Nations?"

"Yes. They're a bunch of socialists and most of the member nations are tyrannies, but it's nevertheless the closest we've gotten so far to a world government."

"That's actually a good idea" Tahm Qaar agreed. "Who's the Secretary General?"

"Al Gore."

*   *   *

The bogey that was flying parallel with one of Strike Group 14's attack cruisers did not register on any of their regular scanners.

"It only shows up on our quantum scanners" said the captain of the cruiser. "The only reason we found it was that we saw a strange blip on our navigation sensors. It blocked a small string of stars."

"Is it matching your speed and course?" asked first officer Mahir.

"Affirmative."

"A Zoh'moorian ship?" asked the chief engineer.

"Don't think so" Mahir said. "They can't even detect our ships when they're practically crashing in to them."

"I agree" said vice admiral Ghaul. "That bogey's cloak is on par with ours."

And yet, it was not quite a cloak. The ship was visible to the naked eye.

The attack cruiser relayed a computerized image of it, based on their quantum scans. It had a shape they had never seen before.

"That's quite remarkable" Ghaul noted. "It's almost two-dimensional."

"Thirty feet high, a half mile long and two hundred feet wide" confirmed the chief engineer. "No visible propulsion systems."

"A vessel shaped like that should not be able to fly through space" said Mahir. "Especially not at that speed."

"Send one hub ship to investigate" Ghaul ordered. "There could be more of those strangers in the area. And I want those attack cruisers free to do their job."

"I'm concerned" Mahir said. "This could be an alien race allied with the Zoh'moorians. I suggest we scan nearby space before we take any action against the Zoh'moorians."

They recalibrated the probes that they had already spread throughout the sector. None of the quantum scans detected any other vessels than the Zoh'moorian fleet and the unknown one that was bogeying the attack cruisers.

However, they noticed that some probes were missing.

"Is there a pattern in what probes are gone?" vice admiral Ghaul asked.

"Yes, sir" the chief engineer said. "They're missing in a u-shape that comes from the direction of Zoh'moor almost all the way to Earth and then turns back on a parallel course with our attack cruisers."

"Did they scoop up the probes as they went along?" asked Mahir rhetorically. "That's quite bold. What if we'd had live data streaming from them?"

"Bold or stupid" Ghaul noted. "Only way to find out is to confront that bogey."

The attack cruisers slowed down to let the hub ship catch up quickly. The bogey matched their speed. As the hub ship closed in, though, it changed course and moved away from them. It was still moving slowly, and when the hub ship came within range it deployed strikers that quickly sped off in pursuit of the bogey.

The intent was not to destroy the unknown vessel, but to establish contact and tell it to get out of the area. Frontline Services did not accept the presence of unknown vessels anywhere within its jurisdiction. That included space where they were conducting any kind of operations, even outside Danarvia. Absolute dominance was the founding strategic principle. If that meant stepping on a few alien toes, then so be it.

The alien vessel kept moving away at a constant speed. The four strikers quickly caught up and took positions behind it and on its sides. They relayed a message from vice admiral Ghaul:

"Alien vessel, this is a military unit from Frontline Services of Danarvia. Identify yourself."

No response. They repeated the message on more frequencies. The alien vessel kept moving at steady pace.

"The shape of that vessel is remarkable indeed" said Mahir. "It's almost two-dimensional."

"And still no sign of a propulsion system" the chief engineer noted. "And it's completely black, no sign of lights anywhere, no shifts in the shape."

"Sir, we are reading strange magnetic disturbances immediately around its hull" reported one of the strikers. "Relaying scans."

While a new image of the alien vessel took shape on a computer screen right next to vice admiral Ghaul's seat, the strikers tried to contact the vessel a third time.

Still no response.

"Sir, it's a magnetic field, alright" said the chief engineer. "But I've never seen anything like it."

"Put your brightest minds to work on it" Ghaul ordered. "Alright, let's turn up the volume a bit."

The two strikers that flanked the alien ship fired energy torpedoes diagonally in front of the alien vessel. They exploded with safe distance to the alien so as to signal that there was no direct harm meant.

That brought the alien to a halt.

"Now, that's better" Ghaul noted. "Let's put some mines in a perimeter around it."

While two bombers left the hub ship to deploy the mines, the battle commander reported that the Zoh'moorians had halted all traffic between their half way point and Earth.

"So now they know we're here" Ghaul said.

"Which means we're dealing with a Zoh'moorian ally" Mahir

noted. "May I suggest we engage the Zoh'moorians immediately so they don't get a chance to adjust?"

"No other aliens in the area?" Ghaul asked the battle commander.

"None, sir."

"Good. OK. Let's roll."

And so, the battle began.

It was not really a battle, though. It was too lopsided. Out of nowhere, the captains of the Zoh'moorian ships suddenly saw someone firing on them, with devastating firepower and chilling precision. And that was about all they saw. The Zoh'moorian vessels proved to be even weaker than the command of Strike Group 14 had expected. Their engines, fuel systems and even weapons systems were built with almost no protection against enemy fire.

"It's a massacre" first officer Mahir noted.

"They're losing tens of thousands of lives" Ghaul muttered. "For what purpose?"

That was the price he had to pay for being militarily superior. If he could have avoided it, the vice admiral would have preferred to set a couple of examples for the Zoh'moorians to witness, so that they could be smart enough to pull back. But there was neither time nor diplomatic opportunities for that.

Still, the vice admiral made a note for himself to talk to his wife when this was all over. She was the only one he shared his deepest feelings with.

"Sir, the alien vessel is moving again!" yelled a young, rookie bridge officer.

"No yelling on the bridge!" Mahir replied sternly.

"Sorry, sir."

Ghaul turned to the screen with live scan feeds from the alien vessel. It was surrounded by a close perimeter of grid mines. They were deployed in a zig-zag formation with beams between them to form a tight grid. If anything tried to pass through the beams all the mines within a certain distance would explode.

The two bombers that had deployed the mines had positioned themselves above and below the alien vessel. The four strikers held positions outside the mine perimeter.

Moving forward slowly, the alien ship approached the mine grid almost cautiously. It seemed as if it wanted to take a close look at the grid. The bombers matched its speed and course.

The alien stopped, pulled back a little bit and stopped again.

Then, without any warning, it accelerated hard and hurled itself straight at the mine grid. Its acceleration seemed to come from nowhere, with no signs of energy build-up. As it shot forward it hit the mine grid with full force.

Five mines detonated. On any normal ship the damage would have been irreparable. But this was no normal space ship. It stopped as the mines exploded and let the shock of the explosions shake its hull. As one of the bombers relayed images of the vessel, Ghaul and Mahir watched in amazement.

"I've never seen anything like it" Mahir said. "Look at the hull. It reacts like a liquid!"

The hull of the alien vessel responded to the shock waves from the mines like the surface of water to a stone. Waves transmitted from the front to the back. The ship stood still while the waves went through its hull and subsided.

Then it accelerated again.

"Bomb him!" Ghaul ordered.

The two bombers let the alien ship have it. A barrage of bombs pounded it from above and below. Two strikers took position and opened fire from the sides. The alien vessel stopped again.

"He can't move when the hull is absorbing shocks" Ghaul noted with great interest.

"Sir!" yelled the battle commander. "More quantum scans coming in!"

The hub ship closest to the alien vessel had picked up another alien ship further out. It was holding position.

"He's watching what we're doing to his buddy" Ghaul smiled.

The alien vessel under fire was still not moving. The waves in its hull continued due to the barrage from the bombers and the strikers.

"I wonder how much beating he can take" said Mahir. "Romschi!"

"Yes, sir" said the chief engineer.

"Give me live scans of the magnetic field around that ship."

"Got it!"

He handed the second officer a laptop-like device with a small three-dimensional screen. Mahir put it on a desk right next to Ghaul's seat. He pulled up a three-dimensional image of the alien vessel, but instead of the hull they saw a magnetic field.

"Quite intriguing" he smiled. "Its entire hull is magnetically charged."

"How is this possible?" Ghaul asked the chief engineer.

"We're working on a theory, sir."

The waves in the hull escalated and the magnetic field showed signs of rupture. The battle commander ordered the bombers and strikers to focus their fire on the rupture spots, and to fire with random pauses in between. The ruptures grew larger and the entire vessel began to shiver badly.

Then it imploded.

Not exploded. It imploded. The hull collapsed and disintegrated.

The vessel was gone.

*   *   *

"Sir... Mr. President..."

"Yes, Andrew, what is it?"

"The... The Supreme General is here to see you."

"What? But I..."

"He demands to see you right now, sir."

"But I have to make some phone... Oh! Welcome, Mr. Supreme General, to the Oval Office of the White House. I would certainly have invited you if..."

"I do not need an invitation, Barry. Tell your servant to leave."

"Andrew, go wait in..."

"I'm leaving right now."

"Thanks, Andrew."

"Barry, you have not kept your promise. The Danarvian forces have not left."

"But I sent you a copy of my TV message..."

"They have launched a full scale assault on our forces, Barry.

They have disrupted our supply line from our home world and destroyed ships with over two hundred thousand soldiers onboard."

"Oh, Mr. Supreme General, I... I am very sorry... Ouch!"

"I can break your neck right now, like this, you filthy little bare-skin sub-being!"

"Mr... Mr. Supreme General..."

"The only reason why I don't do it is that you are so easy to negotiate with. Even easier than your spineless little vice president."

"Oh! Thanks for... for letting go of my throat..."

"I cannot believe a man with such a weak spine was elected president in this country. Are all Americans' as spineless as you are?"

"No..."

"Don't waste your breath. I did not come here to discuss American politics. I came here to let you know that from hereon I will take direct command of your armed forces."

"What? But..."

"I want you to leave immediately for that speech tour. You lay the rest of Earth before my feet and I will reward you. If you don't, I will punish you as the pathetic sub-being you are."

"But I thought we had negotiated... w-without preconditions..."

"How do I know you did not secretly tell the Danarvians to attack us?"

"No! Absolutely not!"

"Perhaps you relayed our coordinates to them?"

"No! Mr. Supreme General, I've been waiting for you to come here for so long... why would I...?"

"Get out and give those speeches you promised me. Make sure they are effective, or I will let my troops subdue your people. And I expect that your military stay in their barracks... or we will pave the streets with their bare, ugly skins!"

*　　*　　*

Goryell had taken up position on top of an office building on the intersection of H Street, 19th Street and Pennsylvania Avenue in the northwest of Washington, DC. The building was actually the International Monetary Fund headquarters. Below was a wide open space that Goryell concluded was a construction site. Right next to it, across 19th Street, was an open plaza with some bushes and sitting areas.

Zoh'moorian elite Fah'marook troops had gathered in large numbers in the open spaces and done considerable damage to the construction site. They had leveled the bushes and made markings in the asphalt on Pennsylvania Avenue. Troops with less equipment and smaller weapons were waiting around the markings. Goryell assumed that they were regular army troops.

A shuttle flew in, landed right where the markings were and the back doors opened. At least 30 humans, all stripped of their clothes, were forced out and led over toward the construction site. There were four small children among them.

The Zoh'moorians picked a couple of men from the lines and forced them to lie down. Then Fah'marook thugs stepped up on them and stood on their backs. The rest were forced up to the edge of the construction site, facing the hole in the site.

Goryell was standing right on the edge of the roof of the building. He was wearing a cloak suit and had cloaked his shuttle, so there was no risk he would be detected. But he also had to keep his mouth shut in order to stay invisible, and that was not easy when he heard women and children cry. All he could do was to switch on a head-mounted camera and direct it toward the women and children. He zoomed in so that their faces would be clearly visible.

He also made a sweep with the camera to show the Zoh'moorian commander who was standing some 20 feet behind the women and children. He also let the camera capture the soldiers who were standing on the back of naked men.

Those soldiers were watching over a half dozen other soldiers whose weapons were now pointing at the backs of the naked women and children. The naked women and children were facing the big hole in the construction site.

Everyone knew what was going to happen.

The commander gave an order. The execution platoon fired.

Goryell counted a dozen burning human bodies falling down

into the hole in the construction site, but he knew he had not counted them all. He estimated that there were now 20 dead people down there.

The soldiers who were standing on two humans stepped down. One of the men was pulled up and forced to stand on his hands and knees. Then one of the soldiers put a big box on his back and yelled something at him while pointing toward the shuttle. The man fell to the ground under the heavy weight. The soldiers took the burden off his back and dragged him to the edge of the hole where they threw him down on top of the dead women and children.

Then the Fah'marook forced the other man to stand on his hands and knees. The big, heavy box was put on his back and he was ordered to carry it to the shuttle. He struggled hard, desperately trying to do what he was told to do, probably hoping to get through the ordeal alive. One soldier beat him over his buttocks and the back of his feet with the rear end of his weapon. The man screamed in pain but kept on moving toward the shuttle. Another soldier stepped on his right hand and apparently crushed his fingers. The man screamed again but was beaten over his legs and feet when he stopped. So he continued.

When he finally reached the open doors at the back of the shuttle they took the box off his back and carried it in to the shuttle. The man was breathing heavily but was still alive. One of the soldiers came out with something that looked like a seat. It had straps underneath it. He fixed the seat on the man's back and tied the straps around his belly. Then he put a leash around his neck and pulled it. The man had to crawl on his hands and knees and follow the soldier over to the point where the execution had taken place. The soldier ordered him to stop. The commander who was leading the execution came voer and sat down on the seat.

The shuttle took off and flew westward. Another shuttle soon came in and unloaded another group of humans. All naked, all except two men led up to the edge of the hole.

Many of them screamed in panic when they saw the dead bodies.

Goryell watched and taped it. He watched and quietly cursed the Zoh'moorians.

But he was not a one-man army. He knew there was not a single thing he could do to stop the executions.

*   *   *

L'Faa did not want the Executive Office to see the latest intelligence report from Earth. She did not want them to hear Barry Oslow ask Danarvia to stay out of Earth's affairs. She wanted to omit that part and present something generic so that the Executive Office would stay focused on defeating the Zoh'moorians and liberating Earth.

But she could not do that. She was not above the law. She was a kind of politician that many Americans would look at with suspicion and wonder when her façade of sincerity would come off and the real, corrupt, power-hungry moron would step forward.

The problem with L'Faa was – there just was no such moron inside her. She was honest, sincere and loyal to death to the people of Danarvia and to the Charter of Liberty. Which was why she presented the latest intelligence report from Earth in its entirety. And let the Executive Office know that the American president wanted Danarvia out of Earth's affairs.

"How did he find out about us?" was the first question that came up when the Executives met.

"The Zoh'moorians know about us" L'Faa reminded her colleagues. "Our agents have performed a couple of high-risk operations on Earth. They must have put two and two together. What this means, though, is that we have to call off the plan to liberate Earth from the Zoh'moorian invaders."

The other Executives agreed, grudgingly. Izah, whose resignation would soon go in to effect, gave away a restrained smile.

"I cannot help but wonder" he said, "what difference it would have made if we had asked the Earthlings first."

That did not sit well with L'Faa.

"Look" she said and leaned over toward Izah. "You know just as well as I do that the American president, and vice president, are collaborating with the Zoh'moorians. You know what that means. You know that leaders don't always follow the will of their peoples. You remember when the Hakai invaded Tamlin Two."

"That was a long time ago" Izah objected.

"Time does not change facts. Only memory does. One faction of the Tamlin government invited the Hakai invasion, and declared on open space channels that this was not a hostile takeover, but rather an invitation to a neighboring world to come and help."

"Nobody believed that" Izah said, but he was clearly on the defensive now.

"And why did no one believe that?" L'Faa continued, a bit upset. "Because the Tamlin leader was such a nice guy?"

She regretted the somewhat edgy tone in her voice. She was upset and frustrated, but it was unfair and undignified to take it out on Izah.

"I apologize for my tone" she said. "I do not mean to offend you."

"This is a stressful situation" Izah said, acknowledging her apology with a nod.

"So the bottom line" said another Executive, "is that we have to call Strike Group Fourteen back and order the Second Armada to make a halt."

"No. According to our laws, the message from the American president is only valid for Earth and its atmosphere. Whatever Zoh'moorian vessels are outside of Earth's atmosphere, we are free to engage."

"That's not entirely logical" another Executive remarked.

"I know" L'Faa agreed. "But this is what our interplanetary territorial laws define a case like this."

"So we will cut off the Zoh'moorians' access to Earth" said Izah, "but we will not oust them from the planet."

"Yes."

"Ah. I see. We're putting Earth under blockade."

"Right. Strike Group Fourteen will bar any alien vessels from entering or leaving Earth's atmosphere. Personally, I hope that this will deprive the Zoh'moorians already on the planet's surface of enough of their resources to allow the Americans to rise up against them. And their obviously corrupt leader."

It was a delicate political balancing act. And militarily absurd. Before the meeting L'Faa had felt a strong urge to go in there and put all her political clout on the line for a full-scale invasion of Earth, just as they had planned. But she also knew that with Barry Oslow's plea to them to stay away from Earth she ran the risk of being hauled before the Charter Court. They would eat her for lunch for having violated the Fourth Principle of the Charter of Liberty.

As much as she disliked their decision to leave Zoh'moorian invaders on Earth, it was the right thing to do.

The question was: would the blockade work? Would it stretch the Zoh'moorian troops on ground so thin that the American forces could size them up? Or would the American forces just sit on their hands and take orders from Barry Oslow?

*   *   *

Tahm Qaar viewed the reports that Goryell was sending back from Washington, DC with rising impatience. He got similar reports from other agents dispatched to New York, Chicago, Los Angeles, Atlanta, Houston and San Francisco.

In San Francisco, the mayor had tried to welcome the Zoh'moorians as liberators. When the city woke up on the day of the invasion he had given a speech where he promised his residents that the Zoh'moorians had come to liberate them of American capitalist oppression. He was so excited he could barely contain himself. He assured the residents of San Francisco that they could all look forward to tolerance, equality and free health care. The convenience stores would begin selling marijuana and polygamy would become legal.

Once the Zoh'moorians got there he became confused. They did not behave like the enlightened liberators they were (supposed to be). And now that Fah'marook troops were taking the mayor's residents to mass graves in the desert in Nevada, he tried desperately to negotiate with them. When that did not work he fled the city by car and was rumored to be hiding at a vineyard up in Napa Valley.

No political leader seemed to want to stand up and call for the U.S. armed forces to defend their country. On the contrary, President Oslow kept talking about how the Zoh'moorians were their new friendly neighbors.

Fortunately, the captain in charge of the ORCA team came in to Tahm Qaar just as his frustration was about to begin to irritate him.

The ORCA captain was a short, sturdy humanoid with short, dark hair, a beard that looked like it had been trimmed with a butcher knife and a left hand that missed one finger. He was wearing a strange combination of military outfit and rugged exercise gear. He had a hunting knife strapped to his calf, a state-of-the-art single-hand weapon at the hip, an urban combat weapon across his chest with six reload packages in a column along the front of his vest.

The ORCA captain sat down heavily on a chair across the table from Tahm Qaar. They looked at one another without a single facial expression.

"So where's Goryell?" the captain asked.

Tahm Qaar looked at the captain with a touch of weariness.

"You flew twelve thousand light years to practice martial arts?" he asked.

"I heard he got his second star."

"You're three ranks above him, Kho. Why don't you try me instead?"

"How's your wife? Still got that cute butt?"

"Cuter than yours."

"That's funny" captain Kho said without a hint of a smile.

They looked at one another without saying anything. A few seconds passed.

Then Kho broke out in laughter. Tahm Qaar laughed with him.

"Good to see you again, you rascal" Tham Qaar chuckled.

"Been a while, buddy!"

"Almost a year."

"So you got yourself into a little mess again?" said captain Kho and hauled out a piece of something that he started chewing on.

"Is that Blinnian bark?"

Captain Kho laughed again and tossed Tahm Qaar another piece.

"You remember" he said. "We had some good times back then."

"I've got some Aquaan ale for you when you're done with this one" Tahm Qaar chuckled and explained what mission he had in mind for the ORCA team.

ORCA was an acronym for something that not even Goryell could pronounce properly. It was a very highly classified special assignments operation within Advanced Retrieval. Not even the politicians in the Federal Assembly or the Executive Office knew it existed. The men who served on any of the four ORCA teams were recruited from the elite forces in Frontline Services and Advanced Retrieval's own Rapid Deployment Group. They underwent excruciating physical and mental tests and were subjected to almost unbearable loyalty challenges. Four out of five cracked under the tests.

The ORCA team members often came across as half mad, which was probably not far off. They lived their lives with their dozen-member teams, with unpredictable breaks between long, challenging assignments all across Danarvia.

And beyond her borders.

Much of the assignments that the ORCAs got were of a kind that no one else could do without breaking at least half a dozen laws.

"So you want me to kidnap the Secretary General of the United Nations for you?" captain Kho asked. "Why don't you go get him yourself?"

"Because the acting president of the United States has asked Danarvia to stay the Hell out of their affairs, including the Zoh'moorian invasion."

"Ah" Kho said. "Politics."

"And the Fourth Principle of the Charter of Liberty" Tahm Qaar reminded him. "The Secretary General of the UN is the only official who ranks higher by our standards."

"Well... sounds pretty straightforward."

"Here's how to contact Goryell. He's in Washington, DC right now. I have an agent watching the Secretary General. Apparently the Secretary General has been called down to a meeting in Washington, DC tomorrow. That should give you a decent chance. Goryell can be your tourist guide and show you the town."

"And when we have the Secretary General... what do you want us to do with him?"

"Bring him to me. I want him to send a plea back home on behalf of Earth."

"And what if he says no?"

Tahm Qaar looked at him for a moment.

"Then I'll make him an offer he can't refuse. I'm not going to let this country... the United States of America... be destroyed by a bunch of thugs who can't tell the difference between freedom and a fart."

Captain Kho smiled.

"So you'd be willing to break a law or two just to promote freedom? My friend, you're growing up. You should join us."

"And have to listen to your rants about the hardball season all day long? No, thanks. Now, get the Hell out of my office and go earn your paycheck."

*   *   *

"So let me see if I get this right" said Goryell as he was sitting in his cloaked shuttle on the top of the IMF building with captain Kho. "You're going to walk up to the White House, ring the doorbell, ask to see the Secretary General of the UN, then ask the Secretary General to come with you, walk out again and take the next regular flight to New Mexico."

"Pretty much, yeah" captain Kho nodded.

Goryell shrugged.

"Sounds like a plan to me."

"It's a piece of cake compared to the last thing Tahm Qaar asked me to do. Then I had to go down five thousand feet into a closed and sealed deep-core mine and retrieve a computer hard drive that someone had hidden there. That was the easy part. The tough part was to fight the... creatures that lived down there."

"Where was that?"

"That's classified information, kid. Now, I need all the info you have on the White House."

"Before we get to that it might interest you to know that Barry Oslow is no longer in the White House."

"Why not?"

"He was sent out on a speech tour by the Zoh'moorian Supreme General. I was there the other night and planted some bugs in their computer system. It's really neat – they have audiovisual surveillance of every room. Anyway. The Supreme General kicked him out because he thought that Oslow was collaborating with us."

"Well, all I want is that Al Gore guy, the head of the UN."

"Yeah, he's meeting the Supreme General in the White House in two hours."

"Got the schematics of the White House?"

Goryell pulled out a blueprint of the architectural layout of the White House. Captain Kho took it and got up to leave. Just as he was about to exit the shuttle he turned and said:

"By the way, tell Tahm Qaar he's lost some weight since I saw him last."

"I'm sure he'll be happy to hear that" Goryell smiled.

"No, he won't."

The captain left. Goryell frowned, shook his head and thought that captain Kho was an inherently dislikable character.

Most people would agree with Goryell. Captain Kho was a rough, rude, crude man who took pleasure in defeating an enemy and would rather kill one of his own team mates than let him be captured. It was amazing that he and Tahm Qaar were friends.

But captain Kho was also exceptionally good at what he did. Kidnapping a high dignitary out of the headquarters of the leader of a big country was among the easiest things anyone had ever asked him to do.

The ORCAs left the rooftop of the IMF building in their ground tactical vessel. It was designed to let them eject from side hatches, one by one, equipped with anti-gravity power packs. They trusted Goryell with piloting it.

"You crash my baby, I crash you" captain Kho smiled before he and his seven crew members ejected from the cloaked vessel.

Using cloak suits they gently descended over The Mall and past the Washington Monument. They landed halfway between the monument and the White House. Normally the area would be filled with people, but because of the Zoh'moorian troops there was almost no humans in sight.

The ORCAs folded away the power packs and marched quickly from the Ellipse by Constitution Avenue up toward the White House. There was a concentration of Zoh'moorian troops, especially Fah'marook, around the White House. They tried to look intimidating, but captain Kho just chuckled inside his cloak suit as he walked right past their noses.

As they got to the high fence that separated the White House premises from E Street they switched on their power packs again. There were more Zoh'moorian troops inside the White House premises, and they were all wearing special markings. Captain Kho assumed that they were some kind of personal guard to the Supreme General. He and his ORCAs neatly snuck past them, still undetected, and moved all the way up to the building itself.

It was mid-morning and usually the White House should be brimming with activity. But since the Supreme General had taken over the place had been eerily silent. He was re-organizing it to make it his personal home. His sub-commander had taken over the vice president's residence and there were several guards stationed throughout the huge structure. But other than that it was quiet and empty.

Goryell had showed them where the president's office and quarters were. It was most likely that the Supreme General would meet with Al Gore there. That would be to the left from where the ORCAs were approaching.

However, before they could make a left in to the West Wing they had to get inside.

The ORCAs would have preferred to sneak in undetected, but they also knew that nobody would really leave the door unlocked on a building like this one.

Two guards were posted at the main entrance from the South Lawn, but there was a small side door that no one was watching. The ORCA team moved over toward it. Two of them disabled its relatively crude computer-controlled electronic lock. Before they opened it two others placed diversion robots on the ground in front of the main entrance. These were small, cylinder-shaped hovering robots that would fly around and distract the guards.

The robots themselves had no cloaks, so when the ORCAs took them out they were obviously spotted by the guards.

This was part of the plan. While the six other ORCAs entered through the side door, the two others started their robots and moved toward the East Wing.

If the robots did not create enough of a diversion maneuver, they would.

The robots triggered a massive operation on the South Lawn. Groups of guards and soldiers came from all directions. The robots flew around, about four feet above ground, in random patterns and sent out harmless electrical charges that made the Zoh'moorians dance around and focus on avoiding being hit rather than shooting them down.

Goryell was hovering right above them and watching. He promised himself to thank captain Kho for the entertainment.

But the Zoh'moorians were not completely stupid. They realized that someone was trying to create a diversion maneuver and dispatched extra guards to the West Wing where the Supreme General and Al Gore were meeting in the Oval Office. Since most of the guards had no idea where to go, the scene inside the White House was pretty chaotic. It was easy for the cloaked ORCAs to move from room to room and down the hallways until they stood outside the Oval Office.

Six guards blocked the door. They were all six-foot tall Zoh'moorians with special markings on their black uniforms. They had big weapons and stood in positions that looked more intimidating than they were efficient for actually defending the door from an attack.

The first thing captain Kho noted was that the weapons that the Zoh'moorians had were bulky and unsuited for combat in such a small space as they were in. The second thing he noted was that they casually talking to each other. Not exactly alert – even though, captain Kho assumed, there should have been some sort of call from the guards outside that there might be intruders on their way.

Captain Kho decided to play a little trick on the guards. He and his seven men took up positions less than two feet from the guards and made themselves ready for hand-to-hand combat. It was the easiest way to take down an enemy without making a whole lot of noise.

Then they turned off their cloak suits.

It was a trick that captain Kho loved to play on people who had no way of detecting cloaked people around them. And it always made people react the same way. A second of stunned silence, a second's deep breath and frantic scrambling for weapons, and a second to realize that captain Kho and his men were way ahead of them.

A couple of swift, hard strikes by the ORCAs and the six Zoh'moorian guards went down. They disarmed the guards and secured them before turning on their cloaks again.

Then they entered the Oval Office.

The Supreme General was sitting in the chair that was reserved for the president of the United States. He was leaning back, casually observing the man at the other end of the desk. There, Al Gore was leaning forward in his chair, his hand stretched out in an open, communicative gesture. You did not have to know anything about reptilian facial expressions to realize that Al Gore was the underdog and the Supreme General was smirking back at him.

The Supreme General and Al Gore were the only men in the room. Neither of them noticed that one of the doors opened slightly for a few seconds, then shut close again.

"But sir" Al Gore said, his voice trembling. "Sir, I can assure you that the rest of the world will cooperate and negotiate with you. We are a peaceful world, with peaceful people. We wish you no harm."

"You are fighting wars among yourselves all the time" the Supreme General said and sounded like he was laughing.

"I know" Al Gore said and bowed his head in frustration. "I know... you are way ahead of us. You must think we are primitive..."

"There will be no negotiations, Al. There will only be cooperation on your end. You are bare-skinned sub-beings, not worthy of our respect. You will tell the other nations of this world that if they do not cooperate we will come down hard on them. With all our might and force."

"They have already begun taking advantage of the situation, sir. China has already invaded Vietnam and Russia is massing forces on the European border. In fact, many of the other nations are welcoming you as liberators. They see you have conquered America, a country they saw as a superpower. They think you will come and help them improve their lives."

The Supreme General broke out in a laughter so big and so uninhibited that even Al Gore realized that he was being laughed at.

"What... what is so funny?" he asked.

"Oh, nothing. Uh... Al... go back to that office you have in... where is it..."

"New York."

"Yes, yes. Go back there and tell the other nations that all they have to do is to give us access to their raw materials and their work forces, and we will leave them alone."

"Is that... all you want?"

"Yes."

"And how will you compensate them? I'm sure you have a lot of technology to share."

The Supreme General looked at him with no discernible expressions on his face.

"Now, go" he said. "I'm busy."

Al Gore seemed a bit unsure what to do. But the Supreme General's body language told him that the meeting was over. He got up and started saying something, but the Supreme General made a discouraging gesture. Al turned around and walked toward the very same door as the ORCA team had come in through. The Supreme General looked at him. Captain Kho, who was used to reptilians and knew how to read their faces, quickly concluded that the Supreme General despised Al Gore.

This was their chance. But they could not let Al Gore open the door.

On their motion detectors they noted that other guards were

approaching the six they had neutralized before. They could not go back the way they came.

But they had to take Al Gore now. If they did, though, the Supreme General would know that they were there and they would have an endless firefight all the way out – dragging along an uncooperative kidnap victim.

There was only one thing to do.

*   *   *

Vice admiral Ghaul really did not have time to leave his bridge seat to go to a secure station and talk to his commanding officer in private. But the admiral would not call him just to chat.

"Admiral Grez, what can I do for you?"

"How is the operation going?"

"Good, sir."

"I am sorry for pulling you away from the bridge" the admiral said. "But we have new orders. You must not interfere with Zoh'moorian vessels or personnel within Earth's atmosphere."

"Sir?"

"The president of the United States has directly asked us not to get involved in Zoh'moorian operations."

"I see."

"And since Earth has no territorial claims to its solar system, we can operate anywhere except in their atmosphere."

"Did Advanced Retrieval relay that?"

"Yes."

"It would be helpful if I could talk to them directly."

"I'll see what I can do."

"Sir, do you have any comments on our report about the alien vessel?"

"That's one curious vessel. I have passed your report on to Military Intelligence."

"Sir, the other vessel we saw took off once we destroyed the first. It moved amazingly fast. It headed for Zoh'moor."

"Could it be one of theirs?"

"I doubt it, sir. The discrepancy between the tin cans they fly around in and those vessels is simply too big. My guess is they have an advanced ally behind them, someone who is not interested in getting involved directly."

"Good point. I will suggest to High Command that we deploy a Deep Space Assault Force."

"Good idea, admiral. They're much faster than we are. We can't keep up with them."

"Alright. I want you to focus on forming a blockade around the Earth system. Hopefully we can starve the Zoh'moorians of their own resources and give the Earthlings a chance to take care of them."

Vice admiral Ghaul did not like his new orders. One of his hub ships and two of his attack cruisers had obliterated the Zoh'moorian halfway station and every ship between that station and Earth. He was prepared to pursue the Zoh'moorians all the way to their home world, but his new orders effectively gave the enemy a chance to regroup and prepare for another attack.

And – the vice admiral noted in his personal log – make plans with whoever was flying those big, black rectangles.

He was not particularly amused by that part of the equation.

* * *

Captain Kho and his team had only seconds before the Zoh'moorian guards outside the Oval Office would barge through the door. They also could not let Al Gore open it.

Once again they uncloaked and used the two-second surprise it triggered to take advantage of the situation. Two of them shot and killed the Supreme General. Two others jumped Al Gore and injected him with a tranquilizer. Two others pulled out a cloak suit and the last two took up position so they could fire at any door that someone might open.

Noise came from the other side of the door where they had left the six guards. They could hear a couple of reptilian voices yelling and screaming.

It was only seconds, now, before someone would open fire at the door.

Four of the ORCAs worked together to get the unconscious Al Gore inside the cloak suit. It was not easy. He was a big guy.

A communications device in front of the dead Supreme General made a couple of crackling sounds.

"They're calling him" said captain Kho. "Let's move."

"In a second" said one of his team members. "Al Gore is not secured yet."

The device made more crackling sounds and relayed someone's message.

"Time to go, boys" said captain Kho.

"In a second!"

The cloak suit was on but they could not close it over the belly.

"He's too fat" said one team member.

"Turn him over on the back!" the captain suggested.

Someone tried to open the door to the Oval Office.

"He's a big boy" said one of them.

"He's a fat boy" said another.

"Shut up" said captain Kho.

The attempts to open the door stopped. There were no sounds from the other side of it.

"OK, they're gonna blast it open" said the captain. "Let's go, boys."

"Wait…"

"Cloaks on now!"

"But wait!"

Four Zoh'moorian laser rifles blasted the door open. Eight guards stormed in, almost stumbling over each other, with another four right behind them. Three of them dashed up to the Supreme General. The others spread out in the Office and tried to find Al Gore. One looked under the desk. Another guard looked under a sofa. Two guards searched under a coffee table.

But Al Gore was gone. Fortunately, one of the guards had heard a side door close just as they got in. Frantically calling out orders over their radios, the guards stormed through it and down the hallway to try to catch up with whoever had escaped through it. The hallway was narrow and looked like an easy exit to the garden just south of the West Wing. When the guards turned a corner and got to the exit they saw a couple of people outside. They raised their weapons and opened fire. The three men outside fell to the ground. Cheering, the guards stormed out the blasted door and surrounded the downed men. The lieutenant in charge of the guard group called his commanding officer and said they had shot and killed three of the intruders.

There was only one problem. The three men were Fah'marook soldiers, stationed by the door to prevent anyone from getting in or out. They had been recklessly careless on their post and not heard or seen the guards. Not that they should have to – after all, they were all Zoh'moorians.

As soon as the last guard had left the Oval Office through the side door, captain Kho and his team put the final touch on Al Gore's cloak. They all stayed cloaked while they did it. The captain had covered the last piece on Al Gore's belly with his own cloak suit glove and then put his uncovered hand inside the sleeve of the other hand. Then they had opened a door and let it close by itself.

"Dumb bastards" captain Kho chuckled as they lifted up Al Gore and started carrying him out.

The ORCAs left the Oval Office, two in the front, two in the back and four carrying the still unconscious Secretary General of the UN. All they had to do now was get outside and have Goryell pick them up.

Piece of cake.

They walked back toward the main hall and aimed to get to the north side of the White House, to the half circle at Pennsylvania Avenue and Lafayette Park. Zoh'moorian guards ran back and forth, yelled and pointed and talked on their radios. No one noticed the ORCA team, a tribute to their awesome cloak suits.

Everything was going just fine.

Until captain Kho's glove came off.

He had re-attached it a bit carelessly after ha had used it to cover the hole in Al gore's cloak suit. When moved his hand too quickly it came off.

And two Zoh'moorian guards suddenly saw a hand in the middle of the air. They started yelling and screaming and pointing.

The ORCAs were almost at the north exit from the White

House Between them and the doors were two Fah'marook soldiers and behind them were a half dozen guards.

One of the ORCAs immediately saw the glove, which was still invisible to anyone not wearing a cloak suit. He threw himself on to the ground, grabbed it and tossed it over to captain Kho. The captain caught it just as he ordered everyone to the ground. He suspected that the Zoh'moorians would open fire as soon as they realized that there were cloaked intruders in front of them.

He was right. They had barely ducked and placed Al Gore between them on the floor before the guards behind them opened fire.

They were apparently very determined. Their barrage of laser-based fire lasted for a good ten seconds. It was very effective. It even killed.

But not the ORCAs. The only ones who died were the Fah'marook soldiers at the northern entrance.

"Friendly fire" captain Kho remarked. "A sad way to die for a soldier."

It was not until an officer behind the guards yelled something to them that they ceased fire and realized that they had just killed two of their own. But it would not take long before they also realized that they had aimed at the invisible intruders as if those were still standing up – and redirect their fire toward the floor.

"Let's give them a taste of superior firepower" said captain Kho.

Four of the ORCAs stayed on the floor while four got up on a knee. On their captain's command they opened up with their urban combat specials.

It must have looked kind of funny to someone who was not at the receiving end of the fire. Out of thin air came blasts of pulsating energy, blasts that killed and destroyed with devastating efficiency. But for the Zoh'moorian guards and their officer it was not fun at all. In fact, it was the end of it as far as they were concerned.

"Bang, you're dead" said captain Kho.

But there was really no time to crack funny comments. He knew that reinforcements would arrive on the double. He and his team members, still carrying the unconscious and carefully cloaked Al Gore, quickly exited the White House.

Only to find about a hundred Fah'marook troops gathered outside, weapons pointed at the White House entrance. The ORCAs were still cloaked, but the Fah'marook, who had formed a crescent around the entrance, were smart enough to realize that the doors to the White House did not open by themselves. As soon as the doors opened, they opened up.

Once again the ORCAs found themselves on the ground. But this time they did not wait to return fire.

There were eight of them against a hundred Fah'marook soldiers. Their weapons were superior in precision, reliability and firepower. Their training and experience were far beyond what any Zoh'moorian soldiers could dream of.

They fought well, and killed many, many enemy soldiers. Their cloaks helped, but the Fah'marook quickly learned to aim at the spots where fire was coming from. The ORCAs had very good suits that not only cloaked them but also resisted enemy fire better than any protective armor used by anyone else in Danarvia. But despite such good odds, not even the ORCAs could walk away from the encounter without a few scratches.

One of them was focused on keeping anyone away who tried to approach them from inside the White House. He other seven fought the Fah'marook with everything they had. By the time they had killed off half of the Fah'marook, two of them had suffered injuries. When another ten Fah'marook had fallen, the weapon of one of the ORCAs was hit point blank – a virtually impossible angle to hit a weapon from – and quit working. He had to resort to his one-hand weapon.

When only 20 Fah'marook were standing their commander ordered a retreat. Captain Kho thought they could regroup and advance.

Until a ship emerged from above the White House.

It was a Zoh'moorian gunship. It stopped right above Lafayette Square and turned around.

It lowered its front slightly so its guns were pointing straight at the north entrance to the White House.

"So that's why no one was trying to attack us from behind" captain Kho concluded.

They threw themselves to the sides just as the gunship opened fire.

The pillars in front of the entrance collapsed. The entire façade behind the pillars also collapsed. Debris flew around in the air and landed in piles all over the place.

The Fah'marook cheered. Captain Kho, on the other hand, asked his team mates to let him know that they had been smart enough to pull Al Gore with them.

"I thought he was with you" said one of them.

"What?"

"Just kidding. Got him here."

"Remind me to kick your ass when this is over."

The group was now split in two halves, one on each side of the debris piles. There were more Fah'marook troops coming in from up Pennsylvania Avenue. Not many, but enough to extend the battle.

And the gunship was taking aim again.

Captain Kho reloaded his weapon. He looked around for another place to take cover and get away from the gunship again. He was ready to fight his way right through the Fah'marook lines if necessary.

Sure, it was probably a bad idea. Their cloak suits had already sustained some damage and would probably stop cloaking them with a dozen more direct hits. And then the gunship pilot could find them with his eyes closed.

The next blast from the gunship hit right above captain Kho. This time they escaped the falling debris with barely an inch to spare.

The four ORCAs on the other side of the debris fired at the gunship, but in doing so they attracted fire from the troops on the ground. They managed to take out one of the guns on the ship but had to disperse in order to evade fire.

The gunship now aimed in their direction.

This was getting tough. Their only chance was to leave the area before their cloaks stopped working. They could regroup on the other side of Lafayette Square.

Just as he gave the order, captain Kho noticed that something was approaching from behind the gunship.

A vessel with a familiar shape.

It was Goryell. He had finally come to pick them up.

When he opened fire, the gunship exploded on first hit. The carnage that followed when it crashed on the Fah'marook soldiers was bloodier than the one Goryell had caused before when he shot down another Zoh'moorian gunship. It was a terrible scene, but captain Kho and his men had no time to sob over dead enemies. They had a mission to accomplish.

Goryell landed on the lawn on the north side of Lafayette Square. Captain Kho and his men quickly moved around and got inside.

Still carrying the unconscious Al Gore, of course.

"What took you so long?" asked captain Kho.

"Well, you know how rush hour is in this city."

Goryell glanced at Al Gore as he steered the ship up in the sky.

"Is that the Secretary General?"

"It better be, or I'll be a damned fool" captain Kho muttered. "Hey, where are you taking us?"

"Space."

"I thought we were going back to your on-ground headquarters?"

"We've been ordered to evacuate."

"What?? Why?"

"Politics. Ask Tahm Qaar. He knows politics. Strike Group Fourteen is in the neighborhood. One of their hub ships is here to pick us up."

As soon as they had docked on the hub ship captain Kho went straight to Tahm Qaar to ask him about the politics.

"Oh, man" Tahm Qaar said wearily. "Where do I start? Barry Oslow… you know, the American…"

"President, yes, I know."

"He gave this televised speech where he asked us to stay out of Earth's affairs."

"Still yesterday's news."

"Why are you so irritated?"

"Why? I'll tell you why. I was just in a battle with a hundred enemy soldiers and one of their gunships, that's why."

"Yes, I'm sorry. Where was I?"

"You look tired."

"I am" Tahm Qaar said and yawned. "I'm getting too old for these time zone changes. Anyway. Because of Barry Oslow's request the Executive Office decided to cancel the invasion and place Earth under blockade. The Zoh'moorians on Earth will remain there for the Earthlings to deal with, but no one gets in and no one gets out. The Executive Office also decided that under the present circumstances it would be a violation of the Fourth Principle to keep an intelligence detail on Earth."

"That's a new one" captain Kho said. "We've had intelligence operations on many worlds were our military has not been welcome."

"But this time one of the candidates for the open seat on the Executive Office threatened to sue the Executive Office under the Fourth Principle if they did not get us out."

"Who is the candidate?"

"Delegate Quim."

"The Teuran?"

"Yes."

"I thought he knew better."

"I thought I knew better than to try to make sense out of politics" Tahm Qaar said and yawned again. "I'm sorry, old friend. I need to get some sleep."

"Yeah, me, too. So I kidnapped Al Gore for nothing?"

"No, no, we'll have a nice, long conversation with him and see if we can convince him to make a formal request for help."

"How about some Kherr-Wa tomorrow?"

"You still only have five stars. I'll kick your butt."

"I bet you two bottles of Aquaan ale."

"You don't have two bottles of Aquaan ale" Tahm Qaar smiled.

"No, but you do" captain Kho smiled back.

"Get out of my quarters, you rascal."

*   *   *

HOPE

When Jack saw a space vessel lower itself and land outside the house, he immediately grabbed a gun and hunkered down by the window. The vessel did not look like any other Zoh'moorian ship he had seen, so he assumed that it was some sort of special unit. Why they would come here, to his house in Lindsborg, Kansas, he did not know. But he was not going to have a conversation with them to find out.

"Put that gun away."

Jack glanced over to the door. He made a gesture to Thor to be quiet.

"It's not the Zoh'moorians" Thor said.

"Not the Zoh'moorians? Then who the Hell is it?"

Thor came up to the window just as a man emerged from the vessel. Thor smiled.

"That's a good friend of mine."

"So you guys have space ships now?" Jack asked and stood up.

"No. He's just a friend."

Jack holstered the gun and made a face at his brother.

"He's from the Danarvian Federation" Thor explained. "Good guys. His name is Goryell. You'll like him."

Thor was right. When Jack got to know Goryell, he really did like him. Especially when Goryell told him about the Danarvian Federation.

"An entire federation of civilizations, built on libertarian principles" Jack smiled. "Sounds too good to be true."

"Hi, Goryell."

It was Carl. He had been working on something in the attic.

"Hi, there, buddy! How are you?"

"Better. My leg is almost back to normal."

Carl turned to Jack.

"This man saved my life two times in a couple of days."

"Thanks for coming" Thor said to Goryell. "I wasn't sure you'd get the message. You guys had already packed up your headquarters."

"Well, I wish I brought better news" Goryell said and sat down. "But our politicians back home have decided not to launch the liberation."

"What?"

He explained the whole political complexity around Barry Oslow's televised speech and the Fourth Principle.

"So basically we're left to fight on our own" Jack noted. "Are you guys too weak to take them on?"

"Not at all. Our military crushed the Zoh'moorian fleet before the invasion was halted. The Second Armada would eliminate the Zoh'moorians here on Earth in a matter of hours. It's not a military decision. It's all politics."

"It's stupid" Jack concluded.

"I can see the logic in it" said Carl. "How else do you guarantee the sovereignty of another world?"

"How long can the Zoh'moorians last without backup from their home world?" asked Thor.

"They could last a long time if they use your resources" Goryell noted. "They landed a lot of troops before Strike Group Fourteen got here. They have troops here and in Europe and parts of Russia. That's a lot of land and resources. It all depends on what your military decides to do."

"The president is obviously cooperating" said Jack. "Although he seems to be little more than a figure head for the Zoh'moorian supreme general."

"Well, it's gonna be tough" said Thor. "We better…"

Carl interrupted him with a tap on the arm.

"What?"

"There's a car coming."

"Where?"

They all looked out the window.

"I better cloak my ship" said Goryell and tapped a few buttons on a remote.

The car made a turn and came up the driveway.

"I've never seen that car before" Thor said and reached for his gun.

He and Carl hunkered by the windows.

"Put the guns away" Jack said.

"What?" Thor said and frowned at his brother.

"It's Jenny."

"Who's Jenny?"

"Jenny Blue Eyes."

Jack went to open the door and welcome her.

"She got my message" he said, sounding like a child on Christmas.

Thor and Carl stood up and holstered their guns.

"He's bringing a girl out here?" Carl said. "Don't we have more important things to do?"

"She's cute" Goryell noted, looking out the window.

"He's always had this thing for blondes" Thor sighed.

"Well, I better get going, guys. Technically, me being here is a violation of a direct order from our Executive Office."

Goryell, Thor and Carl looked at each other for a moment. It was hard for them to say farewell. Goryell had not known the two Earthlings for very long, but they had become very good friends.

"Let's keep in touch, okay?" Thor said.

"Absolutely. You got my e-mail, right?"

"Yeah, right" Thor chuckled.

Goryell put his flat backpack on the table and took out a strange looking communications device, about the size of a laptop.

"This... this is my personal... I guess you can call it a communications platform. I'll leave it with you guys. You can call me on it. I'm not giving it to you. It cost me a fortune, because it has a range of twenty thousand light years. But you can borrow it and send me messages and give it back to me, well... next time."

"Can you play Civilization Five on it?" Carl asked.

"We'll send you some news bulletins" Thor promised.

"That's a good idea."

"We'll give the Zoh'moorians a hard time."

"I've seen many worlds" Goryell said as Thor and Carl walked him to the door. "Few people love freedom as much as you Americans do. You'll be alright."

Goryell saluted them with his home world's two open palms and a brief nod. Thor copied but Carl held up his right hand and formed a V with his fingers.

"Live long and prosper" he said.

"I've never seen that one before" said Goryell.

Thor shook his head and pointed with his thumb at Carl.

"Vintage sci-fi."

When Goryell's ship lifted off, Thor, Carl, Jack and Jenny stood on the front porch and watched it rise to the sky and vanish.

"May the force be with him" said Thor.

"May the force be with us" said Carl.

"So what's next?" Jack asked. "You're gonna gather your buddies from... what's it called?"

"Branch Four" said Thor. "That'll be tough."

"Why?"

"We're the only ones left" Carl explained. "Stanton managed to eliminate the rest."

"That's a setback" Jack noted.

"We can still fight for our freedom" Thor reminded them.

"I'm not sure how to do it" Jack said. "I mean, I know how to use a hand gun. But..."

Thor smiled and put a hand on his brother's shoulder.

"I'll teach you a few tricks."

They stood on the porch for a moment and looked out over the fields. The town of Lindsborg was a mile away. Rolling fields stretched in the other direction. A couple of farm houses broke the beautiful landscape and reminded them of their distant neighbors.

This was America. The America they had grown up in and loved so deeply.

The America they would all give their lives for.

"Whose house is this?" Carl asked.

"Been in our family for four generations" said Thor. "Our grandfather grew up here. He and his sister."

"What was her name?"

"Who?"

"His sister."

"Thora Jane Larson. Why?"

"I was up in the attic. I thought maybe we could build a dojo up there. I looked at some old panel on the wall that was coming off. I found this tape recorder behind it. It was like someone had hidden it there."

Carl took a black Dictaphone-type tape recorder out of his pocket.

"Have you listened to the tape?" Jack asked as they went inside.

"Yeah, you won't believe what's on it" Carl said as the door closed behind them.

E P I L O G U E

I can smell something new. Something fresh. It's coming from up above. The tunnel forks, and the one to the left goes upward. It's still pretty dark here, but there are those strange, glowing stones here and there, so the tunnel is not completely dark.

I have gone so far away from the laboratory and the dungeon that I cannot even believe it. Why haven't they stopped me? And where are they? Usually I can smell them from thirty feet away, sometimes more. But I haven't sensed the ugly smell of the creatures since I left the laboratory.

I wonder what happened. What if they left? What if they decided that their experiments were completed and they abandoned us? The other humans are still in the dungeon. They'd be left to die there.

Maybe I should go back to them. Maybe they need my help. After all, I'm the oldest. I've been here longest. I have the responsibility...

No. I can't go back. At least not until I have been up there, up where that fresh air is coming from.

I've always known this was a system of caves and tunnels. At first, I thought the creatures just had a laboratory down here, then I wondered if they also lived here. There are so many tunnels and strange, dark doors down here... maybe they do live here. But if they do, why are they not stopping me? Why are they letting me go?

It's hard to climb up this tunnel. The ground is a bit slippery. It's water on some kind of rock that's smooth and... wait, what's that? Oh, a stairway!

Wait. It's for... for the creatures, and their... their... feet.

Well. I guess I can use it. My legs are not that strong, I have not had much exercise in a long time. And I'm getting old. But I'll make it. I will make it up to that fresh air.

Ah! I can really smell it now. And there is light up there. Oh, I cannot wait!

There it is! I can see it!! The sky! I can see stars!! It's night. The middle of the night.

This... this opening... it's a big cave. The ground is filled with gravel and small rocks. I better walk carefully.

I'm outside the cave now. I cannot believe this... The air is so different. It's kind of thin, like high up in the mountains.

But... what kind of landscape is this? Those are not mountains. I've never seen mountains like them. And that light? It's coming from over there. Way over there. Far away.

It's a... a lava stream. Like a river of lava. Falling... like a fire fall.

And what a strange night sky! Those stars... I have never seen them before. And that stream of stars – it's like a galaxy arm. And that almost looks like a planet!

Where am I?